# PRAISE FOR THE BLADE MAGE

"The Blade Mage delivers big-muscled magic and high-octane thrills."
— **Gary Phillips**, *Matthew Henson and the Ice temple of Harlem*

"Phillip Drayer Duncan has done it again. First with the Assassins, Inc. series and now with The Blade Mage. His characters and the situations they get themselves into and out of have me laughing out loud—and I don't often, even on the inside. I read two comic writers, Duncan and Robert Asprin's Myth series." — **JC Crumpton**, *Silence in the Garden*

"Witty, action-packed, and never one to shy away from the unexpected. Phillip Drayer Duncan is not to be missed."
— **J.H. Fleming**, *The Queen of Moon and Shadow*

# ...AND FOR PHILLIP DRAYER DUNCAN'S OTHER NOVELS

"Not since the feud between the Hatfields and Mccoys, has anyone made a bunch of hillbillies interesting, and that's just what Phillip Duncan did with Moonshine Wizard." — **Jason Fedora**, *The Truth of Betrayal*

"ASSASSINS INCORPORATED boasts the sort of writing that avid readers crave to come across between the covers of a book." — **Kristofer Upjohn**, *Horror is Art*

# ALSO BY PHILLIP DRAYER DUNCAN

**The Blade Mage:**

The Blade Mage

Of Song and Shadow

The Memphis Knights

Rebel Medicine

**The Moonshine Wizard:**

Moonshine Wizard

The Distilled Shorts Collection:

*First Job*

*The Ogre & The Primates*

*A Sword Named Sharp*

*Hunting one Like Us*

*The Monster Beneath the Bed*

*The Hunt for the Dark Wizard*

**Assassins Incorporated:**

Assassins Incorporated

Assassins Incorporated: Rehired

# NEWSLETTER

Sign up for the Phillip Drayer Duncan Newsletter to receive a **FREE** digital copy of Catalysts, a collection of 3 stories from the Blade Mage & Moonshine Wizard series. Nearly as much content as a full novel, this collection includes:

~

The Generic Mage *(The Blade Mage Series)*

The Last Great Blade Mage *(The Blade Mage Series)*

The Hunt for the Dark Wizard *(The Moonshine Wizard Series)*

~

Sign up for FREE at **PhillipDrayerDuncan.com**

# REBEL MEDICINE

## BLADE MAGE BOOK 4

### PHILLIP DRAYER DUNCAN

ISBN: 978-1-964044-01-9

Publisher: Happy Omega Publishing, LLC

Cover Art By: German Creative

Interior Art By: Phillip Drayer Duncan

Edited By: J.H. Fleming

A Note from the Author:

If you wish to support your favorite authors, the best way is to buy their books brand-spanking-new when you can afford to. If you can't afford to, then this author supports you buying used books. In which case, you can still help your favorite authors by raving about their books to your friends and family. If you can't afford to purchase at all, feel free to stop by **PhillipDrayerDuncan.com**, where I usually have some FREE content available. And if there's a title of mine you really want to read, but just can't afford it, feel free to reach out through my Contact page and we'll see if there's something we can do.

**PhillipDrayerDuncan.com**
Happy Omega Publishing

# REBEL MEDICINE

## BOOK 4 OF THE BLADE MAGE

By

**Phillip Drayer Duncan**

# CHAPTER ONE

I felt like the new kid stepping onto the schoolyard for the first time.

That was ridiculous, of course. I'd been to the Castle countless times. Yet, I couldn't deny this time felt different.

I had thought long over what the Archmage had said. Despite my own reservations and resentments, I knew he was right. If I wanted to be the Blade Mage, I'd have to earn aaamy place. Fair or not, I'd have to convince them I was for real.

Of course, that was easier said than done.

I had no idea what to do.

Hence the anxiety.

But I knew where to start.

The Castle.

I needed to walk in and make a *new* good first impression. And I needed to do it without Axel. He wasn't keen on that part of the plan. In fact, he'd reacted rather poorly when I told him he couldn't come. After getting over his initial sense of betrayal, he'd switched gears and started treating me like an empty nester, sending their baby off to college. Mother Goose asked if I'd brought enough socks and reminded me not to forget my toothbrush. He even packed me a lunch.

It wasn't like I was moving out. I was just going to go stay at the

Castle for a few days to make my presence known and see if I could start fixing my image.

At least, I hoped it would be that simple.

I rolled up to the gate in my old beater truck.

The Castle grounds were protected by high stone walls, undoubtedly enchanted with enough magical energy to turn a tank into a squishy toy. It would've had a very medieval vibe if not for the modern security shack beside the big metal gate.

I pulled up alongside the shack and rolled down my window. The guard on the other side of the glass didn't open his. Instead, he barked at me through a speaker. "State your name and business."

This was new.

Then again, this was the first time I'd actually approached the Castle on my own in several years. During my previous visits, I'd either been unconscious or dragged in by Parker Grimm. In the past, though, the gate guards had never been so uptight. Maybe it was just my fortune to get the grumpy one.

Pointing my mouth back at the speaker, I said, "Wyatt Draven."

"And your business?"

"Seriously?" I asked, making a point of raising one eyebrow. Put aside the fact I was the Blade Mage, I'd also spent a good portion of my childhood on the other side of that wall.

Yet that didn't stop the man behind the glass from glaring at me. "State your business immediately, or you will be treated as a threat."

"I'm the Blade Mage," I replied, glaring back at him. As an afterthought, I added, "Of this Cabal."

Without missing a beat, Officer Friendly said, "That's your title. I'll ask you one more time: what is your business here?"

There was no doubt Little Mr. Power Trip was sitting on the trigger of some really nasty magics that could disintegrate me into dust. The rent-a-cop had the power, and he knew it. *Prick.*

Fortunately, I had the power of not caring and enough stubbornness to back it up.

"My business here is none of yours," I said, keeping my tone sharp. "Now open the damned gate. I'm the Blade Mage, for crying out loud."

He scoffed. "We haven't had a Blade Mage in years."

Despite the insult, the gates swung open, and I started forward before our budding friendship could dissolve further. On the "influencing people" side of things, I wasn't off to a good start.

The Castle grounds were extensive and reminded me of a rich dick retirement community. There were more mansions than I cared to count, all of which were inhabited by the so-called noble families. My family had once been among them, but we'd never had a mansion.

There were also several smaller suburb streets with normal houses for the less pretentious.

The area directly around the Castle was more like a University Campus. There were a handful of schools—some of which I had attended at some point in my life—the giant library, a grand cathedral, the hospital, corporate offices for the important businessy types, a grand auditorium and concert hall, the military barracks and operation center, the Constable Academy, and a number of "colleges" dedicated to the study of different types of magic. All of these buildings were of old stone, just like the Castle proper, which gave it an old college feel, like one might find in Oxford, or the gray-stoned Trinity college in Dublin.

This wasn't Europe, though.

It was Arkansas, and this was a hidden place, a place the local yokels didn't even know about. Nor could they see it. Even from the sky, powerful magics made the whole of the Castle grounds look like tree-covered hills, or so I'd been told.

So basically, the Castle grounds looked like an old European college that a bunch of rich dicks had bought and turned into a bougie country club. There was even a golf course. Do some alchemy in the morning. Play through eighteen holes in the afternoon.

It wasn't all study and fun, though. As far as security went, there were few safer places on the planet. The dark mages who'd plagued me in Memphis would've been squashed like bugs if they'd tried their shenanigans at the Castle.

In fact, there was a reason none of the powerful enemies I'd faced had ever tried their nonsense here. No one would be that stupid. It didn't matter how powerful they thought they were. Attacking the Castle would be suicide. So, it had that going for it.

I followed the quaint little driving trail until it brought me to the

Reception Hall. Also a stone building, it served as a sort of an administrative catch-all. Say, for example, that a mage from another guild had been invited for a visit. The receptionists at the Reception Hall would get their sleeping arrangements sorted. If one of the rich tits was having plumbing problems in their mansion, they could report it to the receptionists at the Reception Hall. If some snobby lady's yorkie went missing, she could report it to the receptionists at the Reception Hall. The receptionists at the Reception Hall took care of all sorts.

So, I was counting on them to help me secure accommodations for my stay.

I even thought there might be a chance I could stay in my dad's old place, but I wasn't going to get my hopes up. I wasn't really sure what happened to his house after he'd died. For all I knew, someone else could've moved in. That was okay, though. I decided I'd be happy to have one of the little rooms inside the Castle itself, like I'd stayed in previously.

My plan was pretty simple, really. I'd get the receptionists to get me a room. Then I'd get the receptionists to help me get meetings scheduled with as many of the masters as I could over the next few days. I wanted to meet with each of them one on one, to show them I wasn't quite the bastard they'd made me out to be. And who knew? Maybe I'd find out they weren't the bastards I'd made them out to be, as well. The latter was doubtful, but I was pinning my hopes on the former.

I stepped into the stone building and strolled up to the counter, feeling pretty good about myself.

The reception area of the Reception Hall was large enough to serve a butt-load of people at once. However, there wasn't a butt-load of people at the moment.

Just me.

And there were only two receptionists present, so the numbers worked out in my favor.

The receptionists could've been twins. Both war charcoal gray jackets with matching skirts, both wore enough makeup to hide their true identities, and both had purchased their smiles at the nearest dollar store. The only thing that distinguished them was that one was blonde and the other was brunette. The blonde looked up first and reeled me in with a smiling set of unnaturally white teeth.

"Hi, there," she said in a bubbly voice. "How may I help you?"

"Uh, hi," I said. "I'm Wyatt Draven, the, uh, Blade Mage. Looking to stay here at the Castle for a few days and I was hoping you could help me get a room sorted."

"I see," she said as she began typing keys on the computer in front of her.

The brunette stood from her desk and slipped through the door behind the counter, disappearing.

I leaned against the counter and tried not to seem impatient. I thought about trying to strike up a casual conversation, since that's why I was there after all, but the blonde receptionist seemed pretty focused on her screen.

After a minute or so, the brunette returned. I smiled her way and thought maybe I'd try to engage her in conversation, but she didn't even make eye contact with me.

Then, after what felt like a lifetime, the blonde finally looked up from her computer screen. The look on her face was almost apologetic. "I'm afraid there're no rooms available."

"No rooms available?" I heard myself repeat back to her. "What, is there a sci-fi convention on this weekend?"

The brunette looked up and gave me an icy glare. "This isn't a hotel."

"No, it isn't," I agreed. "It's a Castle. With big ole castle grounds. Lots of buildings. With lots of places to stay in them. You know, for visitors, students, and important businessy types. You're telling me there isn't a single room available anywhere on the grounds?"

"I'm afraid not," the blonde said. "There's a Super 8 on the south side of Fayetteville, if you don't mind the commute."

I blinked at her a few times. This wasn't going at all how I'd planned it.

Still, I couldn't let myself get derailed at the first little hurdle. I forced a friendly smile and said, "You know what? That's okay. There may be something else you can help me with instead."

"Sure," the blonde said, but with little conviction. The brunette rolled her eyes.

"I was also looking to get some meetings set up with a few of the masters. Is that something you could help me get arranged?"

The blonde chewed her lip. "So, you don't have appointments already?"

"Well, no," I said, feeling a bit like a helium balloon with a pinprick.

More eye-rolling from the brunette, but the blonde attempted to be professional. "And which of the masters were you wanting an appointment with?"

"All of them, actually," I said. "Or whoever is available. But individual meetings for each. That should make things a little easier, right?"

The blonde looked up at me with a twinkle of humor in her eyes and a smirk on her lips. So much for being professional.

Her buddy rolled her eyes again. "You *do* understand the masters are very busy? They don't just *take* meetings with *anyone* who comes in off the street."

"I'm not off the street," I said through gritted teeth. "I'm the Blade Mage. Of this Cabal."

"I didn't even know we had a Blade Mage," the brunette said, glancing at the blonde. "Do you know where we stored the red carpet? I think he wants us to roll it out."

Without missing a beat, the blonde said, "Oh, and we should schedule a parade. Do we have a marching band we could call in?"

"Wow," I said, struggling to keep a neutral tone. "Your sarcasm training is on point."

"So, you're the infamous Blade Mage," the brunette said, looking me up and down. "And I suppose after not showing your face around here for years, you think your title affords you some special privilege?"

"Well..." I said, unsure how to respond. "I would have thought it would be enough to afford me a simple meeting with my peers."

The brunette sort of scoff-shrieked while the blonde merely snorted. Apparently, the idea that I considered the masters to be my peers was a bit of a joke. In fairness, it was, and I had used a poor choice of words.

"Unbelievable," the brunette said. "*Just* unbelievable."

"Okay," I said, trying to think of a way to soothe the situation. "I guess that's an unreasonable ask?"

Before either answered, a side door opened and three security guards stepped through. These weren't mall cops. These fellas looked like spec ops guys who'd just got back from killing terrorists. All three were decked out in full body armor, combat gear, and were carrying assault rifles. The only thing that identified them as mages were the wands holstered on their hips, right next to their sidearms.

One guard, with a particularly lame handlebar mustache, took a few steps forward and asked, "Do we have a problem here?"

All eyes turned to me.

"Uh, I don't think so," I said, glancing between everyone in the room. Had the receptionists called security on me? I forced my most friendly smile and said, "Just trying to get some meetings set up and sort out where I'm going to stay while I'm here at the Castle."

"I believe the nice ladies already explained there were no rooms available, Blade Mage."

The way he said "Blade Mage" sounded like it caused him physical pain.

I tried not to glare at his mustache. I've got nothing against a handlebar mustache, in principle, but as the great and wise Peter Griffith would say, do you know what really grinds my gears? When a fella puts that much time and effort into perfectly grooming his face waste because he *thinks* it makes him look tough.

I took a calming breath. This whole situation seemed to be deteriorating rapidly, despite the fact I was pretty sure I'd been polite. It was pretty clear there was some serious nastiness directed my way, and I really didn't understand why. Sure, most of the masters would not be writing me a letter of recommendation anytime soon, but I wouldn't have guessed that Castle security guards and receptionists had anything against me.

I forced another friendly smile. Those were getting harder to come by. Still, I managed one and said, "They explained that. And then we moved on to my next query and it was going just as well."

The blonde looked up at the security guard and said, "Fred, he expects us to arrange meetings with the masters for him. You believe that?"

All three of the security guards chuckled at this, and Fred the Security Guard asked, "You want them to get you a meet and greet with the Archmage while they're at it?"

"That would be excellent," I said, trying not to let them see I was bothered. Based on the burning feeling in my cheeks, I don't think it worked.

Fred took a few steps toward me. "Do I look like your personal assistant, Blade Mage? You think because you've got that sword on your back we're supposed to bend over backwards? Get serious."

"I don't suppose there's anyone else I could talk to?"

"I'm on the on-duty Security Supervisor," Fred said, pointing at his own chest. "End of the line."

"Right," I said. Feeling desperate, I asked, "Can you at least tell me if Parker Grimm is around?"

"No," Security Supervisor Fred said. "Like I said, end of the line."

"Okay, then," I said. "Thanks everyone."

As I started toward the door, Security Supervisor Fred asked, "And where do you think you're going?"

Turning around, I said, "Well, I get the impression I'm not going to get much help here, so I'm just going to head on to the Castle."

Security Supervisor Fred shook his head.

I raised an eyebrow at him.

"You don't have security authorization," he said.

"Seriously? I've been to the Castle countless times."

"By invitation," he said, and apparently it was his turn to roll his eyes. "What? Now you think that sword on your back is a golden key to just go wherever you want?"

"No, but—"

"You think because you're the Blade Mage you automatically get to stroll around wherever you want? You think you're above security clearance?"

I sighed. "And where do I request security clearance?"

"From me," he said, crossing his arms over his combat-armored chest. A hint of a smirk played at the corner of one bushy handlebar. Clearly, he was enjoying himself. *Asshole.*

"Oh, joy," I said. "And let me guess... You're not going to give me clearance."

"Oh, I'll give you clearance, Blade Mage. Hell, better clearance than you deserve."

He stepped behind the counter and opened a drawer beside the blonde. After rummaging for a few seconds, he withdrew a white badge on a blue lanyard and threw it at me.

I caught it awkwardly and turned the badge over in my hand. The word GUEST was written in giant letters. Below that, in smaller letters was RESTRICTED.

"You're to wear that at all times while on Castle grounds. Failure to comply will result in your immediate ejection from the premises. You're to comply with any order given to you by a member of my security staff. Failure to comply will result in your immediate ejection from the premises."

"Seriously?"

Ignoring me, Security Supervisor Fred continued, "You are not authorized to enter the Castle proper without the escort of a senior-level member of the Cabal. You are also prohibited from approaching any of the houses."

"So, what exactly do I have access to?"

"Common areas. Like the library, the hospital, and the gardens."

"Great," I said, turning and heading for the door. "You've all been a big help."

He might've said something else, but I didn't hear him as I went out the door.

# CHAPTER TWO

Back in my truck, I sat quietly for a few moments, trying to get my blood to simmer from a boil. My initial reaction was to leave. To just turn around and go back home.

But that was what they wanted, wasn't it?

And the Archmage had said this wouldn't be easy. In fairness, he *hadn't* said it'd be an absolute fucking nightmare, either.

So, Security Supervisor Fred, his fellow security guards, and his receptionist buddies wanted me gone. By not giving me a place to stay, nor access to the Castle, they thought they'd run me off.

I was mad.

So mad, in fact, I thought the thought which is typically better left un-thought.

What would Axel do?

An idea came almost immediately.

A *really* bad idea.

I put my truck back in drive and headed toward the exit.

Security Supervisor Fred and his band of misfits would think they'd won.

That was okay. It would only set them up for the much bigger disappointment that was to come.

Oh, yes, they were about to meet the stubborn wrath of the Blade Mage. If they hadn't liked me before, they damned sure wouldn't like me after this.

# CHAPTER THREE

The guard at the shack seemed surprised when I returned. This time, he didn't give me any guff and let me right through.

Security Supervisor Fred just happened to be standing outside the Reception Hall as I drove past, so I gave him a friendly wave. He didn't seem thrilled to see me. *Weird.*

I continued onward, toward the Castle proper and the large buildings surrounding it. Since I didn't have access to the Castle itself, my destination was actually the beautiful and well-manicured lawn in front of it. About the size of a football field, it maintained a lush green, even during the harshest freezes. And there was always a variety of flowers painted across its expanse. The colors changed every time I visited. This go around it was a sea of purple and blue. I didn't know what kind of voodoo magic the gardeners used to keep it so pristine, but it was really something.

In fact, the front lawn of the Castle was so revered for its beauty that few people dared step on it. I didn't know whether there was actually a rule against it, or if folks just thought better of traipsing through the pretty scenery.

I tapped the brakes on my truck and studied the sea of flowers, second guessing my plan of action. It was too late to hesitate, though. I'd just spent a butt-load of money at the nearest Walmart, and I was committed. Despite the risk of further damaging my reputation, I knew it was time to make a statement, good or bad.

I let my foot off the brake and eased my truck out onto the lawn.

# CHAPTER FOUR

I was surprised at how quickly I pitched my tent.

And no, that wasn't innuendo. I was genuinely surprised how not-painful that process was. When I was a kid, that was always my least favorite part about camping. It felt like it took hours to set up my tent. Apparently, tent technology had come a long way. I was done in minutes.

After that, I started laying a fire. It wasn't particularly cold or anything, but I wanted my campsite to have the full effect.

Fortunately, before I'd left the house, Mother Goose had insisted on giving me five hundred dollars cash. On one hand, I was annoyed since I had barely been able to pay the electric bill that month. On the other hand, I was glad to have it to put to the good use of annoying jerk-faced security guards. Axel would've approved.

The cash had been more than enough to purchase a tent, an air mattress, a sleeping bag, a camp chair, a cooler, food, and all the basic camping gear one needed when going camping.

And going camping I was.

Right on the front lawn of the Castle.

I couldn't wait for Security Supervisor Fred to come along. Was it childish and petty? *Yup.* Would it make it harder for me to win people over? *Yup.* Was it worth it?

*Abso-frickin-lutely.*

I already had some spectators watching me from afar. There were five of them, three girls and two boys. All teenagers, best I could tell.

They didn't know what I was up to, but teenagers had a good nose for shenanigans because they hadn't yet been beaten down by the atrocious adulty nature of the real world. And it was clear I was up to some *serious* shenanigans.

I made a point of ignoring them while I got the fire going.

When I looked up again, the entire group had edged closer. It was as though they were afraid of me. As if they'd get in trouble by proxy, just for witnessing my desecration of the Castle lawn.

I continued my work until I heard footsteps approaching.

Glancing up, I expected to see Security Supervisor Fred or some other goon. Instead, I noticed one of the teens standing on the edge of my campsite.

The rest of the group had remained behind, but this one peppy-looking blonde girl had summoned up the courage to approach. The older I got, the harder it was for me to judge the age of younger folk, but I guessed she was seventeen or eighteen. She and her friends were probably in high school.

I offered her a little wave and said, "Hello."

"Uh, what are you doing?" she asked.

I raised an eyebrow and gave her a skeptical look. Then I motioned around my temporary home. "Setting up camp. What does it look like?"

"I mean... Why?" she asked with an equally skeptical look. "Why are you setting up camp on the front lawn of the Castle?"

"According to reception, there are no rooms available anywhere on the Castle grounds." I shrugged. "So..."

"But like... Here? Of all the places... Here?"

"Here is as good as anywhere, isn't it?"

"No," she said, shaking her head. "You're going to get in trouble. Like, *big* trouble."

That made me laugh.

"Seriously... Like some director is going to flip shit. You might even get the attention of a master. Oh, God, what if the Archmage or one of the other Arcane Guardians comes strolling through here?"

"It's all right," I assured her. "I pretty much stay in trouble with those guys."

She stared at me for a few moments, then asked, "Who are you?"

I moved closer and stuck out my hand. "Wyatt Draven. Nice to meet you."

Her eyes went wide and she took a step back. Like my outstretched hand was a rattlesnake.

"You're the Blade Mage."

"I am," I replied, more than a little surprised she knew who I was.

"That makes *so* much sense."

"Does it?"

"Well, yeah. You're the, like, most hated person in the Cabal. Literally the only person I could think of who'd be ballsy enough to pull a stunt like this. This is crazy."

"Uh, thanks, I think," I said, scratching the back of my head. If she thought I was the only person ballsy enough to try something like this, she clearly had never heard of Axel Gunner.

She turned around and started waving and yelling at her friends. "Guys! Get over here! He's Wyatt Draven. The Blade Mage!"

The remaining four teens shared some nervous glances, then collectively approached my camp.

As they closed in, the blonde explained what I'd told her. The kids stared at me with a mix of shock and wonder.

I felt one-part celebrity and one-part zoo animal. Like the rattlesnake from the earlier analogy, but now caged and wearing an adorable little bowtie and hat.

Trying to ignore the awkwardness of the situation, I asked, "Shouldn't you guys be in class or something?"

"We're on our lunch break," the blonde informed me.

I didn't have a chance to say anything more because that's when Security Supervisor Fred showed up. He started by berating the teens for being on the lawn and not in class.

"Pay attention, kids," I said, doing my best professor impression. "This man is a real-life example of why you need to try hard in school and stay out of trouble. You don't want to end up like him, now, do you?"

Fred turned his angry gaze on me, right where I preferred it. This little drama was between him and me. There was no reason to bring the adolescents into it.

The teens chortled among themselves, but backed away, albeit slowly.

"Just what the do you think you're doing?" Fred asked.

"Oh, just gettin' camp together. Got some beers in the cooler. Want one?"

"Are you serious?"

"Well, yeah," I replied as I flipped open my cooler. I pulled out a beer and held it out. Fred stared at my hand like I was holding the bowtie-wearing rattlesnake from my earlier analogies.

"No, I don't want a damned beer," he said, crossing his arms over his chest. Apparently, that was the signature Security Supervisor look.

I shrugged at him, closed the cooler, sat down on top of it, and popped the top. While I was taking my first gulp, Fred said, "You can't camp here!"

"Really?" I asked, taking another chug from the can.

"I'm not playing, Blade Mage. Get your shit and get off my lawn."

"Your lawn?"

"Yeah, asshat, *my* lawn. Right now, I'm the Security Supervisor on duty. Ergo, it's my *fucking* lawn."

"I see," I said in as calm a voice as I could manage. "Fred, have you considered the possibility you've let the inkling of authority you have go to your head?"

"Have you considered what's going to happen if you don't follow my orders?"

"Yes, I have."

"And yet you're still sitting here."

"Well, yeah," I said, shrugging. "Because nothing is going to happen."

"Is that right?" he asked, his hand moving closer to his holstered wand.

"Are you sure that's a good idea?"

His hand slowed, though the murderous rage in his eyes seemed about the same. He kind of reminded me of Sanchez a bit. I wondered if they might be cousins or something.

Fred spat on the ground and said, "There's nothing I'd like more than to teach you some respect."

"Really?" I asked, giving him an appreciative nod. "Bold. Personally, I wouldn't want to be known as the Security Supervisor who picked a fight with the Cabal's own Blade Mage on the front lawn of the Castle." I paused to add the dramatic effect of laughter. "Hell, if you think the masters are going to be pissed about my little campsite, just imagine what they'll say when they find out the Blade Mage and the on-duty Security Supervisor had a tussle, with innocent bystanders around, no less."

"You'd be in trouble, too."

I motioned around my campsite. "Does it look like I care?"

Security Supervisor Fred was still putting on airs because he didn't want to be seen as having backed down, yet I could tell I'd caused him some hesitance. "They might promote me for laying you out."

"Think?" I said, grinning at him.

"You're the Blade Mage who abandoned us, the one who holds the sacred role hostage while the whole supernatural world gets a little more batshit crazy every day and our people are out there getting bloodied. In a time when we need the Blade Mage the most, a punk-ass, spoiled brat hides the sword away in the mountains. They call you the Bastard Mage, did you know that? Yeah, if I put you out of your misery, I'd probably get a promotion."

Of all the things I might've expected, that wasn't it.

I can't lie and say his words didn't sting. They did. Not the Bastard Mage part, although I was surprised the nickname had stuck around. It was the part about abandoning them. That certainly explained the chilly reception. The narrative was that *I* had abandoned them, not the other way around. This was an enlightening, albeit disheartening, discovery.

I did my best to keep my voice even and said, "Fred, there's still one other thing you haven't taken into consideration."

"What's that?"

"The possibility this doesn't go the way you think it will."

The slightest twitch in his eye. That was the tell.

His scowl didn't soften, but that twitch gave him away. He hadn't taken that into consideration. It hadn't occurred to him he might not be able to take me in a fight. In fairness, I wasn't the strongest mage, but when it came to battle, well, that was something different. It wasn't all about who had the biggest magical swinging phallus.

And right then, Security Supervisor Fred was wondering whether his metaphorical magic phallus was, in fact, larger than my own.

Finally, he said, "I'm not too worried about it, chief."

"I'm not your chief, buddy."

"What?" he said. "Look, I know about you, Wyatt Draven."

"But apparently you don't know much about South Park," I replied. "You're supposed to say something like... I'm not your buddy, friend. To which I reply, I'm not your friend, guy. And so on. No? Never mind."

Ignoring me, he continued his tirade. "Yeah, I've heard all about you. You don't deserve that sword."

"That's probably true," I agreed. "What else have you heard about me, Fred?"

"A lot of silly rumors," he said. "Far-fetched nonsense."

"Such as?"

"Such as that ridiculous story about you facing down a shadow army. And how you supposedly uncovered some witch who'd infiltrated the Cabal, then killed her and her pet demon. Or how you fought an army of demons and dark wizards with that biker gang in Memphis. All just stories blown out of proportion. All just bullshit."

"You think so?"

"I do."

"But are you *sure*?" I asked, spreading my hands. "Because if I was going to pick a fight with someone who'd allegedly faced down witches, demons, dark wizards, and shadow monsters, as you have described, well, I'd want to be *real* sure those stories were just...stories. Because if any of that were true... If the individual I intended to bully actually *had* fought and *had* survived witches, demons, dark wizards, and shadow monsters, then what kind of odds would he have against the on-duty Security Supervisor?"

Fred didn't respond straight away. Which, if I'm honest, gave me hope he wasn't quite the dimwitted egocentric moron I'd taken him to be. He was still a moron, just not a completely dimwitted one. Had the moment been appropriate for it, I might've patted him on the head.

Finally, he gave me an extra ferocious scowl and said, "We'll just see what the masters have to say about your little campsite, Bastard Mage. You just wait."

"Will do," I replied cheerily. "Stop by later. I have the fixin's for s'mores."

Security Supervisor Fred stomped away. The teens, a much safer distance away, clapped and cheered.

# CHAPTER FIVE

Once I was done with visitors, I got back to my original mission. The fact my security card wouldn't allow me access to the Castle proper was a problem, but it wouldn't keep me from getting in front of some of the masters. Some worked in the common areas.

For example, Master Healer Cassandra Carter headed up the hospital. That seemed like a logical place to start. After the incident in Memphis, she'd ensured the Knights were healed up, along with the betrayed members of my former team, and me as well. During my meeting with the masters, she hadn't seemed like a particularly big fan of mine, but she had certainly been more even keeled than some.

I was immediately pleased to discover the receptionists at the hospital were much more friendly than the ones I'd dealt with earlier. I mean, sure, they looked at me like I was a bit off my rocker strolling in there and asking to see the top lady, but when I explained I was the Blade Mage, they actually sent someone to track down Master Carter for me.

The hospital wasn't massive, but it also wasn't small. The bottom floor had the walk-in clinic, dentist office, and pharmacy for those who lived or worked on the Castle's grounds. The emergency room was also on the first floor. The second floor consisted of rooms for patients who weren't going to be leaving right away and all the specialists. The third floor was intensive care and home to the school for magic healers. This was where I was told to go.

On the third floor, I was directed to a waiting room where I waited. And waited.

Over an hour passed before Master Carter finally appeared.

Master Healer Cassandra Carter was a striking woman in her mid-forties. She looked the part of serious business type, which wasn't too far off the mark, really. Not only was she so respected as a leader and mage to have promoted to the role of master, but she was also one of the greatest medical minds of the time, or so I was told. She'd received her doctorate at John Hopkins. Since then, she'd been featured in numerous fancy schmancy medical publications and involved in all kinds of research.

Just then, she had her nose glued to a clipboard and only bothered to give me the briefest of glances. "You wanted to see me? I have precious little time."

"Right," I said, rising to my feet. "I was hoping to speak with you for a few minutes."

"Follow me," she said, then abruptly turned and started down the hallway. I had to race to keep up.

Still staring at her clipboard, she said, "You have until we reach the end of this hall. Apologies, but I'm afraid that's all the time I can spare at the moment."

"Oh," I said. "I didn't realize I'd stopped in at a bad time."

"Rarely a good one these days, but just now I have an entire strike team that was mauled by a were-dog gang, and we're short-staffed today."

"That sounds serious."

"We've lost one already. We can save the rest, I think."

"That's good," I said, unsure what else to say. "About the rest of them, that is. Not the one."

I made a mental note to facepalm myself later. Prior to showing up here, I'd had this whole plan about what I was going to say. Now that I'd found my moment, it was all falling to pieces. "So, you're short-staffed?"

"Always," she said. "We've canceled classes today. Our students are getting on-the-job training."

"Is that safe?"

"Of course. First and second year students only observe. Only the experienced ones are allowed to touch a patient, and then only when supervised." She paused and glanced up at me. "I was serious, you know. I've only got about five more seconds. What did you wish to talk to me about?"

"Nothing critical," I said. "Perhaps I could come back to visit with you in a day or two when things calm down?"

"Maybe," she said. "Though I don't expect things to calm soon. More and more of our field operatives have been getting injured out there. The whole supernatural world is going to hell in a handbasket."

"Well, is there anything I could do to help? It seems you have your hands more than full."

"No," she said, and offered me an exhausted smile. "Last time I checked, you didn't have any medical training to speak of. I'm afraid my first-year students would be of more use."

"Right," I said.

"I appreciate the offer, though."

Before I could respond, a woman in a business suit approached with a stack of papers.

Master Carter immediately scowled. "I don't have time for this."

The other woman scowled right back. "I know, but we must discuss the hospital's budget."

"I already told you I'm not going to stop to talk about money until all of my patients are stabilized."

"I understand, but Mr. Spencer—"

"You go and tell our dear Chief of Business Operations to kick rocks."

"If I do that, he'll definitely slash our budget."

"Tell him if he slashes the budget, I'll turn him into a toad."

Master Carter charged through a door, the other woman on her heels. It closed unceremoniously in my face and I knew my time was up.

# CHAPTER SIX

Undeterred by my failed attempt at having a conversation with the Master Healer, I set off for the Forge.

The Forge was where the artificers practiced the art of creating magical trinkets. It was also where students trained to become artificers. That was a recurring theme throughout the Castle. Wherever the specialists did their work, there was also a school for training recruits.

The Cabal's magical education system followed along the same lines as the standard American education progression. As children, we had to attend elementary school, but those of us who showed the ability to manipulate magical energy were also sent to a sort of basic magic school, or Magic Elementary, as we called it. There, we began learning the basics of the craft. Then we had a magical junior high equivalent, and then high school. Afterwards, most would choose a specialty to continue focused training. Others would train in a variety of specialties. Some would go away to actual college and then come back to continue their magical training. There were no age requirements to train in a specialty. A person just had to have a modicum of talent in that particular arena and for a member of the staff to agree on admission.

I had followed none of the above paths. Having barely made it through the high school equivalent, I'd not really excelled in any particular branch of magic, though I had spent some time training with the Battle Mages.

Back to the point, the Forge was where the artificers worked and trained, and therefore, it seemed the most likely place to find the Master Artificer.

I wasn't sure if my limited access badge would get me into the Forge, since it was a highly-secured area. At least, I'd hoped it was. They held the blueprints and recipes to create loads of wonderful and terrifying magical devices. I was sure any number of mages—good, bad, or in-between—would've loved to get their hands on the information stored in the Forge.

Fortunately, it turned out the Forge had a reception desk as well, and again, the receptionists were much nicer than those in my earlier encounter.

I wasn't shocked when they stopped me at the entrance, but I was pleasantly surprised when one of them hopped up and offered to go let the Master Artificer know I was there. I was nearly positive the receptionist was a mage, and likely could've used mind-speak, but they probably got tired of sitting behind the desk all day and wanted any excuse to get away.

Unfortunately, he promptly returned and informed me the Master Artificer was otherwise disposed. Much like Master Carter at the hospital, the artificers were up to their boobs in work, due to an increase in violent supernatural incidents. Apparently, the constables out in the field were under a lot of pressure and Cabal leadership had assigned the artificers with creating new defensive trinkets to be deployed in short order.

The receptionist suggested I try back in a few days or try to schedule a meeting through normal channels, whatever that meant.

# CHAPTER SEVEN

Feeling a little dejected, I started back toward my camp. It seemed all the masters were going to be too busy to make time for me. Perhaps my plan had been a stupid one. And stacking the campsite on top of it was only going to make things worse.

I was so busy brooding I walked right past one of the masters without even realizing it.

"That's not very observant of you, Wyatt."

I whirled around to see where the voice came from.

Leaning against a gray stone wall was none other than Master Watcher Giovanni Jackson. Rather by design, or pure coincidence, his slim fit suit was the same gray as the wall, causing him to blend in like a chameleon.

It wouldn't have surprised me to learn the Master Watcher had a magic suit. The Watchers were basically spies, after all. The spooks of the Cabal. If James Bond had traded his cool personality for magic, he'd have been a Watcher. That's not to say the Watchers didn't have personality. I'm sure many of them knew how to wield it as a tool for their purpose. The Watchers were a scary a bunch like that, and Master Jackson was their leader.

Somewhere on the Castle grounds, or in the Castle itself, the

Watchers probably had a base of operations, or at least an office. I didn't know where it was, though. I'd wager only a very select few outside their order did. Certainly not rent-a-cops like Security Supervisor Fred. Which was why it was so fortunate I'd run into him. And I say "fortunate" instead of "lucky" because there wasn't anything *lucky* about it. There was little doubt he'd sought me out. And that was *fortunate* because I wouldn't have had any way to seek him out.

"Master Jackson," I said, offering him my best smile. "I was hoping to run into you."

"And so you have," he replied, pulling himself from the wall. It reminded me of watching a snake uncoil itself. He fell in step beside me and started forward. "It seems you've been trying to get someone's attention."

"Looks like it worked."

"Perhaps."

A moment of awkward silence passed between us. I broke it by saying, "So, I'm sure you're probably wondering why I'm here."

"Not really," he replied. "I think I've got the gist."

"Okay, so would it be possible for me to get a few minutes of your time, then?"

"No," he said. "I do not need to sit down with you, Wyatt. Nor do you have any genuine need to speak with me."

"But—"

He held up his hand, stopping me.

"I'll be watching you, Wyatt Draven. That's my job, isn't it?"

"I suppose it is."

"Then rest assured, I will learn all I need to know."

"That seems...fair, I suppose," I replied, scratching the back of my head.

He held out a small index card to me.

I took it from him and glanced down at what appeared to be a scribbled address.

When I looked up again, he flashed me a devil's grin. "That address is here on the Castle grounds. There's someone there you may wish to see."

With that, he pivoted and walked away. Apparently, our conversation was over.

Looking around, I realized I was standing in front of the library. Another of the masters ran it, so I figured I'd stroll in there to try my luck. I wondered if Master Jackson had led me there by design, or if it was just happenstance, because if there was any master I had a chance to win over, it was the Master Librarian.

# CHAPTER EIGHT

L ike so many of the buildings on the Castle grounds, the library
was yet another brilliant work of art. Its gray stone pillars
stretched to the sky, giving it the look of some ancient Greek pavilion.
This was no small-town library. No, it was an exceptional piece of archi-
tecture that housed a massive collection.

All three stories were packed with rows of books and quiet study
rooms. However, it was the basement that was of particular interest to
me just then. The levels below ground were where the truly interesting
books, manuscripts, tomes, and grimoires were kept. Rumor had it the
sub-floors could withstand a nuclear blast, which made sense considering the written history of the Cabal was kept there, along with countless volumes about magic.

Mages were allowed to enter the first sub-floor for common books
about magic, but the really good stuff was kept below that, even. I
didn't know how many floors into the earth it went. For the all the extra
security the artificers had, the library had even more. It was, perhaps, the
most valuable building aside from the Castle itself.

As I made my way inside and found the stone steps that would lead
me to the first underground floor, it occurred to me I should've just
started my mission in the library. Master Librarian Santiago Serrano had

been more friendly toward me than anyone else on the Archcouncil. I guess I'd wanted to save him for last, as sort of an insurance policy. However, given my luck so far, it only made sense to move him to the front of the list.

As I entered the sub-floor, I headed straight for the desk and the librarian manning it. The Cabal librarians were a different breed. Mostly, they were bookworms with an abundance of intelligence and strange personalities. It took a special kind of person to dedicate their lives to maintaining the Cabal's prized library. I could but salute their efforts.

When I explained to the young woman working the counter that I was hoping to see Master Serrano, she promptly closed her eyes and said nothing. It took me a moment to realize she was using mind-speak, probably reaching out directly to the Master Librarian.

After a few moments, she opened her eyes again and told me to follow her.

She led me back through a series of shelves, each filled with volume upon dusty volume. It was a maze, and when she finally stopped, I wasn't sure I'd be able to find my way back. However, she motioned down the aisle where I saw a familiar figure leaning over a cart full of books.

Without another word, my guide turned and disappeared back into the paper jungle.

Master Librarian Santiago Serrano was studying a book, and appeared to be trying to determine where on the shelf it belonged. Were he not a master, I might've thought he hadn't noticed my approach, but I knew better. For the many faults I might've found in the masters, none of them were easily surprised.

They were each among the best in their respective fields, but they were all also experts at virtually all aspects of the craft.

And they were all trained battle mages.

And politicians.

And great leaders in their own ways.

I couldn't deny them their skills and experience. The masters were *all* badasses.

The man on the other end of the row might've looked like a jolly

Santa, totally focused on finding where the book belonged on the shelf, but in reality, he knew I was approaching.

"I wouldn't have thought the Master Librarian would be the one to put the books away," I said as I drew closer.

"I find it to be a therapeutic exercise, Mr. Draven," he said, still not looking up at me. "And it's always good to remember where you came from. If my librarians see me putting away books, they certainly won't get it in their heads they're too good for a little manual labor."

I couldn't argue with his logic.

"Ah," Master Serrano said, finally finding the home of the rogue book. Once it slid into place, he finally turned to look at me. A big grin spread across his cheeks. "Wyatt Draven, to what do I owe the pleasure?"

"Well, I was hoping to visit with you for a few minutes."

"Is that so?" he asked, moving his cart a few feet down the aisle and pulling off another book. As he studied the shelf, he asked, "Any particular subject you wish to broach with me?"

I hesitated, unsure what to say. I'd planned for this moment, but when it arrived, again I froze. So, I went for broke. "I was hoping to get your advice on how I might improve my relationship with the Archcouncil."

"I see," he said, still not looking at me. "So, you took to heart the rather critical feedback from your last meeting."

"Yeah, more or less," I said. He didn't need to know the Archmage had come around to drive the point home.

"That's good. Well done. It speaks to your character. However, I'm fairly limited on time currently. Will you be around for a few days?"

"I certainly can be," I said. "Assuming I don't lose my current housing."

"Good," Master Serrano said. "Pop back in tomorrow morning. Perhaps I'll have more time to speak then."

"Thank you," I said. "Will do."

As I struggled to find my way back to the exit, I was thankful at least one of the masters was willing to give me a chance.

# CHAPTER NINE

From the library, I decided to take a break from chasing down masters and try to find the address on the card Master Jackson had given me. If I'm honest, curiosity got the better of me. Who could've been there that I needed to see?

It took some serious walking, but I finally located the right street and found myself in one of the smaller suburb-type neighborhoods.

It gave me the willies.

And not because Security Supervisor Fred told me to stay out of the residential areas.

I'd read *A Wrinkle in Time* when I was a kid, and there was this scene with perfectly matching houses, and fathers mowing in sync, and children bouncing their balls in sync...except for that one little boy. *Fucking no.*

Ever since, standard suburban neighborhoods, with their packed-in mirror image lookalike houses, gave me the creeps.

Not to mention most of the people living in the houses were wizards, and it just seemed so...odd. Even as a wizard, I couldn't help but think that if someone described a neighborhood of wizards, I'd picture gray stone towers, or tree houses, or witches flitting about on brooms, or, I dunno, like, caves or lairs, or something.

But *no*, it had to be *super* normal.

Super normal and creepy as hell.

At any rate, I found the mailbox and checked my card again. This was the place. A little brick home with a well-manicured lawn, just like the rest of them.

Who lived there?

There was no way to know, but one way to find out.

I walked up to the door and rang the doorbell.

A few moments later, an aging woman opened the door.

"Yes?" she asked, giving me a once-over.

"Uh, hi," I said, forcing a smile. "I, uh, I was told there was someone here I should see... And now that I'm saying that out loud, I realize how odd it sounds. It's possible I'm in the wrong place."

"Who sent you?" she asked, and I noticed she looked tired. Not like she'd had a bad night or two, but the kind of tired a face only wore after months of sleepless nights and endless struggle.

"Master Watcher Giovanni Jackson."

"Then you must be here to see my son," she said with a nod. "Lately, I've been turning visitors away, but if a master sent you..."

Her words trailed off.

"Who's your son?" I asked.

"You don't know?" she replied. "My boy's name is Barrett."

"Barrett," I repeated back to her, feeling the lump forming in my throat. The resemblance was slight, but I finally noticed it. "I... I do know your son. I know him well."

Last I'd seen him, he been unconscious and lying in a hospital bed, struggling to survive after being literally stabbed in the back by one of our former teammates.

She gave me a long, hard look and finally said, "You can come in. But don't expect him to talk to you."

"You don't think he'll speak to me?" I asked.

"He doesn't speak to anyone," she said, turning away as she spoke. "Not since... Well, I guess you know, don't you?"

"I do," I replied. "How has his recovery been?"

"They say his lung may never fully recover. Otherwise, physically, he's fine."

"Physically," I repeated at her back as she led me through the house.

"Yeah, physically," she said over her shoulder. "Like I said, he hasn't spoken to anyone since."

She led me to a small room and motioned for me to go inside.

I took a deep breath and forced my feet forward.

The big guy was seated on a bed, his face forward, eyes a million miles away. He might've been staring at something intensely, only there was nothing in front of him save a blank wall.

His mother followed me as far as the doorway and waited, arms over her chest like a prison guard. After all her son had been through, I couldn't say I blamed her.

Barrett was still an imposing figure, even in sweats. But gone was the easy smile.

He didn't react to my presence. Didn't even look up to see who'd entered the room. It was like he wasn't even there.

"Hey, Barrett," I forced myself to say. "It's me...Wyatt."

Nothing. Not even a blink.

I glanced from him to his mother, unsure what to say.

The guilt flooded over me then, almost too much to bear. On some level, I knew it wasn't my fault. There was no way I could've known half my old team had gone to the dark side. But I'd been there... I'd been there when they betrayed him.

I'd seen Zeke, a man who'd been Barrett's best friend, stab the big guy in the back.

I'd watched Zeke drive Barrett to the ground, his fist wrapped around the hilt of the knife.

And they'd gotten away.

I hadn't stopped them.

"I'm sorry, Barrett," I heard myself say, but I wasn't even sure which thing I was apologizing for. "I'm so sorry."

Still, he didn't react.

I couldn't take anymore. I needed to get out.

"I'll find them," I said. "I promise you, we *will* find them."

I turned and started for the door. His mother stepped to the side to let me out and then followed me back to the front door.

On the doorstep, she said, "Wyatt."

I turned and looked at her.

"You're the Blade Mage, aren't you?"

I nodded.

"You used to be on my boy's team, didn't you?"

Again, I nodded.

"He mentioned you," she said, forcing her own smile. "He always liked you."

"He's a good friend," I said, looking away. "He was... He was always looking out for me."

"You were there," she said, forcing my gaze back to hers. It wasn't a question.

"Yes, ma'am."

"You know," she said, motioning at her home. "All this. I never had anything like this. I was just a minor hedge witch. A nobody. My boy, though... He had power. Real power, and an even bigger heart."

"The biggest," I replied.

"He believed in the Cabal. He earned his way, and he got me this place. Moved me here where it would be safe. Got me this big house. He was respected. Loved."

"He still is."

"No," she said, shaking her head. "They took it from him. They took away my boy. They took away everything he worked for. They betrayed him."

"I know."

"You find them, Wyatt," she said, eyes still locked on mine. "You find those sons of bitches and you kill them. You kill them for my boy."

"Yes, ma'am."

# CHAPTER TEN

I made my way back to camp. Security Supervisor Fred did not, in fact, show up to have s'mores with me. The teenagers did, though.

Their names were Katie, Tyler, Aarav, Ashley, and Mallory, and it turned out they were all seniors in high school, and since they were attending school at the Castle, that meant they were all in their final year of basic magical training as well.

Katie was the bubbly blonde who'd first approached my campsite. She had a knack for healing magic, so when school let out, she'd end up training with the other healers at the hospital. Or she might go to regular med-school to get her doctorate, just like Master Healer Cassandra Carter had. She was undecided as of the yet, because while she dreamed of getting her doctorate, she couldn't bear the thought of giving up her pursuit of magic for seven years.

Tyler was a skinny nerd with a strange-looking neck. He was mostly quiet, but when a particular topic of interest came up, he'd jump in the middle of it forcefully, ensuring everyone knew his opinions. It was pretty clear he had it bad for Katie, but I couldn't tell whether she'd caught on. He wasn't sure on what pursuit of studies he was going to follow when the year ended. Apparently, he was pretty talented with enchantments, but found scrying incredibly interesting, and some part of him wanted to pursue the path of a healer, though I couldn't imagine why that might've been.

Aarav was a foreign exchange student from another magic guild in India. I hadn't been aware the Cabal did a foreign exchange program. Apparently, he was supposed to have gone back two years earlier but had liked it here so much that his parents and guild had agreed he could stay with the Cabal, for the time being. He was a shy one. However, his friends explained that despite his timid nature, he'd excelled in offensive magic and was set to train as a battle mage, which likely meant he'd end up in the Cabal's military force, or on a special strike team like I'd been on, assuming he stuck around.

Ashley was a quiet girl, who I learned was not particularly shy. Just not so interested in the group dialogue. An avid reader, her goal was to train under Master Santiago Serrano and to become a librarian, but also to continue her training as a healer and as a battle mage, which on the surface didn't make sense, but I supposed if someone ever attacked the library, they could reflect over their poor life choices as she stitched up their ass after just kicking it.

And Mallory was a heavyset girl with bright blue hair, as vibrant as her personality. That was sarcasm. She clearly had some social issues and felt a need to one-up the others as they spoke, but her friends didn't seem to let it bother them. *Good for them.* She was also undecided on her path forward, and like me, she hadn't had a standout ability. On one hand, that left the possibilities wide open. On the other hand, it made it difficult to pick. This, apparently, was one of her favorite topics of discussion, and perhaps, I negatively assessed, might be the very reason she hadn't chosen. Her group of friends were very concerned about getting it sorted for her, and that kept the attention pointed her way. Then again, maybe I was just a judgmental prick.

Best I could tell, they were good kids with bright futures in front of them. It made me think perhaps I could've done more with my own studies. Here I was, the Blade Mage, and I didn't even have a specialty. How could I expect anyone to take me seriously when I'd never even taken my own training to the next level?

We spoke late into the evening about their plans, dreams, and aspirations. I'd sort of forgotten what that was like. To always be looking forward. I guess that's part of getting older, but I missed it. I missed having a big bright future in front of me with endless possibilities. I supposed I still could, but it's strange as an adult. You get so caught up in life and all the nonsense that you forget to dream sometimes.

What did I have? I would either die alone in the hills or I'd be killed by some evil prick I wasn't strong enough, or clever enough, to kill first.

Still, though, maybe the kids' view of life was the right one to have, regardless of age. I mean, I didn't think that a person should totally focus forward. It made sense to remember and learn from your past, to have aspirations for the future, but to stay focused on the moment. That was probably the right way to live, but it wasn't the way I'd been living. I'd let life beat me down.

Still, for that one evening, as we sat around my camp, eating s'mores, and talking about the future, I caught a glimpse of what it was like to have something to look forward to again. And...it felt pretty good.

Although I hadn't made much progress with the masters, my mission had been to improve my relationship with people in the Cabal. They weren't masters, directors, or even security supervisors, but they were people, and they were a part of my Cabal. So, when I laid my head down that night, it was with the knowledge my mission hadn't been a complete failure.

# CHAPTER ELEVEN

I was never a morning person, but the frigid dawn air roused me from my slumber, and I had no luck falling back asleep. Since I was miserable and awake, I decided I would mess with Security Supervisor Fred. It seemed the only logical course of action.

There were numerous stone paths that led between the gray stone buildings of the Castle grounds. On many of these paths, particularly along busy intersections, there were decorative fountains, sort of like at a shopping mall or fancy schmancy office building.

I chose the fountain at the intersection between the library and the chapel, as I'd noticed it had a lot of traffic the previous evening. I was not disappointed by the volume of commuters in the morning, either. It was even busier. *Perfect.*

I stripped down to my boxers, hopped into the pool at the base of the fountain, and had myself a nice, long bath.

I won't say it was relaxing, because it wasn't.

It was colder than the devil's heart. I didn't just shrivel. I was pretty sure I was poking through the back. My outie became an innie.

Of course, I could've just gone to the gym to shower, and in fact, I planned to do just that later on, assuming my security card got me access. I'd have to be sneaky about it, though, because I wasn't putting on this whole show just to get caught showering like a normal person.

I had just got the shampoo in my hair when everyone's favorite Security Supervisor showed up. With that many people passing by, I'd known someone would tattle.

He had two other security guards with him as well, both younger guys, presumably rookies. I made this assessment based on the fact they were both trying to hide their amusement. Like my young friends from the day before, the world hadn't pistol-whipped the shenanigans out of them yet.

I suspected Security Supervisor Fred might try, so it was up to me to defend the good nature of rookie security guards.

Fred put his hands on his hips in a weird Supermanesque pose, glared at me, and said, "Just what the hell do you think you're doing?"

"Bathing," I replied as I continued shampooing my hair.

"In the chapel fountain?"

"In the chapel fountain," I replied.

Without bothering to rinse out the shampoo, I reached over to the side of the pool where I had my bright pink luffa and body wash. As I began to scrub across my chest, I said, "You know, it's a shame there weren't any rooms available. This water is cold."

"You need to get out of the pool," Fred said. "Now."

"Can't," I replied, looking around. "I don't have anywhere else to wash up."

"I'm not repeating myself."

"Hey, there's an idea. You security guys probably have a private shower. Care if I use your facilities?"

"Absolutely not."

"Then the fountain it is."

"No, it isn't," he said, starting forward until he stood right at the edge of the pool. "Get out."

"If you think this is bad, you don't even want to know what I've been doing when I need to go to the bathroom. I'll give you a hint... It involves a five-gallon bucket."

That staggered him. I'm sure his first thought was that I was bluffing, but when he remembered the restricted access he'd given me, he had to consider which buildings had a public restroom and whether I would've known. The look on his face told me he wasn't confident.

Finally, he asked, "Where did you leave the mess?"

"Which time? There's more than one. Think of it like a scavenger hunt, but without clues or prizes. A really *shitty* scavenger hunt."

This wasn't actually true. Several of the buildings I had access to *had* restrooms, and I *was* aware of them. Still, I liked the idea of him losing sleep over whether I'd actually defecated somewhere on the Castle grounds. I doubled down.

"Fine. One clue, but just one... Someone on the golf course might think of it as a 'hole in one,' if you catch my drift."

"Listen," Fred said, trying to maintain his composure. "You can either cooperate, or we can drag you out of there. I was sent by leadership."

"No, you weren't. If a master, or even a Director, told you to come get me out of this pool, then we wouldn't be having this conversation, would we?"

Security Supervisor Fred didn't reply.

"Do you want to know what I think?" I said.

"What's that?"

"I think there were rooms available. I think you and those little rays of sunshine in reception took it upon yourselves to punish me. Whether I deserved it or not is beside the point, because I think you guys made that decision on your own, thinking I'd tuck my tail and run home. But I didn't. I'm still here. And now you're trying to figure out what the hell to do about me before one of the masters comes along and starts asking a lot of questions."

"Is that what you think?" Fred asked through gritted teeth.

"It is," I said, then pointed toward the bottle of conditioner sitting on the edge of the pool. "Could you hand me that? I like my hair to be soft."

I didn't actually need the conditioner. I still had the shampoo in my hair, after all. But I just wanted to see how he'd react. Which ended up being better than I'd expected.

"This?" Fred asked as he picked up the bottle.

I nodded.

Fred turned and chucked it back down the walking path, where it busted and splattered across the cobblestones.

"Well, see, now someone's just going to have to clean up your mess," I said, shaking my head at him. "And my hair won't be shiny today. We both lose."

Fred turned and snapped his fingers at one of the younger guards, then pointed to where he'd thrown my conditioner. The bastard couldn't be bothered to actually speak to his subordinate. My mind jumped to a particular episode of South Park where there'd been a Biggest Douche in the Universe award, and I wondered idly if Fred could've been a runner-up. I suspected the reference would've been lost on him again.

And he had such a smug look on his face.

As though he'd won.

As though by throwing my conditioner, he'd somehow actually taught me a lesson.

But all he'd really done...

"Well," I said while offering my most innocent smile. "I guess my bath is done, then."

I dropped backward into the pool, causing as much of a splash as I could.

The freezing water was as sharp as a knife against my skin, but I didn't care. I just hoped Fred was in my splash radius.

When I resurfaced, I saw he hadn't escaped the Wyatt Tsunami. In fact, his entire front was soaked from the head down. He shivered once, then the shock plastered on his rosy cheeks dissolved into rage.

I thought he might actually attack, but he didn't. He just continued staring at me like the village idiot.

It was only an unchecked chortle from one of his subordinates that snapped him back to reality. His head whipped around to glare at the rookie, whose poorly-timed chuckle immediately morphed into a cough.

Without another word, Security Supervisor Fred turned and stalked away, leaving me to my bath.

# CHAPTER TWELVE

Back at camp, I'd just put on dry clothes when I noticed something interesting.

A group had just come out of the front entrance of the Castle proper, which wasn't out of the ordinary, but I noticed that three among them were dressed in what I could only describe as Native American ceremonial dress. I wasn't an expert on Native American culture by any means, but it looked like they'd just arrived straight from the seventeen hundreds, or like they'd just clocked out from a history museum.

I sat down in my camp chair and studied them as I sipped on camp coffee. The group, ten or so, moved by, paying no mind to the strange man camping on the lawn. I didn't recognize the three Native American men, but I did recognize Master Battle Mage Zephyrine Castillo and Master Elementalist Thibault Washington. And leading the pack was none other than Grand Enchanter Marius Gunner.

I hadn't counted on seeing any of the other Arcane Guardians while I was at the Castle.

I knew the Archmage wouldn't make time for me. He'd said all he wanted to say to me. The other three, second in command only to the Archmage, would be too busy to bother with me.

That's why I'd set my sights on the next level down and had focused on the masters. But if I had a chance to steal a moment with Marius, I'd jump on it.

I'd known him since I was a kid, and though he was something like an uncle to me, it didn't mean we were close. Still, the last time I'd seen him, he hadn't been *quite* as hostile.

He could've been warming up to me, or maybe he wasn't a dick because he wasn't asking me to murder his own son. Hard to say.

The group stopped at the end of the lawn, just out of earshot, so I couldn't tell what was said. I could tell that the Native American men weren't happy, though.

This provided mild curiosity while I plotted on how to steal a minute of the Grand Enchanter's time.

Although the state of Oklahoma fell within our area of operation, the Cabal recognized the various tribal lands as sovereign nations, only operating in them under strictly agreed terms. During my time with the Kingsnakes, we'd always had to be careful when working jobs in Oklahoma. It was key to understand which tribal lands we were on and what agreement the Cabal had with the tribe. Some allowed the Cabal free rein to manage the whole of the supernatural population. Others didn't want us operating within their nations at all. Mostly, the Cabal respected the tribe's desires, but it was still a game of politics.

The way I understood it, there were occasional disputes, and often, the terms were renegotiated. I could only assume that the three Native American men had come to the Cabal to either negotiate new terms, or they wanted something from the Cabal, but the price had been too high. Either way, it hadn't gone the way they'd hoped. That's how it went when dealing with a giant organized monster like the Cabal. I knew that better than anyone.

I watched as the Grand Enchanter shook hands with each of the men, then turned away and headed back toward the Castle alone, leaving his underlings to escort their guests back to the front gate or wherever they'd parked.

I jumped from my chair, spilling coffee everywhere. I tossed the tin cup aside, then nearly tripped over my own feet, racing toward the Grand Enchanter. I knew I wasn't likely to get another opportunity like this.

Marius walked at a clip, like a very important person off to do very important things. He was halfway back to the Castle when I caught up with him.

"Grand Enchanter Gunner," I said between breaths as I tried to match his pace.

"Wyatt," he replied, not bothering to even look at me.

Trying to think of a conversation topic, I asked, "So, what was that about?"

"None of your concern."

"Okay, well, how's the investigation to find my old teammates going?"

"We haven't found them."

"Anything I can do to help?"

"No."

"Cool. Anything interesting going on?"

He didn't bother to respond.

We were at the steps of the Castle proper and in moments he'd go inside, and I'd be left at the door because of my restricted access. I mean, there was a chance they'd let me through since I was walking alongside the second-highest ranking leader in the entire Cabal, but there was an equally good chance that Marius would tell them not to let me in. So, I had exactly zero seconds to get him engaged in a conversation.

"Listen, I was really hoping you might have five minutes to talk with me. I'd really appreciate it."

"No," he said, and continued on into the Castle.

I stopped and turned around, wondering how he and my father had ever been BFFs. As far as I could tell, Grand Enchanter Marius Gunner had the personality of a mistreated pet rock. I was always amazed that Axel was his son.

Heading back to camp, I was annoyed, but the day was still young. There were hours of crushing defeat ahead of me to look forward to.

# CHAPTER THIRTEEN

I gobbled down a peanut butter and jelly sandwich, then made the long walk to the old training yard.

In the not-so-distant past, when I'd been training as a battle mage, the training yard was where I'd spent a good deal of time, but never by choice. My old shoes had stomped the rugged trails more times than I cared to count, and most of the muscle I'd ever built had been with the old, rusted weights.

Just around the time I'd joined the Kingsnakes, the Cabal had opened a brand-spanking-new gym with state-of-the-art equipment and climate control. It had a huge weight room with every piece of equipment imaginable, a full-length track, yoga studios, and even a rock-climbing station. It had everything one could imagine in a gym. The old training yard was all but forgotten.

It was strange, though, that despite its three pools, saunas, martial arts studios, and basketball and tennis courts, it made me uncomfortable.

The training yard, on the other hand, was open to the misery of the elements and had garage sale equipment—mismatched dumbbells, dinged-up weights, and barbells wrapped with medical tape that had browned from years of sweat and rust. It made me feel right at home.

In fact, it really wasn't all that different from my own setup.

Ever since Memphis, I'd decided it was probably time to get a routine going. It seemed my life was destined to involve a lot of running from, and fighting, scary shit.

I needed to be in tip-top shape if I wanted to stretch my luck as long as possible.

Axel had been on board with the idea, even though he was the type of asshole who'd been blessed with phenomenal genes and stayed in shape with no discernable effort.

Still, he'd helped.

We made our meager living doing the occasional supernatural odd job. When those weren't available, we did normal odd jobs. We'd rake leaves for old folks, help a farmer put up a fence, or even help a local construction crew when they were shorthanded. All cash jobs. Never enough to make a mint, but we managed to barely get by.

This was why it annoyed me when Axel revealed mysterious piles of cash. I didn't know where he'd gotten it from, and I wasn't sure I wanted to know. What I *wanted* was for him to help with the bills, the little asshole.

Still, once we'd had the idea to set ourselves up a gym, we'd taken on a few extra gigs. One of the local contractors had had a house they were behind on, so we'd made a couple hundred bucks helping them hang drywall. Then we'd helped another crew dig a trench. That was fun. Then back to the drywall team to help sand the freshly mudded tape. Side note: I'd rather starve than sand drywall.

When it was done, though, we had enough to pay the bills and a little left over to start our gym.

First, we'd used old lumber, plywood, and discarded sheet metal to slap together a dingy shed. I knew nothing about carpentry, but Axel had claimed to be an expert. The shack didn't immediately fall over, so I had to let him have that one.

Next, we'd started hitting yard sales. At one we'd found a tattered bench with a barbell and a few scattered weights. At another, we'd found a set of dumbbells and a few more weights. And at another, we'd found a punching bag, a jump rope, and a bright pink yoga mat, which Axel had declared we must own.

And I'd been hitting the gym every day since.

Which was why I was more than happy to use the old training yard and its dilapidated equipment. As far as I was concerned, it was an upgrade. Plus, I didn't think anyone else would be using it.

I was wrong.

There was a group of seven people moving between the various stations. My first guess placed them as Cabal military.

Undeterred, I moved to an unoccupied area and began working through some yoga stretches Axel had convinced me to try. At first, I'd been an unwilling student, but it turned out that yoga was pretty hardcore.

I'd always been a believer that weightlifting was the best overall approach to staying in shape. I could even get my cardio in by not resting. Turns out, though, yoga is just as nasty. The combination had me limber, stronger, and faster in no time.

After my stretches, I moved to a free bench, loaded a plate on each side of the bar, and lay down to knock out a warmup set.

At home, Axel worked out with me most days, so I usually had a spotter. But much like a country dog, he wandered off from time to time and wouldn't come home for a day or two. During those times, I'd had to learn how much weight I could safely use without a spotter. It wasn't the brightest idea, but I knew better than to push myself to failure, and I always left the collars off, just in case I needed to dump the weights.

I finished my warmup set and racked the weight only to realize one of the strangers stood nearby, watching me.

She was a middle-aged woman with a piercing gaze, and her face looked like it had long ago forgotten how to smile. She was all business, this one.

Seeing she had my attention, she said, "Well, you're not complete mush."

"Uh, thanks, I think."

"Why aren't you in the fancy gym?"

"Doesn't suit me."

"And this does?"

"Yeah," I said, and perhaps a little more forcefully than was necessary. I'd never been keen on playing twenty questions with strangers. "Is there a point to all these questions?"

She stared at me for a moment longer, then asked, "Do you want to train with us? We've got an odd number."

My immediate reaction was to say no. I'd always been weird about working out with strangers.

That was part of the reason I didn't enjoy going to public gyms. It wasn't that I was embarrassed about working out in front of others or anything like that. It was all about my deeply-rooted paranoia. If someone wanted to kill me, what better opportunity would they find than when I was pinned beneath a couple hundred pounds of weight?

It was the same reason I wasn't keen on spotters I didn't trust. If I pushed myself to failure and they weren't paying attention, I could be in real trouble. I guessed I'd always had trust issues.

But I'd come to the Castle to show people I wasn't the asshole they'd made me out to be, and this had been too kind an offer to refuse.

So, I accepted.

They were called the Honey Badgers. A strike team, just like my old one. And just like the Kingsnakes, between assignments they hung around the Castle and trained, ensuring they'd be ready for the next job.

Commander Harris, as I learned she was called, barked orders and everyone followed them, myself included. One point of interest was in her designation as "Commander." When I was on a strike team, we'd just referred to Malik as our "Team Leader." I supposed he could've taken the mantle of "Commander" as well, but for whatever reason, he hadn't. In fact, our team was considerably less formal and rigid than the Honey Badgers. Either things had changed over the years, or some teams were just stricter.

She paired me off with a burly fella named Garza. He was close to my height, but had quite a bit more muscle. And by "quite a bit," I mean the dude didn't have a neck. He looked like a bulldog and sported a Mr. T mohawk, which showcased the sea of scars scattered about his skull. Like his boss, I got the impression he didn't smile often. He certainly wasn't chummy with me.

Harris didn't allow any slacking during training, nor did she believe in rest. By the time we were done, I was, well...done.

I was super glad I'd kept up with my routine at home. Otherwise, I'm pretty sure my heart would've exploded out of my chest. As it was, I ended up breathing like I was having a baby and was more than a little embarrassed. Still, I didn't quit.

Afterward, sitting in the grass and choking on my own sweat, Commander Harris glanced my way and said, "You aren't as worthless as everyone makes you out to be."

I didn't immediately respond. Until that point, none among her team had made it clear they even knew who I was. Garza hadn't said a word to me while we'd worked out together. Of course, between the running and racing from station to station, there hadn't been much time for idle chat. Or oxygen.

Wiping the stinging sweat from my eyes, I finally looked up at her and said, "Just how worthless do *they* say I am?"

"Well, you're not well loved," she replied with a casual shrug.

"I've caught on to that."

"You didn't know before?"

"Not really."

"Well, that makes sense," she said, shaking her head. "It would take some serious satchel fortitude for someone with your rep to show your face around here."

"Just how bad is it?" I asked, glancing between them. It seemed Commander Harris was the only one who'd do any talking, but I thought I might find an answer in the others' stony expressions.

I did not.

"Do you really want to know?" she asked.

"I do."

"Your name is both a curse and a joke, ever since the day you were chosen. People had just about forgotten you, though. Then you resurfaced, and now your name is a curse again."

"That bad?" I asked.

"Worse, even. In basic battle mage training, when someone fucks up, they call it pulling a Wyatt. Or they'll say, 'don't be a Draven.' "

"Wow," I said, unsure what else to say. It was one thing for them to point fun at my first name, but to degrade the Draven name, well, that had negative connotations toward my father as well. It only cemented the feeling I'd let him down.

Commander Harris pointed at Garza. "You're lucky, actually. Garza has long said if he ever met you in person, he'd just snap your neck and bring the sword back to the Cabal. Consequences be damned."

I stared at my training buddy, feeling validated in my paranoia about workout partners. There'd been plenty of opportunity to take advantage of my vulnerability.

I pictured myself on the bench as he spotted for me. If he would've simply pushed his own weight down on the bar, there would've been nothing I could've done. The barbell would've crushed my windpipe. He could've just said I'd dropped it. No one in the Cabal would've even questioned him.

The hate he was glaring at me suggested the thought might've crossed his mind, and I supposed it said more for his character that he'd decided not to murder me.

"I see," I said, turning my attention back to Harris. "Well, then, I guess I appreciate you guys allowing me to work out with you."

Their eyes were all on me as I pushed myself up on rubbery legs and made to leave.

"Nothing to say to defend yourself?" Harris asked.

I turned back toward her and chewed my lip, considering an appropriate response. Finally, I said, "No, I won't try to convince you. It's funny, though. Since the day I was chosen, I never thought anyone in this organization wanted me to be the Blade Mage. Back then, everyone just wanted me gone. So I left. But now, it seems that was the wrong decision and the narrative has changed. Now, I'm learning that everyone views me as the one who abandoned the Cabal." I chuckled. "You know, I remember just after the ceremony thinking maybe the best thing I could do would be to throw myself in front of a bus so the dice could be rolled again. Might've been the best choice. But I didn't. And now we're here. So, no, I won't try to convince you I'm not the asshole everyone makes me out to be. I probably deserve it, and I probably am."

When no one responded, I nodded at Harris and said, "Thanks again." Then I turned my attention back to Garza. "And thanks for not killing me when you had the chance."

I started off again, but Harris called out once more.

"Hey, Blade Mage. If you're still around tomorrow, we'll be at it again. Same time."

I nodded at her again, then headed back toward my campsite.

# CHAPTER FOURTEEN

There was a note at my campsite informing me I should return to the library. I grabbed my gym bag and headed to the fancy gym for a real shower, then made my way back to the library.

The receptionist once again led me to Master Serrano, but this time he was seated at a table with his face buried in a leather-bound book that looked rather ancient.

And he wasn't alone.

Sitting opposite the Master Librarian, also reading a book, was Master Diviner Agatha Brown.

Neither of them immediately acknowledged my presence, and Master Brown only paused briefly to take a sip from a steaming cup and scratch behind the ears of a black cat perched in her lap.

Master Diviner Agatha Brown was an elderly woman with sharp features who reminded me of a hard-nosed schoolteacher from old cartoons. That probably wasn't a fair assessment since I didn't really know her and had only ever seen her during my few council meetings. Still, she had a condition which Axel had taught me about. He said kids these days called it "resting bitch face."

Master Serrano seemed her opposite in nearly every way. His face didn't know how not to smile. Where she was thin and hawkish, he was fat and jolly.

And watching the two of them, it didn't seem they were engaged in work. It looked like they were just hanging out as friends.

His eyes still glued to the tome in front of him, Master Serrano finally said, "Good morning, Wyatt."

"Good morning, Master Serrano," I said, pulling up a chair.

He made a sputtering sound and pulled his eyes away from the book just long enough to roll them at me. "Please, in this informal setting, just call me Santiago."

"Thanks," I said.

He nodded toward Master Brown. "I'm sure you remember Agatha."

"Yes, of course," I replied, and was just about to say hello when she pounced.

"That'll be Master Brown, thank you very much," she said, tossing a scowl my way.

As if to add insult to injury, the black cat in her lap looked up at me and hissed.

"Don't mind Sir Charles," Santiago said, motioning toward the cat. "He's always moody in the morning."

"He's an excellent judge of character," Master Brown said.

"Oh, stop being a crotchety old shrew," Santiago said, a hint of mischief in his eyes as he studied his fellow master.

Her icy glare turned to meet his. "Remember who you're speaking to, Master Librarian. Keep at it and I'll turn you into a newt."

"A newt?" Santiago replied in his best attempt at a British accent. "My dearest lady, you wound me."

"I'll do more than wound you," she said, returning her attention to her book.

Sir Charles mewed and attempted to nuzzle her, but Master Brown didn't react, so he jumped from her lap to the table, where it might be easier to garnish the attention he desired.

Master Brown continued ignoring her cat, but Santiago did not. "Off the table, Sir Charles. This is a library."

Sir Charles hissed in reply.

"Agatha," Santiago said.

"Hmm?" she replied, eyes still on the pages in front of her.

"Please get Sir Charles off the table. We've been over this."

"He isn't hurting anything."

"Still, this *is* a library. Can't have miniature panthers on the tables."

"Now who's being a crotchety old shrew?"

Santiago shook his head, then winked at me. "I keep telling Agatha that she ought to start her own witch's coven. She already has the cat and the attitude, but I just can't seem to sell her on the idea."

"Maybe she isn't a witch," I offered.

"True," he agreed. "But in the morning, she's certainly a—"

"Say it," she said, whipping her head toward him. "I *dare* you."

"A wonderful and friendly person to be around," he said. "Her smile lights up the entire library. Why, if we could bottle it, we'd no longer have a need for reading lamps."

"Good answer," she replied, then turned her attention back to her book.

Santiago winked again, then said, "Check this out, Wyatt."

I got up from my seat and moved around behind him so I could peer over his shoulder at the book he was studying. On one page was a drawing of an unfamiliar sigil, and on the other page were handwritten words in an unfamiliar language. In fact, the characters were so strange, I wasn't really sure they were words at all.

"What is it?" I asked.

"A spell book," he replied. "One of our constables in Northern Missouri took it off the corpse of a nomad mage who attacked him."

"Truly?" I asked. It wasn't unheard of, but there were so few mages who'd dare risk the wrath of the Cabal. I guessed things really were getting bad out there. As though I hadn't already seen that for myself.

He nodded at me. "Poor young man didn't know when to quit. He might've been all right, but he injured two constables when they attempted to apprehend them. Nearly killed one of them."

"That's terrible," I replied.

"It's happening more and more," he said. "The whole supernatural world seems to be spinning out of control."

"I've heard," I replied, then on second thought, added, "I've seen."

"Would be a good time to have a capable Blade Mage," Master Brown muttered while still reading her book.

"*Agatha*," Santiago said, shaking his head.

"It's fine," I said, giving him a warm smile. Then I turned my attention toward Master Brown. "I didn't come here expecting anyone to roll out the red carpet for me. But I *did* come here to find out how I can help. I don't know where to pitch in to bring the most value."

"Likely at home," she said. "Back in your little exile."

"*Agatha!*" Santiago repeated in a more reproachful tone. "Wyatt has come to us looking for wisdom and guidance."

"Lucky him, then," she said. "I just gave him a bit of both."

"I'm not going home," I replied. "I'm also not going to throw myself in front of a bus."

"Huh?" Santiago asked, raising an eyebrow.

"Never mind," I said. "What I mean is... I'm here to help whether anyone wants me to or not. I keep hearing that the whole world is falling apart and how we desperately need a Blade Mage, yet no one seems interested in giving me the time of day. The sword *did* choose me, after all. Has anyone considered that perhaps it's seen something in me the rest of you haven't?"

Master Brown sighed and set down her book, then turned her full attention on me. "It isn't personal, Wyatt. My desire to see you return to your exile is not a mark against you as a person. It's simply the fact that *every* time you get involved, there's *always* a terrible amount of collateral damage."

"What?" I said. "Really? I don't cause *that* much damage."

"The warehouse outside Branson," she said simply.

"The demon and the half-torso-lady did most the damage. I caused very little myself."

"And the Pattersons' bunker?"

"Mostly the demons again. Well, and the backstabbing Pattersons. How was I to know they'd choose that very moment to have a family implosion?"

"And turning Director Allen's house into a war zone. Am I remembering correctly that you went there and started that fight?"

"Well, I went there, sure, but they attacked me. Well, sort of. They were about to attack me, and Shain Stone fired a grenade into the room. Still, though, someone had to take Director Allen down and stop the obayifo."

"Indeed," she said. "But it could've been handled more gracefully. Bringing in Director Allen alive would've been incredibly valuable. You yourself have indicated that all of these events are somehow linked."

"Fine," I said. "You're right. The whole Branson situation did get a little out of hand. But you guys weren't a lot of help and I was a bit out of practice."

"And Eureka Springs?"

"I didn't start anything there," I said. "And there was very little collateral damage."

"Really?" she said. "Have you already forgotten about the attack at the hospital? Plenty of witnesses."

"It's a *very* small hospital," I said, glancing over at Santiago to see if he might jump in to aid my cause. He didn't. "There weren't that many witnesses. I suppose you'll want to blame me for Memphis next."

"Not at all," she said. "I thought you handled the situation in Memphis perfectly."

"Really?" both Santiago and I asked at the same time.

"No, of course not," she said, rolling her eyes. "Memphis was the biggest disaster yet. There were dead bodies strung halfway across the city."

"Are you seriously going to blame Memphis on me?"

"You're missing the point," she said with a hint of exasperation. "I'm not *blaming* any of it on you. I'm just simply pointing out that wherever you go, you're like a walking nuclear bomb. Even before you became the Blade Mage, there was always collateral damage. Look, when your dog gets loose and tears into the neighbor's chicken coup, you don't just let it wander off again. You take measures to ensure it stays its ass at home."

"That's hardly fair," Santiago said, finally jumping in.

"What does *fair* have to do with it?" she asked. "Fair or not, the fact remains that every incident Wyatt has been involved in has turned from brushfire to wildfire."

"So, you just want me to go home and give up?"

"Precisely," she said, but then her voice softened. "It's likely the best thing for everyone."

"Okay," I said, trying not to feel disheartened. "Another option is that the Cabal could work with me to help mitigate these catastrophes from blowing up. In all the incidents you mentioned, I had little to no help from the Cabal, and was basically on an island. Were that not the case, maybe things would've turned out better."

"Ah, yes, but would you take our direction?" she asked. "Your track record tells me that the first time you disagree with how we decide to handle things, you'll sneak off and do it your own way. Is that not so?"

"Oh, come on now," Santiago said. "Wyatt has come here in good faith to try to work with us. We can't just assume he'll go rogue at the first opportunity. I'm surprised at you, Agatha."

She replied with a wicked grin.

I was just about ready to lose my temper, but it occurred to me then that perhaps something else was afoot. Maybe, just maybe, Master Brown was testing me. As I've said before, the masters weren't fools. Assholes, sure, but not imbeciles.

They were sharp. All of them.

Most of all, they were influencers and manipulators, and I don't mean that second one in the bad way. To reach that sort of level, they had to know how, and when, to push someone's buttons.

So, perhaps she was testing my resolve. Stirring the pot a little to see if I'd boil over.

Or maybe she wanted to see if I'd give up that easily. Was I not the Blade Mage who'd put myself in exile?

On top of that, I was known to show my ass from time to time. It was only reasonable for her to assume I'd either rebel or flee at the first sign of pressure.

*Or* maybe she was just a jerk.

I really didn't know for sure, but one option meant there was no hope at all.

The other meant I was merely under exam and perhaps could still win her over.

Either way, if she thought to goad me into a fight, or to dishearten me into flight, she was going to be disappointed.

Taking a calming breath, I said, "I'm aware the previous incidents didn't turn out exactly how the council desired. They didn't turn out the way I wanted, either. In every case, I was lucky to escape with my life. Others weren't. By all rights, I should be dead several times over. But I'm still here and now I want to do things differently."

"A noble sentiment, to be sure," Master Brown replied. "Though, I think you'll find it challenging to win over many."

"I have no doubt."

"Well, then, you aren't a complete fool," she said, flashing me an insincere smile. "Off to a good start."

"See, that's the spirit," Santiago said, rolling his eyes once again. "Positivity."

Master Brown snorted and returned her eyes to her book. I had the impression our conversation was over.

# CHAPTER FIFTEEN

I tried my hand at the chapel next. And by chapel, I of course mean the beautiful gray stone cathedral that looked like it had been plucked straight from an old European city. Catering to multiple beliefs, the chapel served as the religious center for the Castle grounds.

Despite our work in magic, there was a scattering of belief systems within the Cabal. I suspected most of our mages were either atheist or Christian, but certainly there were a few Buddhists, Muslims, and so on.

Many mages found a strength in their own magic by tying it to their belief system. I couldn't fault them. I'd met the Memphis Knights, after all. Certainly, their beliefs were deeply tied to their own strange abilities. Though I had very little experience with it myself, I supposed the same was likely true for mages, depending on the strength of their convictions.

That was the main reason for the giant gothic church and monastery.

More importantly, this was the stomping ground of Master Spiritualist Matteo Gray. He was another I'd put on my list as a backup plan. My thought was that the kind-eyed and soft-spoken master would almost surely be willing to give me a few minutes of his time.

I wasn't wrong, but I had to wait a while. It was less boring than my wait in the hospital, though. Three different people approached and offered to pray with me. Another asked if I was waiting for confession. A monk sat down beside me and asked what I knew about Zen Buddhism. That was the most interesting conversation.

Finally, another monk led me through a maze and then into a small garden where Master Spiritualist Matteo Gray waited.

It was a little of spot of nature with a tiny coy pond, a single bench, and several bird feeders.

The Master Spiritualist was filling one feeder as I approached, a red cardinal perched atop his shoulder like a pet. Birds of other varieties flitted around him. Blue Jays, robins, hummingbirds, and others I couldn't name.

He looked up from his work and offered me a sincere smile. "Welcome, Wyatt. I apologize for the long wait. Matters of politics delayed me, I'm afraid."

"Politics?" I asked, raising an eyebrow. "In the church?"

"Of course," he replied with a chuckle. "Our doors are open to nearly every religion. Part of my job is to maintain a neutral balance between the various orders who practice, preach, and worship here. Always, they are vying for more influence, or seeking changes which may benefit them to the detriment of others."

"But it's a church," I said, spreading my hands. "For *everyone*. What more could they want?"

"Ha, perhaps I should have you speak to them. If only they saw it as you do."

"Do you need me to get violent with some priests? Break a few legs? See if I can straighten everyone out?"

Master Gray chuckled. "You may find that more challenging than you think. Tread carefully around the Baptists. They're known for their wicked right hooks. And I'd not want to get caught in a clench with a Catholic. Most of all, avoid scrapping with the Buddhists at all costs."

"The Buddhists? I thought they were all one with the universe and whatever."

"Yes, well, trifle with one of the monks and you'll find their fists may become one with your face. Scary bunch, those Buddhists."

"Fair enough. I'll leave the church politics to you."

"Probably for the best," he said, holding out his hand for a Blue Jay to land on. "I understand you wish to speak with me. I have little time to spare."

"That seems to be the case for everyone."

"Busy times," he said, nodding while the jay in his hand danced around. "How can I help you, Wyatt?"

"Well, it turns out my reputation in the Cabal isn't so great."

"This is news to you?"

"Sort of. Well, no. I mean... I knew the Archcouncil hated my guts, but I wasn't aware everyone in the Cabal felt the same way."

"Hate is a strong word. I certainly don't harbor any hatred for you. I would daresay the other masters don't either. Nor the Arcane Guardians."

"Fine. Right. Poor choice of words. I mean to say that, at best, a few of you think I'm not cut out to be the Blade Mage. The rest of you are sure of it. I wish to change that."

"Is that so?"

"Yes, and I mean to improve my reputation with the rest of the Cabal as well. Look, I know I'll probably never be loved or respected like my father was, but I want to do my part. I want to try to *be* the Blade Mage."

"And how do you plan to go about that?"

"Well, that's why I'm here," I said, shrugging. "I thought you might have some guidance or a recommendation."

"So, you mean to say that camping on the front lawn of the Castle and bathing in a fountain was an act of fealty rather than defiance?"

He had me there. "Well, that was... Uh, I felt the need to make a statement."

"Well, you certainly accomplished that. *But,* do you think you made the statement you intended to make?"

"Maybe not," I said, and found myself looking at my shoes. "Felt like the right answer at the time."

"Hmm. I wonder if those feelings betrayed you."

"Are you telling me they did?"

He shook his head. "That's for you to decide. I'm merely suggesting that perhaps you should consider the question. I will point out one observation I see, if you're willing to take my feedback."

"That's why I'm here."

"You *felt* like you needed to make a statement. It *felt* like the right answer at the time." He turned from his birds and met my gaze. "You believe we masters and guardians hate you?"

I started to reply, but wasn't sure what to say, so I practiced the art of shutting up.

"The Arcane Guardians were chosen for their role by the weapons they carry, same as you. We masters, however, obtained our positions via promotion. And while we each have our flaws, we were chosen because we had a track record of making sound decisions. A history of displaying good leadership. Wisdom in our specialties. We had shown we were trustworthy and reliable. We were not chosen lightly, I'd dare say. Would you agree?"

"I suppose I would," I said.

"I don't tell you this to toot my own horn. Nor do I say it seeking your reverence. I'm trying to draw you to a specific point, and that point is... Do you think any among the council have earned their place by allowing their feelings to override their judgment? We are expected to be wise, to be cautious, and to make the best decisions for our Cabal."

"I hear you," I said, scratching the back of my head. "That's probably fair."

"Then is it also probably fair that we might wish to see the same of the person who holds such an important title as our Blade Mage?"

"I..." I could feel the wind flying right out of me. "I suppose so."

"When you say you *felt* like you needed to make a statement, or you *felt* like it was the right answer, you're telling me you allowed your *feelings* to drive your decisions. All I'm saying is that as a master, I expect my peers to drive their decisions with more than their feelings. They expect the same of me. And perhaps we expect the same of you. Something to think about, no?"

"Yeah," I said, unsure what else to say.

"I think your heart is in the right place, Wyatt. In fact, I'd warrant that may be the very reason the blade chose you. I don't think any of us question that. Nor do we think you are a fool. I do not have all the answers you seek, but perhaps start there, with learning to better control your emotions. Consider how your words and actions might be perceived. Perhaps spend some time with one of the Zen Buddhist monks here in the chapel. They may be able to help."

"Thanks," I said, choking on the words. Fortunately, I had a sense that my time was up. "I appreciate your guidance."

As I turned to leave, I considered what he'd said. On some level, I knew he was right, but it still wasn't quite what I'd been looking for. Certainly not what I was hoping for. I'd wanted something a little more tangible.

"And Wyatt," Master Gray called to me. "I'll consider your goals. If I think of something that might help, I will let you know."

"Thanks again," I said, waving as I walked away.

Well, at least he'd given me a few minutes of his time, even if it was just to point out what an ass I'd proven myself to be.

Sulking back to my camp, I was more disheartened than ever. I'd made little progress, and I was running out of options. As it was, it didn't seem anyone would make much time for me. With that being the case, there was little I could do to rebuild my reputation.

It felt pointless. I thought it might be best to return home, clear my head, and come up with a new plan of attack.

I just needed something to do. Some way I could help.

Lost in my own thoughts, I almost didn't notice the man loitering at my campsite.

He was parked in my folding chair and watching me approach. I didn't recognize him, and like me, he didn't look like he belonged.

He wore an ankle-length trench coat that had seen better years. Maybe better centuries. Beneath it he was dressed in slacks, a dress shirt, and a tie, but seemed uncomfortable in dress clothes, so much so that he'd already loosened the tie and left it dangling about his neck. His hair was a scraggly mess he'd failed to comb into submission. His face was recently shaved, though it was clear he'd missed a spot or two and had nicked himself in another.

So, this was a man who'd tried to make himself look presentable, but wasn't used to such behavior, and it showed. Interesting.

Studying his face, I noticed his eyes were sunken and he looked tired.

He also looked pissed.

"Hello," I said as I approached my camp.

His eyes narrowed as he looked up at me. "You're Wyatt Draven? The Blade Mage?"

"I am," I replied.

He shook his head and rose to his feet. Under his breath, just where I could hear it, he muttered, "Should've known. Fucking assholes."

I raised an eyebrow.

"Sorry to bother you," he said, turning to leave.

"Wait, hold on a minute," I said, moving to stand in his way. "You can't just loiter in someone's camp, wait until they show up, then wander off all disappointed like."

"Sorry," he repeated, then forced a smile that was really more of a grimace. "I didn't mean to be rude. Just frustrated is all."

"And why is that?"

"Doesn't matter. I don't think I'm going to find what I'm looking for here."

He started forward again, but I put up my hand to stop him. "And just what are you looking for?"

The man met my gaze and sighed. "I came here looking for help. I was turned away, but was told that perhaps I could try the Blade Mage. They said you had a camp set up out on the lawn, which I thought was strange, but... Well, I guess this was all just a big joke to someone."

"Probably," I agreed. "I'm not even going to ask who you spoke to. However, I am going to ask why you came looking for help. First, though, I'm going to try to not be offended that you took one look at me and disregarded me. Which will take me a moment... Hold... Okay, now, what did you come to the Castle looking for help with?"

He stared at me for a few seconds, then sighed. "You're right. I'm sorry about that. You're just...not what I expected."

"And you don't look like someone who should be wearing a tie. So why don't we start over?" I stuck out my hand. "Wyatt Draven."

"Fair enough," he said, firmly shaking my hand. "August Bones."

"Cool name."

"Thanks."

"You're a wizard?"

He nodded.

"Part of the Cabal?"

"Sort of," he said. "Or, well, I used to be."

"Used to be?"

"I was a constable."

"I see," I said, though I didn't really, but dragging answers out of this character felt like it might take days. I jumped straight to the point. "So, what did you come here looking for help with?"

He still seemed reluctant to speak, but after a moment, he shrugged and said, "I came here to appeal to the council, or anyone in leadership I could get to listen. Where I live... Well, I'm over in Oklahoma, in a little supernatural town tucked away in the hills. On tribal lands."

"Which?"

"Cherokee. And they've been having some trouble."

"What kind of trouble?"

"There's a camp. It's where the elders train the next generation of medicine men and women. Only, some of the youngsters have recently started switching to the dark side, if you know what I mean."

"They're becoming dark mages?"

He nodded. "Seems that way."

"I think you're going to have to explain."

He shrugged. "I don't really know. I guess that's the problem. No one really understands what's going on, but a bunch of the kids have been abandoning the tribe. The elders don't know why. One day they're training, and the next day, poof, they're just gone. There's a gang of them running around the area, and they're dangerous."

"When you say kids...?"

"Mostly teenagers. A few pre-teens."

"Wow. Shit. But wait, hold on. If someone is training dark mages, why hasn't the Cabal gotten involved? What's the agreement between the Cabal and the tribe?"

"That's just it. The Cherokee allow the Cabal to maintain a presence in Lost City, but they're restricted from exercising any authority without the tribe's express permission. So, Lost City has become something of a bastion for rogue elements. They can live right under the

Cabal's nose and practice whatever kind of magic they want without having to worry about the wrath of the Cabal."

"But doesn't the tribe police its territory?"

"It used to," he said, shaking his head. "With the Cabal's help. I used to be a constable in Lost City. We had a great relationship with the tribe and helped maintain order, but the tribe's supernatural element has waned. They're training less and less of their own, and now, there are all kinds of scumbags nesting in the area. I suspect their influence is part of the reason these kids have rebelled."

"Okay," I said, "but wouldn't the tribe want the Cabal to get involved now?"

"They do," he said. "But the Cabal is refusing. Elder Morgan and a few of the others were just here trying to appeal to the Council for aid."

"I saw them," I said, remembering the Native American men I'd spotted with Marius Gunner. "And the Cabal refused to help?"

August spit on the ground and said, "They refuse to help unless the tribe relinquishes some control and agrees to new terms that benefit the Cabal."

"Are you serious?"

"I am. The Cabal won't even step in to help the tribe figure out what's going on."

"But if those kids go too far, they'll end up being hunted down."

"It's already gone too far," August said, rubbing his hands over his face. "A few days ago, one of the tribal elders was murdered in a scuffle. I fear... The elders fear that if they don't remove the rogue element and find a way to bring the kids home quickly, it'll be too late. Some of these kids... They, well, they think they should turn to power. Abandon the old ways and embrace darker magics."

"That's a tough situation," I said. "But...how exactly are you involved?"

"I'm not," he said, shrugging. "Not really. I just... I want to help the tribe. Elder Morgan and the others, well, they were always good to me. I may not be a constable anymore, but I want to help before anyone else ends up dead, or before Lost City becomes a war zone."

I rubbed my chin, considering all he'd told me. "And what exactly would you expect the Cabal to do? Even if the Cabal agreed to help, it might not end well for the kids who've left, especially if they've begun practicing forbidden magics, or if they're truly killers."

"I know," he said. "What we need is help to find the kids and convince them to return to the tribe. And we need to root out who's behind teaching them dark magic. It could only be one of the local gangs."

"But the Cabal won't move in until the Cherokee agree to new terms."

"Exactly," he said. "And the tribe isn't keen on giving them more authority. They've always been able to manage the supernatural elements themselves. They don't want the Cabal telling them what to do."

"Neither do I," I said, shaking my head. "This sounds like a precarious situation, August. If someone in Lost City is truly practicing and teaching dark magic, they won't be keen on being rooted out. And something tells me these kids won't be easy to convince."

"I know," he said. "The situation is all but hopeless. Which was why I came here. I didn't really expect I'd be able to convince the Cabal to help, but I had to try."

"What will you do now?"

He shrugged. "I guess I'll go back and try to figure it out on my own."

"Not on your own," I said. "I'm coming with you."

He raised an eyebrow.

"What?" I asked, offering my most charming smile. "I *am* the Blade Mage, after all. And it was just pointed out to me that if I didn't like the way the Cabal handled something, I'd likely go rogue anyway. It was also pointed out that I shouldn't make decisions based on my feelings, but, meh. One piece of advice a day, right?"

"Won't you get in trouble?"

"Almost certainly. But that's not your problem."

"Fair enough. And not to sound ungrateful, but I was kind of hoping for a posse. You're just one man."

"That's where you're wrong," I said, and this time my smile was genuine. "There'll be two of us. I just need to find a phone."

# CHAPTER SIXTEEN

"Axel, we've got a job."
"A paying job?"
"Nope."
"Is it dangerous?"
"Probably."
"Cool. Are you coming to pick me up?"
"About to leave the Castle now. Do you want to know the details?"
"Not really."
"Okay, see you soon."

# CHAPTER SEVENTEEN

L ost City, it turned out, wasn't much of a city at all.
        According to the Google search Axel did, the town was actually unincorporated. Some years back, they'd closed the school, and that was pretty much all she wrote. The population was less than a thousand and said to be on the decline, which made sense if more spooky shit was moving in the neighborhood. Normans didn't hang around long when the boogeymen started showing up in droves.

It seemed a quiet sort of place.

A town forgotten.

The only publicity it had ever received was when a meteorite crashed outside of town back in the seventies. Otherwise, it was something like a ghost town, just the type of place we freaks liked to congregate. Mix that with the fact that no one was policing the supernatural population and it was no wonder they had riffraff moving in. The poor local Okies probably had no idea what was going on.

We met August at a spot just outside the "town" and got into his car so he could drive us around. According to him, it wouldn't take long for everyone in the area to know the Blade Mage had come to visit, but we didn't want to advertise it just yet.

As we drove into the little town that wasn't a town, August said,

"About the only decent building is the old church house. They have trouble keeping a regular preacher, though. The newest seems pretty good. Everyone is real hopeful he'll stick around."

"What do you mean, it's the only decent building in town?" I asked.

"You'll see. Not much here, other than a few farmhouses nearby. Though part of the abandoned school has been turned into a shady motel for supernatural burnouts."

"Lovely," I said.

"I'm glad you think so," he replied. "Because that's about the only place you'll find to stay around here. Otherwise, you guys will have to make the long drive back."

"That's great," Axel said, and there wasn't a hint of sarcasm in his voice. "It'll be an adventure, Wyatt. Hanging out around doped-up supernatural goons. Kind of like spending the night in the Broken Guitar. Someone may try to rob us."

"I can't wait," I replied.

"It isn't all bad news," August said. "That's just one wing of the old school. They've also turned the old cafeteria into a bar."

"Yeah?" I asked. "And what do they call it?"

August shrugged. "The bar. It doesn't really have a name. And it's pretty awful, if I'm honest. You're just as likely to get stabbed as you are to get a dirty glass. And you won't find a clean glass anywhere near the place."

"This'll be like *Road House*!" Axel said. "Maybe I'll become the bouncer and kick ass in tight jeans. My butt looks great in Wranglers."

August raised an eyebrow at Axel through the rearview mirror, then turned to me in the passenger seat. "Is he...?"

"He's fine," I said. "You'll be glad he's along. Trust me."

"Whatever you say," August replied. "They've also turned the old gymnasium into a sort of farmers market where folks peddle wares. Outside of that, the local gangs have their hideouts, and the local Cabal constables have a tiny shack up the road. The tribe's training ground is up in the hills. Where do you want to go first?"

"I kind of want to see the bar," Axel said.

August ignored him. Clearly, he was a quick learner.

"Hmm," I said, rubbing my chin. "As much as I hate to do it, I think the first thing we should do is visit the constables."

"I was afraid you were going to say that," August replied.

"Don't have a good relationship with the local Cabal people?" I asked.

He didn't respond immediately. "It's not that, really. Johnson has always been a dick. Williams is all right, though. She's the one they brought into replace me when... Well, when I left."

Watching his features closely, I said, "I've been meaning to ask you..."

"Yeah," he said. "I was fired."

"Care if I ask what for?"

"Yeah, I do care," he replied. "It doesn't have anything to do with why you're here."

"Yeah," Axel said from the backseat. "It's none of your business, Wyatt."

"Right," I said, not convinced. On a whim, I'd agreed to come help August with this problem, but I didn't know anything about him. And I didn't know why the Cabal had sent him packing. The way the Cabal worked, it could've been justified, or it could've been complete bullshit. While I didn't care about his personal business, I did want to know how far I should trust the guy.

"Look, I'll take you to see the constables," August said. "Like I said, Johnson is a dick and Williams is all right. I don't have any problems with them. It's just... I don't like being reminded of what I'm not anymore."

"Fair enough," I replied. "But if you aren't tied to the job, why stay around a place like Lost City? There isn't much here."

"It's home," he said, keeping his eyes on the road.

# CHAPTER EIGHTEEN

"Well, would you look at this, Williams?" said a balding man with his bulk squeezed into a squeaky office chair. "Ole August Bones honors us with his presence, and with company, no less."

"I see," replied a blonde woman. She was attractive. No beauty queen, but she could certainly turn some heads. She had that kind of... girl next door, small-town charm.

I pegged the first speaker to be Johnson, since I'm super smart and my deductive reasoning dictated that it must be so.

August confirmed a moment later. With a curt nod, he said, "Constable Johnson. Constable Williams. I hope you don't mind us stopping in like this."

My gaze tracked over to my new friend. In the short time I'd known him, this was the most formal I'd seen him act. As an ex-constable himself, he either wanted to maintain some dignity, or it just came back to him that way, like riding a bike.

"Oh, you know how busy we are here, Bones," Johnson said, followed by a big yawn. "Don't know how we'll ever get caught up on all this work."

When August had described the constable's office as a "tiny shack," I'd thought it had been a bit tongue in cheek.

It was not.

The Cabal had literally bought a Derksen building and converted it into a little office. Through the front door, there was a small room with just enough space for two desks and a little couch. There was also one little table with a coffeepot and a microwave. In one corner was a mini-fridge, and in another was a space heater. There was one small interior door in the back, which I assumed was likely a restroom, mostly because I *hoped* the Cabal had provided them a toilet, at least.

It made sense. The Cabal wasn't going to spend a ton of money just to maintain a tiny presence in an area where it didn't have full authority to operate. The office was probably only there because it'd been added when the Cabal and Cherokee were on better terms. The only reason they'd ever stationed anyone was because they knew it was where the Cherokee did their own magic training, and a presence here was more symbolic than anything else.

"I went to the Castle," August said, his gaze on Johnson.

Johnson rolled his eyes. "Now, why would you go and do a thing like that?"

Williams answered before August could. "He was trying to help. Trying to convince our evil overlords to have a heart."

"They ain't his evil overlords anymore, are they?" Johnson said, his scowl fixed on Williams. He transitioned it back to August. "You don't work here, remember?"

"I remember," August replied.

"Not for a long time," Johnson said.

The two stared at one another, both lost in old history.

Williams interrupted. "So, how'd it go?"

"Uh, well," August said, his staring contest interrupted. He glanced my direction. "In an official capacity, the Cabal wasn't very helpful, but, um..."

Johnson's eyes narrowed. "Why do I get a feeling I don't like where this is going, Bones?"

August pointed a thumb in my direction. "In a less official capacity, these guys have offered to look into things."

Johnson's eyes shifted from August to me, to Axel, and then back to me as they narrowed slightly. "You look familiar..."

At the same time, Williams said, "August, you shouldn't have brought them. I'm afraid it's a wasted trip. We're under strict orders not to get involved."

"Yeah," I said, speaking up for the first time. "Breaking orders is sort of my thing."

"And it's my life's passion," Axel replied. "Which is why Wyatt is my life partner."

I turned and looked at him. "Dude. *No.*"

"What?" he asked. "How else would you describe me?"

"Wyatt," Johnson repeated, still staring at me. His brow furrowed in concentration as he tried to place me. And then I saw the metaphorical lightbulb click on above his head. His eyes went wide and he said, "Oh, no! No, no, no."

Both August and Constable Williams were clearly confused. I wasn't. He'd just placed who I was, and sadly, this wasn't an unusual reaction.

"You shouldn't be here," Johnson said.

"I'm not worried about the Cabal," I said, though that wasn't quite the truth.

"Well, I am," Johnson said, crossing his arms over his chest. "But that ain't what I was referring to. Did August explain the kind of folk who live around here? If they hear the Blade Mage is in town, it'll cause a panic. Half the folks will run off. The other half will want to take a shot at you."

"Worried about my wellbeing, Constable?"

He scoffed. "I couldn't give a shit about you, Blade Mage. But Lost City is, for the most part, a quiet little town. And you know what? I like it when my quiet little town stays quiet. Sure, the Indians have had some trouble—"

"Native Americans," Williams corrected, rolling her eyes. Johnson barely paid her any mind. Clearly, this wasn't the first time she'd attempted to correct him.

He continued, "Sure, they've had some trouble, and one of their elders has been killed, but it ain't *that* big of a deal. I agree with the Cabal's orders. Let the tribe deal with their own messes. And there's no reason to stir up the local gangs."

One of my eyebrows jumped for the ceiling. "A man is dead and it's no big deal?"

"Blade Mage, these gangs 'round here, they're like sleeping dragons. So long as they stay asleep, Lost City is a quiet little place. You go waking up the dragons and it ain't going to be pretty."

"Wow, Johnson," I said, a little of my temper trickling through. "You're quite the constable, aren't you? True Cabal material."

Before Johnson could reply, Williams jumped in. "Forgive my partner."

"Boss," Johnson corrected.

It was her turn to ignore him. Her attention still on me, she said, "Johnson isn't known for his empathy. He means well, though."

"I bet," I replied, and kept my focus on the more sensible of the two. "So, you've been ordered not to help the tribe?"

"That's right," Williams replied. "And while I don't share Johnson's view, my hands are tied. And I think you should reconsider getting involved yourself. If you really are the Blade Mage, then Johnson might be right. Your involvement could cause a fire to spread among the local gangs. And if leadership doesn't want peons like us to take meaningful action, I can only imagine that'll go double for the Blade Mage."

"Not to burst anyone's metaphorical bubble," Axel said, then paused to make sure he had everyone's attention. "But if someone is teaching dark magic to tweens, then one of those sleepy dragons is already awake. It's only a matter of time before it comes down from its mountain and starts eating villagers. And unless Bard the Bowman is around to shoot the bugger down, your little hamlet isn't going to remain quiet either way."

The two constables shared a glance. Then Johnson turned his gaze on August once again. "There's no reason to believe anyone is teaching the runaways dark magic."

Once more, the two old work pals were locked in a death stare.

I sighed. "That doesn't quite match the story I got. Anyone care to explain?"

"Sure," Johnson said, fixing me with a yellow-toothed grin. "I'm guessing ole Bones here told you the kids were being trained in dark magic, but he's always had a taste for the dramatic. Truth is, there's been no sign that anyone is performing forbidden magics. Best we can tell, the kids just don't want to follow the old ways." He paused for a shrug. "Way I see it, if they want to run off and start their own gang, that's their business."

August cut in, "According to Elder Morgan, they've seen—"

"According to Elder Morgan." Johnson snorted. "Yeah, the old bugger will say anything to get someone else to solve his problems for him. Fortunately, ole Bleeding Heart Bones is around to do just that, am I right?"

August took a step forward and I casually stepped between the two men, but my focus remained on August. "What did this Elder Morgan say?"

August sighed. "He said the kids were learning dark magic."

"And you believe him?"

"I do," he said, then glanced past me. "I'd trust Elder Morgan's word over Constable Johnson's any day."

I held up my hand before either of them could start back up again. Then I turned my attention back to Williams. "What do you think?"

She seemed to shrink in her chair, not wanting to take either side. She pursed her lips and looked away. After a moment, she said, "Elder Morgan is a good and honest man. However, as Johnson mentioned, we've seen no evidence that anyone in the area is performing forbidden magics. Elder Morgan and his tribe practice a very specific medicine that has been passed down from generation to generation. They may not be familiar with what the Cabal would consider dark magic. It's possible the teens have picked up some common spells, which might seem uncommon to the tribe."

I rubbed my forehead. This was already taking a turn for the annoying.

"Okay," I said, considering my next question. "Are there many mages in the area?"

"Some, yes," Williams said. "All nomads, of course."

"Of course," I agreed. The tribal lands gave nomad mages a loophole to practice their magic without having to worry about the watchful eye of a sanctioned magic guild. Not that most of them would practice forbidden magics anyway, but some people just weren't keen on having a governing body to tell them what they could and couldn't do.

Another thought occurred to me. "And the local gangs? Any of them have mages?"

"Well, Fatima's crew does for sure," Williams said.

"And who is that?" I asked.

"Renegade," Johnson said. "She's a good-for-nothing lowlife with a band of magical miscreants."

I kept my attention on Williams.

She said, "Fatima was former Cabal military. No one knows the full story, but her and several wizards broke off from the Cabal a few years back. They've been here ever since."

"Any chance she's been recruiting from the tribe?" I asked.

"I don't think so," Williams said. "Fatima and her lot mostly keep to themselves. They don't cause any trouble, really. Only when one of the other gangs bothers them."

"How many gangs are in the area?"

"Several," Williams said. "Though most are just linked together for protection. The biggest is the Red Dirt Riders, a motorcycle gang led by a ghoulish-looking fella named Raymond."

Oh, great. Another motorcycle gang. Just what I needed. "Do they have any mages?"

Williams shrugged. "Not that we're aware of."

"Not that you're aware of? Shouldn't you guys know the local gangs pretty well?"

Constable Johnson let out the heaviest of sighs. "We already told you, Blade Mage. Our job is to sit in this little shack with our thumbs up our butts. We *don't* get involved. This office is all for show."

"And an impressive show it is," I said, shaking my head. I turned back to Williams. "What about the kids? They've started their own gang?"

"Yes," Williams said. "They call themselves the Wolf Pack. They're led by—"

"That's enough, Williams," Johnson said, dragging his bulk out of his chair. "We're under no obligation to tell the Blade Mage anything."

Williams was taken aback. She glanced between Johnson and me, then said, "I just thought, since the Blade Mage was here—"

"You thought wrong," Johnson said, then turned his attention to me and motioned toward the door. "You ain't here on official Cabal business. Like we already said, it's best you forget whatever sob story Bleeding Heart Bones told you and head back to wherever you came from."

"Are you throwing us out?" Axel asked, eyes lighting up. "Wyatt, I think the good constable is kicking us out."

"Damned right," Johnson said with a smug grin. "Until my superiors tell me otherwise, you ain't authorized to be here. Bones, you neither. Go back to doing what you do best and leave the police work to the actual authorities."

A silence fell over the room. It seemed both Axel and August were waiting for me to make a move while Constable Williams found something fascinating to stare at on her desk.

I won't deny I wanted to punch Constable Johnson right in the throat, but it wouldn't do me any good. If anything, when word got back to the Cabal, it would only make my reputation worse.

I smiled at Constable Williams, then nodded to Constable Johnson. "You've both been very helpful. Keep up the good work you're doing."

With that, I let myself out the door.

# CHAPTER NINETEEN

As soon as we were back in August's car, the former constable let out a sigh. "I guess you probably have some questions."

"I guess I probably do," I replied.

"Do you even want to bother?" he asked. "Or do you just want me to take you back to your truck so you can take Johnson's advice and get out of town?"

Axel snickered from the back seat. "You don't know us very well, Bleeding Heart Bones."

August turned around in his seat to scowl at my friend and then at me.

He struck me as a guy the world had beaten down, chewed up, and spit back out. There was some fight in him, sure, but he seemed on the verge of defeat. I noticed again just how tired he looked. Bloodshot eyes and shaking hands. I got the impression he wasn't a bastion of health. Maybe that's why the Cabal had taken his job.

"Listen," I said. "I'm not going home because some lazy slob with a cushy job told me to, and I expect that you're better suited to answer my questions anyway."

"Okay," August said. "Fire away."

"Fatima's gang," I said. "What do you know about them?"

"What Williams said. She's all brass tacks. Left the Cabal for one reason or another, and a pile of wizards followed her. Mostly, her gang likes to keep their noses clean, but they aren't exactly the friendliest bunch."

"And the Red Dirt Riders?"

"A mixed bag. Vampires, were-creatures, and a few uglier things. Possible there's a mage or two in the bunch, but I don't know for sure. They make their living selling moonshine and pot."

"Really?" Axel asked, perking up. "I love moonshine."

August continued, "Out here on tribal lands, they're not only free from the Cabal getting in their business, but there aren't too many normal police officers to worry about, either."

"You think they're likely to try to recruit our runaways?"

"I don't know, but it would make sense. I mean, they're the largest gang in the area, and the tribe is the biggest threat to their business. If they could weaken the Cherokee somehow, it would only strengthen their own position. And everyone could use a few magic wielders in their gang."

"And our runaways are calling themselves the Wolf Pack?"

"Yeah, I guess Williams was trying to explain that before Johnson showed what a dickhead he is. I'll be honest, they're vicious little snots. They're led by two older kids, and their founder is a nineteen-year-old who calls himself Waya."

"Waya?" I asked.

"It's Cherokee for Wolf," August explained. "Hence...the Pack."

"Very creative," I replied.

"Wolves are cool," Axel said. "Wolf packs are cooler. Do you remember the old wrestling team, the Wolfpac, from when we were kids?"

"Sadly, I do," I admitted. "I was a Sting fan."

"I remember," Axel said. "My favorite was 'Macho Man' Randy Savage."

"In hindsight, that makes a lot of sense," I said. Then I turned my attention back to August. "Okay, so Waya started this little band of runaways. And now I guess more are joining up?"

"Most, yeah," August said. "Of particular note, his second-in-command and girlfriend is a young woman who calls herself Pathkiller."

"She's a more recent addition?"

"Yes," he said. "And there's something else you should know. A few of the runaways have simply disappeared."

"Disappeared?" I asked.

He nodded. "They're just gone. No one has seen them around. So, they've either left the area completely, they're in hiding, or..."

"Or they're dead," I finished for him. "Well, that certainly brightens the situation. And what do Waya and his wolves have to say?"

"So far as I know, they haven't spoken to anyone. They're more likely to attack you than talk to you."

"I see. And this talk of dark magic?"

"I don't know specifics," August said, rubbing the back of his head. "I guess I should've told you that up front. I took Elder Morgan's word at face value."

"And what was his word?"

"He said when they found the dead elder's body, there was an aura of dark magic around it."

"Spooky," Axel said. "How did the elder die?"

"Presumably burned," August said. "They found him on the side of the road. Half his upper body was charred to a crisp."

"Fire magic isn't dark magic," I said.

"You're right," he agreed. "But again, Elder Morgan said they sensed dark magic around the body. But, yeah, Williams may be right. Elder Morgan could be wrong."

I shrugged. "It doesn't really matter. If one of the teens killed him with fire magic, that's just as bad in the eyes of the Cabal. It may not be forbidden magic, but that's certainly a forbidden *use* of magic. How do they know it was one of the teens?"

"They don't for sure," August said. "But according to the tribe, this elder's grandson is one of the runaways. He'd set out to bring him back on his own. They found his body the next morning."

"And they sensed the bad aura," I replied. "So, we have reason to believe the murder was done via magic."

"Right."

We lapsed into silence and I considered the situation. There were a great many unknowns.

Too many, in fact.

It was quite possible the whole situation was as simple as Johnson had laid out. Rebelling was part of being a teen, after all. I could imagine that after Waya left, it had only encouraged more of the kids to do the same.

And it was also possible this other kid and his grandfather had gotten into a domestic dispute that had escalated to bloodshed.

And it was also possible that one of the other local asshats had killed him.

And as far as dark magic went, well, Williams had made a good point. The tribal elders might not be familiar enough with a dark aura to properly identify it. I'd known plenty of country folk who'd mistaken every snake they saw for a venomous one.

Then again, it was also possible that darker forces were at work in Lost City.

The Cabal could've easily resolved the matter. They could've sent constables, sleuths, and any other number of investigators to tear right through the noise and find the truth. But no, they were too busy trying to extort the tribe for more power.

And these were the bastards I was trying to build a better relationship with.

The Archmage's words echoed through my mind... *You don't like the way our organization is run? Then start changing it. Show us what's better.*

So I would.

I turned to August. "I think it's time to see Elder Morgan."

# CHAPTER TWENTY

"What should we expect?" I asked as August navigated the dirt road that would lead us to where the Cherokee trained their future medicine men and women.

"Well, it's probably not going to be as exciting as it sounds," August said. "We'll only be allowed near the cabins. The actual training grounds are off limits to outsiders. The tribe is very protective of its medicine."

"So, you don't know much about the type of magic they do?"

He shook his head. "Very few people do. Even among the tribe. And those who know keep their mouths shut. It's tradition, I suppose. Plus, they don't want a bunch of plastic shamans running around."

"Plastic shamans?"

"It's a term for people who pretend to be medicine men. Frauds who act like they know Native American magic, usually to rip people off."

"People do that?" I asked, a little surprised. But even as the question came out of my mouth, I realized how stupid it was. Of course people did that.

"People suck, Wyatt," Axel said from the back seat. "It really shouldn't surprise you at this point."

"Right," I said, shaking my head. "So, are there a lot of students?"

"Usually a hundred or so," August said.

"That many?" I asked.

"Yup. Just like us, those who have the potential are identified at a young age."

"And they're here training full time?"

"Some of them, yes," he said, then swerved a pothole. "Some students are here year-round. Some come and go, depending on how much time their families are willing to give up."

"What about schooling?"

"For most of them, it's done here. Legally speaking, the training grounds are a 'private' school. So, they don't have to worry about that sort of thing. Which is good, because from what little I've seen, very few of the kids become medicine men or women, and much of what they learn is tribal tradition and history."

As we came around the next corner, several rows of cabins appeared among the trees, like we were pulling up to a summer camp.

A sea of faces turned our way. Untrusting, but not quite hostile, twenty teenagers watched our approach with interest.

I glanced over at August. "Are you sure we're welcome here?"

"I'm sure," August said, eyes forward. "I am sure that we are *barely* welcome here."

I raised an eyebrow at him. It was the closest thing to a joke he'd said in the short time I'd known him.

As he parked the car between an old beater truck and a shiny new SUV, one of the teens bolted toward a larger cabin.

"We got a runner," Axel said in a serious tone. "The jig is up. He's surely summoning reinforcements."

"Axel," I said, turning in my seat to give him a serious look. "I need you to be on your best behavior. Please."

"What's that supposed to mean?"

"You know what it means. No shenanigans. You heard August. The tribe isn't big on guests. Let's try not to make them hate us in the first five minutes."

"Okay, fine, but the second five minutes is up for grabs."

"*Axel.*"

"*Wyatt.*"

"Maybe you should stay in the car."

"Maybe you should," he replied. "If you want to take count, I'm pretty sure I've been more successful at making new friends than you."

"Just behave," I said. "That's all I'm asking."

"I always behave," he said. "Well, most of... Some of... Occasionally. Look, I don't know what you're worried about. People *love* me."

I shook my head and turned to look back out the window. Three men were approaching from the larger of the cabins.

The man at the front of the pack looked to be in his mid-sixties, and though he walked with a bit of a limp, he kept his back straight and his head held high. He wore jeans and a western pearl snap with the sleeves rolled up. His long gray hair hung past his shoulders.

Behind him were two younger men in similar garb.

I waited for August to get out of the car before I did the same. Then we waited while he threw his trench coat back on and led us toward the approaching men.

August raised his hand and waved. "Elder Morgan. John. Samuel."

"Welcome, August," the older man said with a curt nod. "I see you have guests with you."

It was a statement, but clearly a question hung on the edge.

"Yes," August said, motioning toward me. "This is Wyatt Draven, Blade Mage of the Ozark Mountain Cabal, and his associate Axel."

I stepped forward and held out my hand to the elder. I wasn't sure if that was the right protocol, but he took my hand in a firm grip.

"Wyatt, this is Elder Morgan," August said, then as I moved to the muscular man behind him, August continued. "And John."

The third man, a wiry young guy, introduced himself. "I'm Samuel."

As the handshakes finished up, August said, "I've mentioned Elder Morgan to you, but John and Samuel are both instructors here as well."

"It's a pleasure," I said while trying to keep one ear on Axel. So far, he'd raised no alarms.

When introductions were completed, Elder Morgan turned his focus back to August. "The Cabal, you say? Have they had a change of heart?"

August looked to me to answer.

I wasn't really sure what to say, so I shrugged and just went with the truth. "I'm not here on the Cabal's behalf."

"No?" he asked.

"We came of our volition. When August explained the situation, I thought the least I could do was come out and see if we could help in any way."

"Your own volition," he repeated back to me, a mischievous twinkle in his eyes. "Do your leaders even know you're here?"

"Well, we stopped and visited with the local constables on the way," I said. "So, if they didn't before, they surely do now."

"The local constables are a joke," John said, shaking his head. His muscled-up neck reminded of me of Garza.

"And not a funny one," I agreed. "But yeah, I'm sure Cabal leadership knows I'm here by now."

"I see," Elder Morgan replied. "And you do not fear you may get in trouble?"

"Not a bit."

He seemed to ponder this over. I could only assume he was considering whether taking our help would cause further fallout with the Cabal. In the end, he either decided it wouldn't, or simply didn't care.

"Well, I won't turn away help. Not in this dark hour. Please, follow me. I will tell you of our troubles."

# CHAPTER TWENTY-ONE

We were escorted into a large cabin that served as an administrative office, then led into a small conference room.

Another elder—called Elder Thomas—joined us there.

John stayed in the room, but Elder Morgan sent Samuel to fetch us sodas. When he returned with the drinks, Elder Morgan said, "Thank you, Samuel. Please give us a few minutes and shut the door behind you."

Samuel flashed a jealous glare at John, who pretended not to notice, then excused himself, shutting the door behind him, just as he'd been told.

Elder Morgan offered us a brief smile. "Thank you for coming. I was led to believe the Cabal no longer had a Blade Mage. It's good to see someone has filled the role."

I blinked a few times and tried to ignore the snicker from Axel. "I've held the title for some time, but I haven't been very active until recently."

"I see," he said. "We'd heard there were some troubles of late."

"Some," I agreed, but didn't feel inclined to elaborate.

"You said your last name was Draven?" Elder Thomas asked. He turned his gaze to Elder Morgan. "Was that not the name of the previous Blade Mage?"

"My father," I said, nodding at them. "He held the role before me."

"Ah," Elder Thomas said, nodding approvingly. "He was a good man."

"You knew him?" I asked.

"Of course," Elder Morgan answered. "In his day, we maintained a healthy friendship with your Cabal. Not so much these days."

"I'm sorry," I said, not sure what else to say.

Elder Morgan only smiled. "Yes, well, it is good the position has been filled once more."

I decided it was time to get to the point. "So, August tells me some of your trainees have slipped away and you fear they may be involved in dark magic."

"Yes, that's the gist of it. Many of our young folks have left. I fear if we don't bring them back soon, we'll lose more still."

"And this has never happened before?" Axel asked. "You've never had students rebel?"

"Of course we have," Elder Thomas said with a dry chuckle. "It is said that even Elder Morgan was a rebel in his day, though that was in the time before the white man came to this land. So, little is known."

His delivery was so dry that for a moment, I thought he was serious. Also, Elder Thomas didn't seem so many years younger than Elder Morgan, which also threw me off.

"As I recall, you're the one who roamed the Earth alongside the dinosaurs," Elder Morgan replied, then turned his focus back to Axel's question. "We've had many students choose to walk a different path over the years. We have *not* had them rebel for the sake of power. And we've not had so many abandon us in such a short time."

"How many have gone?" I asked.

"Too many," John replied with a scowl. "Ungrateful brats. They forsake their heritage, and for what?"

Elder Morgan gave the younger man a pat on the shoulder. "Ever since Salal left, another twenty-two have followed."

"Salal?" I asked, glancing at August. "I thought Waya was the first to leave."

Elder Thomas chuckled. John scowled. Elder Morgan sighed and said, "Waya was, and I hope still is, Salal. He was a good kid once, our little squirrel."

"Little squirrel?" I asked.

"Salal means squirrel," John said helpfully.

"Wait," I said, "So, the wolf..."

"Was once a squirrel," John replied. "A quiet and timid kid who loved to read and was allergic to pollen. Then he left us and became the big bad wolf."

Beside me, Axel burst out in laughter. I couldn't even be mad. He'd held it in this long, which was better than I'd expected. And if I were honest, I could feel the ironic grin creeping along the corners of my own mouth.

"And have you spoken to him?" I asked.

Elder Morgan shook his head. "We've tried. Most of us have tried. August as well. He won't speak to any of us. All he'll say is that he has no words for blind old fools."

"That's quite the personality shift from what John described," I observed. "Same with the other kids?"

"The ones we've seen, yes," Elder Morgan said. "Though some of the runaways..."

"I know," I said. "August told us that some of them haven't been seen at all. But what of the ones you *have* seen? Were they all good kids before? None of them were troublemakers?"

"They were all good kids," Elder Morgan said. "And now not one of them will speak to us. Even my Alyita will not speak to me now."

"Alyita?" I asked.

"Pathkiller," August said.

"Yes, that's the name she's chosen for herself," Elder Morgan said. "I guess she wanted to send me a message. Imagine that, Blade Mage. My own granddaughter will not speak to me, unless it is to tell me what an old fool I am."

His granddaughter.

This was new and rather pertinent information.

It changed things.

While I didn't question Elder Morgan's good intentions, knowing that his own granddaughter was among the runaways made it more complex. Would he bend the truth to see her brought back? Would he make up a story about sensing dark magic just to get some extra help? He was responsible for *all* the kids, sure, but his granddaughter, *well*, that was something else. I could see it in his eyes when he said her name. I could hear the despair in his voice.

"You were close," I said.

"Before, yes," he replied. "Very."

"And she was a good kid, too?" I asked. "She didn't get into any kind of trouble?"

"She always had a fiery spirit," he said, smiling fondly. "Always questioning authority, even as a child. But no, beyond that, she never got into trouble. Like Salal, she was a quiet kid, for the most part. Preferring her books to the more common distractions of teens these days. Before Salal, I'm not sure she ever even had a boyfriend."

I nodded slowly. "Which is why you think there may be an outside influence involved."

"Precisely," Elder Morgan said.

"All these kids," John said, putting up his hands as though he didn't know what to say. "To answer your question before... All good kids. Likely, many of them would've finished their training. All were exceptional students. Not riffraff. Not troublemakers. Though, there is one common denominator: they were all loners."

"Which makes it only stranger that they would've formed a gang," Elder Thomas said. "It isn't like any of them. You must trust us on that."

"We'll take your word for it," I said. "Another question, though. August mentioned another elder was murdered, and that you sensed dark magic near his body?"

"Yes," Elder Morgan said. "It was then we knew the problem was beyond us. It was then that we reached out to the Cabal for help, but..."

"The Cabal refused," I finished for him. "And now you're afraid that if you don't bring these kids back soon, you'll either lose more, or worse... When the Cabal does get involved, it will be to hunt dark mages, rather than to rescue errant teens."

Elder Morgan nodded. "You can appreciate our trepidation when August introduced the Cabal's Blade Mage."

"I'm no child killer," I replied.

An uneasy silence passed between us, and I wasn't sure they were convinced. If I was going to help them, I needed them to trust me. Then again, I had my own doubts about the elder's intentions, so I supposed it was all fair.

"When you say 'dark magic,' though," Axel said, leaning forward with his elbows on the table. His interest level had jumped up a notch. "What precisely do you mean? What did you feel?"

"You've not felt the use of dark magics?" Elder Morgan replied.

"Oh, maybe a time or two," Axel replied.

I kicked him under the table and said, "What Axel means is, what about it made you think it was dark magic?"

Elder Morgan didn't reply immediately. When he did, there was a hint of iron in his voice. "Young man, I was protecting these hills, often alongside your father, before you were ever born. I have seen dark sorcerers at work. I know evil when I sense its presence."

I wanted to consider my words carefully, but knew I didn't have time with Axel likely to blurt out a stupid reply, so I said, "I understand. We only needed to be sure. Neither of us knew of your greater experience. It is a serious matter to implicate the use of dark sorcery."

"This I know," Elder Morgan said. "Your father led a great inquisition to rid the Cabal lands of such filth. Without him, though, I fear it may be returning."

"Is this the first time you've sensed anything like this?"

"In a great many years," he admitted.

"And do you think any of the local gangs might be involved?" I asked. "From what little August has told me, there are a number of rough customers about."

"Yeah, you can thank your Cabal for that," John said, crossing his massive arms over his chest.

"John, this is not the time or place," Elder Morgan said.

"It's fine," I said to the elder, then switched my attention back to John. "You'll find that where the Cabal is concerned, my sentiments aren't much different from your own. The reality of the situation is that you don't have the manpower to police your area, and the Cabal is refusing to help unless you relinquish more control. I have little interest in such politics, but I do understand the result is more unscrupulous characters have moved in, seeking a haven where they can escape the wrath of the Cabal. So, my question, again, is whether you think the local gangs are involved."

"Who else?" John asked.

"I don't know," I replied, keeping my voice even. "That's why I'm asking."

Elder Morgan once again patted John on the shoulder, trying to calm him. "Yes, Blade Mage, your assessment of the situation is spot-on. And yes, we fear one of the local gangs may be behind influencing our youngsters. But we don't know who, why, or how."

"The kids are always here during training?" I asked.

"Yes," Elder Morgan said. "And we allow few visitors. The kids are protected. Our medicine, though different from your magic, is great. While on these grounds, they are protected. You can take my word on that."

"Fair enough," I said. "So, who from the area would you suspect?"

"I thought I covered this," August said, stepping in. "I told you about the locals. As did Williams, before Johnson cut her off."

"You did," I said, casting him a sideways glance. "But I'd like another perspective."

"Johnson was a real Johnson," Axel said. "If you guys know what I mean?"

John scoffed, but the two elders shared a dry chuckle.

Trying to cut off Axel before he started a standup routine, I said, "I understand there's a former Cabal mage here. Fatima, I believe was her name."

"Yes," Elder Morgan said. "And I'm sure they told you she has several wizards with her."

I nodded. "Would you consider her a suspect?"

"I'd not rule out anyone at this point, save my fellow elders and teachers, the two constables, the local pastor, the old woman who runs the bar in town, and August, of course," Elder Morgan said. "So, yes, I suppose I would, though I can't think of what she'd hope to gain from it."

"Perhaps she wishes to grow her own cabal," I said, shrugging. "I don't know anything about her. Just grasping at anything we should take into consideration."

"Fair enough," Elder Morgan replied. "Then that is the only real motivation I could see, though people's motives are often hidden. So far as I know, none of the children have taken up with her gang, or any other, save Salal's Wolf Pack."

"Squirrel Pack has a better ring to it," Axel replied.

I elbowed him in the ribs, though I had to admit his comment summoned a chuckle from John. Before that, I thought the muscled-up fella didn't have a sense of humor.

"All right, and what about this motorcycle gang?" I asked.

"The Red Dirt Riders," Elder Thomas said. "They're troublemakers, for sure. And I'm sure they'd love to see our influence crumble. Raymond is probably giddy knowing our students are abandoning us, but outside of that, I don't know what his motivation would be."

"Are there any other gangs who would want to hurt you guys?"

"Well, I'm sure August mentioned the Evans brothers," Elder Morgan said.

"I don't think he did," I said, glancing toward August.

"You're right," he said, shaking his head. "Apologies. I completely overlooked them."

"If any of the locals wish us harm, it would be them," Elder Morgan said.

He seemed a little surprised that August would've let them slip his mind, which made me wonder if they had, in fact, "slipped" his mind. I took a quick glance at our new companion, noting that his expression seemed earnest, but I reminded myself that I didn't really know August Bones. Would he have kept something from us intentionally? And if so, why?

That was something to consider later, however.

I turned my attention back to Elder Morgan. "Why would these Evans brothers wish you harm?"

"Because they're fucking tweakers, is why," John said. "They cook and sell the shit. We should've sent them packing ages ago."

"And?" I asked.

Elder Morgan sighed. "And only a month ago, one of our instructors had an altercation with them in town."

"An altercation?" John asked, turning to Elder Morgan. "Is that what you call it? They beat him nearly to death. He was in the hospital for a week."

"Yeah," I said, glancing over at August. "That seems like pertinent information."

"Yes," Elder Morgan said. "They threatened all of us. Said they'd kill the whole lot of us if we didn't stay out of their business. As if they could. I should've summoned a war party, but this business with our kids takes precedence."

"That was before the kids started disappearing?" I asked.

Elder Morgan shook his head. "No, Salal and some of the others had already left by then. But yes, the more recent uptick has been since."

"But the Evans brothers aren't mages," August said. "They're a bunch of mangy were-dogs."

"I agree," John said. "And I doubt they could influence a hooker with a handful of cash, much less convince a bunch of teenagers to give up their heritage to become rogue sorcerers."

"John," Elder Morgan said, shaking his head. "You must learn to control that tongue of yours."

"Yes, Elder," John said, but it seemed more an automated response than a real acknowledgment.

Elder Thomas said, "The Evans brothers seem like dumb hicks, but they're as crafty as they are dangerous. I agree with Elder Morgan and John both. We should've removed their cancer from Lost City before now. They are unscrupulous, but as far as taking our kids... I can't imagine what they would have to gain."

"Okay," I said. "And there's no one else you guys can think of?"

Elder Morgan shook his head. "Like I said, I'd suspect just about anyone. Someone, or something, is influencing our kids. I can feel it, Blade Mage. I can't explain it to you beyond that, but I need you to trust me... Something more is going on here."

"All right," I said, nodding. "Well, thank you guys for meeting with us. You've given us much to consider."

"Do you think you can help us, then?" Elder Morgan asked.

"I don't know," I replied honestly. "But we can poke around town and see what turns up. Otherwise, I don't know how to help. Not that I doubt your feelings, but is it not possible the kids just rebelled? Teenagers do that."

A little hope seemed to disintegrate from his features and I immediately felt bad for even asking the question.

"I don't think so," Elder Morgan said. "But thank you, Blade Mage. And Axel. John will show you out."

I nodded at him and rose from my seat. The others followed suit and only Elder Morgan remained seated, looking just a little deflated. As we started toward the door, he raised his hand and said, "One more thing, Blade Mage."

I paused and waited for him to continue.

He remained quiet for some time, then said, "You may not believe me, but I've learned over a lifetime to trust my instincts. I listen to the Earth and what it tells me. And now...something isn't right. I don't know if it's just here, just our little area, or if it's wider, but I can feel it in my bones. Like the first cold snap in autumn. Something is slithering beneath the surface, begging to break free. To wake up. I'm not the only one among us who's felt it."

"And you don't know what it is?"

"No," he said, shaking his head. Then he looked up at me and met my gaze. "No, Blade Mage, I don't know what it is...but I am afraid."

I nodded at him and headed out the door.

# CHAPTER TWENTY-TWO

As we left the training grounds, August asked where we wanted to go next. I didn't have an immediate answer. Truth be told, I considered driving all the way back home just so I could ponder over all we'd learned. But something clawed at the back of my mind and I decided it would be best for us to stay local.

So, we had August deliver us to my truck. Then we followed him back to the dilapidated and formerly abandoned elementary school. From the outside, it still looked pretty abandoned. The exterior hadn't had a paint job in years, and no one had kept up with the yardwork. The weeds were waist high in places and the grass had forced its way through the concrete path, as though the greenery waged war to reclaim all human creation and return it to its original shrubbery state.

We followed August to a secluded lot in the back, where a few other vehicles were parked out of sight of the main highway.

He led us in through an old glass door into a long hallway of classrooms and rusted lockers. August turned into the first classroom and I followed, noting a hand-painted sign above the door that read, "Motel."

A makeshift counter had been placed near the front of the classroom and a weasel of a man stood behind it, eager to take our money.

And take our money he did. At twenty bucks a night, Axel and I each got our own rooms.

The slimy fella dropped a key in each of our hands and we were off on a grand adventure, barely able to contain ourselves. What surprises awaited us in our rooms?

Walking further down the hall, I wondered how one would go about turning a school into a motel. Well, it turned out that each classroom contained three small rooms each, or at least that was the case of mine. They'd framed in three rectangular boxes with lumber, then covered the walls with plywood rather than drywall. Basically, they'd built three shacks in each classroom.

My room was at the end of the row, so I was fortunate to have two of the original concrete walls and two plywood walls. I say "fortunate" because I wasn't convinced they had bothered insulating between shacks. I wasn't keen on hearing whatever noises my neighbors might make. Luckily, I'd only have to worry about one side. Better than being the meat in the middle.

Axel's shack wasn't in the same classroom as mine, which was fine. I wasn't keen on hearing his noises, either.

The other plus side of having one of the original walls was that it provided me a window, though it was foggy from years of neglect, so I could barely see out of it.

I supposed what impressed me most was the fact my room had its own bathroom. They had managed this by creating a step-up platform, which meant the plumbing pipes must have been right across the tile of the old school floor.

What impressed me least was the state of my bathroom. Sure, someone had "cleaned" it, but there were stains in there I'd rather not describe. My first task was going to be to find the nearest store that sold Lysol and load for bear.

My room didn't have a television. However, there was a rickety old desk with a rocking chair beside it. And a space heater in one corner, which I counted as a win, so long as it didn't catch on fire and murder me in my sleep.

The bed was adorned with a faded comforter I'd bet was picked up at a yard sale or thrift store. If I slept in it as it was, I feared I'd have to burn my clothes, or myself. So, I was going to waste more money on getting my own sheets. Afterwards, I'd burn them. The bed did have a little nightstand, though.

Supernatural accommodations at their finest.

I reminded myself that many in the underworld community were forced to live this way, especially those with non-human appearances. Plus, it wasn't the worst place I'd ever spent a night.

After the rooms were sorted, August offered to drive us to the nearest "real" town for food. Tahlequah, it turned out, wasn't terribly far away. They had a Walmart and a Burger King, so all my highfalutin requirements were met. We didn't talk much. Well, neither August nor I spoke much. A part of me wanted to use the time to get to know him better. To get a sense of who he was and why he cared so much about the tribe. It was clear he was used to keeping to himself, though.

That was all right. Everything we'd learned was an awful lot to process, and I wanted time to consider our best course of action. I still wasn't convinced that anything truly nefarious was going on in Lost City, but I also wasn't ready to call it quits.

After dinner, August returned us to our five-star accommodations and agreed to meet with us in the morning.

I disinfected the hell out of my bathroom and put new sheets on my dingy bed, cursing just how broke we were going to be after all of the recent purchases. I regretted going overboard with the camping gear, but that was a worry for another day. I also regretted not bringing it with me because I could've set up my tent outside.

Finally, I put on my pajamas, or as I liked to call them, my pashamas. In my mind, that was what every wizard should call their pajamas. Like shaman pajamas. Gave them a bit of magical flare, even if they were Ninja Turtle pajamas, which mine were.

With my Ninja Turtle pashamas equipped, I sauntered off to bed.

# CHAPTER TWENTY-THREE

D*yrnwyn!*

I awoke with a start.

My sword had trembled.

It was trying to warn me of something.

I rolled toward it, reaching for where I'd left it leaning against the nightstand, along with my staff.

That move saved my life.

The door crashed open and I saw a blur flying at me through the moonlight. That "something" thudded into the headboard, just above my pillow. Whatever it was, it would've struck me in the face.

I continued to roll right off the bed and onto the floor, just in case any other UFOs came for my head.

A second later, my sword was in one hand and my staff was in the other, which was good because a dark figure was racing toward me.

I fired a simple burst of raw energy that hit my attacker in the chest and hurled them back out the door. There was a skidding crash outside, followed by curses from a male voice.

On my feet, I was about to pursue my attacker when I caught the faintest whiff of smoke and stopped in my tracks. Flames burst through the open door, just as I was raising my magical shield, which again, was the only thing that saved my life.

Still, the heat was incredible, and I wasn't able to block it all. Whoever was on the other end of the fire spell was no slouch. I took a few steps back, noting that the plywood walls of my little hovel were catching flame.

Magical shield or no, if the makeshift shack that was my "motel" room went up in flames, I was done for.

I only had one option...

The window.

Backing a few steps toward it, I kept my staff focused on protecting me from the oncoming flames, and with my other hand, hurled my sword right through the glass window.

I've never studied fire science, but shattering the window only created something of a vacuum, which sucked the flames toward me with more veracity.

Or the spell caster knew I had a means of escape and was pushing even harder. Either way, the intensity of the heat increased, and I knew my poorly summoned shield wouldn't protect me much longer.

I turned and dove out the window, tearing my flesh and Ninja Turtle pashamas on broken glass, even as the flames licked at my heels.

I landed on my back with a thud, thankful the tall grass had softened my landing. Above me, the flames roared out of the window and I had to cover my face to shield it from the heat.

A moment later, the flames cut off, as though my attacker had released the trigger of a flamethrower.

I quickly rolled to my feet and realized I wasn't alone.

Glancing over, I saw a middle-aged man standing by the road. He looked like he'd been out for an evening stroll, and he was studying me with wide eyes. When he realized he had my attention, he said, "Uh, are you all right?"

"Sure," I said, realizing for the first time that my pashamas were smoking. I didn't have time to share pleasantries with a concerned local, though. My assailants could've been preparing their next attack, or worse, making their escape.

I glanced back through the window and saw nothing but smoke and burning embers. I wasn't going back in that way.

"Are you sure you're all right?" the stranger asked in a concerned tone.

"Yeah, just had my heater turned up too high."

I ignored him and set off, hoping he wasn't a local Norman who'd find it necessary to call the police or fire department.

As I raced around the school looking for another entrance, it occurred to me that the new sheets I'd just bought were almost certainly ruined, along with my duffel bag of clothes. That was going to cost me even more money.

Fortunately, I'd been so worried about letting my guard down in such a seedy place that I'd slept with my keys and wallet in my pashama pockets.

Being paranoid paid off from time to time. In hindsight, though, I wished I would've slept with my shoes on. And I wished I would've set up a simple ward as well. Rookie mistakes.

Around the corner, I found the main entrance to the school and pushed through the door, staff and sword at the ready.

I peered into the "motel" office first, but found it empty.

I headed back down the long hall toward my room and the sound of excited voices. I was just about to use mind-speak to check on Axel when he appeared from his classroom, a drumstick in each hand, wearing nothing but a bright pink speedo and Darth Vader slippers.

Several other guests had also sauntered into the hall. Most were in their pajamas, and I quickly determined none of them were my attackers. More likely, they'd been woken up by the commotion. It certainly wasn't due to the fire alarm, which hadn't gone off. Probably hadn't worked for years.

Most of the other "guests" were of a human variety, but one individual had a very reptilian appearance, and another had the face of a hamster. I ignored all of them and headed back to my room.

Axel caught up just before I got there.

As I rounded the corner into my classroom, I found the weasel of a manager standing in the entryway with a fire extinguisher, spraying bursts of white powder into my ruined lodgings. The unnatural flames were long gone, leaving only small, random fires, and the extinguisher was quickly resolving that problem. In a matter of seconds, my room was just a stinky smoldering mess rather than a burning one.

At least I didn't I have to worry about the heater catching fire any longer.

A quick study through the smoke revealed that one of the plywood walls was damaged beyond repair. The cheap desk and rocking chair were also toast, and about half the bed was ash. My unqualified guess was that the room was a total loss.

The motel manager must've come to the same conclusion.

He glared at me over his shoulder and said, "You're going to pay for all this damage."

I was so taken aback that I didn't have an immediate response. Axel did, though.

My friend smiled pleasantly at the manager and said, "You got here awfully quick."

"What?" the manager asked.

Axel ignored him for the moment and turned to me. "What happened?"

"I was attacked," I said, sliding past the manager and into the smoke.

It was hard to breathe, but I pushed forward anyway, toward the bed. The lower half had been eaten by the fire, but the upper half was still intact. I waved the smoke from in front of my face and reached through the dim light until I felt my hand closed around the object embedded in the headboard.

I gave it a hard tug and tore it free. Waving the smoke from my face once more, I saw I was holding a tomahawk.

A shiver ran down my spine.

Were it not for Dyrnwyn, and the fact I'd rolled when I had, it would've been stuck in my skull rather than the headboard.

It hadn't been a warning.

Whoever had attacked me had done so with the intention of killing me, and they'd damn near succeeded.

The head of the ax was of nondescript dark steel. The haft was wood wrapped in leather. The only thing to give it any flare were two feathers fastened with little strands of leather, just near the top of the shaft. This, of course, gave it a "Native American" sort of vibe, but whether it truly belonged to one of the local Cherokee, I couldn't say.

I started back toward Axel, and when I saw I had his attention, I tossed him the tomahawk.

In a smooth motion, he moved both of his drumsticks to one hand and deftly caught the ax with the other.

He studied it for a moment, then looked up. His eyes scanned the blackened room again, then landed on me. "How long would you say it was from the time you jumped out the window until you saw me?"

As always, Axel was an astute investigator. At least when he wanted to be. I hadn't told him what had happened, but seeing the room, he'd already pieced together that someone had attacked me with fire magic and I'd escaped via the window. I supposed it wasn't rocket surgery, but I figured the average individual would've asked why I'd come from a direction other than my room to start with.

I shrugged. It wasn't liked I had a stopwatch. "Maybe thirty seconds."

"And I assume the fire wasn't long before that?"

"Seconds," I replied.

Axel's face took on a predatory look as his gaze shifted back to the motel manager. "So, within thirty seconds of when the fire started, you were already here with an extinguisher."

"So?" the manager asked, though he seemed to shrink a little under Axel's gaze.

"So, it's very fortunate," Axel said. His voice was soft, but his eyes maintained their menace. "Why, you must have been walking down the hall with the fire extinguisher at the ready. Maybe doing the monthly checks? And it just so happened this fire occurred just as you were passing by. But wait... How would you have known this particular room was on fire?"

"Well, I, uh... I saw the smoke."

"Saw the smoke," Axel repeated back to him. "Why, that *is* most fortunate. Were it not for your quick response, the entire building might've gone up. Yet, somehow, you saw the smoke from outside the classroom's shut door and took immediate action. Bravo."

"Well, I wasn't going to let the place burn down," the manager said a little defensively.

"Of course not," Axel replied. "Your response was both timely and fortune, indeed. Why, you should probably be awarded a medal."

"Look, if you're trying to say I knew anything about... Well, whatever happened in here—"

"Not at all," Axel replied, smiling wickedly. "But you should be aware that my best friend was attacked in your motel. And that makes me feel a bit smitey." He paused and looked around the room for dramatic effect. "Yet, I don't have any enemies to smite. So, if I were to happen upon someone who might have knowledge about the attack, well, that person would probably be in for a rough evening, if you know what I mean? They'd likely get...smitten?"

He sort of lost it there at the end, but his desired impact remained intact, which was extra impressive in Darth Vader slippers and a pink speedo.

The manager took two quick steps back, then looked my way. "If you were attacked, then, well, this certainly wasn't your fault, was it? So, don't worry about paying for the damages and all that."

With that, he turned and bolted out of the classroom.

We might've given chase, but as he disappeared, another face emerged. It was the concerned citizen from outside.

He looked at Axel and me, then at my smoldering room, then back at me. "Everyone okay here?"

"We're fine," I replied. "Like I said, I just left my heater turned up too high."

The man raised an eyebrow at me. "Is that so?"

I didn't reply.

It wasn't that I was trying to be a jerk, nor was I trying to go for a cool kid vibe. I genuinely didn't know what to say. I didn't know who the man was, nor why he'd followed me. Studying him more closely, I guessed he was in his early forties. He had soft features and an earnest face, as though he were genuinely concerned. Perhaps he was simply a good Samaritan, but after having a tomahawk thrown at my face and nearly being burned alive, my paranoia was on full alert.

"I couldn't help but overhear," he said, biting on his lip. "Did you say you were attacked?"

I glanced at Axel, who shrugged in reply.

"Yeah," I said, pointing toward the tomahawk in Axel's hand. "Someone tried to bury that in my face. Then they tried to burn me alive."

"Goodness me," the man said, shaking his head. "I fear Lost City is on the cusp of disaster. Such a small community cannot sustain such acts of violence. And more ruffians roll in by the day. Whatever shall we do?"

"Um, look," I said. "Not to be rude, but, uh, who are you?"

"Oh, dear me," he said, as though it had only just occurred to him. He stepped forward and put out his hand. "I'm Pastor Wright."

"You're a pastor?" I asked, taking his hand in what would go down in history as one of the limpest handshakes I ever had the displeasure of suffering.

"Yes," he replied, beaming. "Of the only church in town. And you gentlemen are?"

I paused, unsure exactly how to answer. Finally, I said, "Wyatt Draven, Blade Mage of the Ozark Mountain Cabal."

"Axel Gunner," Axel said, raising his hand in a little wave. "Red-headed Stepchild of the Ozark Mountain Cabal."

"Wizards, then," he said, eyes widening. "And a Blade Mage, no less. I'd heard of Blade Mages, but never had the chance to meet one. Why, this is certainly out of the ordinary, isn't it?"

"Not for me," Axel said. "I meet holy men like, all the time. They usually love me, except when they don't. I'm usually dressed better, though."

Pastor Wright chuckled. "Well, you're an interesting one, aren't you?"

Axel raised his nose like something smelled bad. Clearly, this had not been the response he'd wanted.

"What will you do now, Wyatt?" he asked. "You can hardly stay here."

I pointed at Axel. "My friend still has a room."

"But what if your attackers return?"

"I kind of hope they do. I want to give them their tomahawk back."

"Do you know what I think?" Pastor Wright asked.

I wasn't sure I wanted to know, but I forced a smile and asked, "What's that?"

"Well, you know, I don't always walk the streets this late at night. It just so happened that I couldn't sleep, and when that happens, I like to walk, you see? Lost City is usually such a peaceful little place, that... Well, I'm rambling, aren't I?"

"A little," I admitted.

He chuckled. "Sorry, I do that from time to time. Anyway, my point is... I think God sent me down the street at just the right time, so that I would see you coming out of that window."

I fought down the urge to groan. I've never cared whether someone wanted to chalk pure coincidence up to faith. That was their business. And that was my problem, really. If he wanted to think that God had put him where he was, that was fine, but it didn't mean I had to go along for the ride, did it?

Before I could respond with tired grumpiness, Axel said, "Seems logical to me."

I had to suppress my urge to slap him.

The pastor continued, "Yes, exactly. I think the Lord wanted me to see you and come to your aid."

"You think?" I asked.

"Indeed," he replied. "You see, I have a spare room at the church with two beds and you are both welcome to them. What do you say?"

"I say that we already have a room here," I replied. "Though I appreciate the kind offer."

Pastor Wright scrunched his nose up and fidgeted, as though he had something he wanted to say, but couldn't quite think of the words. Finally, he said, "Okay, look, it's not really you two I'm worried about. You're both wizards, and one of you is a Blade Mage. Certainly, you can handle yourselves."

"It's the other people," I said, realizing where his concern really came from. "You're concerned about the other people staying in this motel."

He smiled and lowered his voice. "Many of them don't have much.

For some of them, this is home. I'm sure your business in Lost City is of the utmost importance, but I'd like to avoid any of my flock being caught in the crossfire."

"We're usually pretty good about that sort of thing," I said, though Master Brown's words echoed through my skull.

"Yes, I can tell," he replied, his eyes shifting toward my husk of a room. "But this time... Had those flames spread..."

"I hear you, Pastor," I said. "I assure you, I had no idea I was going to be attacked. Nor do I know who the attackers were. Until a few minutes ago, I didn't even know I had enemies in Lost City."

"Still," the pastor said, "I'd love to host you for the night. I'd warrant that my spare beds are considerably more comfortable."

"No, thank you," I repeated.

"And there's a TV," he said.

"Sold," Axel said, moving toward the door. "I'll just get my things. This has to be the most boring motel I've ever stayed in. If you've got a television, then I'm with you."

"Well, I guess that settles it, then," the pastor said, turning back to me with too warm of a smile.

"Fine," I said. "We'll stay with you. Hopefully, it'll work out better than the last time we spent a night in a church."

# CHAPTER TWENTY-FOUR

I n big letters, the sign read, "Lost City Church." Beneath the words, in smaller print, it said, "A Haven for the Lost."

It had neither the beauty of the Memphis Knights' chapel, nor the charm of the little church we'd hid from the Valravn in. This was a simple country church, in a town forgotten. The buildings surrounding it were long since vacated, just like the old school, which was just down the road. We could've walked.

We'd followed Pastor Wright in my truck, and he'd even been so gracious as to wait while Axel attempted to track down the elusive manager. Unfortunately, the weasel of a man had disappeared. No surprise there. As Axel had sussed out, there was a good chance he'd known something about the attack. Apparently, once we'd let him out of our sight, he'd disappeared into the night. That was all right, though. Axel assured me he had "collected" the means to track him down the next day.

On the short drive over, Axel asked, "So, who do you think tried to kill you?"

"Well, from what we've heard, there's any number of people in the area who might want to take a stab at the Blade Mage. I just don't know how they figured out we were in town so quickly."

Axel nodded. "Unless August told someone, only the tribe and the constables were aware."

"But it's not out of the question that we could've been recognized at the motel. I mean...we're not exactly famous, but I suppose people in the area might know who we are."

"Speak for yourself," he said. "I'm famous."

"What's of most interest to me is the tomahawk," I said. "Notice the feathers? Either it belongs to someone from the tribe, or someone wanted it to *appear* that it belonged to someone related to the tribe. After it was buried in my face, of course."

Axel had a thoughtful look on his face. "What if it was Squirrel and the Squirrel Pack who tried to take you out?"

"Waya and his Wolf Pack," I said. "It's possible."

"More than possible," Axel replied. "If they got word that the Blade Mage was in town, they could only assume you were here for them, and likely not under peaceful terms."

It made sense. And they were just as likely as anyone else. Until we tracked down my attackers, or they came for me again, we wouldn't know.

At the church, Pastor Wright led us straight inside, assuring us that no one in the community would dare attack the church. I wasn't convinced, but if the kindly minister was naïve enough to believe the local ruffians would keep his church off limits, I wasn't going to try to convince him otherwise.

Like the exterior, the interior looked about like I'd expect of a small-town church. The walls were a stained white that needed a fresh coat a decade ago. There were a few stained-glass windows, but nothing exceptional. The pews were a worn-out tan. The dark blue carpet didn't match anything else in the room, but might've been stylish in its day, which I would guess was about when I was a toddler.

Wright led us to the back of the church, where the living quarters had been built on. I didn't think pastors normally lived at their churches. But hey, what did I know? He showed us our room and Axel dropped his stuff. I had no stuff left, so I dropped nothing.

Then the preacher offered to make us a cup of tea. I was about to politely decline when, once again, Axel voted "yes" for both of us. A few minutes later, we sat around a small dinner table, which was likely older than the carpet, sipping tea with the town's only holy man.

Wright didn't hesitate to cut right to his burning questions. "I suppose you're in town because of the trouble the tribe has had?"

I nodded.

"I see," he said slowly. "And I don't suppose you'd consider a different path?"

"Why would we do that?"

He forced a smile. "Those kids... They're not bad. They've simply lost their way."

"I can understand that," I said, shrugging. "That's why we came to help."

He stared at me for a long moment before asking his next question. "So, you're not here to...take them out?"

"Take them out?" I repeated. It took me a moment to realize what he was asking. It finally clicked. "Oh, no, of course not, Pastor. Not at all."

"But I thought..." He paused, seeming to collect his thoughts. "Well, I don't know much about wizards, but I was under the impression that was sort of what Blade Mages did."

"Yeah," I said, forcing a bitter smile. "That's a common misconception. Don't get me wrong, I've met my fair share of dark sorcerers. I'm here and they are not. But I am not in the business of butchering kids. That isn't what Blade Mages do. At least...it isn't what this Blade Mage does."

"Then why come at all?" he asked, and I could tell he wasn't quite convinced.

"A local man, August Bones, approached the Cabal looking for aid for the tribe."

"Ah, August," he said. "A good man with a good heart, troubled though it is."

"You know him?"

"Of course," he said with a more sincere smile. "I consider him one of my flock, though he's never attended church. I know he's a good man, though. Always wants to help."

"Can you tell me about him?"

"No, I don't think I can," Wright said in an apologetic tone. "It isn't for me to talk about others behind their back."

"It's important," I replied. "He's working with us, and I need to know if I can trust him."

"That is something you'll have to discover on your own, I'm afraid. Though, I'll say that I think August means no one harm. And even saying that, I feel I've stepped beyond what is appropriate."

"Fair enough," I replied. "Well, anyway, I only came to town to see if there was something I could do to help."

"And is there?"

"It's yet to be seen. Though, the fact someone tried to kill me is a pretty good sign someone is up to no good."

"So, do you intend to stick around?"

"Worried what will happen to your town?"

"A little, I admit."

"As I said before, I didn't come here looking for trouble. And I assure you, I have no ill will toward these youngsters. My only goal is to help them. If they don't want to be part of their tribe, that's their business. But if they're in danger..."

"And who do you fear they're in danger from?"

"That's the question, isn't it?" I replied, taking a sip of tea. I wasn't sure on the flavor, but it was clearly an herbal mix he'd sweetened with honey. It was quite good. "I'd warrant they're mostly in danger from themselves, at the moment."

"That may not be all," Wright replied.

I raised an eyebrow. "Oh?"

"You aren't the first person to show up asking after them. Thus, my interest in your intentions."

"Who else?"

Throughout the entire conversation, Axel had been flipping through channels on a small TV on the counter. For the first time, he turned his attention to us.

The preacher shrugged. "He didn't give me a name. But another man came by the church just yesterday, asking about Waya and his pack."

"And he concerned you?" I asked.

"Yes," Wright said, looking down as though a little embarrassed. "He...kind of scared me."

"Did he threaten you?"

The preacher shook his head. "No, he didn't threaten me. Not with words. Nor with his actions, really. It was more... There was just something about him. He was dangerous, I could tell."

I shared a look with Axel, but my friend only shrugged in reply.

"What do you mean?"

"Well, it's like... You two. I could tell by looking at you that you were both men accustomed to violence. Yet, you didn't strike me as evil men. Nor did I sense I was in any immediate danger from you. But I suspect if your attackers kicked down the door right now, you'd be ready for action while I would curl up in a ball on the floor."

"Okay," I said. "And this man?"

"This man seemed like he lived for violence. Like a ticking time bomb. Not that he was evil per se. Just someone who thrived on conflict. And I fear that his presence in Lost City can mean nothing good. I think he aims to find Waya and his friends and hurt them."

"Did he say something to that effect?"

"No, he only asked if I knew where they were. And what I could tell him about them. He referred to them as dark wizards, or something like that, but I don't know anything about that kind of stuff. I only told him the truth, same as I told you. They're good kids. And I do not know where to find them."

"So, when you ran into us, you feared we were on the same course," I replied.

He nodded.

"You invited us to your church not only to avoid collateral damage at the motel, but also so you could try to sway us not to harm Waya and his buddies."

He nodded again. "Perhaps I should've been upfront about my intentions."

"It's all right," I said. "I don't blame you. And again, I want to assure you I have no intention of harming any rebellious teenagers. But what you've said changes things some. Whoever this man is, I think we need to find the Wolf Pack before he does."

Pastor Wright smiled. "On that, we can certainly agree."

# CHAPTER TWENTY-FIVE

I awoke to the smell of delicious meat stuffs and stumbled into the kitchen to find Pastor Wright cooking eggs, bacon, and biscuits. We certainly wouldn't have gotten that kind of service at the janky motel.

As we ate, he brought me a pair of old loafers that were just a tad tight. Still, it was worth having to scrunch my toes to have shoes on my feet again. Plus, he'd hooked me up with a pair of socks so I'd have something to wear with my dress shoes. *Win.*

I had to admit, despite his overfamiliar demeanor and talkative nature, Pastor Wright was a good dude. Knowing what he'd known about us, he had invited us into his home, fed us, and put shoes on my feet. I knew I'd have to find some way to repay his kindness.

August was already waiting for us at the motel. He seemed relieved to see us. "I heard you had an eventful evening."

Axel shrugged. "Pretty boring, really."

Ignoring my friend's comment, I asked, "Where'd you hear that?"

August motioned toward the motel. "One of the locals. When I first got here, I thought to check in at the office, but the manager wasn't around."

"Imagine that," Axel said, giving me a knowing look.

August continued, "I walked down to your room and saw the mess.

Grabbed the first person I recognized. All they could say was there was a fire and a fight. Didn't know any more than that. So...I've been a little worried."

"We're all right," I said.

"Yeah, they mentioned no one got hurt," he replied. "I was more worried you'd gone on the warpath."

"No," I said, shaking my head. "Pastor Wright was in the neighborhood around the time of the attack. He offered to let us crash in the church." I paused and lifted one foot. "Even loaned me these swanky loafers."

"Ah," he said, nodding. "That's no surprise. He's a good guy. A little on the naïve side, but he means well. He's done a hell of a lot of good for the folks around here. Certainly better than the last fire and brimstone pastor."

Axel tapped his finger on his chin thoughtfully. "Well, he didn't slit my throat while I slept, so he's all right with me."

"You have low standards," August said with a smile.

He seemed in better shape than the day before. His eyes still looked tired, but a lot of the previous day's exhaustion seemed to have dissipated. He wasn't shaky like before. Perhaps he'd gotten a better night's sleep than we had.

"Elder Morgan reached out to me," he said. "He wants to visit with you guys again first thing this morning."

"Hmm," I said, making a face. "It's going to be a busy day, then. I was rather hoping to head for the big town to get some new apparel."

Also, I smelled like I spent the night around a bonfire, and if I didn't get something more comfortable on my feet, I was going to end up with blisters. And then we had some other things to check in on. Still, I supposed we shouldn't keep the elder waiting. So, him first, then new clothes and shoes, and then we could get down to the real business of finding out what kind of evil was plaguing the happy little town

# CHAPTER TWENTY-SIX

This time, more elders were present, and I couldn't remember all their names as we were introduced. John was there as well, along with Samuel and a few other younger members. This was the entire consortium of medicine men and women responsible for training the next generation. To a stranger, they just looked like an assembly of teachers.

Instead of the little meeting room, we'd been led to a larger conference room. I suspected this was where they usually held their staff meetings.

They told us about each of the missing kids in turn, which ones had been seen around and which hadn't. More importantly, we were informed that another had disappeared in the night. He was only ten.

In turn, I told them about the attack.

A silence fell over the room when I showed them the tomahawk.

I handed it over to the nearest elder, who passed it around until it reached Elder Morgan's hands. He didn't pass it on. Instead, he stared down at the tomahawk, as though in a trance.

When no one else seemed inclined to speak, I asked, "Do you recognize it?"

"I should," he said, turning it over in his hands. "I made it, after all."

"You made it?"

He gave me a soft nod, sadness burning his eyes. "It was a gift for my granddaughter."

"Pathkiller," I said.

His lips twisted into a scowl. "Alyita."

"Yes, of course," I said, realizing my error. "Apologies."

"So, it was them," John said, looking around at his elders. "It was Waya's Wolf Pack who attacked the Blade Mage."

"I can scarcely believe it," Elder Thomas said, rubbing his eyes. "You're sure it was not meant as a warning?"

"I'm sure," I said, despite wanting to lie. It was clear this was taking a heavy toll on them, but I couldn't bring myself to be dishonest. "If I hadn't moved when I did, that tomahawk would've been implanted in my forehead."

Elder Thomas's gaze moved to August.

August nodded in reply. "I saw the room. It was blackened to a crisp. That was no warning. It was attempted murder."

Various conversations broke out. Some argued there was no way the kids would've tried to murder me. This crowd, it seemed, still didn't believe the teens were responsible for the other elder's death. The other side took it as proof that the kids had fallen from the path. They'd seen enough evidence.

Only Elder Morgan was silent, staring down at the tomahawk as he rolled it between his gnarled fingers.

I put up my hands to get everyone's attention. "Look, there's no point in arguing. Maybe they heard the Blade Mage was in town and thought the worst. Maybe they figured they'd get to me before I got to them. Or someone else could've stolen the tomahawk and used it so that when my corpse was found, it'd look like your kids were responsible. It doesn't really matter. What's important is finding them before anyone else gets hurt."

Elder Morgan's eyes shot up to meet mine. "Does this change things for you?"

"No," I said. "If anything, it has only shown me how dire your situation is."

"You will still try to help us?" he asked, swallowing the foul taste of his next question. "Without seeking to harm them?"

I wasn't sure what to say, so, like an idiot, I glanced over at Axel. I supposed I wanted to be sure that he and I were on the same page. He took it as his opportunity to take the floor.

"Of course we'll help," he said, grinning like an asshole. "I have the utmost confidence that Wyatt will come up with a happy resolution that suits everyone. You'll see."

I blinked three times, cursing myself for allowing him the chance to speak. Yet, I was so flummoxed by what he'd just said that I failed to stop him from continuing.

"In fact, I'd say we're your best hope. Wyatt and me, well, we're great with teenagers."

That wasn't true.

"And experts at tracking people down."

No, we weren't.

"I'm *absolutely* sure we can handle the situation."

I *absolutely* wasn't sure of that, at all.

"Right, Wyatt?"

Every face in the room turned toward me. And despite the boldness of Axel's claims, there was a glimmer of hope etched across their collected faces.

*Well, fuck.*

There was no backing out now. We were committed.

I coughed to buy myself a moment, then said, "Look, uh, I can only promise that we'll do our best to bring your missing kids home unharmed."

"Right," Axel said cheerfully. "So, can we get any of their personal possessions to try our tracking spells on?"

"You can," Elder Morgan said slowly. "Though, we've already tried several of our own."

"Which are probably better than ours," Axel said, a little of the wind coming out of his sails. "Guessing you didn't have great results?"

Elder Morgan stared at him like he was a potato.

"Right," Axel said again, rebuilding his cheer. "So, we'll have to hunt them down the old-fashioned way. Never fear, Axel and Wyatt are here!"

I sighed. What had we gotten ourselves into this time?

# CHAPTER TWENTY-SEVEN

J ust before we left the training grounds, Elder Morgan offered Axel and me a small cabin, which took care of our lodging. I couldn't tell whether they did this out of guilt because I had nearly been killed the night before, or out of fear that if it *were* their kids, and they attacked me again, I might hurt one of them. Perhaps a bit of both.

Our next stop was the Walmart in Tahlequah so I could get some fresh clothes. I was damn near out of money, but once more, Axel produced a wad of cash and paid for my loot.

And yeah, I bought my clothes at Walmart. Of course I did. I never felt the need to spend ridiculous sums of money at designer stores to impress people I didn't give a shit about. Jeans and black t-shirts were all I needed. And socks and underwear, of course.

Shoes, on the other hand, well, thankfully there was a small shoe store in town where I was able to walk out with a fresh pair of Vans.

On the way back to Lost City, August asked, "So, what's the game plan?"

"Well, we need to catch up with the motel manager," I said, thinking it over. "Any chance you know where he lives?"

August nodded. "You think he knew something about the attack?"

Axel answered for me. "Only enough to be standing there with an extinguisher moments after the fire started."

"And he disappeared after Axel called him on it," I said, turning to glance at my friend. "We should've never let him slip away."

"Pastor Wright sort of got in the way," Axel said.

"Right," I replied. "It's best to avoid interrogating witnesses in front of holy men."

"Well, that's silly," Axel said. "Holy men have been some of the greatest torturers throughout history."

"Fair enough," I said. "Then why did you refrain from grabbing the manager there and then?"

"Well, because I have the attention span of a cocker spaniel. Plus, I thought the preacher might've been your attacker and was back for a second round."

"Pastor Wright?" August chuckled. "One look at his face and you could tell he's about as aggressive as a teddy bear."

"You never know," Axel said defensively. "I've met some mean teddy bears. Never judge a book by its cover. Unless it has a really cool cover, of course. Or if it's a nudie mag. Or a coloring book. You can judge those by their covers."

"So, the manager first, then?" I asked before he could continue listing things.

"Yes," Axel said, rubbing his hands together like a cartoon villain. "I have some rather creative ideas on how to make him crack."

August laughed again. "I'm pretty sure you can look at him wrong and he'll crack."

"Then look I shall," Axel said, adding an exaggerated, "Mwahahaha."

This was going to be interesting.

# CHAPTER TWENTY-EIGHT

The weasel who ran the seedy motel lived in a small yellow house outside of town. It was a quaint little cutesy home. Not at all what I expected of the sum lord.

According to August, his name was Bill, and he mostly kept to himself. He was known to be stingy, but other than that, August didn't really know much about him. He'd been running the motel for years, but there was no indication he had a family, any friends, or more importantly, any affiliation with the local hooligans, outside of renting them rooms.

We approached the front door cautiously. If it turned out he had a family, our visit might get awkward. But there was only one car in the drive: an ancient rust-covered station wagon that seemed out of place in front of the well-kept country home.

As August and I approached the front door, Axel slipped around to the back, just in case Bill tried to run off again.

Axel used mind-speak to let me know when he was in position, and I raised my hand to knock on the door.

Three quick knocks and I pulled my hand away. Just to be clear, I didn't knock like I was serving a warrant. I hadn't wanted to freak him out, so I'd gone for a softer, Jehovah's Witness type of knock.

Despite that, the door pushed in a few inches, opening.

It hadn't been closed all the way.

I turned and raised an eyebrow at August. He shrugged in reply.

Looking closer, I realized the latch was broken. In fact, when I tested the knob, there was no tension at all. It, too, was broken.

I gave August another look, this time more concern than confusion. He replied in kind.

I warned Axel, then let myself in.

It didn't take us long to find Bill. He was in the living room, seated in a dusty recliner.

And he was dead.

His throat had been slit wide, revealing his severed jugular. Judging by the dried blood caked on the front of his wife beater, he'd been dead for hours.

His glossed-over eyes were open but staring up at the ceiling. His hands sat on the armrests of his chair, his finger sitting on top of a remote. The TV was still on. There were no signs of struggle.

Whoever had killed Bill, they'd crept up on him.

Did him in quick before the poor bastard even had time to register what had happened.

We stared at him in silence for several seconds. I can't say what August was thinking, but for me, I was already considering our next steps. By that point, death had become old trade.

I didn't think we'd find anything, but certainly we'd check the house for any other bodies or clues.

It was pretty obvious, though. Axel had been right.

Bill had known who'd attacked me, and someone had come along to ensure he kept his mouth shut. If only Axel or I had stopped him from getting away, the weasel would've still been alive.

That said, I didn't feel bad about it. I just couldn't find it in myself to summon up any empathy for someone who'd played a role in trying to have me murdered.

And that...

That lack of guilt made me feel guilty.

Once more, I found myself questioning my own mental state. What had I become that I could stare down at a murder victim and feel nothing? What kind of monster had I turned into?

Axel's footsteps broke through my thoughts as he entered the room.

My friend took one look at the body and said, "Well, I guess we won't be getting any answers here after all."

Apparently, he was short on empathy as well.

# CHAPTER TWENTY-NINE

"What's next?" August asked as he took the wheel once again.

It was a fair question. Our best lead was dead, and we'd not learned anything of value. As we left, though, August had called it in to Constable Williams so she could get the right authorities involved. I wasn't sure how the tribe handled supernatural-related murders on their land, or if the Cabal played any role, but surely they'd know what to do.

Apparently, Constable Johnson had demanded we make ourselves available for questioning. We wished him luck with that and went about our business. The way I figured it, I was going to be in enough trouble with the Cabal anyway. What was walking away from a murder scene on top of it?

I was a little worried about the consequences for August, but he was a big boy, and seemed about as bothered as we were. I kept my concerns to myself.

Instead, I considered where we should go next, and finally answered August's question. "It's time to learn about the local gangs. Up close and personal."

"All right," he replied. "You want me to show you where the Red Dirt Riders have their base of operations? Or Fatima's crew?"

"Actually, I was thinking of starting with the Evans brothers."

"The Evans?" he asked, taking his eyes off the road to glance at me with surprise. "Why them?"

"Well, they're the ones who threatened the elders recently."

I decided to play my cards close to my chest. I didn't want him to know the main reason I wanted to speak with them was because he'd conveniently forgotten to mention them previously.

But then Axel said, "And they're the ones you conveniently forgot to mention previously."

*Well, so much for that.*

"I didn't *conveniently* forget them," August said, taking a defensive tone. "They're just two-bit redneck thugs. Nobodies."

"Then it'll be easier to discount their involvement in... Well, whatever the hell is going on around here." I gave him a toothy smile. "After we see for ourselves, of course."

August didn't argue, which spoke volumes. He either didn't want to believe they were suspects, or he didn't want us to look in their direction. That only made me want to scratch the itch even more.

# CHAPTER THIRTY

"See there," August said, pointing into the distance. "The single-wide with the smoldering burn barrel. That's Braedon Evans's house. He's the alpha."

The distance was great, but fortunately, he'd had the foresight to bring along a pair of binoculars. I raised them and studied the trailer he'd pointed at.

We were spying from a tree-covered hilltop and had a good view of the clearing where five single-wide trailers sat in various states of redneckery. The place was littered with junk. There was a fleet of old pickups, most of which I doubted would ever run again. There were a couple of rusted lawn mowers, a poorly stacked woodpile, some graying lumber, and various other hillbilly lawn ornaments.

"So, they all live here?" I asked.

"Yup," August replied from beside me. "All seven brothers."

"And what do they do?" I asked. "I mean... What role do they play in the community?"

"They make meth, mostly," August said. "Not exclusively, of course, but that is their bread and butter. They service the Normans around Tahlequah and the supernatural community around Lost City."

"Lovely," I replied. "Sound like a nice bunch."

"Yeah, well, they're not," he said, ignoring my sarcasm. "The whole deal with the tribe... Well, one of the brothers sold pot to one of the students. Not even sure how he got it to him. But it happened, somehow. Anyway, one of the elders approached Braedon Evans and told him not to deal to their kids."

"And that's when the trouble started," I said.

"That's when one of the elders nearly ended up dead," he corrected.

Waiting impatiently beside me, Axle said, "Wyatt, either let me have a turn on the binoculars, or let's go burn down their meth shack. I'm getting bored."

August turned to Axel and said, "You didn't strike me as the strait-laced type."

"Who? Me?" Axel said, raising an eyebrow. "I've got no problem with herbal remedies. Pot, mushrooms, hell, maybe even peyote. Meth, though, that's another story. I've seen the way it ruins people's lives. Anyone peddling that poison needs a swift kick, as far as I'm concerned."

Before August could reply, Axel turned his attention back to me.

"Seriously, Wyatt, let me have a turn with the noc-nocs!"

"Hold on," I said. "There's a car coming up the drive."

It was a black sedan. Looked fancy from a distance. Certainly not the type of car I'd expect to see pulling into a meth lab trailer park.

As it drew closer, I saw the symbol that identified it as a Lexus. Definitely not a dirt road kind of car.

As the Lexus came to a stop, the screen door to Braedon's trailer opened and a hulking man in a sleeveless pearl snap stepped outside. Between the shitty tats and the long beard, he looked like he was just home from his latest stint in the big house.

"Someone just came out of the trailer," I said. "Big hulking brute."

"Most likely Braedon," August said. "Though I don't think you'd say any of the brothers are small."

The driver's door of the Lexus opened and a middle-aged man in an expensive black suit stepped out of the car. I was willing to bet the sunglasses he wore cost more than my house.

I watched as the two men engaged in conversation. They certainly weren't strangers, but I didn't get the impression they were old fishing buddies, either. It appeared to be a business conversation. Neither man seemed thrilled to be talking to the other, but the businessman maintained a professional, relaxed salesman demeanor. The brute, on the other hand, seemed cocksure and ready for action.

I glanced over at Axel, intending to ask him to do his magic trick where he could hear over distances, but found that he already had a drumstick in one ear.

"No good," he said. "Too far and too much wind. I can't hear them."

I handed the binoculars over to August. "Do you recognize the other guy?"

August studied the scene for a few moments, then said, "No, can't say that I've ever seen him before. The other *is* Braedon, though."

Axel tried to snag the binoculars as August handed them back to me, but much to his dismay, he failed. He stomped away, pouting.

When I looked again, I felt as though the rich dick in the suit was looking right at me. That was silly, though. There was no way. We were too far away and there was too much coverage between us.

Still, the man smiled, as though he'd noticed I'd noticed him noticing me. Then his eyes shifted back to Braedon.

They spoke a few more words. Then the businessman got back into his car while Braedon stood on his porch with his arms crossed.

I turned and held the binoculars out to Axel, who took them from my hands like a greedy child.

"So, what now?" August asked.

"Would they speak to us?" I asked.

"Not a chance," he replied. "Hell, if they knew we were up here, they'd shoot first and ask questions later. Expect the same if you approach their homes."

I stared at the distant trailer. My own thoughts weren't that far from Axel's. A big part of me wanted to torch their meth lab for sport, but that would almost certainly result in Norman authorities prowling the area. And we hadn't come to Lost City to play drug cop. The fact of the matter was, there were assholes all over the place cooking dope, some Norman and some supernatural. Even if we put the Evans out of business that day, they would set up shop again the next. No, we weren't in

Lost City to fight the war on drugs. We were there to help the tribe find their missing kids.

"Let's go," I said.

"That's it?" August asked.

"For now," I replied. "I've seen what I wanted to see."

The former constable didn't argue. He understood. We were just getting a feel for the local gangs. And he'd shown us where they lived. Axel and I could get back there with or without him after that. If we wanted to find the Evans brothers, we knew where to look.

# CHAPTER THIRTY-ONE

A bandoned factories and dank caves.

Those were prime locations for supernatural baddies to call home. The Red Dirt Riders were no exception.

They'd chosen an old warehouse a short drive from Lost City. There was no sign of what had once been manufactured there. Not that it mattered.

There wasn't a decent spot to spy on them, so we opted for a small clearing off the side of the road. Far enough away that we hoped it wouldn't be obvious we were spying, but close enough we could get a decent look at the place. Not that there was much to look at.

We raised the hood of August's car, letting it play the part of a broken-down old beater. It was a gamble, since most people wouldn't believe an old Honda had broken down.

When we were confident no one was watching us, we used August's binoculars again.

The old metal skeleton was quiet, and no one was roaming around outside. If I'd happened by the place at random, I would've never known it was the base of operations for a local gang. I guess that was the idea, though. I could only hope that one day I'd run into a villain who did their evil plotting someplace nice.

"Well?" August asked.

I wasn't sure what to say. The whole point of this excursion was to learn about the local gangs. So far, all I'd learned about the Red Dirt Riders was that they were good at disguising their base.

The question then was whether it'd be a good idea to approach them directly and reveal our presence. There was a chance they already knew the Blade Mage was in town, and if they were in any way involved in my attack the night before, they might try to kill me on the spot. It wasn't like anyone would notice out there.

I was chewing on my lip and weighing the options when I heard the throaty rumble of a car in the distance. Glancing up out of habitual curiosity, I noticed something interesting.

The approaching car was a black Lexus.

The very same black Lexus we'd just seen at the Evans's trailer.

"You guys seeing this?" I asked, just as the car turned down the long driveway to the factory.

"No," Axel replied in a pout. "I can't see anything because you're hogging the noc-nocs again."

August, on the other hand, asked, "Is that the same car?"

"I think so," I said, handing him the binoculars. "Are you sure you don't recognize that guy?"

"Positive," August replied. "People with that kind of money don't visit Lost City, and when they do, they stick out. It sure looks like the same car."

Much to Axel's dismay, August handed the noc-nocs back to me.

I looked again, just as the man was getting out. There was no mistaking him. It was the same guy, all right. The same smarmy chap in the same smart suit.

We were far enough away that it shouldn't have been obvious we were spying, but once again, the man's head turned in my direction, and once again, I could've sworn he looked right at me. Only for a moment, then his eyes shifted away.

I followed his gaze back toward the side of the factory, where a gaggle of bikers walked out to greet him. Most appeared to be human, though there were a few who clearly weren't. One guy looked like he'd just stepped off the set of a classic werewolf movie. Another had skin that was ashen gray.

And the guy walking out to meet our dapper fella looked like a straight-up zombie. No, that wasn't quite it. More like a less attractive Freddy Krueger, minus the hat. His entire head looked like it'd been dipped in acid or had survived a raging brush fire. He didn't have any hair, and I didn't see a single spot of healthy skin.

"The half-baked guy is Raymond?" I asked.

"Charismatic leader of the Red Dirt Riders," August replied.

"So," I said, watching the exchange between the rich tit and the bikers. It looked like a repeat of the same conversation he'd had with Braedon. "Didn't you tell me these guys were moonshiners?"

"Primarily, yeah," August replied.

"So, what sort of business does a guy in a fancy suit have with the local meth dealers *and* moonshiners?"

"Two for one special?" Axel offered.

I glanced over at August, who shrugged in reply. "Hard to say. I wouldn't be surprised to learn that the Riders have branched out into more lucrative illicit business. Raymond has been recruiting recently. His gang is getting bigger and bigger."

"Hard to finance a big gang on moonshine sales," Axel said. "Unless we've stepped into a portal and have traveled back to the 1920s. Wait... You guys don't think that's possible, do you?"

I stared at the both of them. "Seriously, what sort of business would a guy in a thousand-dollar suit have with meth dealers and a biker gang?"

I supposed the question lent itself an answer, which was just as well because August didn't say anything, and Axel... Well, Axel said, "No, *seriously*, do you think we could've gone back in time?"

When I didn't take the bait, Axel began listing off several reasons the businessman might've been meeting with both gangs. However, I wasn't convinced they were starting a flash dance group together. Nor was he going to sell me on the idea that the guy in the Lexus was a door-to-door Bible salesman.

The whole situation didn't add up. Something funky was going on, and it was time to pack up and head out. I had a bad feeling. More than that, I felt naked on the side of the road.

Too late, though. Before I could suggest we leave, I heard the distinct rumble of a motorcycle engine coming down the road. In fact, it sounded like several. I'd gotten rather familiar with the sound recently.

"Quick," August said, moving closer to his car. He started fidgeting with things under the hood, pretending like he was working on something.

Axel and I moved alongside him, trying to help facilitate the façade. I really wanted to reach for my staff and sword, but that would've been a dead giveaway.

The riders appeared from the direction opposite the factory, about ten of them.

My initial impression was that they were all merely returning to base from some mission, or perhaps an afternoon joy ride. I thought they might glide right past us.

It wasn't to be.

The whole lot of them pulled off the road and surrounded us. Most parked their bikes and got off, but three began circling us like sharks.

I almost laughed. I knew it was meant to intimidate us, but if things went south, they'd be much better off on their feet.

A burly fella with a long beard started toward us. In one hand, he held a long skinning knife. His other hand hovered over the revolver holstered on his hip.

The outriders let off their throttles and the burly guy yelled over the hum of their motors. "August Bones, who are your friends?"

"Just some acquaintances." August pointed toward his Honda. "We're having a little car trouble."

"I bet," the big man barked, eyeing us suspiciously. "Old Hondas don't break down, Bones."

Well, I'd certainly called that one.

"This one did," August replied.

The man moved closer. "Is that why you were spying on us with your binoculars?"

August said, "We were just checking to see if anyone was home. Thought you guys might be willing to lend us a hand."

The big man grinned. "The boss wants to speak with you. He ain't happy. In fact, I think he might finally put you in the ground, you fucking interloper."

Axel and I shared a look, and then I spoke up. "You're bad at making threats."

"What?" he asked.

I couldn't tell whether he legitimately hadn't heard me over the obnoxious motorcycles or if he was confused because people didn't normally talk to him like that.

So, I repeated myself. "I said you're bad at making threats."

"Is that right?"

"Yeah," I replied. "You don't say your boss wants to talk to some-body, and then follow that up by suggesting your boss might want to kill them."

"Yeah," Axel said, jumping right in. "You've removed any incentive for August to go peacefully. Should've invited him in for tea and cookies."

The dude was big. Like, my-eyes-barely-came-to-his-nipples big. Clearly he wasn't used to being challenged by people he thought he could crush under his sweaty man-boobs.

"Maybe I don't want him to come peacefully," he said.

I knew what was coming next, and even if I hadn't, his eyes gave him away. Just the briefest of glances toward the bikers who were circling behind us again.

I dropped and spun, and at the same time, called Dyrnwyn to my hand.

With my head lowered, the tire iron swung through the vacated place where my precious brain case had just been. The hit would've killed me, but he missed.

I didn't.

As soon as I'd dropped, I'd spun, slashing Dyrnwyn through the front tire of his bike. The magical blade tore through the metal as easily as the rubber on the tire.

The whole bike took a nosedive, launching the outstretched rider over his handlebars.

The second bike slammed into the first. The third slammed into the second. They all went down.

For a moment, it was like being back in Memphis again.

And that made me wonder how Uriah was getting on. And that, in turn, made me think of Eilidh. But only for a moment, because I didn't have time to reminisce.

I turned back just in time to see the big guy barreling toward me, his skinning knife raised over his head. His eyes were wide with surprise, like he'd seen what I'd just done to his sneaky buddies, but his brain hadn't quite registered what had happened. As the realization finally hit, he paused, but only for the briefest of instances.

That was all I needed.

I swung my wizard staff toward his head, connecting with a solid *thunk*.

He staggered back, but to his credit, didn't go down. His eyes blinked rapidly, though. And again, I figured his brain was trying to process what had just happened.

Despite having revealed my staff and sword, I thought there might still be a chance to hide the fact we were wizards. Then Axel fired a lightning bolt, zapping the two bikers trying to attack him. They both went down, convulsing.

*So much for that.*

August Bones drew his own magical instrument then. Bigger than the typical wand, it appeared to be made of bone and was shaped an awful lot like a spine.

A red wave of energy emanated from the end of it. The three nearest bikers dropped to their knees, shrieking and clutching at their own faces.

No, I realized, not their faces. They were scratching at their own eyes.

What had he done to them?

There was no time to ponder it just then as another biker raced toward me with a rusty machete.

Blade met blade and Dyrnwyn won, slicing the machete right in half. The biker paused and stared, dumbfounded, at his ruined weapon.

He was only more surprised when the blunt end of my staff slammed between his eyes as I Spartan-lunged at him.

By that point, all the extra noise from the bikes had been silenced, and the only sounds were those of the surrounding melee.

The first burly biker had recovered and was glaring at me. He spat and said, "Wizards."

The rest of his pals realized what they were up against and all took a collective step back.

The advantage was ours.

A new roar of motors sounded and I turned my gaze toward the factory. The black Lexus was gone. Instead, a stream of motorcycles poured from the warehouse, along with a few pickups, beds loaded down with pissed-off goons. I didn't care to count, but we had a small army descending on us.

The Red Dirt Riders were bound for war, and we were their targets.

The sheer numbers were a problem, even if they didn't have any sorcerers among their ranks, and that was yet to be determined.

Axel glanced over at me and asked, "Memphis?"

It was a good question. He was asking whether I wanted him to fire a lightning bolt into their ranks like he had in Memphis. It had been a very effective tactic.

I shook my head.

If we attacked, they'd certainly defend. So far, there hadn't been any serious injuries. Further provocation, however, would certainly end in bloodshed. It was likely to end up there anyway, but this, again, wasn't why we'd come to Lost City. We were there to help the tribe, not start a war.

"Oh, shit," August said, watching the oncoming horde. "This isn't good."

Keeping my voice low enough the nearby bikers couldn't hear me, I asked, "What do you think the chances are they'll be willing to talk?"

He shook his head and shrugged at the same time, which I took to mean there was a chance. Maybe it was about as good as Jim Carrey's chance in *Dumb and Dumber*, but it was a chance.

I didn't know August Bones very well, but I decided right then I rather liked the guy. Any wizard with half a brain would've fled. But I didn't have any plans to run, and so, despite his obvious fear, he didn't, either.

We'd just have to see how he'd handle himself if shit *really* hit the fan, but this was a good start.

The horde fell upon us and circled around us. Only this time, they all stopped and dismounted. A few were brandishing melee weapons, but the vast majority were armed with guns. Most of these were either shotguns or pistols, but I spotted a couple of AR-15s and at least one Kalashnikov. On the other end of the spectrum, however, there were a few rusted revolvers and some deer rifles.

What I found most impressive was that after they dismounted, most dropped behind their bikes, using them for cover. This wasn't just a ragtag band of bikers. These asshats practiced for the big game. I just hoped this wasn't it.

If they all opened fire, I knew my shield wouldn't hold up. Even Axel wouldn't be able to maintain for long. I didn't know anything about August's ability to shield, but given that he'd once been a Cabal constable, I could assume he was at least better at it than me. However, I didn't care to find out if my guess was accurate just then.

Best guess... We were screwed.

The crispy leader of the gang approached at a casual gait, his eyes scanning the wreckage and his men.

Raymond's gaze finally landed on the burly guy with the beard, and he asked, "So, what have I missed?"

Before the burly fella could reply, Axel jumped in and asked, "Have you heard the good news?"

One crispy bacon eyebrow rose.

Yup, we were screwed.

# CHAPTER THIRTY-TWO

"About our lord and savior," Axel said. "You see, sir, we're door-to-door Bible salesmen."

Raymond stared at Axel for a moment, then back at his underling.

"They're wizards," the burly biker said.

Both crispy eyebrows rose, and Raymond made a *tsk tsk* sound as his eyes shifted to August. "What is this, Bones?"

"Your men attacked us, Raymond," August said in a matter-of-fact tone.

The gang leader grinned, and I really wanted to ask whether it caused him physical pain. His face didn't look any better up close. I couldn't tell whether he was a human who'd survived a terrible accident, or if his appearance was the natural result of some obscure supernatural breed. A ghoul of some kind, perhaps?

"Only after we caught you spying on us, *former* constable," Raymond said. "So, let me ask you another question... Why have you brought wizards to our front door? And why are you spying on us?"

"We weren't spying," August said.

"Bones," Raymond replied, feigning a hurt expression. That wasn't a hard sell with his messed-up face. "I thought we had an understanding, you and me. And now you show up on my doorstep uninvited, spy on us, and then hurt my people... Whatever should I do with you?"

"Your people attacked first," August repeated, and I could see he was getting frazzled.

I didn't know the history between him and Raymond, but clearly the gang leader was the type to twist the narrative. And he needed to make a strong showing in front of his people. The only reason he hadn't ordered them to attack us yet was because we were an unknown entity. Also, he probably wanted to know why we were there. But that didn't mean this friendly charade would hold up.

I needed to jump in to help August, but it was crucial I chose the right words.

I took a moment to weigh what I could say that would help the situation. It turned out that pausing was a bad idea. Axel had no such reservations.

"We weren't spying," my friend said. "We were just making sure you didn't have company before we popped in for a visit."

"Is that right?" Raymond asked, turning his attention to Axel.

"Of course," Axel said in a serious tone. "It's called being polite. Ever heard of it?"

"Excuse me?" Raymond said.

It was hard to read his face, but I had the impression he was stuck somewhere between anger and bewilderment. Axel had that effect. And it was most enjoyable when it was directed at the hardened baddies who took themselves too seriously.

"Well, if I'm being honest," Axel said, "you're being kind of rude. You've pointed out that we're standing on your doorstep, yet you haven't invited us in for tea and cookies. You haven't told us to make ourselves at home, nor have you pointed me toward the restroom, nor subtly bragged about your fine furnishings or family photos. You, sir, are a poor host."

Raymond turned back to August. "Is this guy fucking serious?"

August turned to me, his face pleading for help. I shrugged. *Fuck it.* Sometimes you just had to let Axel have the floor.

"I am *deadly* serious, sir," Axel said. "And furthermore, to add insult to injury, you're pointing guns at us. I'm sure I've seen ruder behavior, but frankly, I can't remember when."

Raymond kept his eyes on Axel, but said, "Bones, I'm about two seconds from having my boys wipe the smug grin off your new friend's face."

Axel's grin spread ever wider. "Straight to threats of violence. Very original. Just so you're aware, much scarier people have tried to keep me from smiling, but you know what? The only time I quit smiling is when I accidentally sit on my balls."

Raymond snorted. "You seem too young to have that problem."

"They're just that big," Axel replied.

"Maybe I'll keep them as a trophy, then," Raymond replied.

Axel raised an eyebrow. "Well, now, that's just a weird thing to threaten someone with."

"It's not a threat," Raymond said. "Consider it a promise."

Axel mimicked Raymond's *tsk tsk* from earlier. "And the rude behavior continues. My balls are already promised to the Smithsonian, due to their abnormally gargantuan size and beauty. There's some argument about whether they should be studied for their splendor or displayed in the art museum for their grandeur, but either way, you won't find them easy to claim. Rescind your vow, good sir, or consider me your mortal enemy."

"We won't be enemies long," Raymond said. "One of us will be dead soon."

"I see," Axel said. "I'm sure you will be sorely missed. Well... I'm guessing you might be missed. Well... I'm thinking maybe some of these guys might miss you. Can't imagine who else, if I'm being honest."

"All right, you annoying little fuck," the gang leader said, his patience running out. "The time for jokes is over."

He was about to order the attack and we all knew it. Axel had goaded him too far.

We were on the brink of violence.

*Sigh.*

I guessed it was my turn.

"I agree," I said, taking a step forward. All eyes were on me. "We didn't come here to fight, but if that's what you're set on, then let's get after it. I've got shit to do today."

The bikers were silent as their leader sized me up. The look in his eyes told me he wasn't impressed. That was okay. It just made the next part better.

"And who the fuck are you?" Raymond asked.

White flames raced down the length of Dyrnwyn's blade, burning bright for all to see. "Wyatt Draven, Blade Mage of the Ozark Mountain Cabal."

An unease shredded the gang's bravado. They may not have known who I was, but *everyone* in the supernatural world knew what a Blade Mage was.

Raymond stared at me. I could tell he wasn't sure how to proceed. He couldn't risk losing face in front of his gang, but the game had just changed.

I offered him a friendly smile. "But like I said, we didn't come here to fight."

"Then why *are* you here?" he asked.

I considered my answer. They were unnerved, but we were still on the razor's edge of violence.

So, I told them the truth, or at least part of it. "We're in the area investigating a case involving dark magic. Likely tied to the missing students from the Cherokee."

"What's that got to do with us?" Raymond asked.

"You tell me."

"Nothing."

"Perhaps," I said, shrugging. "But I wanted to know about the local gangs. I asked August to bring me for an introduction."

"Why not the local constables?"

"Would *you* recruit the local constables?"

He chuckled. "I might recruit Constable Williams for a special job or two."

Several of his men laughed.

"But I hear your point," he lamented. "So, what? You think the Red Dirt Riders are hiding a dark mage in our ranks?"

"It's possible someone is," I replied. "I was more interested in what you knew about the kids who've bailed on the tribe."

"Waya and his little Wolf Pack?" Raymond asked, scoffing. "I know when we catch up to that little bastard, I'm going to put him over my knee. Or I might just send him back to the Cherokee in pieces. Not really decided on that point."

"You've had trouble with Waya?"

"Nothing we can't handle," he said with a grin. "Now, I've got a question for you. Has the tribe given the Cabal authority to operate in Lost City?"

"There's a longstanding partnership," I replied.

"That doesn't answer my question."

"I'm here at the tribe's request," I said.

"I see," he said, biting his lip as he stared at me.

My worry was that if I told him the whole truth, they might go ahead and attack. On the other hand, if he thought the Cabal had full authority on tribal lands, they might skip town. And while that'd likely be better for the tribe long-term, if they were involved with the missing teens, I didn't want them slinking away.

"Tell you what, Blade Mage," Raymond finally said. "I'll let this little transgression slide this time, since you're new in Lost City. But out here...the Red Dirt Riders run shit. Not the Cherokee, and not your fucking Cabal. I don't want to see you anywhere near our base again. That goes for your weird friend as well."

I didn't bother to reply. This was his way of avoiding conflict while saving face. If I acknowledged the threat, he'd think we were scared. If I threatened back, he'd have no choice but to respond, likely with violence. So, I just stood there, staring back at him like I didn't have a care in the world.

He turned to August. "And you, Bones. I'll be seeing you."

He motioned for his guys to pack it up and started away. I was just about to sigh with relief when Axel coughed obnoxiously loud.

The gang leader turned back to face him.

"There's still one matter which requires resolution, *sir*," Axel said, crossing his arms over his chest. "Rescind."

And just like that, we were standing on the edge of the knife again.

Raymond stared at Axel for several long seconds, the tension growing with each passing moment.

Finally, the gang leader shook his head and said, "For fuck's sake. I rescind. Keep your balls, you fucking weirdo."

# CHAPTER THIRTY-THREE

"What approach would you like to try this time, Blade Mage?" August asked with a hint of a smirk.

It was a fair question after our close encounter with the Red Dirt Riders. In hindsight, we'd acted foolishly.

If Fatima and her band of nomad wizards were just as inviting, it wouldn't pay to get caught snooping around their house. And we were more likely to get caught, considering their place would be warded.

Based on what little I'd learned about Fatima, it was safe to assume she wouldn't be receptive to anyone affiliated with the Cabal showing up on her doorstep. She and her crew had left the Cabal, after all. And if what was said was true, they were ex-military. A whole gaggle of battle mages.

Which meant if we were caught snooping, we'd be in for a fight, and likely one we couldn't win.

On the other hand, they might attack us just for pulling in their driveway.

Decisions, decisions.

I turned my attention back to August and other matters. "Are you sure Raymond won't be a problem? I mean, you really don't think he'll come after you once Axel and I leave town?"

"It'll be fine," August said.

He'd already said as much the previous few times I'd asked him. I wasn't convinced. So far, all I'd accomplished in Lost City was getting a motel manager murdered and setting August up for future trouble.

In the backseat, Axel happily hummed "MMMBop" to himself. August focused on maneuvering the windy roads. I practiced my wizardly brooding.

Finally, I asked, "Do you think Fatima will be more receptive to a direct approach?"

"Hard to say," August replied. "I've only interacted with her a handful of times. Her and her crew mostly keep to themselves. But I will say she'll be less receptive than Raymond was if we're caught snooping."

"Direct approach, then," I said.

"Okay," he replied, though he didn't seem too excited about the idea. "Their place is just up ahead. Once we pull up the drive, I'm sure their wards will alert them they have visitors."

"Right," I said, picking up on the underlying message. Once we turned up their driveway, there was no turning back.

August turned on a busted-up dirt drive that led into a dense cover of trees. "There used to be a cult that lived up here. Moved out years ago. Not sure how Fatima acquired the place, but there's a number of small cabins they all live in. You'll see when we get up there, but this is their driveway."

I was about to reply when I noticed something terribly interesting.

Ahead of us, another car was coming around a sharp corner from the direction we were headed.

A black Lexus.

August pulled over as far as he could without going off the road. The Lexus driver did the same so they could squeeze by one another.

Through the windshield, I saw the businessy-looking fella. He wore dark sunglasses, completely hiding his eyes, but yet again, I couldn't escape the feeling he was looking right at me.

After we passed, August glanced at his side mirror. "Weird. It's the same car again."

"Yeah," I replied. "I thought you knew everyone around here."

"I do," August replied. "That's what makes it so strange. I have no idea who that man is, or what business he has with the Evanses, the Riders, and now Fatima."

From the back seat, Axel said, "If only there were some sort of system that would allow you to track a person down based on the details of their vehicle."

I turned in my seat to look at him. "You got the plates?"

"Of course," he replied. "We just need a way to run them."

"Okay," I said. "We'll worry about that later, after we visit Fatima."

Below his breath, August mumbled, "If there *is* an after."

# CHAPTER THIRTY-FOUR

I t was a cozy spot for a gaggle of wizards to hide from the world.

Just as August had described, there were several cabins hidden among the trees. Like a summer camp for brooding wizards. I kind of dug it.

I wasn't surprised to see several of them waiting for us, staves and wands at the ready. There were likely more in hiding, ready to pounce. I liked our chances against Raymond's army more than our odds against the handful of battle mages who watched us approach with silent contempt.

"This might've been a bad idea," August said as he put the car in park.

"Too late to back out now," I replied, opening my door and stepping out.

August and Axel followed suit.

A tall, middle-aged woman with a "fuck-off" demeanor stood at the front of the gang. Her sandy blonde hair was tied back in a ponytail, and despite her simple jeans and t-shirt, she held herself like a five-star general.

"You must be Fatima," I said, offering my most friendly smile.

"And you must be the Blade Mage," she replied.

"Wyatt Draven," I said, holding out my hand.

She stared at my outstretched hand like it was covered in dog shit. When I realized she wasn't going to take it, I lowered it, feeling like Ricky Bobby and not quite sure what to do with my hands.

Fatima's attention turned to August. "I'm surprised at you, Bones. Bringing the Cabal's own Blade Mage to my home without invitation. Have you finally lost your mind?"

"Most likely," August said. "Apologies. I thought you might want to speak to him."

"You're full of shit," she said, crossing her arms. "If you ever bring someone from the Cabal to our home again, I'll kill you. Understand?"

August nodded but didn't reply.

Once again, it seemed like August needed a save. This time, I didn't hesitate to jump in. "If it makes you feel any better, I'm not exactly the Cabal's favorite son."

"So I've heard," she replied. "You also didn't make friends with the Red Dirt Riders."

I raised an eyebrow. "News travels fast."

She gave me a wicked grin. "According to Raymond, you attacked his people unprovoked and were headed my way to do the same. He said you declared us dark mages and were coming to put us down."

I chose my response carefully. "Judging by the fact you didn't attack us the moment we arrived, I'm guessing you didn't believe him."

"Raymond is also full of shit," she said. "More likely you pissed him off, and he was hoping we'd take care of the problem for him. Sound about right?"

"Just about," I said, nodding. "He must have had someone follow us. Or he assumed we'd be coming here next."

"Do you guys think this is about my balls?" Axel asked, glancing between August and me, a genuine look of concern on his face. He glanced up at Fatima. "He wanted them *real* bad."

"You weren't willing to part with them?" Fatima asked.

"No, ma'am," Axel said. "But I thought we left it amicably enough."

She grunted a laugh. "You must be the infamous Axel Gunner."

"That's me," Axel said, delighted she knew who he was. "My reputation precedes me."

"Your reputation is that you're a pain in your dad's ass," she said. "And your dad is a real ass, so I approve. In fact, both your reputations are the only reason you aren't dead right now. From what I've heard, you've both been a pain in the ass for the Archmage, the Arcane Guardians, and the whole damned Archcouncil. And apparently Parker Grimm, too, the uppity prick."

I chuckled. "We do our best."

Her eyes hardened. "But don't think that endears you to us. It's bought you your lives and a conversation. That is all. You're still an enigma, and a dangerous one at that."

"An enigma?" I asked, genuinely unsure what she meant.

"Yeah," she said. "I remember when you became the Blade Mage. I was there. We all were. But then you just fell off the map. You disappeared for years, only recently resurfacing. And the rumor mills are churning out stories about you now."

"I see you keep informed," I said, for lack of anything better to say.

"We always have an ear to the ground. It pays to be in the loop, even when you just want a peaceful retirement. The Cabal has a way of not letting go, if you know what I mean."

"I do," I said. "As you just called out, I've only recently resurfaced."

"Why?" she asked. "Why did you go back after all this time?"

I opened my mouth to speak, then shut it. We were standing on a precipice again. It wasn't what she'd said, or even how she'd said it, nor any shift in the tension, but my gut instinct warned me that the next words out of my mouth might be the difference between life and death.

My gazed shifted from Fatima to her people, then to the small cabins they lived in. It occurred to me that perhaps I wasn't so different from them.

They'd sought their exile from the Cabal just as I had, but I'd gone back.

So, perhaps I was the very thing they feared most.

As she'd said, the Cabal had that way about it. Love it or hate it, we'd all grown up to believe in the mission. We'd all felt the call of duty, and yet we'd walked away from it. That was no easy decision. I remembered my own fears that the Cabal might one day come knocking and drag me back into this world, kicking and screaming.

And that was just what had happened. But not to Fatima and her crew. Not yet.

My focus back on Fatima, I asked, "Did you know my father?"

She nodded.

"He was a great Blade Mage, wasn't he?"

"The best," she said without hesitation. Behind her, a few of the others nodded. "Were he still around, we might not have left."

"Me, too," I said. "When Dyrnwyn chose me as the next Blade Mage, I thought it had to be a mistake. No one was more shocked than me. And it didn't surprise me that no one else wanted me to be Blade Mage. Though I'll admit it still stung a little. On top of that, I'd just left my team and my father had died. Even if anyone had wanted me to be the Blade Mage, I wasn't prepared to take on the responsibility. I knew I couldn't fill my father's shoes. And so, right or wrong, I left."

"The leaving part makes sense to me," Fatima said. "It's the going back that doesn't sit right. Did you have a sudden epiphany that you were ready? I want to know. Why did you go back?"

"Is that what you think I've done? You think I'm serving the Cabal?"

"You're working on their behalf, are you not?"

"Did you know, just before he died, my father warned the council of a threat of dark mages? They all but laughed at him. You'd be hard pressed to find anyone who would speak ill of my father now, but at that time, they believed he was just an old man trying to hold on to his glory days. Did you know that?"

"I heard rumors, yeah," Fatima said. "But you're still dancing around the question. Are you doing the Archmage's bidding? Yes or no?"

"Yes *and* no," I said. "You're right that I've been more involved recently, but I'm no loyal servant to the Archmage, nor anyone else on the council. See, I haven't forgotten how they treated my old man. And I haven't forgotten how they treated me. I'm little more than the Cabal's miscreant bastard. More trouble than I'm worth, as far they're concerned. And to answer your question, I didn't just go back to the life. It keeps coming to find me. So, I guess I've decided to just embrace it. Sure, I'll try to play nice with the Cabal, but most of them would rather see me dead."

"Hmm," she said, then shrugged. "Can't say I'm convinced."

"I don't see any reason you need to be," I replied with a shrug of my own. "I didn't come here to pitch myself to you."

"Then why did you come here?" she asked.

"The tribe," I replied. "I'm trying to help them figure out what's going on with their missing youngsters."

"Missing?" she asked. "Is that what you call it when a bunch of rebellious teens rebel? Didn't think 'missing' applied to people who up and left of their own volition. Do you think that's how the Cabal refers to us? We're just missing."

"I have no idea," I replied.

"Those kids aren't missing," she said. "They're kids. They probably got bored of old medicine men preaching at them all day and made a break for it, as kids do."

"I don't suppose you've spoken to any of them?"

"So what if I have?"

"Are you always this defensive?"

"Yes," she replied. "Next dumb question?"

August took a step forward. "Fatima—"

"You be silent," she said, glaring him into submission. "You brought the Cabal dog here, so you've lost speaking privileges."

I sighed. "If I'm the Cabal's dog, then I'm the dog who pisses on the floor and digs in the trash. They'd just as soon swat me on the nose or send me to the pound. Even now, I've snuck away to the neighbor's chicken coup. When I get back, there will be hell to pay. Trust that, at least. I'm not the Cabal's puppy."

"That's yet to be seen."

I tried to think of something clever to say, but it seemed she was immovable. There was still one card to play, though. "Look, I just want to help these kids, and make sure the rumors of them going down a dark path aren't true."

"What are you talking about?" she asked, studying me suspiciously.

*Bingo.*

I went for broke. "We have reason to believe dark magic may be involved with their leaving the tribe."

She watched me for a few moments, perhaps assessing whether I was full of shit like Raymond. Then her scowled hardened. "And so, naturally, you came suspecting us."

*Damn.*

She was a tough one.

Like Raymond, Fatima knew how to twist words to match her narrative. She was good at it, too. I wondered if she'd ever considered being a lawyer. The whole time, all I'd been doing was throwing her easy pickings. I'd have to be more careful.

I forced a smile. "Are you really implying that we would come strolling into your camp like this if we thought you were dark mages? You must really think we're idiots."

"Why else?"

"Because rebellious teens with the ability to do magic have rebelled. If I were a rebellious teen who knew how to do magic, and I was rebelling, well, I might seek out other rebellious mages who had also rebelled. And if what I've come to understand is true, these kids want to learn battle magic rather than just become medicine men and women. And, oh, look, it just so happens that the other local rebellious mages who rebelled happen to be former Cabal battle mages."

A ghost of a smirk played around her lips. "Let's say you're right, Blade Mage. What if the kids did come looking to us for guidance? Do you think I'd betray their trust?"

"Having met you now," I said, dragging out my response, "no, I don't think you would."

"Well, then, it sounds like your whole trip would've been pointless. *If* that were the case."

"No, I don't think so," I said. "Because I'd leave you with a message for them. I'd ask you to tell them I don't give a shit whether they go back to the tribe and finish their schooling. But I'd also tell them they've left a bunch of elders awfully worried about them. So, don't go back, but at least try to make peace with the elders, and whatever they do, don't dabble in forbidden magics."

"Is that all you'd say?" she asked.

"No. I'd also say that some people have gotten hurt, and whether or not they were involved, I suspect they could help end it. I'd ask them to do the right thing."

"Well, that's very touching," she said.

"Really?" Axel said. "I thought it was a bit dry and corny."

Ignoring him, Fatima continued, "But it's a moot point. The kids aren't here, and we haven't heard from them. Whatever trouble they've gotten themselves into, it has nothing to do with us. Furthermore, this talk of dark magic is nonsense. If someone were using forbidden magic around Lost City, we'd have found out."

"A bold statement," I said, holding her gaze. "How can you be sure?"

"This is our home now, Blade Mage. We protect it, just the way the Cabal taught us to."

"I hear you," I said. "And I don't doubt your vigilance or abilities. But keep this in mind: those rumors my father warned the council about... Well, he was right. I met a witch in the Branson compound. She hid in plain sight, right in front of some of the Cabal's greatest mages. And I met a demon summoner who'd been a long-standing member of the Memphis Knights. No one in their order had a clue. Did you ever meet my old team, the Kingsnakes?"

"I met Malik once," she said. "Bit full of himself, but otherwise, he seemed like a total ass."

"Yeah, well, he's dead now," I said. "Shot in the head by the woman he loved, who was also second-in-command of his team. Turned out that a few of my old friends were in league with an army of gray-cloaked demon summoners."

"I see," she said.

"I wasn't finished," I replied. "I've spoken to an immensely powerful necromancer. I solved a magical puzzle written in blood magic. I've been face-to-face with a fucking revenant."

"Don't forget the shadow army," Axel said. "Or the abasy. Or the half-torso flying lady. Oh, and the evil villain party we crashed. Or the fact the Cabal's own Director of Accounting was an evil douche. And all the other demons, of course. Creepy buggers."

When Axel stopped talking, I realized how quiet it was around us.

Fatima still had her gaze locked on mine, and I wasn't going to look away.

"Jesus Christ. You're telling the truth," she said. Finally, some of her harsh demeanor melted away. "We'd heard stories, but...we figured they were just rumors. Shit blown out of proportion."

"I can't speak to what you have or haven't heard," I said. "But I'll swear on Dyrnwyn that everything we just said was true. Those were very real threats. Many of them still are, though a few we managed to put in the ground. Most are still out there, still plotting, and no one can seem to find them."

"I understand what you're saying, Blade Mage." She sighed and looked around at her own people before turning back to me. "Look, I told you the truth as well. We don't know where the kids are. Nor have we seen, heard, or sensed anything that would lead us to believe there's anyone in the area practicing the forbidden arts. Though we'll take your warning on deck. But that's all I can tell you."

"Thank you," I said.

She waved my thanks away and said, "Now, please leave. Our door is rarely open for visitors, and never for anyone who still associates with the Cabal. Truth be told, you'll probably only cause yourself more trouble if they find out you approached us. If what you said is true, trouble follows you around like a bad cold. Cabal dog or not, I'd rather not have your pee on my doorstep."

With that, the conversation was over.

I nodded at her once and started back to the car.

# CHAPTER THIRTY-FIVE

As soon as we were on the road again, August put in a call to Constable Williams.

Once he confirmed Johnson wasn't around and that it was safe to talk, he put his phone on speaker so we could hear.

After pleasantries, she said, "You guys really should come by. Johnson is having a shit fit. He's been on the phone with the higher-ups from the Castle all day."

"Any idea who he's been talking to?" I asked.

"Can't say for sure," she replied. "Our own chain of command, I suppose. Outside of that, I don't know."

"It's cool," Axel said from the back seat. "I'll just call my dad and get the whole thing sorted."

I turned in my seat to ensure he saw me staring at him like he was a potato. "Axel, what in the hell makes you think your dad will help us out?"

"Well, he's never really helped us out before, and I'm his son, so it's about time," he said, as though this line of reasoning was perfectly logical. "The way I figure it, he owes me one for all the favors I haven't asked of him."

"You *do* remember your dad wanted me to execute you, right?"

This brought a surprised looked from August, and even Williams said, "Damn, that's cold."

Axel doubled down. "Yeah, I remember. And I figure he owes me one, right? I'll be sure to mention it."

Deciding it was past time to ignore him, I returned my focus to Williams. "Sounds like they're awfully worked up over one body."

"People around here don't usually get their throats slit while they're kicked back watching TV," she said.

"I'd have thought violence would be more prevalent," I said. "Based on what I've seen."

"Oh, violence, sure," she said. "And we have some homicides occasionally. Just...not like that, you know? At least, we didn't use to. It sure seems like the whole area is just a big ole zit ready to pop."

"I get that impression as well," I said. "Though I don't know if I could've described it so eloquently."

"That's me. Miss Eloquent," she said, then switched gears. "Look, I'm guessing you guys didn't call to socialize, and it won't be long before Johnson is back. What did you need?"

August said, "I was hoping you could do us a small favor."

"Depends how small," she said. "I'm not looking to get myself strung up for pissing off the higher-ups, but I do want to help you guys."

"We want you to run a license plate for us," I said.

"Oh," she replied. "I really shouldn't."

"Worried you'll get in trouble?" I asked.

"Yes," she admitted without hesitation. "My job might not seem glamorous to you, Blade Mage, but I worked my ass off to get this shithole job. I don't want to lose it."

I paused, realizing I'd made light of her fear. Yet I understood where she was coming from. If not for my magic sword, the Cabal wouldn't have let me get away with half what they did.

"I get it," I said. "Your fear is warranted. But, let me ask you something. Why did you become a constable?"

"Why do you think?" Her tone was defensive. I probably deserved it.

"I wouldn't want to assume," I replied.

"Because I wanted to help people," she said.

"And that's still what you want to do?"

"Of course."

"Then you have to decide whether it will help more people to sit at your desk doing nothing all day, or to help us."

She was quiet for a few seconds, but finally said, "Give me the damned plate already."

Axel yelled the info at the phone from the back seat and we waited in awkward silence while Williams got to work.

As we sat there, still on speaker, August's phone buzzed. Glancing down at it, he said, "It's Elder Morgan. I'll have to call him back."

He swiped the screen to send the elder to voicemail, but a few seconds later, it was buzzing again.

"Hey, Williams," August said. "Elder Morgan isn't giving up. Do you think this will take long? Should we drop off and call you back after I find out what the elder wants?"

"Sheesh. Just hang on," she said, then mumbled, "don't be so impatient, Bones."

Glancing at his phone again, August said, "I'm not being impatient, but this will be the third time now I've sent him to voicemail. He's persistent, I'll give him that."

"Must be important," I said, wishing I had my own phone so I could call him back.

The problem was the damned things never lasted long for me, so I wasn't in the habit of toting one around. I tried off and on, but I tore through burner phones at a rate that would put me in the poorhouse. Axel had better luck with it than me, but he always said that carrying a phone was like tying a leash around your neck. I'd noticed most of the other mages I'd spent any time around didn't seem to have as much trouble as me, either. I often thought about trying to figure out what they were doing differently, but then I remembered Axel's leash theory and decided I was better off. It wasn't like I wanted to walk around staring at Face Hugger all day.

"All right," Williams said, breaking me from my rambling thoughts. "It doesn't normally take this long, but this is pretty weird."

"Oh, I love weird," Axel said, leaning forward between the seats. "Tell us about our mystery man, Watson."

"It's Williams," she said, missing his reference. "Did you know undercover cops get special IDs and licenses plates that cause a flag in the system if they get pulled over? That way, the cop who pulls them over will know not to arrest them and send them on their way without blowing their cover."

"Yes," I replied. "Did his plates flag as an undercover car?"

"That's the thing," she said. "It flags the plates like an undercover cop car, but it doesn't have any of the normal information. Like, it doesn't say who the officer is. Or what jurisdiction they're from. Doesn't even have any information about the vehicle. It's all just...blank."

"Is that normal?" I asked.

"I've never seen it before," she said. "I ran it twice to be sure."

"So, there's nothing useful at all?" August asked. "No bit of information we might use to track the car or the driver?"

"Nothing," she said. "It's like a ghost."

"Well, that's...something," I said, shrugging at August. "Thank you anyway, Williams. Appreciate you doing that for us."

"Hey, no worries," she said. "Let me know if there's anything else. I'll do what I can to help."

"Thanks, Williams," August said. "We'll let you know. I'd better call Elder Morgan back."

Williams said bye and ended the call. Then August dialed Elder Morgan and put his phone on speaker once more.

"Hello," Elder Morgan said, a sense of urgency in his voice. "August?"

"Hey," August replied. "I've got you on speaker with Wyatt and Axel."

"Thank you," Elder Morgan replied. "The situation is most urgent."

"We're listening," I said.

"Our tracking spells picked up on one of the kids."

"Okay," I replied. "That's good news, isn't it?"

"Yes, it's the first time it's occurred."

"So, do you want us to go after them?" August asked.

"We can't seem to agree," the Elder replied. "Some think we should go ourselves, and bicker over *who* should go. Others think that may cause more harm than good and that you should try to speak with them."

"And which camp do you fall in?" I asked.

"I suggested we let you try to speak to them. All our attempts have fallen on deaf ears. Perhaps they'd see reason from an outsider, especially one with such a prestigious role as the Blade Mage."

"But some of the others fear what may happen if we go?" I asked.

"Yes," Elder Morgan said, pausing. "Some are worried how you might react if they attack you."

"I won't hurt the kids," I replied. "You have my word."

"I believe you," he replied. "But the others aren't convinced. I fear we'll bicker until we lose our chance."

"Uh, Elder Morgan," Axel said, leaning forward again. "Are you someplace where any of the others can hear you?"

"No," he replied.

"Good," Axel said. "Then just keep them bickering a little longer, and in the meantime, we'll go check on this missing kid of yours. What do you say?"

The elder chuckled. "I like that plan very much."

# CHAPTER THIRTY-SIX

The kid in question was named Ben.

He was ten years old.

Elder Morgan explained they'd tracked his location to an old farm off Killabrew Road. Not sure who'd named that road, but I kind of dug it. At any rate, our missing ten-year-old had been pinged at an abandoned farm. More specifically, his aura was pinpointed in an old chicken house, of which there were three, along with an old house and a giant barn. All of which made a lot of good shelter for a pile of runaways.

By why had only one kid pinged?

And why now?

From what Elder Morgan had said, this was the latest kid to have abandoned his education. Perhaps he'd realized he'd made a mistake and had fled the care of the others?

But if that was the case, why was he out at an abandoned farm alone?

There wasn't much point in speculating, but we couldn't help ourselves during the drive over.

I'd pictured some ancient farm with rickety buildings, but that wasn't what I got. The grass was grown up tall, sure, and clearly no one had cared for the place in some time, but the structures were in fairly good shape. And it was a modern farm rather than some dead relic from the turn of the nineteenth century. The house might've had some years on it, but the barn was covered in red sheet metal and was quite large. The chicken houses appeared to be in reasonable shape as well.

We parked up the drive and hoofed it the rest of the way in. If there was a skittish runaway about, we didn't want to scare him off with the grumble of a petrol engine, nor the slamming of car doors.

As we walked up the path, I wondered about the previous owners. Where were they? Why had they abandoned their farm? Had they made so much loot off of chickens that they'd retired to the Bahamas? Had they left Oklahoma for greener pastures, figuratively or literally? More likely, the farm hadn't produced and had been retaken by the bank. The bank just hadn't found a new purchaser to screw over yet.

Still, I liked to imagine that old couple from the *American Gothic* painting sitting on a beach somewhere sipping Mai Tais. That was the American dream, wasn't it? Work your ass off for fifty years, go into debt for a bunch of shit you don't really need, then, at the end, if you were just smart enough to invest enough in your retirement account, you could fuck off on a beach somewhere until you died.

The thought made me want to vomit. I'd take witches and warlocks over a "normal life" any day.

As we approached the first chicken house, I noticed the door was ajar.

Both August and I agreed on just walking in and trying our best to appear non-threatening. Axel had other ideas, of course.

He wanted to sneak around the back to "flank our quarry," as he put it.

And just before he dropped into a ninja crouch and sauntered off into the weeds, he demanded that we wait a solid thirty seconds to give him a chance to get into position.

As soon as he was gone, August whispered, "Should we wait like he asked?"

I turned, met his gaze, blinked three times to get my point across, and walked into the chicken house.

Despite growing up in the Midwest, I'd never ventured into a chicken house before. Chicken coups, sure, but not a full-length industrial-style chicken house. So, I didn't know what to expect. Well, I supposed I knew not to expect any chickens, since the farm was clearly abandoned. I was not surprised in that regard.

The chicken house was primarily one very long open room with a dirt floor. The lights weren't on, so it was somewhat dark, but there were places near the roof where plastic had been placed to let some daylight through.

There was a small toolshed just beside the door on the way in, and its door was open as well. However, without the lights, it was nearly pitch black in there.

Drawing my staff from my back, I summoned a small amount of energy to light up the tip.

No kid in there. Just a few discarded tools and a bit of junk.

I killed the light and walked alongside August into the main area.

Whoever had abandoned the place had left some old crates, drums, and various other junk piled near the center of the room. If there was a kid hiding in the building, it had to be in there.

We started in that direction.

Just before we got to the rows of junk, a door swung open on the far end of the chicken house and Axel rolled in. And yes, I do mean that he rolled in. He somersaulted through the door, kicking up a flurry of dust and old white feathers.

He made no shortage of noise either.

A gasp sounded from the junk piles.

*Bingo.*

August and I rounded the corner of some crates and spotted a small boy sitting cross-legged in the dirt, a pile of action figures laid out before him. I immediately identified an Incredible Hulk, followed by a Boba Fett. I liked this kid.

He looked up at us with wide, red-rimmed eyes. Tears were drying on his tiny cheeks.

"Hey there, little man," I said. "You all right?"

He stared at me for a few moments, then slowly nodded.

Axel appeared between two rows of barrels, blocking any escape the little dude might've had. If he bolted, he'd either have to go through Axel, or both August and me.

"Are you all by yourself?" I asked.

He looked down at his toys again, fidgeting with the Hulk.

"Why are you here alone?" I asked. "It isn't safe to be all by yourself, you know."

Still the kid didn't respond. I looked to August, who shrugged, then glanced over at Axel. If he noticed I needed a save, he didn't jump in to help.

I drew on a little magic and used mind-speak. *"Axel, you're better with kids than me. Why don't you try talking to him?"*

*"You'll never get any better without practice."*

*"Now isn't the time."*

*"Oh, really? So, then, when we get back home, are we going to go on that Chuck E. Cheese trip I keep asking about?"*

*"Axel, we're two grown-ass men. Two grown-ass men can't go into a Chuck E. Cheese without a kid."*

*"Why not?"*

*"Because someone would suspect of us of something foul."*

*"Hmm, I'm sure someone would loan us a child."*

*"That's... That's even worse,"* I said. *"Look, are you going to help me out here or not?"*

*"I'm not talking to you until you promise to take me to Chuck E. Cheese."*

Ignoring my grown-ass child of a friend, I looked down at the kid again. "Is that a Boba Fett?"

The kid looked up at me and once again responded with a slow nod.

"That was always my favorite Star Wars character. What about you?"

Another nod.

I was trying to think of another question when the kid looked up at me and said, "I left him. I left Boba Fett. He must've fallen out of my bag. I didn't zip good. I never zip it good. I always get in trouble."

"So you came back for him?" I asked.

He nodded again and looked at the floor. "I always get in trouble."

"You're not in trouble now," I said.

"Yes, I am," he replied, nodding so hard I thought his head might fall off. The dam that held back his tears reopened and a fresh batch started down his cheeks. "They told me not to leave. They told me to stay close to the others. But I couldn't leave Boba Fett."

"It's all right," I said, slowly edging a little closer. "I don't blame you. I wouldn't have wanted to leave my Boba Fett, either."

He looked up as though to agree, but upon noticing I'd moved closer, he jumped to his knees and began grabbing toys and hurling them into his little backpack. "Did they send you? Did the bad man send you?"

"No," I said, putting up my hands and taking a few steps back. "Who's the bad man?"

"I don't want to go with him," the kid said, still shoving toys in his bag. "I don't want to. I won't. You can't make me."

"I'm not going to take you to him," I said. "I promise."

The child sniffled again, and with the last of his toys packed up, he zipped the bag and rose to his feet.

"Looks like you got it zipped good this time," I replied. "And I don't think you missed any."

He glanced down at the dirty floor, then back up at me. "You're a stranger."

"I suppose I am," I replied. "My name is Wyatt. And I'm guessing you're Ben?"

"How'd you know my name?" the kid asked, still wary.

"Elder Morgan asked me to come talk to you," I said, then added, "He's not the bad man, is he?"

Ben shook his head.

"We could take you back to him. Back to the tribe, if you want."

"I can't. Waya told me I can't go back."

"Waya isn't here," I said. "I am. And I can take you back."

"No," he said, taking another step back. He glanced around, perhaps only then noticing that Axel had the other path blocked. "I can't go back. Waya says I can never go back. He says I'll be in trouble."

"That's not true, Ben," I said, shaking my head. "You won't be in trouble."

"They'll hurt me." More tears streamed down his cheek. "Waya said so."

"I won't let them hurt you." A silence dragged between us for a moment and I asked again, "Ben, who is the bad man?"

"He's... I don't know," he said, shaking his head. "He's a man. He says nice things. The others all say he's nice. But he's not. I know it. I know he's not a nice man."

"Okay," I said, trying to think of something smart to say. "Do you know his name?"

"No, he didn't tell me his name. But I don't like him. I don't want to go with him."

"You don't have to."

"Waya says I do. He says I'm too young to stay with the pack and that I have to go with the bad man. Waya says the bad man will protect me, but I don't want to go with him. He's not nice. I don't care what the others say. He pretends. He's a liar. Why won't Waya let me stay with the pack?"

"I don't know," I said. "I don't know Waya. But I do know Elder Morgan, and Elder Thomas, and John, and Samuel. None of them are the bad man, right?"

"No," Ben said. "The bad man isn't part of the tribe."

"Well, there you go," I said. "The tribe wants you to come home. They're very worried about you."

"Waya says they hate us. He says the tribe is weak. He says the bad man is powerful."

"The tribe isn't weak," I replied. "They are strong. And so am I. And I won't let the bad man have you, Ben. I promise."

"How do I know?" Ben said. "You're a stranger. They told me not to trust strangers. Waya said I shouldn't trust anyone outside the pack."

"But the pack isn't here, is it?" I said. "So, you've got to decide for yourself, Ben. Elder Morgan won't send you with the bad man. Waya will. Why don't you let us take you back to the tribe?"

"No," he said, backing up further until he was just a few feet in front of Axel.

He seemed on the verge of panic and I wasn't sure what to do. I had never been particularly good with kids, not like Axel. The best I could think to do was to grab him and just take him with us, but I really wanted to avoid that. I hoped Axel would jump in, since he had the same maturity level as the ten-year-old and would surely know what to say.

"Hey, bud," Axel said, taking a step closer. "Listen—"

Ben turned, saw how close Axel was, screamed, and punched him in the balls.

Axel dropped to his knees.

Ben sprinted past him into the darkness.

"Wow, Axel," I said as I raced past him. "Well done, buddy."

It looked like taking the kid by force was going to be our only option after all. I hated it, but what else could we do? I certainly wasn't going to leave him by himself in an abandoned chicken house.

By the time August and I came out the back side of the junk pile, Ben was already at the door. Even with a backpack, the kid was quick.

I considered what magics were at my disposal to slow him down and decided none were appropriate for the situation. If it were an adult, sure. But I wasn't going to risk injuring a little kid by force pushing him into a metal wall.

Ben made it out the door and we raced to follow, leaving Axel alone in the chicken house to cry over his egregious injury.

We hit daylight, and the weeds were nearly tall enough to hide Ben's escape, but I could just barely make out his head bobbing above the top.

He was headed for the big red barn.

I was just about to inform August when I heard him cry out and looked over to see him lift off the ground and disappear into the weeds, as though he'd been whacked by some unseen force.

And then I sensed it.

*Magic.*

I ran the final few steps to the barn and slowed to a walk as I stepped inside.

I was surrounded.

# CHAPTER THIRTY-SEVEN

There was little doubt who they were. It was either Peter Pan and his Lost Boys, or it was Waya and his Wolf Pack.

Most were teens, though a few among their ranks looked younger.

And they were dressed like teens, mostly in jeans and t-shirts, but they were armed to the teeth.

Those on the ground level carried spears, tomahawks, wands, and staves. A few more were above me on the second floor. These had bows pointed at my chest.

Standing in the center, just ahead of me, were the two oldest, a young man and young woman.

Waya and Pathkiller.

Well, we'd found them quick, so that was something.

But this wasn't ideal.

I mean, it was ideal I'd found them, since that was sort of the whole point. On the other hand, they'd caught me chasing one of their pack members, and clearly assumed I was a threat. If they attacked me, there wasn't much I could do except try to escape. I certainly wasn't going to fight them.

On the other hand, I was sure a lot of people in the Cabal would've found great joy in learning their bastard of a Blade Mage had died at the hands of a bunch of children.

*Fuck my life.*

Unable to come up with anything clever to say, I offered them a friendly wave and said, "Hi there."

"Don't come any closer," Waya said, his arms crossed over his scrawny chest.

Ben huddled behind the older boy, staring at me like I was the boogeyman.

Pathkiller turned to the younger boy and asked, "Did he hurt you?"

Ben shook his head.

With his eyes still on me, Waya said, "We protect our pack."

"That's good," I replied. "You should. I meant little Ben no harm, though, I assure you. I take it you're Waya?"

The eldest teen nodded.

"My name is Wyatt—"

"We know who you are," Waya said, cutting me off. "And we know why you're here. The Elders sent you to kill us. You won't find our pack to be easy prey, Blade Mage."

"Whoa," I said, putting up my hands. "I'm not here to kill anyone."

"Don't lie to us," Pathkiller said, also crossing her arms. "We see through your deceptions. The truth is clear to us."

"Clear as mud, apparently," I replied, desperately trying to think of something to say that would diffuse the situation. When in doubt, I usually just tried the truth. "Look, whether you guys believe it or not, the elders are worried about you. Since they haven't had much luck communicating with you, they reached out for help. That's why I'm here. Just to talk."

"You lie," Waya said.

Before I could reply, I heard the distinct roar of a motorcycle engine. Followed by another. And another, until a chorus was picked up.

We had company.

One of the kids upstairs bolted over to a top-floor window, then called back to the others, "It's the Red Dirt Riders!"

"How many?" Waya asked.

"They're moving," the kid replied. "I can't count."

"Make a guess," the leader replied with a hint of frustration.

"Uh, like, twenty or so."

"Is Raymond with them?"

"I don't think so," the kid said, shaking his head. "But they have guns. A lot of guns."

Waya groaned, then looked at Ben, who was still hiding behind him. "This is why I told you not to get too far from the pack."

"I'm sorry," Ben said, tears flowing again.

"Sorry won't keep us alive," Waya replied, and for a moment, I thought he might strike the kid.

Then Pathkiller stepped in. "It's all right, Ben. What's done is done. We have to deal with it now, but you must stick with the pack from now on and do what Waya tells you. You must be brave."

"I will," Ben said, rubbing the tears from his eyes. "I'm sorry. I didn't mean it. I'm sorry."

"What's your trouble with the Red Dirt Riders?" I asked.

"It's none of your concern," Waya said.

"They intend to hurt you, though, right?"

"Them and everyone else," Waya said. "Yourself included."

And that gave me an idea. One of my classic bad ideas.

I sighed and said, "I'll take care of the riders for you. I'll keep them busy while your pack escapes. In return, you agree to have a conversation with Elder Morgan. Deal?"

Waya laughed.

Laughed right in my face.

"Fine," I said, shrugging. "It doesn't have to be Elder Morgan, or anyone else from the tribe, for that matter. It could be someone with the Cabal. Parker Grimm. Have you ever heard of him? I'll cover your escape, and you just agree to reach out to the Cabal, ask for Parker Grimm, tell him I sent you, and he'll help you guys out. Will that work?"

"We don't need your help, Blade Mage," Waya said. "We take care of our own."

Outside, the engines cut off and a gruff voice called out, "Little wolf pack! Come out, come out! We know you're here. We have unfinished business to discuss."

"I don't doubt you take care of your own," I said, trying to keep my voice calm and patient. "You have magic and I know you know how to use it, but those brutes outside have a lot of guns, and *they* know how to use *them*. Why risk any of your pack when you can risk me? Why fight when you don't have to?"

Waya snorted. "You still don't get it, do you?"

That was true. Whatever he was referring to, I definitely didn't get.

He seemed about to say something more when Pathkiller moved closer and whispered in his ear.

Outside, the biker called again, "We're going to find you, little puppies. And I promise you, it'll go a lot easier if you just come out to talk. I'm gonna get *real* impatient."

I kept my focus on Waya, watching the arrogant smirk on his face transition into a wolfish grin as his girlfriend spoke in his ear.

When she stepped away, Waya said, "All right, Blade Mage. You've got a deal. Go run those bikers off and we'll do as you ask."

I stared at him dumbfounded, wondering what Pathkiller might've whispered in his ear that had made him do a full turnaround.

"Uh, okay," I said for lack of anything clever to say. I couldn't help the feeling that these kids were playing me. That somehow I'd gone from trying to protect them to being their tool. Still, what else could I do?

I nodded and glanced over at Ben. "Keep track of your Boba Fett, kid."

Then I turned and walked out of the barn.

August was still down in the grass where he'd fallen. Whatever they'd hit him with, he was either out cold or stuck. Either way, he was keeping quiet, and I doubted the bikers could even see him through the weeds. I had no idea where Axel was, or whether he was still crying over his hurt balls in the chicken house or trying to sneak somewhere to be helpful.

I turned the corner, drawing my staff and sword, letting the white flames spring to life. Even in the daylight, they were an impressive sight.

The riders had parked their bikes in a circle, just as before, and were using them for cover. Twenty or more firearms pointed in my direction as I stood before them. I summoned my shield to full strength and tried not to think about how many rounds it would take before I'd lose it.

"You," a voice near the center said.

It was the same burly biker who'd accosted us before.

"Hi there," I replied. "Nice to see you again."

"Where are the kids?" the biker asked.

"Not here. It's just me."

"Bullshit."

I shrugged. "Guessing you got a similar tip to the one I got. But I beat you here, and I can assure you, if Waya and his pack were here, they're long gone now."

"Yeah, and where are your pals? The weird one and August Bones?"

I shrugged again.

"I have a mind to put a bullet in you," the leader said, licking his lips. "You're a real pain in the ass."

"That's what I'm told," I replied, and decided it was probably a good time for a bold bluff. "But are you really sure you want to do that? You don't have the rest of the gang to back you up this time, and last time, things weren't really going your way."

He spat. "Last time you got the jump on us. This time we know what you are. And we ain't afraid of no goddamned wizard. We've dealt with your kind before."

"Have you now?" I asked. "You've dealt with a Blade Mage, have you?"

*Crack.*

A gunshot sounded and the round smacked against my shield, then fell harmlessly to the ground at my feet.

Another of the riders held a smoking gun and had a surprised look on his face.

The burly leader looked over at the shooter. "What the fuck? I didn't order you to shoot."

"It was an accident," the biker said. "I didn't mean to."

"Hold your goddamned fire until I say," the leader said, but an unease passed through the group.

The burly fella was losing control. The draw to violence was coming in like a storm, and I wasn't really sure anything could stop it.

"No harm, no foul," I replied. "As you can see, I'm unharmed. Don't bring bullets to a magic fight."

The burly biker scowled. "You arrogant son of a—"

*Crack.*

Another gunshot.

The burly rider's head exploded in a spray of red.

As his body toppled to the ground, I realized two things: one, there was no smoking gun among the riders, and two, the gunshot had sounded from further away.

*What the hell now?*

# CHAPTER THIRTY-EIGHT

Another gunshot echoed across the farm.

Another biker went down.

The Red Dirt Riders scattered in a mass of panic, shouting and searching for the unseen shooter. There was no sign of them, but they could see me.

And then they opened fire.

I dove to the side, hoping none of the children were on the other side of the barn wall. Sheet metal wouldn't stop bullets. The walls might as well have been made from paper for all they'd do to stop the rounds.

I kept on the move, keeping my shield up and trying to find a spot where I could get cover without the barn directly behind me.

Glancing up at my attackers, I saw another one of them topple over, taking a bullet in the chest.

Who the hell was shooting at them? The kids? I hadn't seen any of them wielding a gun.

As another biker's head exploded, I realized that whoever it was, they were a hell of a shot.

I had no more time to contemplate the shooter on the grassy knoll because one biker rose from cover and hurled a Molotov at me.

A bullet hit him in the chest, but not before his arm started forward.

The Molotov hit the tall grass a few feet from me and flames licked at my heels as the grass ignited. Behind it, the barn wall was bathed in fire as well. The sheet metal would stop fire, but not if any of the flames caught hold of the wood frame. Certainly the grass at the base of the barn was going up quickly.

Fewer gunshots were aimed in my direction as the bikers realized they were being picked apart from elsewhere.

That afforded me an opportunity to strike back.

Summoning a simple force spell, I fired into the nearest bike, knocking it over right on top of the man hiding behind it. It also bumped another of the bikes and caused it to tump over, but the man behind it managed to get clear. And then a bullet took him in the chest.

The fight had barely begun and already a quarter of their number had been reduced by the unseen triggerman.

I considered the possibility of whether Axel could've secretly brought a gun along with him. It wasn't out of the question, and he was an excellent shot, but the rapport of the weapon told me it was a high-powered rifle. I think I would've noticed if Axel had been hauling a rifle around all day.

It seemed that at least one biker had spotted where the rogue shots were coming from and was screaming at the others, pointing and firing his weapon in that direction. It was from the opposite side of the yard from the chicken houses, over in a thick tree line.

I glanced that way, but couldn't see anything.

Still, the bulk of the remaining Red Dirt Riders focused their attention and gunfire in that direction.

I noticed one still had eyes for me, so I hit his bike with a force spell and pinned him beneath it.

One biker raised another Molotov, but threw it toward the mysterious shooter instead of me, which I was grateful for.

As the flames went up, I saw some kind of movement. Some kind of... Creature? It kind of reminded me of Swamp Thing, if Swamp Thing ran around with an M-4.

*Not a creature, you dingus.* It was a man. A man in a ghillie suit.

He ran a few paces and disappeared among the tall grass again.

The riders had a general sense of where he was, but honestly, if I were them, I wouldn't have known exactly where to shoot, and clearly, they didn't.

Another of the bikers fell.

And then another.

I stood and fired a force spell into another bike and this time managed to knock two over.

The remaining bikers stopped shooting, except to lay down cover fire as they helped their comrades who were pinned beneath bikes. They didn't have any injured to care for. The mysterious shooter hadn't aimed to wound; he'd aimed to kill.

When their stuck members were freed, they jumped on their bikes, some riding double, and attempted to flee.

Three more fell dead in the dirt before they began tearing back down the driveway.

Another two fell before they made it to the end of the lane.

And then the riders were gone and the shooting stopped.

I lay where I was for a moment, keeping my shield at full strength. I had no reason to think the shooter was trying to help me for any other reason that it suited their motives to get the riders out of their way.

That didn't make them friendly.

The fire was still raging in the grass and was growing. I had little doubt the barn would go up soon enough.

And August was still pinned down with some strange magics, and eventually, the flames would make it to him.

What of the kids, though? Had they taken the opportunity to escape?

I glanced back toward where I'd last seen the shooter, but didn't see any movement. I was just about to give up and race back toward the barn when I caught a movement out of the corner of my eye.

It was Swamp Thing, all right, but he wasn't where I'd last seen him. He was moving across the grass and headed toward the other side of the barn.

*Damn.*

I rose to my feet and raced back the way I'd come out. If the pack hadn't fled, I needed to get to them before Swamp Thing. I didn't know whether the mysterious figure meant harm to the kids or not, but I wasn't taking any chances.

Glancing over at August, I made a snap judgment that he would be all right for at least a few more minutes, assuming the wind didn't pick up and blow the fire right on top of him.

I rounded the corner and went into the barn. Waya and his Wolf Pack had taken up defensive positions.

My first thought was to scream at them for being idiots. The barn wall was riddled with bullet holes and there was a fire raging just outside the door. It was no place for a bunch of angsty teens.

I didn't get to explain this to them, however, because as soon as I rounded the corner, one of the kids let fly with an arrow that harmlessly bounced off my magical shield.

I might've taken that as yet another accidental attempt on my life, but then Waya raised a fist and hurled something at me that looked like a rock. When it struck my shield, it erupted in an explosion of green flames.

I'm not sure what it would've done to my flesh if my shield hadn't stopped it, but I *was* sure I didn't want to find out.. A sulfuric stench filled the air and my defenses were just about done for.

Glancing past the teens, I saw Swamp Thing appear at the back of the barn. He raised a strange-looking fat gun. It looked more like a cannon than any kind of rifle.

There was a metallic *thunk* and a metal canister hit the floor, right in the middle of the pack.

My first thought was grenade.

My second thought was that my shield wouldn't withstand a grenade.

My third thought was that it must be a dud because instead of an explosion, a bunch of white smoke was pouring from the canister.

My fourth thought was that I was an idiot and it wasn't a grenade at all.

It was tear gas.

I ran to the side as two more arrows flew my way. One bounced off my dying shield while another stuck into the wall above my head. These kids were serious. And so was Mr. Ghillie Suit Man.

Trying to kill me or not, my first order of business was to protect the pack from whoever this new player was. Whatever his intention, he'd fired his tear gas at the kids rather than me, which meant I wasn't his target. They were.

I raised my staff to hit him with a force spell, but he disappeared around a support beam. When he came out the other side, he had a firearm raised and pointed at me.

Trusting my shield to hold up a little longer, I raced toward him and hurled my sword in his direction.

I missed.

Not just a little.

Like, I thought I'd gotten pretty good at throwing my sword, and even suspected Dyrnwyn magically helped with my aim. I mean, I had no logical reason to suspect that other than I was so damned accurate most the time.

This time, though, my sword didn't help my cause, and I threw high and to the right, sticking Dyrnwyn into a support beam rather than my opponent's face.

Behind me, Waya and Pathkiller were both barking orders, and it sounded like the kids were finally going to try to make their escape. Which I thought was a relief, right until a tomahawk planted in the wall just above my head.

This whole situation was getting rather frustrating. I couldn't remember a time when someone I was trying to help was trying so hard to kill me.

I didn't have much time to think about it, but the thought crossed my mind. Why would they have allowed me to cover their escape from the riders only to ambush me when I returned?

*Oh, right. I'm an idiot.*

Maybe that's what Waya had meant when he said that I just didn't get it. Perhaps, they'd been planning to kill me the whole time, but Pathkiller had been smart enough to suggest letting their mutual enemies have a crack first, so they could just mop up.

They *had* played me.

*Fucking teenagers.*

The pack was running to and fro now, while the better part of the barn was filling with the noxious gas. I wasn't even close to the thick of the cloud, but already my eyes were burning and I was finding it harder to breathe.

I had to keep my focus, though. My target was the man who looked like Swamp Thing, and my objective was to protect these ungrateful little brat asses from him.

I saw him move out of the shadows and raise a handgun, only he didn't have it pointed at me. I glanced back over my shoulder and saw one of the younger kids running and coughing on this side of the white cloud.

The gunman fired.

The kid went down, screaming and crying.

Pathkiller appeared through the fog then, using some kind of spell to push the smoke from her. She reached down and grabbed the smaller kid, lifting him off the ground. With a surprising show of strength, she threw the kid over her shoulder and disappeared behind the tear gas cloud once more.

I couldn't tell how injured the kid was, but one thing was clear: that bastard had shot him.

All bets were off.

I summoned Dyrnwyn back to my hand and pressed forward, trying to get closer to the child-killing Swamp Thing wannabe.

He appeared again, this time with the gun leveled in my direction.

I hurled my sword again, and once again, missed completely, sticking it in the sheet metal wall instead. I blamed that one on the tear gas.

The gunman fired at me twice, but I was on the move and the rounds never even hit my shield.

Then I saw Axel across the way from me, drumsticks at the ready. It seemed he had the same idea in mind.

He raised one drumstick and fired a force spell at the gunman, knocking him from his feet.

He might've finished the job then, but one of the teens charged him from behind with a spear and nearly skewered him. Axel turned to face the kid and used a gentle force spell to scoot him back a few feet.

I tried to think of something I could do to help, but everything I came up with would hurt the kid, and while I was quickly running out of empathy and patience, I just couldn't bring myself to intentionally hurt them. Even if I was becoming a monster, as I feared, I had to draw a line somewhere. And that line, I knew, ended with harming angsty teenagers.

So, I rushed the gunman while keeping my eye on Axel.

The kid charged Axel again, but he sidestepped, then gave the kid a good push back into the tear gas cloud.

Axel seemed about to say something clever, but a gunshot rang out first and Axel stiffened.

I glanced back at the gunman just in time to see him fire again.

Axel flinched a second time.

He'd been shot. Twice.

In the back.

My best friend cried out and collapsed to the ground, out of my field of vision.

I didn't need my vision, anyway, because all I could see was red.

Forgetting magic, or my sword, or anything else, I rushed the gunman.

He turned toward me and raised his gun, which I batted away with my staff, then swung for his head.

The gunman ducked and charged forward, slamming a fist in my gut and knocking the air from my lungs. My fury didn't need oxygen, though, and I tried to swing again.

It turned out I was wrong about that whole oxygen thing, and my attack was clumsy.

My opponent caught hold of the end of my staff and yanked me toward him. I caught a glimpse of ghillie suit face as he head-butted me. I saw stars and nearly fell over, but somehow kept my footing as my attacker came at me with my own staff.

I summoned Dyrnwyn back to me again, but the sword didn't make it in time.

He slammed my staff against my arm, and for the first time, I felt what my opponents felt when they got walloped by a mage's staff.

It wasn't pleasant.

The pain only fueled my rage. This asshole had just shot Axel. My best friend was dying on a barn floor because of this prick. I was going to take him apart, dammit.

As he raised my staff to strike again, I howled like a rabid wolverine and charged him like a rhino, slamming my weight into him and driving him to the floor. I intended to rain blows into his skull until I turned his brains into jelly.

And then I wasn't on top anymore.

Somehow, he'd quickly maneuvered my weight against me, hit me in the gut again, and tossed me to the side like a sack of potatoes.

One side of my brain knew I was in a race against time to recover before he finished me while the other side of my brain questioned why he'd let off the pressure when he had me.

Then I saw he was going for his gun.

Still out of breath and not quite back to my feet, I launched myself at him, trying to get to him before he could pick up the gun. I closed the distance a second too late, but grabbed hold of his mask and pulled.

The fabric tore away and I staggered back, looking up at my attacker, who was now pointing his sidearm right at my chest.

I blinked twice and said, "Stone?"

He pulled the trigger.

# CHAPTER THIRTY-NINE

"Ouchie," I heard a voice say.

Axel's voice.

He'd been shot.

Only, I hadn't "heard" it in a traditional sense, had I?

It was in my head. Mind-speak.

Trying to piece things together was proving a real challenge. There was an immense amount of pain in my chest, and I couldn't quite catch my breath. Each attempt felt like I was sucking fire into my lungs.

Why was that?

*You were shot, dummy.*

Oh, right. I'd forgotten about that.

So, this was it, then. This was what dying felt like.

I could only imagine the size of the hole in my chest and the amount of blood that was probably pouring out on the dirt floor of the barn. It was odd, but I never would've guessed dying would burn so much.

Again, Axel's voice sounded in my mind. *"Owwie oww."*

"Axel!" I yelled, not bothering with mind-speak. "Axel, how bad is it?"

"Well, it doesn't feel good, Wyatt. I'll tell you that."

"Can you move?" I asked. "I think we're dying, Axel. I think this is it."

"Speak for yourself. Death would be a blessing right now."

"I've been shot. Right in the chest. I'm dying."

"Oh, quit being dramatic, Wyatt."

"I'm not being dramatic! I got shot in the chest! I can barely breathe."

"Get up. We need to move before this whole barn burns down on top of us."

"I can't get up. Didn't you hear me? I've been shot. Wait... Didn't you get shot too?"

"Yeah, but I'm feeling much better."

"Huh?"

"Wyatt, open your eyes."

I forced open my eyes and saw Axel standing over me.

I blinked a couple of times, then looked down at my chest.

There was no pool of blood.

No big hole.

Though, in fairness, the entry wound wouldn't have been. It was the bigger hole in my back I had to worry about. Still...

I raised a hand and felt around my chest.

I hissed at the immediate pain, but upon further inspection, there wasn't a hole in my chest. There wasn't even a hole in my shirt.

"What the hell?" I said, looking back up at Axel.

He shrugged. "Maybe we're bullet proof?"

"I don't feel bullet proof," I replied, testing the tender flesh on my chest. "It still hurts. And my eyes burn. What the hell?"

"Umm, Wyatt, while I am truly enjoying your dramatic display of dying, we don't have a lot of time. So, I'm just going to go ahead and point out that while you were shot, it wasn't by a bullet."

"It wasn't?"

"No. I believe our attacker was using non-lethal pepper spray rounds."

"Non-lethal pepper what?"

"Your eyes are burning from the combo of pepper spray and tear gas. You're having trouble breathing because of the pepper spray and tear gas."

"So, that means..."

"You're being a big baby over pepper spray and tear gas. That said, if you'd like to lie there a little longer whining, I'm sure this burning barn will be happy to *actually* kill you. It'll be via asphyxiation, burning you to death, or crushing you when it falls on your head. I hope that meets your criteria. *Or* you could just get up."

"Right," I said, forcing myself to sit up.

"So, can we go now?" Axel said.

"Help me up," I said, raising my hand.

Axel rolled his eyes but helped me up.

On my feet again, I realized I wasn't in all that bad shape.

As we started toward the door, I said, "It was Stone, Axel. That was Shain Stone."

"Wow," Axel said, chuckling. "Then I guess we were lucky."

"Yeah, I guess so."

We stepped out into the daylight and found August Bones headed our way.

"About time you show up," I said.

He put up his hands defensively. "I was stuck. What could I do?"

I turned to Axel. "And you. Where were you when the bikers were trying to murder me?"

"Well, at first I was massaging my balls. Then, when I saw you were in trouble, I was planning a sneak attack. Then I saw you had help and went back to massaging my balls."

"So, I guess the pack got away?"

"Yeah," August said. "Otherwise, I'm their spell would still have me pinned to the ground."

"Cherokee magic is a bit different from what I'm used to," I replied.

"You and me both," August said, studying the fire. "I suppose we should get out of here and call this in. No telling how long before someone notices the smoke and calls Norman authorities."

"Right," I said, glancing around once more. "And no sign of Stone."

"Who?" August asked.

I shook my head. "Trouble."

"Worse than the trouble you're going to have with the Red Dirt Riders when they find out what happened?"

"Yeah," I said, glancing over at the corpses and discarded motorcycles. "He's the one who killed them."

"And he's after the pack?" August asked.

"Yup," I said. "We'd better find them first."

# CHAPTER FORTY

Back in the car, August had several missed calls from Elder Morgan again. But before returning them, he put in a call to Constable Williams and let her know about the pile of dead bodies we'd just abandoned.

As before, Constable Johnson was none too impressed, and demanded we bring ourselves back to the constable shack. August hung up.

Next, he called Elder Morgan back, but this time he didn't put it on speaker, so all Axel and I could hear was his side of the conversation. And since August was doing more listening than talking, it was the boring side. We were forced to endure our curiosity and anticipation, a skill which neither of us were particularly good at.

Finally, August said, "I see."

A few moments after that, he said, "We're on our way."

The call finally ended.

From the backseat, Axel burst. "Dammit, man! What did he say?"

"Well," August said, pausing as though he had to gather his thoughts. "Umm, the elders think they know what's been influencing the kids. And why they're leaving."

"Okay?" I asked. "We're listening."

"Right, um... It seems that the tribe has found evidence of some, uh, some sort of creature... Or being, or something, nearby. Something that could influence the kids."

"Okay?" I repeated, unsure what else to say.

August shook his head. "I don't know. He said he'd explain when we got there."

"All right," I said, realizing we were only getting more questions than answers. I didn't particularly like this game.

"That's not all," August said. "Apparently the tribe has sent some warriors."

"Warriors?" Axel asked. "Like the fictional gang from that movie? You know... 'Warriors, come out and play?' "

"More like Cherokee warriors."

"Uh, okay," I said. "And...why did they do that?"

"Well," August said, "for the war party, of course."

"Of course," I replied, then turned to stare out the window. "Of course it's for the war party. Why wouldn't it be?"

# CHAPTER FORTY-ONE

On the trip back to the camp, we gave August a brief rundown on Shain Stone. Not too much detail, but just enough that he knew the guy wasn't a joke. Mage or not, it was best to approach Stone with a bit of caution.

Naturally, August asked, "Do you think this guy means to harm the kids?"

"I don't know," I replied, and that was the truth. "Look, if you asked most anyone in the Cabal, they'd tell you Stone is a psychopath with ill intent. That's not been my experience, and certainly not my father's. In fact, if it weren't for Stone, both Axel and I would be dead right now."

"Yeah," Axel said, poking his head up between the seats. "He fired a grenade into the middle of a room we were standing in."

August raised an eyebrow and glanced over at me. "That doesn't sound like he was trying to save your lives."

"We were about to be murdered by a pile of supernatural baddies," I replied. I realized as I said it that it did little to illustrate Stone's good side.

Fortunately, Axel came to the rescue. "It was amazing, August! You should've seen it. They were all smug and arrogant, thinking they had us right where they wanted, and BOOM! Stone lights 'em up! There's no one I'd rather shoot a grenade at me than Shain Stone. I'll say that for him."

I realized Axel's statement required further elaboration. "What Axel is saying is that Stone knew exactly what he was doing. He was sure of his aim and understood we'd be as safe as he could keep us from the blast."

"Uh, sure," August said. "Sounds like a swell guy."

"He also took on an Abasy demon in hand-to-hand combat to save my life," I said. "The guy is a different sort. But the point is, I don't think Stone meant the kids harm."

"Then why did he attack you?" August asked.

"Heat of the moment?" I replied. "In fairness, I think I might've attacked him first. And I'm guessing he wouldn't have known we were here."

"And he was using non-lethal," Axel replied. "Isn't that right, Wyatt? You dramatic little man, you."

"Yes, Axel," I said, gritting my teeth. "He was using non-lethal."

"But even non-lethal can be dangerous, right?" August said. "I mean, you said he shot one of the kids. And he fired tear gas in the middle of them."

"Well, I never said he was gentle," I replied. "Look, there's a bigger question still. If Stone is here, that means there must be something bad going down. He doesn't just go harassing packs of runaway teens for nothing. My best guess is he was planning to capture one of them."

"You're not making a good case for this guy," August said. "Now you're saying you think his intent was kidnapping."

"Right," I said, unsure what else to say. "But that's not Stone's normal operating style. And he wouldn't be in the neighborhood if he didn't have good reason to think something wicked was about."

"So, what is he?" August asked. "Some kind of supernatural vigilante? That's *exactly* what we need in Lost City."

"That's not what he is at all," Axel said. "He just moves about in secret, staying hidden from the Cabal, and when he gets wind of something nasty, he goes and takes care of it when the Cabal can't or won't... Oh, yeah, I guess he is kind of a vigilante, isn't he?"

"With no qualms about killing," August said. "And if what you say is true, he won't be easy to stop."

"Which is why we'll need to prioritize finding him," I said. "If we can talk to him, he'll see reason. He may even help us."

"After he shot you," August said, keeping his eyes on the road. "You want the guy who shot you to help us?"

"Stone shoots lots of people," Axel said, shrugging. "You can't hold it against him."

To that, August didn't reply.

By the time we pulled up the driveway to the camp, the sun was setting. There were no kids outside this time. Nor did anyone come out to greet us as we parked.

Someone did walk out to meet us as we approached the big building with the meeting rooms.

He stood in the doorway like a figure chiseled out of stone. He was easily a head taller than me, and rippling with muscles, which we could see because he wasn't wearing a shirt for some reason.

Fortunately, he was wearing jeans and boots. He had long dark hair that hung past his shoulders, a dark complexion, and a "fuck you" scowl planted firmly between his cheeks.

I glanced over at August and whispered, "Do you know this guy?"

"Nope," August replied. "And he doesn't look excited to see us."

As we approached the door, he didn't seem inclined to move, so I put on my best smile and said, "Hi, there."

He crossed his arms over his massive chest and said, "You aren't welcome here. Leave."

I glanced at August and Axel, both of whom shrugged. I turned back to the big, angry man. "Is Elder Morgan around?"

"You are outsiders," the man said. "You aren't welcome here."

"We were welcome here a few hours ago," I said.

"No longer."

"All right, then," I replied. "So, I guess you guys aren't interested in hearing about our run-in with your missing students?"

His eyes narrowed. "Speak."

"Nah," I replied, shaking my head. "I don't know you."

"And you're kind of an ass," Axel added.

"I think we'll share our story with Elder Morgan," August added. "If he happens to be around."

For a moment, I thought the big man might attack us, but then another figured appeared behind him in the doorway. It was Elder Morgan. "Let them through, Ahuli."

The big man turned to face Elder Morgan. "We have spoken about this, Elder. Outsiders are not permitted."

"These outsiders are working to bring our children home," Elder Morgan said. "You may be War Chief, Ahuli, but here at this camp, I lead the medicine men and women. If you wish for mine to follow your lead, you must meet me somewhere in the middle. And I say these men are friends to our tribe."

Ahuli stared down at the older man, not speaking.

"How you've grown, Ahuli," Elder Morgan said, shaking his head. "There was a time you trusted my judgment. Am I so old now that I've lost not only the respect of the young, but those I once swaddled and trained?"

Ahuli sighed. "No, Elder. Your council is still wise. Though in this, I fear I disagree. Yet, I will submit to your wisdom. I must go prepare the hunting party."

With that, the big man turned and went back inside.

"Um, what just happened?" I asked, looking at Elder Morgan.

"Tribal politics, my friend," he said with a forced smile. "Tell me, what of the children? Did you see my Alyita?"

"I did," I said, and told him of what occurred, leaving out few details. Whatever I missed, Axel or August were sure to correct. By the time we were done, I think he had a pretty clear picture of what had happened.

"So, you think they intended you harm?" Elder Morgan said, staring at the ground. "And the Red Dirt Riders are after them, as well as this other man you know."

"It's not great news," I said. "But I'm most concerned about what Ben said. The bad man. Who the hell is that? And the kid was convinced if he came back to camp, you'd hurt him."

Elder Morgan was silent for several moments, then finally said,

"Well, if the hunting party is successful tonight, perhaps our troubles will be over."

I glanced at the other two, but again, they were no help. I turned my attention back to the medicine man. "Um, what exactly is going on, Elder Morgan?"

He looked up and met my gaze, perhaps assessing me, as though he weren't so sure we should be included.

"Look," I said, putting up my hands. "I understand your tribe has its secrets, and probably for good reason. So, if you aren't comfortable telling us, or including us, that's fine. No hard feelings. We just want to help. We certainly don't want to compromise your position with the tribe, nor do we seek to learn any sacred knowledge. We can leave, if that's what's best."

"Perhaps it is best," Elder Morgan said, turning his eyes up to the sky. "Certainly it would seem so, but my gut tells me otherwise. The Earth speaks to us, Blade Mage, if only we're able to listen. I think it's speaking to me now, and that it wants me to share this with you. That it is right, you should be a part of the hunt."

I wasn't sure about that at all.

If the Earth was speaking, I was reasonably confident it wasn't speaking to me, and I felt very uncomfortable. Whatever was going on, it was clear it had dire consequences for the tribe, and my instincts were telling me it was time to go. I almost insisted, but a slight tremor on my back made me stay. Whether the Earth was trying to tell me something, I couldn't say, but Dyrnwyn certainly was.

*Damn.*

Played by my magical sword again.

"Okay, Elder Morgan," I said, nodding. "Whatever your decision, I will follow."

"You and your friend are to say, if you so desire. It will be a long and likely dangerous night," he said with a forced smile. Then it melted away, and he turned to August.

He didn't say anything, but August understood the message. And once again, he just looked tired.

August Bones put on his own fake smile and said, "I understand. I'll go."

With that, he turned and started toward his car.

"Wait," Axel said, glancing between the elder, me, and the retreating wizard. "Bones can't stay to play?"

"Not this time," Elder Morgan said, and there was an edge of sorrow to his words.

August glanced back over his shoulder. "You kids have fun. Try not to get into too much trouble without me. I'll be around to pick you up in the morning."

With that, he got in his car and started the engine.

Elder Morgan let out a long breath, then turned his attention back to me. "Come. There are things you must see, things you must hear, and things you must know. Then, perhaps, you may join us on this hunt."

# CHAPTER FORTY-TWO

E lder Morgan led us through the cabin and out the back.
We approached a large structure which appeared to have been handcrafted by gluing saplings together with mud. Smoke rose from a single hole at the top. I could only assume it was some kind of meeting house.

I wasn't an expert on Cherokee history, but I suspected this was how they'd built houses back in the day. It made sense that they'd continue the tradition. That was exactly the type of thing I'd want to pass on to the next generation. A reminder of how people once lived, and super practical in the event of societal collapse.

As we approached the entrance, Elder Morgan paused and said, "If you come in, there's no turning back. Do you understand?"

I met his gaze and weighed his words. "I understand and will accept the consequences, so long as you are willing as well. It is your decision."

The elder stared at me for a few moments, then said, "Come."

With that, we followed him inside the hut.

The light was low, a single fire burning within.

Several senior members, including some newcomers, sat around the inside in a large circle, most on the floor.

My gaze stopped on a single figure sitting atop a crate.

It was a little person.

Not a little person by standard conventions.

Like...a small humanoid.

He only came up to my knees.

The tiny fella was speaking to the others in a language I could only assume was Cherokee, and they were listening intently.

Elder Morgan nudged me to get my attention and pointed to a vacant spot on the floor where Axel and I were to sit.

As we plopped down, Elder Morgan whispered, "You must remain silent unless spoken to, and at times, I may ask you to wait outside."

I nodded.

"I'm sure you have questions, but they must wait. And many may remain unanswered."

Axel put up his hand.

I tried to swat it back down before the elder saw, but he evaded me.

Elder Morgan turned to him and said, "Yes, Axel?"

I tensed up, prepared for him to say something stupid. Instead, he said, "Elder, if our presence is causing undue burden, we can wait outside. If we are to hunt a monster, we only need to know what to look for, what to watch out for, and how to kill it."

"It is as it should be," Elder Morgan said. "I wish for you to be present for this part. Just now, our friend is explaining what he found to the others."

"Who is he?" I asked.

"You've not heard our legends of the little people?"

I shook my head.

Elder Morgan smiled. "They are friend to the Cherokee, more often than not. It was they who first saw signs of the beast. He is explaining this now, so there can be no doubt among our members of the validity of his claim. All must agree."

"They won't act because you tell them to?" I asked.

"That is not our way. Only those who agree will support the hunt. Any who doubt may choose not to participate."

"And the creature?"

"The less you know the better. Hush now. I must speak with the others."

Elder Morgan addressed the group then, and their conversation continued. Aside from the occasional head nods, shakes, and facial expressions, I had no idea what was going on. That was okay, though. It wasn't really my concern. As Axel had put it, if we were to join them on the hunt, we didn't need too much information.

Truth be told, I wasn't sure I was on board with this story about mythical beasts anyway. Ben had mentioned a bad man. That was who I thought we should be hunting. It made more sense to me that some ill-intended adult had somehow persuaded the kids to abandon their tribe, not some mythical monster.

This felt like a wild goose chase. But what did I know? Well, I knew it was better to keep my opinions to myself.

As time dragged on, I lost count of how many times were asked to step outside while they continued conversation and ceremony. It was pretty obvious neither Axel nor I understood a lick of the Iroquoian language they spoke. Which meant they were asking us to step outside to avoid seeing something we shouldn't see.

I actually didn't mind being asked to leave occasionally. Sitting in the stuffy room and not understanding a word of the conversation made it tough to stay awake after our rather exciting day. The fresh air helped to perk me up a bit.

After what felt like days—but was probably only a few hours—I'd garnered very little we didn't already know.

The little person had brought news of the monster to the medicine men and women, who in turn had sent their own people to look for signs. And signs they'd found, though this was apparently debatable by some. Still, at that point Elder Morgan had reached out to the greater tribe, and more Cherokee shamans and warriors had arrived. I still knew nothing of the creature, but at least half of the attendees weren't convinced. Whatever this thing was, it was rare, even among their legends. This further convinced me we were wasting time chasing ghost stories when we should've been trying to track down the kids, the bad man, and Shain Stone.

Still, I kept my mouth shut. And despite my reservations, both Axel and I had the sense that our being invited to take part in this council was a great honor and rare privilege. And we were both doing a great job of behaving ourselves.

After our last stint outside, Elder Morgan joined us once more. "Our council has concluded. It is time to hunt."

"Okay," I said, nodding. "Anything we need to know?"

Elder Morgan's face took on an apologetic expression. "It was voted and agreed that you should come along, but that no further information concerning the nature of the beast be shared with you. Only this: if we find the creature and it is slain, you must leave the area immediately. You may not look upon its corpse, nor the ritual that follows."

I glanced at Axel, who shrugged, then turned back to the Elder. "That requirement is no issue, but shouldn't we at least know what we're looking for? Or how to defend ourselves if we come across it?"

"I'm sorry, Wyatt," the elder said. "But no. It was voted. And though I do not agree myself, the majority rule says you're to be told nothing further. If you wish to back out, I will understand, though know it will permanently damage your reputation with our tribe. You'll have to leave Lost City and refrain from engaging with us further, or helping to find our missing children."

"That's not much of a choice, then."

"No, I fear it is not. Though I will understand and accept whatever decision you make. And for what little it is worth, you will not be lessened in my own eyes."

"We're in," Axel said. "I mean... Half the time we have no idea what our enemies are capable of anyway. This isn't any different."

I nodded my agreement. "You can count on us. Just tell us what you want us to do."

"Stay close," the elder said. "Keep your eyes and ears open, and know this... If we come across the beast, your magic will be of little use."

I blinked a few times and said, "Well, that is..."

"Also pretty much par for the course," Axel said, jumping in.

"Yeah," I said, feeling even less confident about what we'd just gotten ourselves roped into. "That *is* pretty standard."

# CHAPTER FORTY-THREE

The chirping of crickets and the dim glow of lightning bugs were my only companions. Them, and perhaps the shining stars I glimpsed through the treetops.

Cherokee County, it turned out, had a healthy amount of forest. The woodlands surrounding the training grounds were vast, and in the dead of the night, I felt lost and a little alone, though I knew Axel was somewhere nearby.

Well, I knew Axel was *supposed* to be somewhere nearby, but it had been some time since I'd seen or heard from him. I liked to think he wouldn't abandon me in the middle of a forest, but for all I knew, he might've just walked on until he found a road and hitchhiked to the nearest McDonald's.

I had seen none of the tribe in some time, either.

As directed, we'd stayed near Elder Morgan during our long march into the wilderness. Among the Hunting Party, the only other Cherokee I knew by name was the big angry fella, Ahuli, and the muscled-up young medicine man, John. A few of the other elders I recognized had taken part, but I didn't know their names. Elder Thomas and the younger man, Samuel, had not joined the hunt.

Even at our best, with some training on infiltration, compared to the Cherokee, Axel and I might as well have been a marching band. The tribe moved through the hills like ghosts, never making a sound that wasn't intended.

When Elder Morgan ordered me to stand and wait, it wouldn't have surprised me if they'd decided to leave us behind because of all the noise we were making. I wouldn't have blamed them.

It was also possible they were all around me. That's how effectively they moved through the brush. I just didn't know.

And the sounds of the night were no help. I couldn't distinguish the hoot of an owl from the hoot of a Cherokee communicating back to the group. I certainly didn't know what the messages meant as they reverberated through the trees.

So, I just stood quietly, feeling like a fool and waiting for someone to come along to get me.

I also considered whether this was all some kind of cruel joke, like snipe hunting. Come morning, would I find myself alone and lost in the woods?

At least it felt like home.

Despite the anxiety and adrenaline of the day—and the sore spot on my chest from my horrific gunshot wound—there was something soothing about standing quietly in the trees. It was my kind of meditation, so long as I didn't fall asleep on my feet or get nibbled by a copperhead.

At some point, I lost all track of time. I could've been standing there for minutes or hours. There was just no way to know. I had a tendency to get lost in my own head.

A whispered voice called out to me, "*Psst...* Wyatt."

"Axel?" I whispered back.

"Did you hear that?" he asked.

"Hear what?"

"Never mind."

Never mind? *What?* I almost used mind-speak to call out to him again, but remembered that Elder Morgan had further advised us that not only did the tribe think our magic would be ineffective, but that it might draw the beast to us, so it'd be advisable to refrain from manipulating any magical energy.

There were a few times I'd thought about doing it anyway, just to get the show on the road, but... I didn't fancy the idea of some mythical beast flinging me around like a chew toy until I squeaked.

But Axel could shove his "never mind."

"What did you hear?" I whispered.

"Shh," he said. "I'm trying to listen."

"Do you know where the others are? Have you seen Elder Morgan?"

"Wyatt, be quiet," he said. "You aren't supposed to be making any noise."

"You started this conversation."

"And I ended it. Shush now."

I considered walking toward his voice, just so I could hit him, but thought better of it. I'd only make a bunch of noise.

And then I heard something, too.

A cracking of a twig followed by a short rasp that sounded like a breath. Not quite human, though. It had been too...husky.

What was it? And how close?

I didn't know the answer to either of those questions, and in the quiet forest, judging distance by sound was next to impossible for someone as unused to hunting as I was.

"Did you hear that?" Axel asked.

"Yes," I replied. "Do you know what it was?"

"Shh."

I was going to murder him.

I remained silent, listening intently. At least he'd confirmed the sound wasn't my imagination playing tricks on me. There was something out there, and Axel had heard it, too.

Another gap of time passed, and I heard limbs shaking somewhere in the night, followed by more ragged breathing.

Whatever the hell it was, it sounded big.

"Axel," I whispered. "Did you hear that?"

No reply.

"Axel?"

Nothing.

*What the fuck?* This was no time for him to go silent on me.

Any other time, I couldn't get him to shut the hell up, but now that there was some beasty out in the darkness, he wanted to play the quiet game?

What if something had happened? What if the creature had attacked? What if Axel was lying dead, his neck severed and blood pumping out in the dead leaves?

*Calm down*, I told myself. *Relax. Breathe. Listen.*

Silence.

I tried to wait.

I tried to be patient.

I just couldn't take it anymore.

Just before I called out again, I heard movement: the padding of feet on the ground. A rustling of leaves.

Another twig snapped.

More heavy breathing.

*What the hell was out there?*

In one hand, my grip tightened around my staff. In the other, my sword. I fought the urge to summon my shield or to fill the night air with magical light.

Something was definitely close, and it was big.

And where were the Cherokee? Why weren't they doing something? Had they really left us behind?

The thing was moving again. I could hear it clearly now, and it sounded like it was getting closer. I tried to tell myself it was just my nerves, but I could sense it. At one point, I thought I even saw a flash of movement in the darkness.

"Wyatt," Axel whispered again, but this time, there was an edge of concern.

The movement stopped and the heavy breathing stilled.

"Axel?" I replied.

"Wyatt," Axel said again, quietly.

Then I heard the movement again, and it sounded like it was coming right toward me.

Like it was *running* toward me.

I tried to calm myself.

I tried to convince myself it was just Axel trying to find me, or one of the Cherokee approaching. But it sounded like something tearing through the forest.

It sounded like it was coming for me.

And then Axel screamed, "Wyatt, watch out!"

I dove to the side as a hulking shadow charged into the space I'd just occupied. I tried to rise, but the creature was on me, and I tumbled to the side as it made some inhuman cry.

I rolled again and hit a tree.

There was nowhere else to go, and the monster was bearing down on me.

I lashed out with my sword, stabbing at the black mass of death trying to consume me.

There was a sharp intake of air followed by a squeal, and the creature backed away from me, falling over on its side.

Useless or not, I summoned my magic and cast a light spell through the end of my staff, nearly blinding my unadjusted eyes.

But I could see the horrifying monster who'd tried to make me its supper.

And it was...

A pig.

A wild boar, to be more accurate.

I'd stabbed it in the shoulder and now the beast was flopping on the ground and squealing out its death throes.

*Damn.* I felt like a *real* asshole.

I blinked at it a couple of times and then Axel crashed through the trees beside me. "Wyatt, are you all right?"

"Yeah," I said, struggling to find my voice. "It was just a pig."

"Poor thing," Axel said, looking down at it. "Finish the job, you monster. Don't let it suffer."

He was right.

I moved forward and ended the boar's misery with a quick stab.

It lay still in the leaves as the Cherokee began appearing all around us.

None of them spoke at first, their eyes focused on the dead creature at my feet. Then a few of them smiled.

Elder Morgan appeared, followed by John, then Ahuli.

The War Chief stared down at the dead boar and shook his head, then turned to Elder Morgan and spoke some words in Cherokee.

Elder Morgan sighed while a few of the others chuckled.

I had a feeling the War Chief hadn't paid me a compliment.

Ahuli and some of the others turned and disappeared into the darkness.

"What did he say?" I asked.

Elder Morgan glanced down at the pig, then back up at me. "He said you might've ruined the hunt, but at least you killed us dinner."

"That's not as bad as I expected," I replied.

"Eh, I cleaned it up a bit," the elder said.

Axel chuckled. "Wyatt Draven, Blade Mage and world-renowned pig hunter."

# CHAPTER FORTY-FOUR

Oh, the jokes.

They just kept coming, all the way back to camp.

Pig Killer.

Swine Sorcerer.

The Bacon Blade Mage.

Ham Hacker.

They were quite clever, those Cherokee medicine men and warriors. And Axel was a *big* help.

That was okay, though. I didn't mind receiving the brunt of their jokes, and after the anxiety of the hunt, it seemed everyone needed to vent.

The important thing was everyone was okay. No one had been mauled to death by some ancient monster. So, I counted it as a win, and if I had to pay a little dignity for that blessing, well, then by all means, I could be the butt of the jokes.

I just hoped my new titles, like the Swashbuckler of Swine, didn't make it back to the Cabal. I was already going to hear it from Axel for the foreseeable future.

My biggest worry had been that I'd have to carry the oinker all the way back on my own, but I hadn't made it far when John relieved me for a bit. After a time, another among the Cherokee took the burden from him, and so on. The hunting party shared in carrying our kill, and even Axel took a turn.

Our return trip was uneventful, and by the time we'd made it back to the training grounds, most everyone was in good spirits.

Elder Morgan explained that they would hold council again to determine if the hunting party would go out the following night. It was likely they would.

Back at the little cabin they'd provided for Axel and me, I was surprised to find I didn't at all feel ready for sleep. For all my aches and pains, and of course my eye-rolling gunshot wound, I was wide awake.

Axel was much the same, so with nothing else to do, we took a little walk around the camp. Elder Morgan had made it clear where we were, and weren't, allowed to go. As long as we stayed near the established modernized cabins, we were free to travel as we pleased.

It was late, but a few folks were out and about. Between the missing kids and talk of a monster in the forest, I suspected they had several guards in place.

The night air was cool, and the stars were still bright in the sky. And for once, Axel was quiet.

It occurred to me that even in my teenage years I would've appreciated the serene setting of the tribe's training grounds. I didn't know what their training was like, but I would've enjoyed doing my schooling years out there. Beat the hell out of the stuffy confines of the stone-walled school on the Castle grounds.

We walked slowly between cabins, minding our own business, until I heard voices ahead. I thought at first to move back the way we'd come, but didn't want anyone to think we were trying to hide anything. So, I rounded the corner and walked directly toward the figures outlined in the moonlight.

The conversation dropped off as we approached. I recognized the young instructor Samuel speaking to a teenage lad, his face white as a ghost beneath the moon.

Samuel was holding something up in front of the kid, but as the teenager noticed us, Samuel turned our way as well. Both seemed a little surprised by our appearance.

"Evening," I said, offering a little wave. "Didn't mean to interrupt. Was just having a walk."

"Ah, it's you," Samuel said with a sigh of relief. He turned back to the kid. "Run along now, Jathan. And remember what we discussed."

The teen took a quick look at me and Axel, then looked back at his teacher. He nodded and disappeared into the shadows.

"Everything all right?" I asked, not sure what we'd just witnessed. I let my gaze drop to Samuel's hand and what he held.

In the darkness, it was hard to tell, but it looked like a sandwich bag. It wasn't empty.

Samuel smiled and pocketed the bag. "Yes, of course. Just commandeering a bit of contraband. You know how teens are."

"Pot?" I asked.

Samuel nodded. "Yes. They know it's forbidden, but they're still kids, aren't they? And despite our efforts to teach them the old ways, they still live in a modern world."

"Pot isn't particularly modern," Axel said, shrugging. "Certainly not anything to have a fuss over."

"I'm glad you see it that way," Samuel said, rubbing at his shoulder nervously. "Some of the elders wouldn't agree, and I'd ask that you keep this encounter to yourselves. I'd hate to see a talented kid turned away because of a little mistake."

"Is this a common occurrence?" I asked.

Samuel shrugged. "From time to time. Our training isn't easy on them. Often, kids who fall behind their peers look for alternate ways to blow off some steam. I don't see it as a big deal."

"But the elders do?" I asked. "Elder Morgan?"

"Look, I have nothing but respect for the elders. Especially Elder Morgan. But if he found out, I fear he'd send Jathan home in shame."

"I see," I said. I didn't like the idea of keeping anything from the elders, but I could get on-board with his concern. I thought of Kate, Tyler, Aarav, Ashley, and Mallory, and how their teachers at the Cabal would react if they were caught with a bag of pot. I feared they'd face similar consequences, which were just a bit extreme for a kid. I nodded. "We can keep this to ourselves."

"Thank you," Samuel said. "I appreciate your discretion."

"Hey, no problem," I said.

"Yeah, it's not like we were the most well-behaved kids, ourselves," Axel said, then pointed at me. "Some of us still aren't."

Samuel laughed. "Well, thanks again."

"Can I ask you something?" I said, as he was about to turn away. "I noticed you weren't on the hunt this evening. Why? If you don't mind me asking."

Samuel opened his mouth to speak, then shut it again. After a moment, he said, "The elders didn't think I was ready."

"But aren't you a medicine man as well?"

"Yes," Samuel said. "But... Well, look, there're some things that should remain private, no?"

"Yeah, Wyatt, sheesh," Axel said.

"I meant no offense," I said, putting up my hands. "I was just curious, is all."

"No offense taken," Samuel replied. "I am... Let's say I'm not the favored son of the Cherokee, though I am, as you put it, a medicine man. My magics aren't as strong as some. Nor am I a great warrior. Not in the eyes of the elders, at least."

"I'm sorry, Samuel," I said, feeling bad for asking.

"It is not your fault, Blade Mage," he said with a forced smile. "In time, I may yet prove myself. But as of today, I am the least seasoned among our trainers. The elders would say I have much to learn."

"And what would you say?" I asked.

He shrugged. "I would say good night, Blade Mage."

"I understand," I said, smiling at him. "Good night, Samuel."

With that, he turned and headed into the darkness.

# CHAPTER FORTY-FIVE

I woke up feeling like a brand-new man. A brand-new man who'd just been run over by a bus.

Axel was already up and bouncing around a like caffeinated child. Apparently, he'd experienced no hangover from the previous day's adventures. *Asshole.*

But our cabin had a hot a shower and there was a mess hall nearby where I was able to get some late breakfast and a cup of coffee, so that was something.

By eleven, there was still no sign of August, but Axel and I visited with Elder Morgan and Elder Thomas. Once again, we recapped our encounter with Waya and his wolf pack. They had little commentary about the teens, but many concerns about the Red Dirt Riders and the appearance of Shain Stone.

Elder Morgan asked, "And you're sure the Riders were looking for our kids?"

"There's little doubt," I said. "They called them by name."

Elder Thomas turned to me. "And the Riders made no indication why they were hunting our kids?"

I shook my head. "When I spoke to Raymond, he made a comment about wanting to find them, but he didn't elaborate. I think it's a safe assumption they've had some kind of disagreement."

"And now he will hunt them with even greater enthusiasm," Elder Morgan said, shaking his head. "It is not good."

"I've been wondering," I said, considering my words. "Would Raymond declare war against your tribe?"

Neither elder was quick to respond.

Finally, Elder Morgan said, "It is possible, though I don't think it's likely. It is true, we've struggled some as of late, but we are still strong. Raymond must know this."

"I'm not so sure," I said. "He isn't a fool. I could tell that much. But he struck me as ambitious and power-hungry. And he's recruited himself an army."

"This is true," Elder Morgan said. "Yet, few know how deep our own numbers truly run or what we are capable of. We have protected these lands from supernatural threats since our tribe was forced here well over a hundred years ago. We are strong yet, Wyatt."

"I don't doubt it," I replied. "But does Raymond know that? You guys play it close to the chest. I've gone hunting with you once, and I could scarcely tell you the difference between your warriors and your medicine men."

"You speak true," Elder Thomas said. "Raymond doesn't know what we are truly capable of. Yet, if he underestimates us, then he must know there are other tribes who would support us, as well as the Cabal. Surely, even in his arrogance, he must know that to declare war on us is to bring on his own downfall."

"I'm not sure," I said. "I think you'll need to be vigilant."

"Always," Elder Morgan said. "If Raymond seeks war against the Cherokee, he will find nothing save disappointment. Yet, for our children..."

"Right," I said, rubbing a hand across my face. "We need to find them. Or find out why Raymond is after them. If it weren't for how many of his people died yesterday, I might've suggested we could offer to make amends. Now, I'm not sure he'll listen."

"I agree," Elder Morgan said, "Though I still think it is worth the conversation. Perhaps I should reach out and see if he will meet with me."

"No," I said, shaking my head. "I don't trust that snake."

Elder Morgan smiled at me. "Afraid I can't take care of myself?"

I opened my mouth to speak, then shut it again.

From where he sat nearby, nuzzling a cup of hot chocolate and reading a comic book, Axel finally spoke up. "And Wyatt puts his foot in his mouth. At least he made it past breakfast today. Progress."

I glared at my friend and turned back to the elder. "It's not that. Well, it is, actually. I don't know whether you can or not, frankly. I suspect you can in some situations, though I don't know whether your medicine will protect you from an angry gang of thugs with guns. But I know my limitations and abilities, so, I will try to make contact somehow. I can at least ask if he'd be willing to have a sit-down, or if there's something that can be done to broker peace."

"That is admirable of you, Blade Mage," Elder Morgan said. "Though, there is still one matter concerning the Riders we have not yet considered."

"Yes?" I asked, unsure what he was referring to.

Axel jumped in again. "How did the Riders know to go looking for the teens at the abandoned farm?"

I paused, glancing between the lot of them. The thought had crossed my mind briefly at the time, but since then, everything had been a blur of movement and I'd never gotten back to it.

A few silent moments passed as we all considered. I shrugged. "I didn't get the impression that the Wolf Pack had been hiding there long, though it's possible. In which case, they could've gotten a tip somehow. Or...they have a mage in their midst."

"And the same question stands for Shain Stone," Elder Thomas recalled. "How did he know to approach the farm? Last heard, he knew no magic."

Elder Morgan's eyes narrowed as he stared at Elder Thomas.

"Oops," Elder Thomas said, offering an apologetic smile to his peer.

"Wait," I said, glancing between the two of them. "You guys know Stone?"

"Of course," Elder Morgan said, turning to meet my gaze. "I'd intended to withhold that from you for a short time, just to see how you might describe him to us."

"What do you mean?" I asked.

Axel let out a big sigh and put down his comic book. "He means to say that it was an integrity check, Wyatt. To see if we would hold back information on just how dangerous Stone is and to see if our perception of him matched their own."

"It was meant as no offense," Elder Morgan said.

"None taken," I replied. "I'm pretty used to people not trusting me."

Elder Thomas grunted. "For me, it wasn't to check your integrity so much as to see if you viewed him much the way we do."

"And how do you view him?" I asked. "How do you know him?"

"He was your father's loyal ally, was he not?" Elder Morgan said.

"Right," I replied. "So, you met him when working with my father?"

"A few times," Elder Morgan said with a nod. "And frankly, the man scares me. Not that he has some powerful magics, but that he simply embodies all the rage and anguish of the world. And yet, he keeps a level head. He will stop at nothing. A man like that..."

"Yeah," I said, nodding. "He's dangerous."

"And he is after our children," Elder Thomas said. "Which means he's against us."

"Not necessarily," Axel said, thumbing through the pages of his comic book.

Both the elders and I turned to stare at him, waiting for him to elaborate on his meaning.

Finally, Axel slapped his comic book on the table and looked at the lot of us with disdain. "You know, for being three of the smartest people I know, you lot are awfully thick. Just because someone appears to have ulterior motives doesn't mean they actually have a different goal."

"You told us he attacked the children," Elder Thomas said, then pointed at me. "Wyatt even saw him shoot one of them."

"Yes," Axel said, shrugging. "So what? We know he was using nonlethal pepper spray rounds. Despite the drama queen complaining about his chest, it left little more than a bruise. So, what does that tell us?"

"That he intended to take one of our children alive," Elder Morgan said.

"Which doesn't necessarily mean he intends them harm," Axel replied. "We all know Stone. If he'd sought to kill anyone, then they'd be dead. So, that leaves only one logical conclusion..."

Axel spread his hands, perhaps waiting for one of us to fill in the blanks. Yet so often his theories were so mad that I usually found it was best to let him do it himself.

After a moment, he did just that. "Stone knows something we don't. He wouldn't be out to punish runaways. There's a connection there. Something they can lead him to. And that, my friends, is what he's after."

"We need to find him," I said.

"Good luck," Axel replied. "Though now that he knows we're here, there's a good chance he'll find us. If he wants to."

"Right," I said.

Just then, August finally made an appearance.

He seemed somewhat haggard, as though he'd had a bad night's sleep again. I wasn't sure what was going on with that guy, but it wasn't my problem, so long as he didn't put me in a bad spot. I didn't need him falling asleep behind the wheel or snoring through a fight.

"Sorry," he said. "I meant to get here earlier, but I got held up."

"We had a long night anyway," I said, shrugging. "No harm, no foul."

"We've got a problem," he said, turning to look at all four of us.

"Seems that's about all we have," Elder Morgan said. "Tell us, August, what new joy do you have to share with us?"

"Raymond wants a meeting. Now." He turned his gaze to me. "He wants to speak with you."

"Me?" I asked, raising an eyebrow. "That's surprising."

"He says you represent the tribe now. So, he wants to talk to you."

"Wyatt doesn't speak for the Cherokee," Elder Morgan said. "It should be one of the elders to meet with him."

August shook his head. "No, I already told him that. He said he wants to meet with the Blade Mage. Alone."

"Well, that doesn't sound like a trap," I said.

Axel shrugged. "It sounds so much like a trap that it might not be."

"A fair point," I replied. "What do you think, August?"

"I honestly do not know," he replied. "All I can tell you is that he's pissed. Real pissed."

I turned to Elder Morgan. "It's your call, but I don't know that we have much of a choice."

The elder nodded. "We'd already discussed this idea, anyway. Perhaps there's a chance you can talk him from the path of violence. At the very least, maybe you can find out why he's after our missing kids."

"Right," I said, nodding. "Did he say where he wants me to meet him?"

"At the bar."

"The bar?"

"The only one in town. I might've mentioned it. It's attached to the school you stayed at your first night."

"And he wants to meet now?"

"Right now," August said, glancing down at his watch. "I'm due to call him with an answer in less than five minutes."

"Okay, set it up," I said, turning my attention back to Elder Morgan. "I won't make any promises on behalf of your tribe. If he has some kind of demand for peace, I'll act as nothing more than a messenger. You have my word."

Elder Morgan smiled. "And you have my word that you won't actually be alone. Not completely."

"Are you sure that's smart?" August asked. "If he even gets a hint you have anyone nearby, it won't be good."

Elder Morgan's grin transitioned into something dangerous. "August Bones, we are Cherokee. No one knows of our presence unless we choose for them to."

# CHAPTER FORTY-SIX

The bar was a shit-hole.

I mean, I've been in some dingy shit-hole bars before, and have adored many, but this... This was on another level.

It was the cafeteria of the old school, and other than hanging some posters of super models and a few faded beer signs, not much else looked different. There was a pool table with a giant tear in the felt and some warped cues. I suspected if I actually went and checked, there wouldn't have been a full set of balls.

The original cafeteria had had giant windows to let the kids see some daylight, but these had mostly been boarded over. Except for a few peeping glares, the place was mostly dark. What little light there was consisted of a few lamps placed about and a construction light behind the bar.

The bar, as it was, was the same bar where children used to pick up their trays from the lunch ladies. There were no lunch ladies now, just an aging fella with an eyepatch and a long beard.

A pit bull was curled up on a gross towel by the door. It opened one eye and gave me a half-hearted growl as I passed.

The only patrons were Raymond and a gaggle of his gang members. I guess he'd felt he hadn't needed to come alone.

That was okay because Axel and August were just outside, and all I had to do was use mind-speak if I got in trouble. At least, that was the plan. There was still the possibility they could kill me silently and my allies would never know, though I was trying awfully hard not to think about that.

And somewhere nearby, the Cherokee were keeping a lookout.

I moved directly toward Raymond and his gang, doing my best to look unafraid and uninterested.

Those who were seated, save Raymond, jumped to their feet the moment I walked in. All of them started toward me, forming a circle around me.

Three particularly big fellas moved in front of me, as if to block my path.

The one in the center had a teardrop tattoo above one eye and a prison-quality neck tattoo, which was indiscernible as anything beyond a black smudge. His head was shaved, but he had a long beard hanging down to his chest. He was shirtless beneath his motorcycle vest, and it was hard to tell where his beard ended and his chest hair began.

He was mean-mugging me, as the kids would say, with his chest puffed out and one hand near his crotch where a stainless-steel revolver was tucked.

I wasn't in the mood and it's always a good idea to make the right impression.

"Get the fuck out of my way."

He didn't reply, but rolled his shoulders and moved his hand a little closer to his gun.

I grinned. "My money says you'll shoot yourself in the dick if you try to draw that thing. Now, move along. The grown-ups need to talk."

"Boys," Raymond said from where he still sat at one of the cafeteria tables. "Give the Blade Mage and me some space."

The big dude made a little tough-guy snorty sound, then moved aside. The lot of them cleared out and moved to the other side of the cafeteria.

Yeah, I decided I was just going to refer to it as a cafeteria rather than a bar. I had a friend who, under the influence of alcohol, had said something about putting a dress on a donkey and making it look nice. I think what he'd meant to say was that if you put a dress on a donkey, it was still a donkey. At least, that's what I hoped. Point was, this wasn't a bar. It was a cafeteria.

I took a seat opposite the Freddy Krueger-looking leader of the Red Dirt Riders.

"Howdy, Raymond," I said. "Nice day, isn't it?"

"It's never a nice day when I have to bury my people."

"I suppose not. Perhaps you should tell your people not to be so quick on the trigger."

"Is that how you're going to tell me it went down?" he asked, smiling. "Not what my boys tell me."

"I don't really care," I said, shrugging. "You asked for this meeting. What did you want to talk to me about?"

Raymond stared at me for a few moments before he finally said, "I'm in a difficult position, Blade Mage. A lot of my people were killed yesterday, and my club demands blood, which I'm inclined to give them. But whose blood should it be? Should I have you killed? Those snot-nosed Indian kids? Or should I have the Cherokee's whole training grounds razed to ash and the lot of them butchered?"

"Why were you after the kids to begin with?" I asked.

He was silent for a few moments, then finally said, "When I heard they had abandoned their tribe, I thought I could make use of them. Get them to join my club. Thought it would be useful to have some little Indian mages on my crew. I had an idea where to find them, and I sent some of the boys to talk to them. Those damned kids attacked on sight, and one of my crew ended up dead."

"And you're still hunting them?" I asked.

He shrugged. "I couldn't allow it to go unanswered. The kids have to be punished. Though, until yesterday, I hadn't planned on killing them. I thought I could rough them up a bit, and still maybe recruit a few of them. Now, though... They have to die."

Ignoring his earlier comment about me, I asked, "And you think to punish the rest of the tribe as well?"

He chuckled. "Not all. There're far too many Cherokee here in Cherokee County to punish them all."

"The medicine men," I said, not hiding my annoyance. "You know

I'm referring to the medicine men and the trainees here in Lost City. Not the tribe as a whole, or every Norman walking around with Cherokee blood in their veins."

"Sure, fair enough. My men expect blood, Blade Mage. And those bastards are the ones who trained the whelps and couldn't keep them under control. Give me one good reason I shouldn't make them all suffer."

"I can give you several," I replied. It was my turn to shrug. "First, don't think for a second the Cherokee are weak. If you declare war on the tribe, it won't go the way you think. From what I've seen, you've done all right for yourself and your club. They've mostly let you be. Do you really want to risk screwing that up?"

"You think I should fear them?" He laughed. "The Red Dirt Riders aren't weak, either. Make no mistake."

"Fine. Let's assume you're right and your little gang is strong enough to take on the Cherokee. Then what happens? Do you think you'll run this area unmolested? No. The moment the Cherokee can no longer maintain law and order in their territory, the Cabal will sweep in. Do you really want to try the might of the Red Dirt Riders against the full weight of the Ozark Mountain Cabal?"

"The way I hear it, the Cabal ain't as strong as it used to be," he said, though I caught a trace of doubt in his words.

"Not as strong as it used to be?" I asked. "What does that mean, huh? There are fewer mages roaming about? The Cabal still has thousands. Hell, its non-magic military outnumbers you. And don't underestimate the Cherokee. They seek peace, but they aren't weak. The best scenario for your gang is to maintain the status quo. If I were to guess, the Cherokee have never come down hard on you because you've never given them a reason to. Don't be cocky and think you'll bulldoze them over, because I suspect it won't play out the way you think."

"Perhaps."

"Secondly, they aren't to blame for the mistakes of their runaways. And for fuck's sake, they're teenagers. Teenagers do dumb shit. If you were as smart as you'd like everyone to think, you'd be trying to help the tribe bring their kids home safely. That protects your status quo and gives you a better relationship with the tribe who, again, have pretty much left you alone."

"There's wisdom in your words," he said, flashing me a wolfish smile. "And perhaps you are right, but it's too late for that now, isn't it? I have dead bodies under my banner, and the only recompense is blood."

"Then why are you talking to me? If you have no interest in peace, why did you ask for this meeting?"

"Because I *do* want peace with the tribe," he said, pausing to pull a cigarette out and light it. "But my men need to see vengeance done for their lost brethren. This you must understand?"

I didn't reply.

He waited and took a long drag on his smoke, then said, "So, here's the deal. I'm going after the kids, and I want the tribe to stay out of my way. They let us do what needs done, and I won't destroy them. They just have to stay out of the way."

"And you think they'll agree to that? You think they'll step aside while you hunt down and murder their missing children?"

"Not just them, Blade Mage," he said, smiling his devil's grin again. "You as well. From all reports, you were standing alone when my men approached. Which means that weird little pal of yours was the shooter."

Again, I didn't reply. If he thought Axel was the shooter, that meant he didn't know about Shain Stone. That could work to our advantage somehow. And Axel wouldn't be disappointed for the Riders to think he was some kind of badass sniper.

Raymond continued, "Not all of the boys have pieced that together, but they all know you were there, and they all want your head as well. Still, if you agree to stay out of our way, I can manage them away from demanding your life."

It was my turn to smile.

"And you think I'll stand aside and let you kill a bunch of teenagers?"

"Never said I was going to kill *all* of them. I just want to see little Waya humbled, and yeah, I'll probably take his head. His little girl-friend Pathkiller, though? I think she's going to be a cute little piece of ass in a few years, so I think I'll keep her as a toy to remind the tribe what happens when you fuck with my club. The rest will join us."

I tried to keep my emotions in check, but I could tell by the spreading smile on his scarred cheeks that he could read my thoughts. It was all I could do not to take out Dyrnwyn and claim his head right on the spot.

He continued, "Think about it, Blade Mage. You'll sacrifice a couple of lives to save countless more. This is the best-case scenario for everyone."

I was silent for a moment, considering my words. Finally, I asked, "When you asked for this meeting, did you ever really think I would agree?"

"I was hopeful," he said with a shrug. "It really is the best solution for all parties."

"And you think the elders will agree?"

"If they know what's best for them."

"Then you really aren't as smart as everyone seems to think you are."

He laughed. "Maybe not, but then, while you're here talking to me, you ain't where the kids are. And you know what? My boys are."

I felt myself blink a few times.

*Shit.*

They had a line on the kids again, and he'd figured if they did, then so did I, and he'd called the meeting to keep me away.

He confirmed it by saying, "The Mickey Mouse club is in trouble, and their little protector isn't there to protect them."

I tried to keep my voice neutral. "Maybe. But then, you told me to come alone, didn't you?"

"I already know your weird little friend and that interloper Bones are both outside."

"And were you wise enough to bring more than ten to protect yourself from me?" I asked, feeling my voice drop into a snarl.

"Oh, yes," he replied. "I was hoping we could come to some kind of arrangement, but I can see you won't. So, perhaps it's best if you don't walk out of here."

"And are you sure you can stop me?"

He shrugged. "Either way, those snot-nosed little fucks are alone out there, and my riders are bearing down on them."

Before I could reply, another voice said, "No, they aren't, Raymond."

I turned and saw Fatima standing a few feet behind me. She'd traded her jeans and t-shirt for combat garb and held a gnarled oak staff in her hand.

"The fuck are you doing here?" Raymond asked.

Fatima smiled at him. "I just wanted to stop by and let you know your boys are currently searching a vacant barn. The runaways aren't there and they never were."

A silence hung between the three of us.

Fatima ended it. "Whatever you're planning here, you probably don't want to try it. I have no great love for the Cabal or its Blade Mage, but if you try to take him out right now, you'll have me and mine to face as well."

"What is any of this to you?" he asked, his frustrations clear.

"None of your concern," she said. "If you're wise, you'll get up and walk away. And you'll leave those missing kids be."

"Is that a threat?"

"No, it's a warning," she said. "There's something bigger at work here, and I suspect it's over your head. Best you keep your gang out of it."

"Club," he replied. "And don't forget who you're talking to."

"It's just us here, Ray," she said. "No need to act tough. Trust me, whatever is going on in Lost City right now, your boys and their little guns won't keep you safe. Best you stay out of the way."

"We'll see," he replied.

Fatima shrugged. "It's neither here nor there to me. I was just providing a friendly warning. Now, run along. I want to speak to the Blade Mage."

Raymond scowled at her. And for a moment, I thought he might choose violence. Instead, he rose slowly to his feet and started toward the door. He paused once and turned back to her. "I won't forget this, Fatima."

"You won't forget that I just saved your gang on two different fronts?" she asked, nodding. "Cool. I like the idea of you owing me a favor."

Confusion played out across Raymond's disfigured features, then he turned and walked out the door.

Fatima sat down in his spot across from me.

"Uh, hello, again," I said. "Thanks for jumping in, I think."

"He was planning to have you and your friends ambushed."

"I suspected as much."

"And yet you walked right into the trap."

"Yeah, I've got a bad habit of that," I said. "What did you mean about his gang searching a vacant barn?"

She stared at me for a few seconds, then said, "After we spoke, I got to thinking about what you said. There is little known about Cherokee magic, but I do know their tracking spells are second to none. There's no way those kids could be developed enough to block the tracking spells of their elders."

"Right."

"So, that means someone very powerful is trying to keep them hidden."

"I agree, which is why I came to talk to you."

"Yes, and whether you believed me or not, I know that I'm not the one hiding the kids. Frankly, I don't think any of my group would be powerful enough to block the elders' spells, either. Then I heard about what happened yesterday."

"Word travels fast around here."

"That it does. But I was curious how Raymond could've found out where the kids were. Best I can guess, one of the kids strayed from the group and the elders pinged their location immediately. And that's how you found them. Right?"

I thought to not reply, but finally nodded.

"But how did Raymond?" she continued.

"I've been wondering that myself."

"He must have a mage," she replied. "At least one with a reasonable tracking spell. So, after your encounter, a contingent of Cherokee and our dearest Cabal constables went out to clean up the mess and set a narrative with local Norman law enforcement. Once they'd cleared out, we went to snoop around."

"And did you find anything?"

"Just an action figure lying in the dirt."

"It wasn't a Boba Fett, was it?"

"What? No, it was the Incredible Hulk."

"Whew," I said, shaking my head. "Poor Ben."

"What?" she asked again.

"Never mind," I replied. "You were saying?"

"So, the Incredible Hulk had a hint of one of the kids' essence. Just a short time ago, we dropped the toy off at a barn and amplified that essence. Just enough that I didn't think the Cherokee would ping it from up on their hill, but anyone directly around Lost City would. Or Raymond and his gang."

"Like a beacon," I said. "Brilliant."

"We wanted to see who would come running."

"And?"

"So far, just Raymond and his gang."

"Which means they definitely have a mage or mages on their team."

"Right," she said. "But Raymond is small potatoes. Whoever is hiding your kids, Blade Mage, that's who you should fear."

"You think?"

She nodded slowly and met my gaze. "I think you're right. I think something bigger and darker is going on here. I think someone or something is manipulating those teenagers and is hiding them."

"We just have to figure out who or what," I said, mostly to myself.

Fatima shook her head and rose. "No, this is all the help you'll get from me, Blade Mage. Don't let Raymond get the jump on you again. Next time, me and mine won't be around. And whatever other powers are at work here, we want nothing to do with it."

"I understand," I replied. "And thank you."

"Don't mention it," she replied. "I wouldn't want anyone to get an idea that we were helping you. And I certainly don't want to get caught up in any drama."

"Do you think Raymond will let your insult slide?"

"We'll see. Raymond isn't a complete idiot. He knows his gang is no match for us, even if they do have some two-bit hedge mage.

Whatever is going on here, Raymond's wrath is the least of my concerns."

With that, she turned and walked away.

I sat a moment longer, trying to wrap my head around everything I'd just learned.

After a few moments, I got up and headed toward the door. The pit bull raised its head to growl at me once more on my way out.

# CHAPTER FORTY-SEVEN

O ur trip back to the training grounds was uneventful. Whether any of the Cherokee were indeed in close proximity during my meeting with Raymond, I never knew.

Back at the training grounds, we met briefly with Elder Morgan and I described what had occurred.

After that, we were left somewhat stumped. Elder Morgan had business to attend to, so Axel, August, and I hung out in the little cabin and debated what all of it meant and what our next steps should be.

Problem was, we didn't have any clever ideas.

At one point, Axel had brought up the idea of simply storming the Red Dirt Riders' hideout and putting an end to that particular problem. It was a surprisingly brutal idea for him to come up with, yet it didn't completely lack merit. We all knew they were going to be trouble. We all also agreed that if he had a mage of any real talent, we wouldn't have avoided a fight during either encounter.

But Raymond wasn't our real problem.

Waya and his Wolf Pack were. And we did not know where to look for them. Which meant that little Ben was still without his Incredible Hulk action figure, and that made me sad. At least he still had Boba Fett.

We had nothing.

No plan. No actions. Nothing.

Axel's next best idea was to just start going door to door. Which sounded absurd, but he made a good point... It was a rural area, and there weren't that many houses. Of course, most of them were owned by Normans. So knocking on random doors and asking people if they'd seen any magically-trained teens roaming about probably wasn't the best idea in the world.

As we sat debating our options, I glanced over at August Bones, who looked in desperate need of a nap.

"You all right, August?" I asked.

He nodded. "I'm good."

"You don't look good," I said. "You always look tired."

"I don't sleep much."

I sighed. Whatever his story was, he wasn't interested in sharing it. I tried a different tactic.

"You're awfully dedicated to helping the tribe," I said.

He shrugged. "Compared to the two strangers who showed up and are helping despite having their lives threatened multiple times?"

"True, but this isn't really your fight, either. Why are you so keen to help them?"

"It's like I said. The tribe was always good to me."

"Do you guys smell that?" Axel asked, lifting his head and glancing around the room. "Something smells like bullshit."

August glared at him.

Axel smiled in return. "Oh, come on now, Bones. Why do you keep avoiding Wyatt's questions? It's obvious there's something more here. I mean, by your own words, we've risked our lives to come aid your cause, and you can't even say why it matters to you."

The former constable looked between the two of us, then rubbed a hand across his tired face. "Look... You're right, okay? I don't like to talk about it."

"If it's that big of a deal, you don't have to tell us," I said, shrugging.

"Agreed," Axel said. "But just know that we won't trust you, is all."

"Fine," August said. "A long time ago... Well, let's just say that Elder Morgan's daughter and I were friends, okay?"

"Close?" I asked.

"Like, *really* close?" Axel asked.

"Yeah," he said. "She was my best friend, and...more."

"Alyita's mother?" I asked.

He nodded.

"Okay," I said, glancing at Axel, who only shrugged. "So, what happened?"

"She died," August said. "A long time ago. It doesn't matter now. Just... I think she would've wanted me to help the tribe. To watch out for her daughter and her old man."

He looked away.

"All right, August," I said. "Thank you. That makes sense. We won't pry further."

"Thanks," he said. "Now, what the hell are we going to do next?"

And then, as happens on occasion, our next step came to us.

It was late afternoon when Elder Morgan approached the cabin with news.

"Salal has reached out," he said.

"Waya?" I asked, trying to keep the names straight in my head.

"Yes, that is what he prefers to be called. He will always be Salal to me. Just as I will never refer to my Alyita as Pathkiller."

"I'm sure you don't need to take advice from me," I said, shrugging. "But maybe humor the kids for now. No reason to widen the gap between you and them."

Elder Morgan sighed. "Yes, I know. Fortunately, it didn't come up."

"What did come up?"

"He wants you to meet him," Elder Morgan said with another sigh. "Alone."

"Yay!" Axel said, clapping his hands. "Another trap!"

"And the closest thing we have to a chance," August replied. "It's something."

It was my turn to sigh. "When?"

"Dusk," Elder Morgan said. "He said he would call back within the hour to hear whether you agree and to provide a location."

"He didn't say anything else?" I asked.

Elder Morgan shook his head. "No, he refused to speak of anything else. Only that he wanted you to meet with him."

"I guess I don't have much of a choice," I replied. "What does the rest of the tribe say? If I've learned anything in my short time here, it's that I'm sure you've already discussed it as a group."

"Ahuli and some of his followers think we should agree to the meeting and attempt to capture the teens. By force, if necessary. Others, myself included, think we should give you this chance. to talk some sense into them. It is why you're here, isn't it? We hope that a voice outside the tribe might be able to talk some sense into them."

August jumped in. "And you wouldn't be here speaking to us about it if they'd voted against you."

"Correct," Elder Morgan agreed. "Though I fear the tribe's patience for outsider involvement is dwindling. Ahuli would see you gone and sent back to your Cabal. So we must make the most of this, Blade Mage."

"I understand," I said. "And I guess this time it would be too great a risk to have your people hiding nearby."

Elder Morgan rubbed his chin. "We have struggled with this question. And though we could have our people get close without Alyita, Salal, or any of the others detecting us, if they did, I suspect it would be bad. Same goes for August and Axel."

"So, this time I'm truly on my own?"

"Yes," Elder Morgan confirmed with a nod.

"Well, hell," I replied. "Set it up."

# CHAPTER FORTY-EIGHT

F inally, someone invited me to an ambush some place nice.

The spot was out in the middle of nowhere and Elder Morgan had dropped me off himself, then gave me directions through the forest to find my destination.

I wasn't convinced I would find the place, but as I walked along through the woodlands, I saw there was indeed a trail, just as he'd described.

The location of our meeting was a spring-fed pond out in the middle of the forest. It was a place where many among the tribe would take their children and grandchildren to fish. Elder Morgan and his Alyita were no exception.

I followed the trail until I came out into a glade and indeed found a large pond hidden amidst a sea of trees.

It was beautiful.

The water was a dark blue and clear, a sharp contrast to the greenery surrounding it. The sky above was cloudless and painted in the bickering hues of blue and orange.

There were no signs of the teens yet, though I suspected they lay in hiding nearby.

I moved out along the bank and stared at my reflection on the water's surface.

After a time, I heard footfalls and saw Waya approaching me, a spear in one hand and a hatchet in the other.

"You came alone?" he asked.

"I suspect you already know the answer to that."

He gave me a curt nod. "Pathkiller."

I heard footsteps behind me and turned to find Elder Morgan's granddaughter approaching. She was also armed with a tomahawk and knife.

"He is alone," she said.

"Good," Waya said, grinning like a wolf.

There was something about the look on his face I didn't like. "Why did you ask me here?"

"Why do you think?" Waya said.

All around me, I sensed the other kids moving closer.

"I don't know," I replied, shrugging. "I'd hoped perhaps you'd seen wisdom in what we discussed yesterday. I guess I was optimistic that perhaps you sought my help."

Waya laughed.

"Waya," Pathkiller said. "We shouldn't waste time."

"There's no rush," he replied to her, then turned his evil little shit-head gaze back to me. "Why would my pack need your aid, outsider?"

I shrugged. "Why else summon me?"

"You still don't get it, do you?"

"Apparently not. I was never the smartest kid in school. Why don't you explain it to me?"

"Waya," Pathkiller said again, this time with an edge of concern.

Waya ignored her and kept his focus on me. "We've summoned you here to die, Blade Mage."

"Is that so?" I asked, my guts turning. It wasn't that I feared these kids, but more that I feared what defending myself meant. If they intended to attack me, my own defenses would likely hurt them. I was an asshole, but I wasn't the kind of asshole who hurt misguided kids. I still hoped for a peaceful resolution.

"It is so," Waya said. "Who do you think it was that tried to kill you on your first night in Lost City?"

"That was you?"

"Yes," Waya said.

"May I ask why?"

"No, Waya," Pathkiller said again, nearly in a panic. "Let's do it. He should know nothing."

"I do not fear him," Waya said, puffing his chest a little. His gaze never left mine. "Our new benefactor decreed it. Said it was how our pack would prove itself."

"Then your new benefactor must not be too happy. You've had two opportunities and have failed both times."

Waya snarled, showing his teeth. "This time we will succeed."

"You should listen to your girlfriend," I said, shaking my head. "You may be the alpha, but I fear she is the wiser of the two of you. If I'm reading this correctly, her preference would've been for you to just kill me outright. Had you done that, you would've succeeded already."

"That is not the warrior's way," Waya said, shaking his head. "It is better that you know and can defend yourself."

"Tell me more about this benefactor of yours. Who is it? And why are they supporting you? Why would you kill for them?"

"No," Pathkiller said from behind me. "That is not for you to know."

"What difference if you're planning to kill me anyway?"

Waya hesitated, then said, "You're playing word games with us, Blade Mage. But no, you're right. My Pathkiller is wise beyond her years. Prepare to defend yourself."

I stared at the kid, then pulled my sword and staff from my back.

My staff, I tossed into the weeds. My sword, I stabbed into the ground in front of me.

Then I dropped to my knees.

"What are you doing?" Waya asked.

"I won't fight you," I said, shaking my head.

"Get up!" Waya hissed. "Face me like a man!"

"But you aren't one," I said, glancing up at him. "You aren't a man,

Salal. You're a boy. Want to know how I know? Because you're acting like one. Acting like a pissy little child. You're no man. No leader."

Rage contorted his features, but he didn't move. "I have killed before. I do not fear battle."

I shrugged. "But will you kill an unarmed man? Is that who you are?"

I heard footsteps behind me and suspected Pathkiller was closing the distance between us.

"No," Waya said, looking past me. "He must face us."

"He refuses," Pathkiller said. "He must die either way."

Waya hesitated again. This clearly wasn't going the way he'd planned.

"And you'll do it, Alyita?" I asked, not turning to face her. "Are you so cold of heart that you'll bash my head in from behind?"

"And I'll take your scalp as a trophy," she said, though her words seemed to force conviction.

"Then get on with it," I replied, my eyes locked with Waya's. "I will not fight you. You will have to murder me. You will find no glory in this."

"Stand!" Waya screamed. "Stand and fight!"

Spittle flew from his mouth and frothed around his lips.

What the hell was wrong with him?

There was more here... Something wasn't right with Waya. He wasn't...stable.

"No," I replied. "You want to be killers, then be killers."

"Waya, we must," Pathkiller said, her voice on edge. "We have no choice."

"He must stand," Waya said. "He must die as a warrior!"

"I won't," I replied, my eyes on the ground once more.

*Holy shit.*

I was serious, I realized.

*Holy smoking shit balls.*

I was going to let these kids murder me.

*Holy smoking Bahama mama shit balls.*

What else could I do?

I tried not to think about it and focused on my breath. I needed to clear my mind before I slid into a panic.

This was it.

I was going to die.

*Holy smoking Bahama mama steaming gourmet shit balls.*

I felt myself relax.

My mind cleared. Their shouts became nothing but background noise as I fell deeper into myself.

This was going to happen.

They were going to kill me, and I was going to let them.

Somehow, the moment I accepted it, a calmness swept over me.

I vaguely heard footsteps running toward me. And I heard Pathkiller's voice as she screamed, and behind me I could almost see her raising the tomahawk, intent on burying it in my skull.

*Crack.*

A gunshot.

I spun, seeing Pathkiller tumble to the ground beside me. Her weapons had fallen from her hands and she was holding her side, though I couldn't see any blood.

I turned back toward Waya, who screamed and charged toward me, spear raised.

*Thump.*

A canister hit the ground between us and a cloud of gas began to spread.

I was pretty sure I'd seen this play out once before, and I had little doubt what the gas was.

It formed up in front of me and I rose to move out of its way.

Sure, I'd been prepared to be murdered, but I wasn't prepared to suffer unnecessarily.

Tear gas equaled very little fun.

I moved to the side and crashed right into Pathkiller. We both went down, rolling over the side of the pond's embankment.

Coming to a stop, I sat up just in time for a thrown spear to bury itself in the ground right between my legs. I took a moment to thank the Maker I wasn't more well-endowed or I might've lost a part of myself.

I spotted the thrower and realized I'd almost been neutered by a ten-year-old.

Dangerous little fella.

Conveniently, my staff was lying just beside me then, from when I'd tossed it down before. I grabbed it.

Then Pathkiller leaped at me with her tomahawk aimed for my skull and I rolled further down the hill to avoid her attack.

Kids these days.

And yes, the irony that I'd been ready to give up my life a few moments prior was not lost on me. But what had changed?

Stone had shown up.

That changed things.

I'm not sure I understood how exactly, but it did. If nothing else, I needed to find out why he was hunting these kids, and I couldn't help but to feel I needed to protect them from him. Though a part of me argued that Stone wouldn't really hurt a kid.

More importantly, I wanted the answer to a question. What did Stone know that I didn't?

I couldn't very well have that answered if I had a tomahawk embedded in my skull.

So, as Pathkiller leaped at me again, I force pushed her back up the hill, then rose to my feet, summoning my shield to full strength. Which was just at the right time, because an arrow bounced off of it immediately.

At least the playing field was a bit more even, then. A random arrow or spear wasn't going to do me in, nor sever my nethers. Which meant I had a moment to think.

Stone had to be my focus.

I needed to stop his assault before one of these kids got hurt and then figure out what the hell was going on.

Turning my attention to Pathkiller, who was crouched up the hill like a mountain lion ready to strike, I said, "Get your pack out of here! I'll deal with the shooter!"

Based on how that idea had gone last time, I didn't even bother to wait on a reply. Instead, I turned and trotted up the hill in the direction Stone had fired from.

Back at the top of the bank, I recovered my sword, then raced toward the tree line where I thought he'd fired from. I searched for any sign of movement in the trees.

That focus nearly cost me my life.

I was just in the middle of my sprint when a nearby tree took a swipe at my head.

Yeah, a tree.

A *tree* tried to punch off my face.

I saw the limb aimed for my head and stumbled to the side, narrowly avoiding having my brain turned to syrup. Pun intended.

Then the whole fat branch, with all its many smaller branches, opened like a hand. I was so surprised by this turn of events that I stared at it like a moron while the tree hand wrapped its grip around me. As though I were one of Ben's action figures, it scooped me right off the ground and left my feet dangling while it tightened its grip.

Stuck, I wondered how it would crush me to death. Slow and crunchy until it squeezed out all my goo? Or would it just pop me like a zit?

I couldn't wait to find out.

Fortunately, it hadn't secured my arms, so I swung Dyrnwyn through the main branch, severing its grip.

I fell to the ground and the tree reeled back as though I'd hurt it. It was more likely the magical wielder had simply relinquished their control and the tree was snapping back to its former position.

Still, I couldn't help feeling bad, as though the tree were sentient and I'd just hacked its arm off. I chalked these thoughts up to my adrenaline and reminded myself the tree had started it.

I turned my focus back to finding Stone, but I still didn't see any sign of him. I continued running that direction anyway, at least until the pond punched me.

Yeah, the pond punched me!

I didn't know what I'd done to piss off Mother Nature, but she was clearly not on my side.

I saw the movement out of the corner of my eye, but before I could react, a fist-shaped fountain of water punched me like the Incredible Hulk.

My shield took most of the impact, but still it was enough to throw me off balance.

I could only assume it was the pack who were summoning these murderous earth spells, which meant they were more powerful than I ever could've guessed.

A bunch of angsty teenagers who were already powerful enough to convince the Earth to murder me.

Here I was, the Blade Mage, and I could do little more than force push people around like a Jedi youngling. No wonder the tribe wanted to get them back to the safety of their training grounds.

It was also why they were so damned arrogant about taking care of themselves.

Wet now, and a little disoriented, I looked up and saw the faintest hint of movement in the trees ahead.

Stone.

I forced my feet forward again, but not at a run. I didn't want to get that close. I'd learned from my past two encounters with my father's old enforcer. My chances were better if I could keep my distance and lean on my magic, rather than get in his striking range.

On the other hand, I wanted to ensure I kept a safe distance between him and the pack.

And then the birds attacked.

At first, I noticed little more than a lot of cawing in the background, but with all the excitement, I paid little heed to the growing birdsong.

It quickly became too much to not be noticeable.

After being attacked by a tree and a pond, I suppose it shouldn't have been a surprise when a crow swooped in low and tried to peck out my eyes.

I waved my staff in front of my face, shooing the thing away.

The first backed off, but another immediately took its place.

In moments, a great swarm of birds was on me, pecking at my head and neck.

I swung my staff around my own skull with reckless abandon, trying to scare the creatures away.

And smacked myself right between the eyes.

Next came a searing pain in the back of my head as some feathered beast latched on to the back of my noggin with its talons. Then it began pecking at the top of my head, tearing through hair and flesh.

I was nearly at the point of using Dyrnwyn to save myself, but that would've meant killing the poor creatures. It wasn't their fault they'd been magically convinced to attack me. Or it was, and I was just the unluckiest person in the world. I figured it was much more likely a magical attack, though.

A new idea occurred to me. I began firing little force push spells from the tip of my staff like shotgun blasts. This proved somewhat effective, as the bird perched atop my head was ripped right off, taking bits of my flesh with it.

Blood ran down my eyes, clouding my vision. I just kept launching minor spell after minor spell, and thinking that if I survived, I'd have to work out how to block birds from slipping through my magical shield.

First was survival, though, and I knew I couldn't keep up my little force blasts forever. So far as I could tell, it wasn't hurting my feathered friends, so I counted that a minor win.

The birds were circling around me in a black mass, more than I could ever hope to count, and in all different shapes, sizes, and varieties. There were crows, and falcons, and even littler birds like robins and blue jays. All had come to the call.

I spun in a circle, trying to spot the caster.

And then I did.

A short distance away, I saw Pathkiller standing with her arms outstretched, and her eyes rolled back into her head.

It was her.

I didn't know how. I knew nothing about the magic she was using, but somehow, she was the one who was targeting the birds on me.

*Damn,* she was strong.

I mean, the strain on her face was evident, but still, I couldn't have done it. I couldn't even imagine the amount of power it would take to pull something like this off. And she was little more than a kid.

If she'd been another mage, like, say, the gray-robed mages in Memphis, I could've just thrown my sword at her. I could've pierced her right through the heart and ended this madness.

But I couldn't. Not this time.

I turned again and saw Stone just ahead. At least, I assumed it was him based on the ghillie suit. He was also being set upon by the ever-growing flock.

Forgetting Pathkiller, I started moving closer to him. My thought was that maybe I could use my little force pushes to protect both of us until we came up with a better idea.

Stone already had a better idea.

I saw him toss what appeared to be a grenade on the ground between us and had a moment of panic because I knew I wouldn't be able to block the explosive power just then.

Instead, a white fog ascended from the canister, filling the air around me.

I almost panicked again, thinking it was more tear gas. That would not end well for me, either. I imagined myself on the ground choking while a flock of birds pecked out my eyes. Of course, the tear gas probably would've affected the birds, but I wasn't bright enough to consider that in my panicked state.

It wasn't tear gas, though.

It was a smoke grenade. And even as it made me cough, the birds backed off. They didn't care for the white fog. Whatever control Pathkiller held over them, it wasn't enough to break their own survival instinct.

I turned back toward her, barely able to see through the growing cloud. I could just make out her form a few feet away.

She realized she'd lost her hold and gave up, then collapsed to the ground.

I started that direction, still hacking and coughing, stumbling and bleeding.

Another figure, presumably Waya, appeared over her and began lifting her from the ground.

Then I lost sight of them in the cloud and tried to force my legs further forward, knowing if I didn't get clean oxygen soon, I might pass out.

A great weight hit me and I felt myself lifted off the ground.

In a rush of movement, I was out of the smoke cloud and tumbling down the side of the hill. A ghillie suited monster was on top of me.

I tried to fight, but I was still short of breath and seeing stars among the treetops.

I forced myself up to my knees, but a booted foot put me back on the ground.

"I'm getting real sick of you getting in my way, kid," Stone's voice said.

"Ditto," I managed through a ragged cough.

Then I tried to raise my staff, but Stone yanked it from my hand. Remembering how this had gone last time and not wanting to repeat the loss of dignity when he beat me over the head with my own magical instrument, I tried to tackle him.

That was dumb.

I ended up on the ground again, not sure what had even happened.

"Would you stop?" he asked.

"You first," I replied, forcing myself upward again. "I won't let you hurt these kids."

His foot slammed into my chest, knocking me down again.

I heard him let out a sigh as I tried to rise again.

"Goddamn, you're a stubborn pain in my ass," he replied.

I was just about to reply with something incredibly witty, but instead, the lights went out.

# CHAPTER FORTY-NINE

"There he is," Axel's voice said. "There's my little guy."

I groaned.

"Wakey, wakey," Axel said. "Or else I'm going to pour cold water on your face."

I forced my eyes open. My vision was blurred, but I could make out Axel's face just above me. As promised, he was holding a glass of water.

He dumped it on my face anyway.

I sat up spluttering, but immediately forgot about the water as an unholy pain seared through my head. It felt like my skull had been tossed in a vat of hot bacon grease.

"Easy there," Axel said, putting an arm around my shoulder. "Your head has been chewed up a bit. If it were any worse, you'd look like our pal Raymond."

"Axel," I said with a parched throat.

"Yes, Wyatt?"

"I'm going to kill you."

"Hey, I just didn't want you to miss all the excitement."

"Excitement?" I asked, then I remembered. "Where's Stone?"

"He's here," Axel replied. "And a little annoyed with you."

"The feeling is mutual." I glanced around and realized we were in our cabin.

"That's hardly fair," Axel replied. "He did bring you back here."

"He's the one who knocked me out."

"And he's the one who patched you up and brought you home. So, it kind of balances out, doesn't it?"

I swung my legs over the side of the bed and saw I was still dressed. That was good, because I wasn't sure I could manage putting clothes on. Every movement made my head hurt worse. What I wasn't sure about was whether it was a concussion from being knocked out or just the torn flesh all over the top of my skull. I assumed it was a bit of both.

"You might want these," Axel said, holding up a bottle of Tylenol.

I took the bottle from him and asked, "Do you have any water?"

"Well, that's what the glass was for, but, no, I guess I don't now."

A few minutes later, I had choked down a couple of Tylenol and forced myself back on my feet.

Outside, I found Stone sitting in the back of a big utility van. He was in the process of cleaning an AR-10 and around him sat piles of guns, ammo, and grenades.

He offered a nod as I approached.

"Stone," I said, watching him reassemble the weapon with expert hands.

After he was done putting it back together, he checked it over and began loading magazines.

"What the hell is going on here?" I asked.

"No one's told you?" he asked.

I shook my head.

"We're about to go hunting," he replied, as if that were answer enough.

I turned to Axel, who was standing just beside me.

"Can someone bring me up to speed, please?" I asked, switching my gaze between the two of them.

Neither seemed concerned with answering.

"Stone, why are you here in Lost City?"

"Same as you," he replied, eyes still on his work. "Got a tip about dark magic. Came to have a look."

"I'm here because the tribe's teens ran off," I said. "I'm here because I'm trying to help them."

"Yeah?" he asked. "How's that working out?"

"Well, not too good, because every time I've had a chance to talk to them, some asshole in a ghillie suit showed up and started shooting everyone."

"You mean the asshole who's saved your sorry ass twice now? You ungrateful little prick," he replied, still not looking at me. "Don't worry, kid. Not looking for thanks."

"You could've tried talking to me," I said. "You were the one who opened fire on me first, remember?"

He shrugged. "First time, I thought it'd be easier to just get you out of my way, then talk to you after. Wasn't a lot of time to converse. The second time, I saved your ass and figured you'd get the hint. Clearly, you didn't."

"Clearly," I replied.

"Clearly," Axel added. "I think I can help. You see, Wyatt, Stone got a tip that the kids are tied to a dark mage. He was trying to protect them from the Red Dirt Riders, but also trying to capture one or more of them to see if he could find out where their evil overlord is hiding."

"And how's that going?" I asked.

"Not so good," Stone replied. "Some asshole in jeans and a t-shirt keeps getting in my way."

"Where'd you get this tip from?" I asked.

Stone didn't reply.

"Stone?" I said.

"Sorry, kid. Not in the mood to answer dumb questions."

"That's not a dumb question," I replied, then turned to Axel. "Is it?"

"Of course it is," Axel replied as though he were speaking to a child. "Why would Stone give up his sources to us?"

I blinked at him a few times, unsure how to respond.

Finally, Stone said, "Don't be an ass, Axel. You asked the same damned question."

"How were you tracking them?" I asked.

He didn't respond. Of course he wouldn't. Stone didn't give up his secrets.

"Right," I said. "Okay, fine. So, you had a tip about dark magic and that led you to the missing teens. So, your whole plan was to capture one of them and then hope they'd give up whoever they're actually working for?"

"Is this where you're going to explain how much better your plan was?" Stone asked. "Because your plan was just to let them kill you. Real winning strategy, Wyatt."

"Wyatt!" Axel said, putting his hands on his hips. "This is the first I'm hearing of this. Unacceptable."

"It was the best plan I had at the time," I replied. "The kids were sent to kill me. It wasn't like I could fight back and risk hurting them."

Stone and Axel both snorted.

"Well, it's not like I'm running around with little pepper spray bullets," I replied.

"Maybe you should be," Stone replied.

"Yeah," Axel said. "Maybe you should be."

"Fine, I'm the asshole here," I said. "What's the plan, now?"

"We're going hunting," Stone replied.

"We're going hunting," Axel echoed.

"What does that mean?" I asked.

"The teens are going after the Uktena," Stone said.

"The what?" I asked.

"That's the monster we were hunting the other night," Axel said. "Apparently, it's called an Uktena. I haven't Googled it yet."

"Well, I have," Stone said. "It's a giant horned serpent."

"Uh, what?" I asked. "A horned what?"

Ignoring my questions, Stone continued, "According to Cherokee lore, whoever kills the beast will be rewarded with great power."

"So, the kids are going after it," I said, glancing between the two of them. "But wait... I thought the tribe was afraid it was the monster who was influencing the kids."

Stone shrugged. "Don't know, but I'd guess that was wrong. If the beast is really out there, they want to find it and slay it."

"So they can be more powerful," I replied, rubbing my hands

against my face. "I feel like we've gotten this wrong every step of the way."

"We've just got to beat them to it," Stone said. "And be the ones to kill it."

"Do you know how to kill it?" I asked.

Stone shook his head.

"Damn," I said. "The tribe won't share that information with us."

"And they shouldn't," Axel said, glancing at me. "Stone and I already talked about this. Whatever this thing is, it's important to their lore. They really shouldn't be taking us along for the hunt. If they kill it, we can't watch what comes next. None but a Cherokee can see."

"But they're still inviting us to come along?" I asked.

Stone pointed at the pile of magazines and ammo around him. "You think I'm loading these for my health?"

"I figured loading magazines was therapeutic for you," I replied. "Like masturbating."

He paused, then shrugged. "You're not wrong."

"The elders have agreed to let you join in the hunt, too? They barely let Axel and me."

He snorted again. "Don't compare yourselves to me, kid. I'm known to the tribe."

"Right," I said. "Then I guess I better get my gear."

I started back to the cabin when I spotted Elder Morgan and August Bones standing a short distance away. I might not have been invited to their conversation, but I headed that direction anyway.

As I approached, they were speaking in low voices, but I could tell August was upset. Well, it looked like they were both upset, but August in particular.

"Our decision is final," Elder Morgan said. "I am sorry, August."

"But the others..." August trailed off. "You know what this means to me."

"I know," Elder Morgan said. "And I am sorry, August. But it must be this way."

Elder Morgan turned, noticing me. August turned as well and I met his gaze. I stopped in my tracks, realizing there were tears lining his eyes.

The three of us stood there, awkwardly staring at one another for a few moments, then August shouldered past me and disappeared into the night.

"Uh, what was that about?" I asked.

Elder Morgan forced a smile. "August is disappointed he's not allowed to partake in the hunt. That is all."

"Why?" I asked, and for some reason, I had a feeling I needed to know. "What are you both hiding?"

The elder stared at me for a few moments and said, "You agreed to help us without asking too many questions."

"Nope. Wrong strategy," Axel said from just behind me. I hadn't even realize he'd followed me. He continued, "Wyatt has that stubborn, frustrated tone in his voice that suggests he isn't going to let this lie. He thinks it's somehow related to everything else, so you might as well just tell him."

Elder Morgan stared between the two of us and finally said, "This creature we're hunting..."

"The Uktena," I said. "Stone heard the name."

Elder Morgan nodded. "So he did. Yes, you know that August Bones was very close to my daughter, yes? And that his loyalty to the tribe is based on that loss."

"Yes," I replied.

"We..." Elder Morgan started, then paused. "We believed she was killed by an Uktena, but the beast was never found. We never located it."

"And now it's back," I said.

"Perhaps," Elder Morgan said. "We have reason to believe it is, yes."

"And that's why August wants to come," I said, nodding. "He wants to help kill the beast that took his friend."

"And to protect her daughter from the same fate." Elder Morgan said. "Yet the tribe voted against allowing him to come."

"Can I ask why?"

Elder Morgan shook his head. "No, you may not. But know that our missing children intend to hunt it down and try to kill it. And they are in grave danger."

"Because they failed to kill me," I heard myself say.

"What?" both Elder Morgan and Axel said.

"They said their new benefactor wanted them to kill me. I had commented about how they'd failed the first two times and their overseer wouldn't be happy. Now, they've failed a third time, so their hope of redeeming themselves is to kill the monster and secure the power."

Elder Morgan's face showed concern. "Speak nothing of what you know about the beast we hunt. Keep it to yourself. If the others think you know too much, they'll fear you'll try to gain its power for yourself."

"I understand," I said. "But Stone found that much online. It's no real secret for anyone with a smartphone."

"Still," Elder Morgan said. "It's better if the others don't know that you've learned the name of the monster, nor anything about it."

"We'll keep it to ourselves," Axel said. "We're great at secrets."

"Your fears may be right," Elder Morgan said. "Had we known that our children were ordered to kill you, we would've never sent you to meet with them."

"There was no way you could've known," I replied. "It is what it is. All that matters is what we do now."

"Yes," Elder Morgan said. "And now, we hunt."

# CHAPTER FIFTY

This time, Axel, Stone, and I were ordered to stick near John. This direction was provided along with several jokes about wanting to avoid the Blade Mage killing pigs. Apparently, this was still hilarious to everyone.

So once more we were in the heart of the forest, but at least this time I wasn't alone.

The moon was high, and when we weren't directly beneath the trees, I could see my companions well enough, though I couldn't always tell them apart. Still, the loss of time and feeling of being left alone in the wilderness weren't an issue this time. The continued pain in my skull was another matter, however. The Tylenol had done little to help.

Nor did the long, slow slog through the wilderness. There was a part of me that felt like I should've just stayed behind, yet the tribe's view was that if I turned away, I would no longer be welcome to help them. Which, in fairness, might've been better anyway. I'd done a bang-up job so far.

I didn't want to give up.

Maybe it was stubborn stupidity, but I couldn't just walk away.

If Stone thought there was wickedness about, it only further confirmed my suspicions. Something wicked had come to Lost City, and it needed to be rooted out. That was the job of a Blade Mage, wasn't it?

So I continued forward, my head bandaged and aching. I hadn't bothered to remove the bandages to see just how severe my injuries were. From Axel's accounts, it sounded like I might have trouble passing myself off as ruggedly handsome going forward, but that was okay. I didn't think many people bought it anyway.

I tried to not think about the pain as I followed the shadowed figure in front of me, who I assumed was John.

At some point he held up a hand, motioning for us to stop. At that moment, I didn't see anyone else, so it might've just been for me.

The young medicine man moved back nearer to me, and I almost jumped when I saw Axel and Stone both appear beside me.

In a whisper, John said, "I've been told we should head further west."

"Okay," I replied, not really caring which direction we went.

In the dim light, I noticed a mischievous look on the younger man's face. "But Elder Morgan and Ahuli are moving north."

"Okay?" I repeated, but this time as a question.

"Our prey will stay by the water. To the west, we'll find woodlands. To the north is a creek."

"You think the creature is more likely in that direction?" Stone said.

John shrugged. "Elder Morgan and Ahuli do."

"Won't you get in trouble for disobeying?" I asked.

He shrugged again, still smiling. "Probably. But we are here to hunt the beast, and they believe the creature is that way."

"I like your style, John," Axel said. "Let's break the rules."

John turned to Stone, who nodded. He looked at me last. I sighed and nodded.

To the north we went.

If the rest of the hunting party noticed our turn north, no one moved in to intercept. So, either they didn't notice, or they didn't really care. The way the Cherokee viewed leadership seemed strange to me. It was as though they valued it greatly in some ways, but valued personal freedom and choice just as much. And it seemed they voted on most things, and once a vote was done, that was law. Yet after the short time

I'd spent around them, I suspected they'd accept John's decision to lead us north without issue.

Or I could've been totally wrong. What did I know?

We didn't see any of the other hunters as we traversed north, and though I could still see John ahead of me, I lost sight of the others again.

We trekked on for what felt like hours when I heard a shout somewhere in the forest ahead.

That wasn't normal.

Based on my last experience hunting with this group, they believed in total silence. What did it mean?

There was more commotion then. Another shout. Splashing water. Limbs cracking. A scream.

"Onward," John called over his shoulder, and sprinted off into the darkness.

Some part of my mind suggested I should turn and run the other direction, back the way we'd come.

I didn't, though.

I chased after John, but I couldn't see him any longer. Nor the others. I was on my own, racing in the shadowed wilderness toward the sounds of combat and a giant fabled serpent monster.

I'd never been a clever man.

For a few moments, I was lost in total darkness. Then the trees parted above me and I saw moonlight reflecting off the water ahead. The creek.

Further downstream, I saw a few figures moving through the shadows.

Then I saw something else.

Just a movement—not enough to make out what I was seeing—but something inhumanly large slithered out of sight on the opposite bank.

Before I had time to decide if that was my overactive imagination or the Uktena, I noticed a figure lying nearby on the ground.

I ran over and found myself looking into the face of Ahuli, the War Chief.

He was lying with his back against a tree trunk, one hand on his side, where a dark patch of blood was growing. His other arm hung limp, twisted unnaturally.

No surprise, he appeared to be in a lot of pain.

"War Chief," I said, kneeling in front of him. "What can I do to help you?"

"Go, you fool," he said, spitting blood at me. "Forget me. Help the others!"

"But you're bleeding to death."

"Help the others. The Uktena is worse than I could've imagined."

*Great.*

"Go," he repeated. "I'll be okay."

Despite my better judgment, I did as he asked. All things considered, he was probably right. If the rest of the hunters were engaged with the great beast, they needed help. Sadly, I wasn't sure what help I'd be, since they hadn't seen fit to tell me how to fight the damned thing.

I certainly wasn't prepared to trust the results of Axel's Google search. Oh, yes, he'd borrowed Stone's phone to read up before we'd left. According to what we found online, we needed to attack the seventh spot from its head. That shouldn't be too hard in the dark, right? Plus, I was sure it would hold still long enough for us to count.

What did that mean, anyway? The seventh scale? Or did the big bastard actually have spots? Was that information even reliable?

These were the thoughts in my head as I glanced downstream again. I didn't see any more human figures scurrying in the darkness, so I didn't have anyone else to run toward. There was no sign of John, Stone, or Axel, either.

But I had seen the direction "something" had gone. And whether that "something" had only been my imagination at work, it was the only lead I had.

I went the way it had gone.

Again, not a clever man.

I found a shallow spot and ran across the creek. My new Vans got soaked, but that was okay because they were still damp from when the pond had punched me anyway.

Racing up the hill on the opposite side, I noticed two Cherokee nearby. I was about to call out to them when I noticed which direction they were looking. Past me. I turned and saw...

Well...

What did I see?

I saw...a giant fucking snake with horns.

Axel's search had suggested the creature was as big around as a tree trunk.

That was *bullshit*.

It was as fat around as a redwood.

Big enough to eat a damned bus.

And horned, like a giant elk, its antlers stretched from its head like tree branches.

In the center of its skull, just between the eyes, was a white glowing diamond. Not like a little wedding diamond, either. Like the Hope diamond had been slammed in the center of its forehead. This was rap video bling.

And despite all of this—the fact it was a giant snake with horns—I found myself running toward it, as if in a daze. Some part of my mind knew this wasn't right, but I couldn't seem to stop my own feet. And the two Cherokee I spotted, well, they were running with me. Past me, actually, because they were much faster.

Still, I couldn't help myself. I was running toward it.

Then Dyrnwyn vibrated on my back, trembling in such a way I thought it might pop right off.

My mind cleared.

*An enchantment!*

*The diamond!*

Apparently, looking directly at it clouded a person's mind and convinced them to race toward it. That had to make getting snacks easy.

I drew Dyrnwyn from its scabbard and as soon as the sword was in my hand, the enchantment broke completely and I came to a stop.

I tried calling to the others, but it was too late.

The snake reared back its head and blew a breath at them, like the big bad wolf trying to blow down a piggy's house. A black cloud of burp mist exhaled from its maw, covering the two men. Both dropped.

Its *fucking* breath was poisonous?

*Shit.*

The Uktena stared at me for a moment, its slitted eyes locked with mine. Best guess, it was trying to figure out how the hell I was immune to its enchantment.

Then it turned as if to flee.

*Ha, small victories and all that!*

At least, that's what I was thinking until its big-ass tail hammered me off my feet.

I hit the ground rolling, the wind knocked from my lungs.

Regathering my senses, I realized the snake was gone. Maybe I'd weirded it out after all. That was no small blessing.

Just in case I was wrong, I held really still and tried to convince myself that the Uktena was too big to sneak up on me without making some noise.

When I still didn't die, I counted it as another win.

*Now what?*

I didn't see any of the other members of the hunting party, nor had I seen which way the snake had slithered off.

A gun shot roared through the night.

Stone.

And the Uktena.

Because Stone wouldn't have been shooting his rifle for the fun of it.

Problem solved. I knew which way I didn't *want* to go.

And I knew which way I *was* going to go anyway.

I heard three more shots and saw the muzzle flash downstream.

Cursing my stupid stubbornness, I set off in the direction of certain death.

I passed through the trees and brush, quick as I could, while trying not to trip over unseen obstacles. At least I didn't have to worry about accidentally stepping on a copperhead any longer. There were much worse snakes in this here forest.

Stone fired his rifle a few more times, and I saw where he stood on the creek bank.

And I could see the Uktena as well.

Our prey was no longer trying to sneak. The diamond atop its head was ablaze and its scales were glowing as if made of starlight.

I could see some of the others as well, racing to and fro around the beast.

Arrows and spears bounced from the serpent's flesh, when they managed to strike at all. It was too *damned* quick for something so *damned* big.

As I raced toward the chaos, the Uktena impaled a man on its horns. With a flick of its head, it sent the dying man sailing into the darkness of the forest.

*Jesus! Fuck!*

This *had* to be the stupidest fight I'd ever run toward.

The next unlucky hunter met an even worse fate.

The Uktena struck, opening its mouth and scooping the man up.

I'd seen snakes eat before, and while always an impressive sight, this was something else entirely. It took the Uktena about a half second to swallow the man whole, and then it was on its way.

No time to savor its meal. There was rampaging to be done!

I closed the distance then and raised Dyrnwyn over my head. My sword took the form of a heavy throwing knife.

The seventh spot.

That was what the Axel had said. You had to hit it in the seventh spot to kill it. And with it all lit up like its flesh was a rock concert, I could see that seventh spot. On my own, I knew there was no way I could hope to hit the moving target, but with Dyrnwyn's help...

I let fly.

Dyrnwyn sailed end over end, transforming into a double-edged longsword as it covered the distance between me and the snake.

The strike thudded home, right into the middle of the seventh spot.

And...

Nothing.

The Uktena didn't even care.

Generally speaking, snakes didn't have the human features to pull off a look of disdain. The Uktena was a special snake, though, and it did. The creature looked at me like I was a mosquito, then whipped its tail at me.

The first time it had hit me with some girth and just swatted me away.

This time, however, it struck with the tip, which was still as fat around as a baseball bat.

Right in the kneecap.

My knee exploded.

There was a devastating pop, I was falling, and then I was in the creek, my head below water.

I sat there for a moment, shocked and sure the pain was coming.

And, *oh,* did it.

Fuck-loads of pain.

I forced my head above water and scrabbled toward the bank with my arms, trying not to scream.

My leg was dead weight. Just a seething fierce misery, lighting up my world.

Whatever I'd felt on my damaged skull, it was forgotten in a new eclipse of agony.

I couldn't breathe.

I could scarcely think.

It was bad. *Oh, fuck,* it was bad.

*Breathe, Wyatt. Breathe. Just breathe. 'Tis but a flesh wound.*

Rolling to my side, I raised my staff with shaking hands and summoned light, terrified of what I'd find.

My fears were proven true.

*Ah, fuck.*

At the kneecap, my leg was bent completely over. Not backward. Bent up. I was looking at the bottom of my shoe. My own foot was looking me in the face.

It was ruined.

Shattered.

Broken.

My leg was fucked.

The pain raced to the front of my mind, pain unlike anything I'd experienced before. An agony so pure, I could've just bobbed my head back into the creek and sucked in a breath of muddy water to make it go away.

*Breathe, Wyatt,* I told myself again. *Just breathe.*

I felt myself edging toward shock, the mix of pain and panic too much.

*Breathe, goddammit! Focus!*

My friends were in trouble.

That was what mattered. Not my knee. My friends.

Forcing my focus back on the Uktena, I saw it had its eyes on Stone. Maybe it didn't like the bright flashes of his muzzle, or all the concussive racket, or maybe Stone's bullets were breaking through its armored flesh and causing some pain. I couldn't say.

Either way, he was the next target.

Stone must've switched his selector from semi to full auto, because he dumped a mag in the span of a few seconds. He hit the release, letting the empty mag fall while he slammed in a full one.

The creature slowed its charge while Stone focused fire on its head. It didn't look like his gunfire was doing any damage, but the snake must've been annoyed, because it turned its face away.

And hit Stone with its tail, just like it had done to me.

He hit the water and came up sputtering. I could only hope he wasn't hurt as bad as me.

He wasn't.

Stone rose from the water and kept firing until he was empty again.

The Uktena raced toward him, seeing its opportunity.

Stone tossed his gun aside and drew something else.

I saw a glint of steel in the moonlight.

A knife? Surely, he wasn't going to attack the bus-sized serpent with just a knife.

Of course not.

With his other hand, he raised something toward his mouth like he was biting an apple.

Now, I didn't know Stone *that* well, but I knew he was a supreme badass. Literally the only person I could imagine who would *actually* do that. Just take out an apple while a giant horned snake was baring down on him.

The safer bet, however, was that it was a grenade.

I didn't think anyone really bit the pins out of them. Had to be hell on the teeth, but then, this *was* Shain Stone. He was a different kind of person.

With a roar, Stone charged right toward the oncoming monster.

The Uktena opened its great maw to swallow Stone up like it had that other poor sap, but as soon as its jaws parted, Stone hurled the grenade.

Right in its mouth.

The giant serpent seemed a little taken back by this, and at the last possible moment, closed its mouth and use its antlers instead.

It struck with such speed and power that Stone was skewered through. I watched as the horns came right out of Stone's back, impaling him.

Stone didn't care.

He pulled himself further on and started stabbing at the snake's head with his knife. Again and again, he jabbed and jabbed.

And there I was, feeling bad about my little shattered kneecap.

Thunder roared as the grenade went off in the serpent's gullet. Light burst from its mouth like a dragon's burp. Stone's body was hurled from the blast and crashed on the opposite bank.

The Uktena kept moving like nothing had happened.

If a throat grenade couldn't kill it, what could?

It still had its eyes set on Stone.

I saw Axel then as he raced toward Stone's still form. He hurled a lightning bolt at the creature, and once more, it responded with its tail, sending Axel airborne. He hit the ground close to Stone.

The Uktena continued toward them. I suspected it planned to scoop them both up like a vacuum cleaner.

Using my staff like a crutch, I struggled up to my good leg.

Then did something incredibly stupid.

I fired a force spell under my body and sent myself airborne. My aim was true, and I crashed onto the bank between my friends and the Uktena. The bastard would have to swallow me first.

Which probably would not be a challenge on account of the fact I'd knocked the air from my lungs and felt several somethings in my ribcage pop when I landed.

I didn't care. The pain was nothing like what I felt in my leg.

I had to help my friends.

Reaching my hand toward the oncoming snake, I called Dyrnwyn to me. It leaped from where it was still lodged in the snake's back and was in my grip a moment later.

At the same time, John raced past me with his spear.

I hurled my sword again, this time aiming for the monster's head. Dyrnwyn's blade sliced right through the top of one antler and buried at the base of the Uktena's skull.

That didn't hurt it, either.

John raised his spear as it pressed in on him, but it was of little use. I felt the weight of my failure as the young medicine man was impaled upon its antlers, just as Stone had been.

John cried out as the monster lifted his body into the air.

With a flick of its head, it hurled John at me like a missile. His body hit mine like a car wreck, the impact blinding.

There were more popping sounds and I hit the ground, not even caring what was broken this time.

The coppery taste of blood filled my mouth, and I felt jagged chunks of broken teeth. *My* broken teeth. I spat them out along with a glob of blood.

It was a struggle to breathe, and I realized I couldn't move one of my arms. It felt an awful lot like my leg. *Ah, well.* What difference did it make?

I turned to John, who lay motionless beside me. He was breathing, but only barely. His fingers were wrapped around his ruined guts, holding in his own entrails. The blood pumping from around his fingers told me he wouldn't last long. He was a dead man.

And so was I.

Gritting what teeth remained, I rolled to my side and realized my staff was still beside me. Using my good arm, I wrapped my fingers around it. I wasn't sure what the hell I was going to do with it, but its presence was some small comfort.

I looked up at the Uktena, who was staring down at me, that look of disdain on its face once more.

It no longer viewed me as a threat. Maybe it never had.

Slowly, it turned its attention back to where Axel and Stone lay a short distance away. I couldn't say whether either of them still lived, but I assumed they must, based on the fact the giant serpent still seemed interested in devouring them.

It was as if it knew.

As if it knew it could hurt me worse by hurting them.

I screamed and cursed at the monster, even while I tried to focus enough energy to summon some kind of spell. Anything.

All I managed was a meager force spell the snake didn't even notice.

It was going to eat my friends, and there wasn't a goddamned thing I could do about it.

Not. A. Thing.

I was helpless.

Useless.

All I could do was watch them die.

Some fucking Blade Mage.

*No!*

*Goddammit*, I wouldn't just lie there! There had to be something. Something I could do.

Fury tore inside my chest. I called on every stubborn ounce of will I had. Everything.

There were stories of wizards who'd burned themselves out summoning too much power at once. I'd never known if it was true or just stories. For my part, I'd only ever used enough in one go to make me want a nap. I couldn't fathom summoning so much power that I'd get one big boom, then an untimely demise.

I went for it anyway.

I reached deep, calling on every bit of magical energy I could summon.

I cried out for help, begging the gods, if any existed, to lend their aid.

No help came.

The Memphis Knights may have drawn their powers from a higher authority, but I could not.

So, I called out to the Earth itself.

I pleaded for its aid against this unnatural beast. In this place, surrounded by the mighty hills, the ancient trees, and the water flowing by, I thought maybe, just maybe, something might answer my call.

Anything.

And then...

Something *did* answer my call.

And something snapped inside of me.

A key turned.

A dam burst free.

A door swung open.

Something unlocked in my mind, as though a new well of power had just opened to me. Maybe it had been there along, but was a hidden thing. Something I couldn't reach or touch with my consciousness. Yet somehow I found it. It was beyond my comprehension, like discovering my powers all over again.

The Earth had answered my call.

I felt its power all around me, welcoming me, offering itself to my will.

And I used it.

I lacked the mental fortitude to aim this new well of power. All I could think was to keep the monster from my friends. I had to stop it. I didn't know what I was doing, but I pushed with everything I had.

The ground trembled beneath me and the Uktena stopped, for just a moment, slithering back, eyes watching me.

*Stay away from my friends.*

It was all I could think. The only thing that mattered. I repeated it over and over in my mind as the ground grumbled and groaned beneath me.

There was a split, a crack, right in the earth. I felt it. I felt it splitting apart at my will.

I was tearing the land in half.

On one side, the Uktena. On the other, my friends.

The Earth felt my desire to keep the monster from my friends and it responded in the only way it knew how: by splitting the ground between them.

The Uktena slithered back further as the crack spread between it and its prey.

I pushed harder still and the crack broke apart further, separating the land. Like an earthquake tearing a new canyon in the creek bed.

The antlered head turned toward me, its slitted eyes studying me.

And then it threw back its head and barked a hissing laugh before starting for my friends again. It seemed to think my efforts were in vain. Funny, even.

I dug deeper still.

My pain became a distant memory as I pushed every last bit of my being into this spell, whatever it was.

And still, the land answered my call.

I could feel it.

All of it.

Every leaf of every tree. Every blade of grass. Every minnow swimming in the creek. The dirt itself. Every dead leaf slowly decaying and returning to its mother. I could feel them all.

And they would *all* answer my call.

As the Uktena leaped across the divide, I called upon the trees.

Their roots launched from the ground, catching and encircling the mighty serpent.

Even that wasn't enough, and the creature's mass tore against them, refusing to be held.

But there were others still to answer my call.

More and more roots shot out of the ground, entangling the creature.

And from above, the trees did the same, reaching down and wrapping their branches and trunks around the mighty beast. The roots pulled, and the trees pushed, forcing the Uktena into the hole I'd created.

And still...

I knew it wouldn't be enough.

The mythical beast wouldn't be held. Not for long.

But it was all I could do.

A single figure darted past me, sprinting toward the bound Uktena. They grabbed hold of the roots and leaped up, climbing atop the monster's back and racing toward its head.

I was near delirious, but I recognized her still.

Pathkiller.

She climbed atop the Uktena's head and raised her tomahawk to the sky. With a roar, she began hacking at the great beast's head.

The horned serpent struggled against its binds and was just about to break free.

Any moment, and her fate would be the same as ours.

And then...

The beast went limp.

The horned serpent let out a final shuddering breath and went still.

It was dead.

She'd done it.

Pathkiller had killed the Uktena.

I let go of my spell and returned the land to itself.

The Earth quieted. All was silent.

And somehow, I didn't pass out.

Instead, I lay in the mud, struggled to breathe, and welcomed back the pain my body felt inclined to inform me of. My state was such that observing reality was more like watching a grainy film than being alive.

"What have you done?" a familiar voice asked.

Elder Morgan.

I raised my head and watched as he limped toward his grand-daughter.

Pathkiller, still standing atop the Uktena, turned to face him. "I've done what you were too weak to do, Grandfather."

"Oh, Alyita," the old man said, dropping to his knees. His voice cracked as he spoke. "You don't know what you've done."

"I know," Pathkiller replied. "I know your secrets, old man. I know what lies you've kept."

"Then you know..."

Pathkiller pointed a tomahawk at the dead beast beneath her. "I know this Uktena didn't kill my mother."

"Don't say it," Elder Morgan said as the tears streamed down his cheeks. It wasn't a command. He was pleading with her. "Please, don't say it."

Pathkiller jumped from the snake and strode to her grandfather. "Don't say what?"

Elder Morgan didn't reply.

"You know the truth," she said. "And you never told me."

Elder Morgan looked away.

"It's true, isn't it? My mother wasn't killed *by* the Uktena. She *was* the Uktena. Look at me! Say it, Grandfather. Tell me the truth!"

"Like you, your mother sought a different way," he replied, finally looking up at her. "She sought power. She killed her path, just as you've done, and this was the cost. This is what I didn't want for you."

"Your weakness led to this," she said, pointing her tomahawk at him. "And you were too much of a coward to see it made right. But I have. I have fixed your mistakes, Grandfather. You should be thanking me."

"How did you know?" Elder Morgan asked. "Who told you?"

"My new elder," she replied. "He promised me a chance to set things right. And so, I have. He will lead the Cherokee back to glory. We will set right all the wrongs you were too weak to face. We will see revenge is met on those who've hurt our tribe. And we will wash away the weakness that plagues us."

"Who?" Elder Morgan asked. "Who do you serve that has such power?"

"A name long forgotten," she said. "A name our tribe has forsaken. Our great betrayal."

"What are you talking about?"

"Think, Grandfather. Before the white man ever came to our lands. When the Cherokee were still strong. Who led us then? Who could've protected us?"

Elder Morgan was silent for several seconds, contemplating. His head jerked upward. "It can't be."

"They have returned. The rightful rulers of our tribe. Through fire, they will see us made whole again."

"The fire priests," Elder Morgan said. "No, Alyita, it can't be."

"Say their name. Say the words long forgotten."

"I won't."

"I will," she said. "The Ani-kutani have returned, Grandfather."

"No. It can't be."

"It can. All those years ago, we betrayed them and thought them slain to the last. But we were wrong. They have existed through all this time, and oh, how they laughed when the white man came and pushed us from our lands, for they knew they could've protected us. But the Cherokee, we turned our backs on them. Worse, we tried to kill them all."

"Alyita, they're—"

"My *name* is Pathkiller!"

Elder Morgan was silent for a moment, then continued, "The Ani-kutani were vile. The things they did to our people..."

"They were our rightful leaders," she said. "And now I serve them. And I will have a place beside them. Fear not, Grandfather, for our family will be accepted as Ani-kutani. Not mere servants, but as Ani-kutani ourselves."

Elder Morgan dropped his head and wept. He begged and pleaded.

And Pathkiller only looked down at him, the snake's blood—her mother's blood—still dripping from her tomahawk. "You are weak."

With that, she turned and started toward the Uktena again.

"Wait," Elder Morgan said. "You intend to claim the Ulun'suti?"

"Of course," she replied.

Elder Morgan pointed toward me. "None but the tribe may see it. We must turn him away and ensure the others are not watching, if they live."

Pathkiller laughed and started toward me. "Turn him away? Come now, Grandfather. You can't be serious. My new master wishes the Blade Mage dead. And he'll not escape me this time."

Looking down at me, Pathkiller raised her tomahawk.

"No, Alyita!" Elder Morgan said. "No!"

The tomahawk came down.

I felt a crunch, but saw only darkness.

# CHAPTER FIFTY-ONE

I awoke with a start.

For a moment, I thought it had all been a bad dream. The Uktena, my injured friends, and me, dying from a tomahawk to the skull, delivered by an angsty pubescent teen. Just a bad dream, right?

Then I realized I didn't know where the hell I was.

Glancing around, I saw I was in a room similar to the thatch shelter where the Cherokee had held council. The main difference was that the walls appeared to be made of clay rather than just thatch.

The room was lit by a small fire with a chimney leading up through the roof.

I could see I was in a homemade bed and covered with a handcrafted blanket. It felt like I'd been transported back in time a couple hundred years.

Across the room was another bed. John lay in it, and he appeared to be breathing. That was no small miracle after the wounds he'd suffered.

So, the rest of the hunting party had found us and somehow gotten us back to camp. But why hadn't they put me in my cabin?

And why wasn't my head hurting? Or my leg?

A flap at the door opened and a beautiful woman stepped through. Her garb was homespun, and she appeared to be of Native American ancestry, but I didn't recognize her. Such was her beauty that there was no way I could've forgotten meeting her. And the tribe all wore modern clothing. Who was she? Where the hell was I?

"Oh, you're awake," she said, flashing me a smile.

"Uh, yeah," I replied, sitting up.

I realized I actually felt pretty all right. I'd suspected the Cherokee's healing medicine was second to none, but this was exceptional.

"How are the others?" I asked. "How are Stone and Axel?"

"Who?" she asked as she moved over to a table and began tinkering with some dishes.

I blinked a few times.

Glancing over, I saw John was awake as well.

The young medicine man lifted his sheets and looked down at his torso, then back up at me, wide-eyed.

Apparently, he was even more surprised than me.

I paused.

I'd seen John get disemboweled.

I'd seen him lose buckets of blood.

Yet there he sat across the room, wide-eyed and every bit as confused as I was.

My knee had been shattered. The bottom of my foot had looked me in the face.

And Pathkiller had split my skull.

Cherokee medicine wasn't *that* good.

No medicine was *that* good.

I reached a hand up to my head and felt around. There were a few spots that were still tender, but it didn't feel like a fractured skull.

And I could I breathe, I realized. The rib I was sure was broken didn't even hurt.

Then again, in my excited state, I might've exaggerated the damage.

What about my leg, then?

It was my turn to lift the sheets. And there was my leg, sitting there straight and normal. I tried to move it and felt a lightning bolt of pain, but it wasn't broken. It was tender, sure, but I couldn't see the bottom of my foot.

Lastly, I ran my tongue over my teeth. They were all there. Every last one.

*What the hell?*

I turned and looked at John again. He looked back at me, and the expression on his face told me he wasn't any clearer on what was going on than I was.

"Um," I said, trying to think of something clever to say. "Where are we?"

"You're in my home," the woman replied, as though that were obvious.

"Right," I replied, then turned to John to shrug. He was staring dumbfounded at the woman.

"We're not at the Cherokee camp, are we?" I asked.

The woman laughed as though I'd made a funny joke. "No, of course not. You are in my home."

"And where is that?" I asked.

"Anywhere," she replied. "Wherever I rest, that is my home."

"Uh, okay," I replied. "Maybe these are dumb questions, but the last thing I remember was a pretty rough fight. Then I woke up here. So, I'm just a little confused."

"You fought the Uktena," she said as she moved toward John, carrying a plate of food. "It is a very terrifying creature."

"Yes, it is," I replied. "But the thing is... How did we get here?"

"I brought you here," she replied. Moving back to the table, she picked up another plate and brought it to me. "You must be hungry. Eat."

Taking the proffered plate, I saw it held some delicious-smelling meat stuffs and a pile of vegetables.

I realized how hungry I was.

I glanced up at John, who met my gaze and shook his head ever so slightly.

*Well, damn.*

But it looked *so* good.

The message was clear, though. Don't eat the food.

I'm not sure I'd ever find this advice in a textbook, but the way I saw it... I had woken up in a strange place. I had been miraculously healed of all my grievous injuries, including death. A strange, beautiful woman was trying to feed me. The most normal thing in the whole place was the honest-to-God medicine man who was telling me not to eat the stranger's food. Good enough for me.

"Why did you bring us here?" I asked.

"You were in trouble," she said. "I sensed the magics of the land crying out. And when I came, I found you two, and I knew it was one of you who'd called upon the Earth, and so I mistook you for one of our friends."

"Friends?" I asked, glancing over at John. "You mean the Cherokee?"

"Yes, of course," she said, motioning toward John. "He is of the tribe. He is my friend."

With her back to him, John put up his hands and made a face that said, *I've never met this baffling woman, but I think I might know what she means.*

"Um, John," I said, turning her attention to him as well. "Maybe you can help me understand?"

John spoke to the woman in Cherokee and she responded in kind. Her responses remained positive and friendly, though John's face looked more and more like he'd seen a ghost.

Finally, the young medicine man turned my way and said, "She is of the Nunnehi."

"Is that another tribe?"

"Not exactly," John replied.

The woman laughed. "We are friends to the Cherokee."

"And I'm not Cherokee," I said, glancing over at the steaming pile of delicious food. My stomach was grumbling, and I was struggling with John's warning like I would struggle with a bowl of ice cream. I forced my attention back to the woman. "Does that mean I am not a friend?"

The woman shook her head, studying me. "You are something else. I mistook you for one of the Cherokee, though, for you called upon the land. But I do not know what you are."

"I'm no danger to you, though," I said, not really liking where this was going.

"Of course not." The woman giggled. Apparently, I'd made another funny joke.

"So, you sensed my magic, and then brought John and me here?"

"Yes."

"And healed us?"

"But of course. It would've been wrong not to."

"And what of the others?"

"I could only carry two of you," she said. "And I knew one of you had used great Earth magics. The Earth answered your call, and so I thought I would lend you my aid as well."

"I am very grateful," I said, risking a glance at John. "But we should see to our other friends. They could still be in danger."

"I fear all the Cherokee are in danger," she said. "I feel it upon the wind."

"Then you understand why we need to go to them."

She shook her head. "But you are safe here. Rest. Eat. You can stay for as long as you like."

I glanced over at John again, who'd gone as white as a sheet.

I turned back to the woman. "I appreciate your hospitality and everything you've done for us. Truly, I do. I can never repay you. But we must see to our other friends. Some of them were badly wounded. Others... Others I fear are dead."

"Yes," she said with a sad look on her face. "Some did not make it. The others, however, I checked that they were alive. I offered what little medicine I could."

"You healed them?" I asked.

She shrugged. "Not as I did for you two. Without bringing them home, I could not offer as much aid. And you two were in such poor shape."

"Thank you," I said. "There were others... Others like me who were not of the Cherokee. Did you see if they lived?"

She shook her head. "I know not."

"I see," I said. "May we return to the Cherokee?"

"Of course," she said, but her smiled transitioned to a frown. "If that is what you desire, but you *could* stay. Here, you would not have to fear anything. You could rest. Many of the Cherokee have stayed with us."

"I'm not of the Cherokee," I reminded her. "And as lovely as that sounds, I cannot leave my friends behind. Do you understand?"

"Of course," she said with a soft smile. She turned to John. "You wish the same?"

John nodded but didn't speak.

She sighed. "Follow me, then."

She moved toward the flap entrance at the door and stepped outside.

John and I shared another shrug, then we both followed.

On my feet again, I realized I was walking with a limp, every step painful, but I could move, and I wasn't able to see the bottom of my foot, so I was pretty happy.

Outside, I saw nothing but gray fog past the woman. She reached out a hand to me and I accepted it. She reached out her other hand to John, who also accepted it.

Then we walked through the fog.

We'd only gone a few steps when the mist dissipated and gave way to a bright orange sun above the treetops. It was morning.

Ahead, I saw the outline of a cabin.

I heard voices and shouting.

It was the Cherokee camp.

And apparently, our misty arrival had gotten someone's attention.

I noticed Elder Thomas first, hobbling toward us with his gnarled old cane. A few of the others were with him, and I felt a surge of relief as I saw Axel among them.

Our guide stopped just before Elder Thomas and smiled at him. "I have brought home your friends."

"You have," Elder Thomas replied, studying her. "We feared them lost."

"They were not," she replied simply. "Only taking rest in my care."

"Thank you," Elder Thomas said, his face paling. "Thank you."

"It is my pleasure, friend," the woman said. "Though I fear I did them little favor. There is a darkness descending upon your tribe."

"Yes," Elder Thomas replied. "These are dark times, I am afraid. Elder Morgan is not with you?"

"No," I said, shaking my head. "He isn't here?"

"He did not return from the hunt," Elder Thomas said. "He was missing, along with you two. We feared the Uktena... You didn't see what happened to him?"

"I might have an idea," I said. "But it isn't good. We should talk."

"Understood," Elder Thomas said.

I turned to my guide. "You are a friend to the Cherokee. Will you lend them further aid in their time of need?"

The woman was silent for a few moments, then said, "It is not yet decided. Much has changed."

"We understand," Elder Thomas said. "And we thank you for what help you've given."

"It was my pleasure," she said, smiling. "I will return home now."

With that, she took one long look at me, turned, and walked back into the fog.

Moments later, the unnatural mist was gone.

I turned to John. "There better be a good reason you told me not to eat that delicious-looking pile of food."

John shrugged. "Some say, if you eat of the food of the Nunnehi, you can never eat human food again, nor return to live with humans again."

"That's a pretty damned good reason," I said, thinking maybe that advice *should* make it into some kind of textbook. I turned to Elder Thomas. "We have a lot to discuss, but I'm starving."

"Yes, of course," Elder Thomas said, forcing a smile. "Come. I'm sure there is some bacon still."

"Very funny," I replied, turning to follow him back toward the cabins.

"Wait, hold on a second," Axel said. "What the hell is going on? Who was that lady? Where were you, Wyatt? And does anyone know if she's single?"

We all ignored him.

# CHAPTER FIFTY-TWO

Apparently, Elder Thomas had been joking about the bacon.

All that was left for John and me were cold eggs and luke-warm coffee. Both were delightful.

Elder Thomas, Ahuli, and a few of the other elders huddled around us. The rest of the eating hall was vacated, except Axel, who was on strict orders to keep his mouth shut.

I wasn't surprised to learn he'd been a ginormous pain in the ass while I was gone.

He'd been out cold when they found him, and hadn't woken until they'd dragged him back to camp. At which point, they'd given him my sword and staff. When I was not also provided, he'd caused quite the ruckus.

Axel had spent the better part of the night trying to round up another hunting party to come looking for me. When the elders had refused, he'd attempted to incite a rebellion. When that was squashed, he'd attempted to set out on his own and had to be restrained. After he broke out, he again attempted to slip away. Once more, they'd caught him.

His logic was simple...

They hadn't found my body. So, I was still out there.

One elder had foolishly suggested the reason they hadn't found my body was because the Uktena had probably eaten me.

Axel's response to this bit of news was that he'd use my sword to cut through the Uktena until he found my body. They thought he was joking.

And the cycle started over.

The second time around he'd nearly succeeded in inciting his rebellion, winning over most of the youngsters to his cause. This was followed by a few more rounds of detainment and escape. Fortunately, I showed up before things go too out of hand.

Elder Thomas brought us up to speed on the rest of the hunting party.

Eight had died in battle. Many more were injured. Between the tribe's own medicine and what help the Nunnehi had offered, they were all stable.

That included Ahuli, who seemed alert and angry as usual, despite my leaving him bleeding to death in the forest. He seemed to have plenty of blood now, and it was boiling. He wore a bandage around his waist and one arm was in a sling, but he seemed more than capable of violence.

Shain Stone was alive as well, which was no small miracle, even with his unnatural healing ability. He wasn't conscious, but he was alive. Which was impressive, considering I'd seen him skewered through the ribs.

The rest of the hunting party, scattered through the forest, had raced toward the sounds of battle. By the time they'd arrived, the Uktena was dead, but there had been no one around to explain what had happened. Elder Morgan, John, and I were missing. Everyone else was unconscious or dead.

As the morning sun rose, the tribe had wept for their losses, but gave thanks for the defeat of the mythical horned serpent. Yet they were unnerved. I could tell.

And I knew why.

They'd not recovered their prize.

And I knew who had. They were not going to like what I was about to tell them.

As soon as we were up to speed, they switched gears and asked about the Nunnehi. Most of the questions were directed at John and spoken in their native Iroquoian language. That was all right by me. Gave me a chance to finish my eggs.

Ahuli cut the conversation short and Elder Thomas turned everyone's attention to me. "You said you knew what happened to Elder Morgan."

I nodded slowly. "I'm afraid it isn't good news. I know many of you feared the Uktena was to blame for influencing your missing kids, but in the end, it was Alyita who slew the serpent."

A hush fell over the room.

Ahuli shattered it with his booming laugh. "You expect us to believe that? We sensed the magic in that place. We saw what it did to the Earth. You expect us to believe a child did that? Elder Morgan alone was the only one of us in proximity with medicine powerful enough to pull that off."

It took a moment to restrain my temper. I was getting a little sick of his pompous hostility. So I met his gaze and said, "I don't care what you believe, War Chief. I'll tell you what happened and you decide whether or not to believe it."

"Please," Elder Thomas said, casting a hard glare at Ahuli, which softened as he turned back to me. "Tell us what happened."

And so I did.

All of it.

I was a little hesitant to point out that I was, in fact, the one who'd summoned the great Earth magics. I told them anyway. It was strange. In all that had happened, I hadn't had a chance to think about it again. It was beyond me to comprehend. I wouldn't have believed I'd done it, and I said as much.

I went on to explain how Pathkiller had arrived and killed the monster.

Ahuli turned his attention to John. "Can you confirm any of this?"

"Only up to where the Uktena had me," he said, his face whitening as he replayed the memory. "It... It gored me. Right through my gut. I thought I was dead."

Ahuli turned to me. "So only you saw your magic. And only you saw the beast slain."

"No," Elder Thomas said. "Were you listening? Elder Morgan saw as well."

"Yet he is not here," Ahuli said. "Might he have betrayed us? And left with the Ulun'suti?"

"That isn't the end of it," I said. "There's more."

"Please," Elder Thomas said. "Go on, Blade Mage. Tell us."

"Before Alyita bashed my skull in, she and Elder Morgan spoke briefly. She told the elder she was serving the Ani-kutani. Does that mean anything to you?"

There was a sharp intake of breath, and then it was as if the entire room froze. Clearly the Cherokee were familiar with the name.

Ahuli's eyes narrowed to slits. Elder Thomas rubbed his face. Most of the others looked like they wanted to cry, or break things, or both.

Finally, Ahuli said, "That cannot be."

"Elder Morgan had a similar sentiment," I replied. "Yet Alyita was convinced. Who were they?"

Ahuli didn't answer me.

When it was clear he wasn't going to, Elder Thomas did. "Fire priests. The Ani-kutani were once our tribe's religious leaders. Much of our ceremony and custom, as well as our medicine, descended from them."

"But the Cherokee turned on them?" I asked. "That's what Alyita said."

"Yes," Ahuli said through gritted teeth. "Like so many with power, they abused theirs, or so the story goes. They would take women, married or otherwise, and have their pleasures with them. Some were even used in dark rituals. Any who opposed them were destroyed. They were a plague on our tribe."

"Yes," Elder Thomas said, nodding. "But one day they took a young warrior's bride, and they abused her. The warrior started an uprising. And for all their atrocities, he had little trouble finding allies. A bloody conflict it was, but, as our legends say, every last member of the Ani-kutani was slain. None remained. The Cherokee were forever free of their tyranny."

"Alyita said they somehow survived. That they've just been buying time. Waiting for the day they could reclaim their rightful place as your leaders."

They were silent for a time.

Then Elder Thomas said, "And it was Alyita who took the Ulun'suti from the Uktena?"

I nodded. "I believe so. She buried her tomahawk into my skull just before that, so I didn't see."

"Elder Morgan didn't try to stop her?" Ahuli asked. "Has he betrayed us?"

I shook my head. "Elder Morgan tried. He begged and pleaded with his granddaughter. Tried to get her to see reason."

"He did not use force?" Ahuli asked. "He did not use medicine? He just stood by while his granddaughter killed you and took the Ulun'suti, and you would still defend him?"

"In fairness, I don't think he thought she was actually going to kill me. Though also in fairness, he was the one who pointed out I was awake. But I don't believe for a moment he wanted her to kill me. I think he just wanted her to move me, or roll me over, or to do something so I couldn't watch. It's forbidden, right? So, that was his intent, but I think she surprised him when she attacked me. Look, I don't believe for a second that Elder Morgan has betrayed you. And I'd be willing to bet that wherever he is, if he's still alive, he's in grave danger."

"On that much, we can all agree," Elder Thomas said, again rubbing his hands over his face. "This news doesn't sit well, Blade Mage. We will need to hold council."

"I understand," I said, rising to my feet. "Axel and I are at your disposal, if needed. Otherwise, we'll crack on seeing what we can learn around Lost City."

Axel and I started for the door, but Elder Thomas called out. "Wyatt, if what you say is true, if that really was your magic..."

"Yes?"

"Well, I guess it explains why you were chosen as Blade Mage."

I nodded and walked out the door.

As soon as we were outside, Axel hugged me like a child whose parents have been away on a business trip.

"Get off of me," I said, but couldn't help but laugh.

As he stepped away, he was grinning like a maniac. "I knew it. I knew you had stronger magics. Oh, man, I wish I would've seen it!"

"I don't know, Axel," I said, shaking my head. "I can only vaguely remember it. Feels like a dream. I don't know how I did it. I couldn't do it again."

"What?" he said, shaking his head. "Of course you can. You just need to learn how."

"No, it wasn't like that. It was.... I don't know how to describe it. It was different, Axel. It was magic in a different sense. Truly, I don't understand it, and I don't know that anyone could explain it or teach me. I guess what I'm saying is, it wasn't magic in the traditional sense. Not the way we were taught. It was something...different."

Axel shrugged. "That's not a bad thing. You always were kind of an odd duck."

"Right. Well, it's not our main priority at the moment. We need to find Elder Morgan and the teens, and whoever the hell is pulling their strings. And I've got *no* idea where to start."

"Well, I do."

"You do?"

"Have you forgotten the man in the black car?"

It was my turn to rub my face. "Honestly, with everything else going on, I sort of did. You think he might be our guy?"

"Who else?" Axel said. "August said he didn't recognize him, but we know he had some kind of dealing with all the local gangs. He must be some kind of scum-fucking asshole. It's the best lead we've got."

"Except it isn't much of a lead, since we don't know how to find him. Any word from August this morning?"

Axel shook his head. "No, and I've been calling him. When I was raising hell and trying to get a search party together, I got annoyed and started calling August. He wouldn't answer."

"That's...concerning."

"Agreed," Axel said. "As frustrated as he was when he left, I assumed he'd want to know how things had turned out."

"You think he's in trouble? That Raymond or someone went after him?"

"Don't know," Axel said, then he got a mischievous look on his face. "But I know how to find him."

"You didn't."

"Oh, yeah, I did," Axel replied. "I put a tracking spell on his car."

"That was bold. Weren't you worried about causing it to break down?"

"It's an old Honda. Nothing aside from a tank could stop that thing. I was going to put it on his trench coat, but apparently he has some magical protections on that thing."

"But you think you can find him?"

"Yup."

"All right, you work your magic. I'm going to take a shower."

Ten minutes later, I was showered, dressed, and ready to go. I found Axel pacing in our cabin.

"Any luck?" I replied.

Axel nodded, but I didn't like the look on his face.

I grabbed my staff and sword. "Well?"

"His car is at the Evans' place."

# CHAPTER FIFTY-THREE

We parked a short distance away and approached the Evans's private trailer park on foot, just the same way August had brought us last time. From the same covered hilltop, we could see August's old Honda parked in front of Braedon Evans's house. There was no one in sight.

What was he doing there?

We'd argued about it on the way over. Neither of us could come up with a good reason for him to be there, though Axel had thought of several nonsensical ones.

Yet neither of us had forgotten how he'd conveniently forgotten to mention them when we'd first arrived.

Question was, was August here of his own accord? Were his reasons nefarious? Or was he in some kind of trouble? All of the above?

We hadn't forgotten what August had said about the Evans shooting on sight. But after facing down the Uktena, I wasn't so worried about some backwoods were-methers.

So, we snuck through the trees, keeping a watchful eye and trying to stay out of sight.

As we closed in on Braedon's trailer, we agreed to split up. We could stay in contact through mind-speak.

Axel approached from the side of the trailer and found a window to look through. He informed me he saw nothing of value, except that Braedon clearly needed a maid.

I went behind the trailer and noticed the back door was open.

Anywhere else, and this might've been mighty suspicious. But country folk—and I mean *real* country folk—had a tendency to leave doors open. So, I didn't think much of it, except that it gave me a way in.

I let Axel know what I found, then eased my way up the back porch and crept inside the trailer.

My first impression was that Axel was right: Braedon really needed a maid.

I didn't have a second impression.

Something struck the back of my head and I was looking at a dirty linoleum floor.

Then I passed out.

# CHAPTER FIFTY-FOUR

"Wakey, wakey," a voice said.

I opened my eyes to find myself face-to-face with the ugly mug of Braedon Evans. His yellow teeth revealed themselves behind his asshole smile, which was tucked behind a filthy beard. I immediately felt bad for anyone who'd ever woken up beside him.

Looking around, I saw I was no longer in his trailer. Instead, I was in an abandoned warehouse, and I was bound to a chair. My sword and staff were nowhere in sight.

Axel was to my right, and August Bones was to my left.

They were both awake, but neither looked particularly happy. Of course, they were bound, same as me. Axel looked like he was just grumpy enough to set off his plans for world domination. August, on the other hand, looked haggard and worn down, like he was trying to get over the flu.

I closed my eyes and reached out with my mind. I could feel Dyrnwyn. It was somewhere nearby, which gave me a modicum of hope.

I turned my attention back to Braedon Evans. "Hi there."

The brute chuckled. "Don't know where you're from, fella, but you ought to be more careful. Around here, walking into someone's house uninvited will usually get you a belly full of buckshot."

"Noted," I replied.

He showed me his yellow teeth again. Then he turned to the others standing behind him. It was no stretch to imagine they were brothers. There were seven of them in all. They all had the same big, brutish, burly, hillbilly thing going. And they were all holding guns.

"See?" Braedon said to his brothers. "After all these years, and you morons still want to argue with me. It was easy."

"I still think we should've just killed them," one of the brothers replied. "He's still a Blade Mage."

Braedon chortled to himself and turned back to me. "Are you a Blade Mage?"

"That's what they tell me."

"Yeah, but I don't see your blade," Braedon replied. "Is a Blade Mage still a Blade Mage without a blade?"

"That's a reasonable point," Axel said.

I glared at him.

"What?" Axel said. "It's a valid argument."

I ignored him. At least I knew Axel was okay.

Turning my attention to August, I asked, "Are you all right?"

Braedon answered for him. "Oh, ole Bones is just fine. We're old friends, Bones and us."

"Fuck off," August said, though it seemed like he had to go through some effort to even say that.

"What's wrong with him?" I asked. "What'd you do to him?"

"I didn't do nothing to him," Braedon said. "He done that to himself. Didn't you, Bones?"

August didn't reply.

"Um, I have a question," Axel said. "If anyone's interested in taking questions."

"This look like Jeopardy to you, boy?" Braedon said.

Axel seemed about to reply, then faltered. Finally, he said, "You know, actually, if there was, like, a hillbilly version of Jeopardy, I bet this is exactly what it would look like. I bet the theme song would sound really cool on a banjo."

"What's your question?" Braedon said. "Before I decide to have your mouth sewn shut."

"Well, I was wondering why you didn't just kill us. In fact, it seems like you set a trap for us. Like you knew we were coming."

Braedon proffered Axel with his charming banana smile. "Well, I reckoned it. You see, your friend Bones here is a customer of mine. Aren't you, Bones?"

August turned his head and looked away.

I studied him for a moment, and then it all made sense. How some days he seemed so spry, while at other times, he seemed so haggard. He was an addict.

Braedon must've seen the realization on my face and found it quite humorous. "You didn't know? Really? You didn't know ole Bones was carrying a monkey on his back?"

"No, I guess I didn't," I replied.

"That's why he ain't a big bad constable no more. He can't keep off the junk. He hides it well most of the time, but he's a junkie, make no mistake."

"Is that true?" I asked, looking at August. I already knew the answer.

It was just as well he didn't respond. The more I thought about it, the more it made sense. That was why Elder Morgan had kept him at an arm's length. That was why the tribe had decided he wasn't welcome to join the hunt. They knew they couldn't count on him. And Braedon was probably right. That was why he wasn't a constable anymore.

"Oh, it's the truth," Braedon said, delighted with himself. "Pills are his poison. Ain't that right? Kills the pain. Opiates. Vicodin and Percocet, or even an oxy here or there. When he's in a real jam, really feeling sorry for himself, he'll opt for something a little stronger. Something in a needle, I'm ashamed to say."

"Fuck you, Braedon," August said, still not looking my way.

"I have another question," Axel said, then hummed the theme song for Jeopardy.

"What?" Braedon asked.

"Well, if August is a good customer of yours, then why do you have him tied up?"

"Ah, well, that brings us to it, doesn't it?" Braedon said, walking over to pat August on top of the head. "It's really all about you boys. August here was just the bait. And sure, I don't mind making a few bucks off the ole boy, but you see, I have a new business partner that's very interested in the two of you. Offered more money for your heads than I'd make off Bones's pill problem for years. So, when Bones showed up in need of a fix, well, I saw an opportunity."

It was my turn to laugh. "So, you took him prisoner in hopes we'd come along?"

"Bingo," Braedon said.

"We was up all night," one of the other brothers said. "Hell, by morning, we were all convinced y'all wasn't coming. But Braedon said to keep a vigil."

"I said to stay vigilant, you moron," Braedon said, shaking his head. Then he shrugged. "Brothers."

It made sense, I had to admit. When August had left the camp all distraught, he'd probably headed straight for Braedon's to get a fix. Braedon had taken him hostage, and we'd played right into his hands.

Arrogance. It'll bite you in the ass every time. *Oh, sure, Wyatt, a few were-methers won't be a challenge after the Uktena.* Yeah, the only problem with that logic was that I hadn't really handled the Uktena, had I? *Such an idiot.*

"So, we're trade bait, then?" Axel asked. "That's cool. Always nice to know I'm worth something to someone."

"You're lucky to still be breathing, is what you are," Braedon said. "Our friend wanted you alive. Otherwise, I would've just presented him your heads."

Axel turned to me. "We should go to the casino after this. I mean, our luck *just* keeps stacking up."

"You won't have to wait long," Braedon said. "He should be here any minute."

"And who is this new friend of yours?" I asked.

Braedon shrugged. "He can tell you himself. Now, just sit quiet and behave. He wanted you alive, but he didn't say nothing about putting a .38 special through your kneecaps."

I took his advice, but reached out to Axel through mind-speak, which was marginally harder without my staff for focus. *"Axel, what the hell happened?"*

*"I don't know,"* he responded grumpily. *"I got hit in the back of the head or something."*

*"Same,"* I replied. *"Any clever ideas to get us out of here?"*

*"I'm working on a plan."*

*"So, no?"*

He didn't reply.

*"I can sense Dyrnwyn. It's here somewhere. I could probably call it to me, but I'm not sure if I could get it through my binds."*

*"Good plan, Wyatt. I'm sure they won't shoot you full of buckshot the moment they see a magical sword floating across the room."*

*"So, it's a backup plan."*

*"No, it's not. Leave the planning to me, genius."*

*"Hey, you haven't come up with anything yet!"*

*"That's because you won't shut up long enough for me to think."*

"Hey, Braedon," I said. "Would one of you do me a favor and slap the shit out of my friend?"

Braedon chuckled. "Bones or the weird one?"

"Actually..." I replied, glancing between the two of them. "Both."

"Why does everyone keep calling me the weird one?" Axel asked. "It's the rest of you that are odd. I'm as normal as a ray of sunshine. It's the rest of the world that's got their heads stuck up their asses. Incapable of seeing through their own bullshit. Miserably slogging through life like dreary vampires on a vegan diet."

"Vampires on a vegan diet?" Braedon snorted, then looked at me. "Does he always talk like this?"

"Why do you think I want you to slap him?" I replied.

"Tell you what," Braedon said. "I'll smack the shit out of him and tie a gag in his mouth. How's that?"

"Kinky," Axel said before I could reply.

"Sounds like a plan," I replied. "Better than any idea he's come up with."

"Braedon," one of the brothers near the door called. "He's here."

Braedon gave me an apologetic shrug. "Guess it'll have to wait. Our guest of honor has arrived."

It would be an understatement to suggest I was a little nervous about meeting whoever had offered the brothers money for my head. I was downright scared, and if there was anything I really didn't like, it was being bound. That feeling of helplessness threatened to drive me into a fit, but I took a calming breath and tried my best to look nonplussed.

I studied Axel and tried to emulate his calm presence. Problem was, I wasn't sure Axel was faking it. I wasn't convinced that being tied up in a warehouse by a bunch of burly hillbillies seemed like anything out of the ordinary for him. It was *just* what he was doing that day. No big deal.

The door of the warehouse opened, and I can't say I was surprised to see the smarmy chap in the smart suit.

He was grinning ear-to-ear, and clearly pleased with himself.

This was the first time I'd gotten an up-close look. He appeared to be in his mid-forties, and his hair was groomed to the same perfection as his thousand-dollar suit. Everything about him screamed money.

"So, here are my prizes," he said, his eyes on me.

"All yours," Braedon said.

"And this one?" the man asked, nodding toward August.

"He was the bait," Braedon said with a shrug. "We can take care of him. Make him disappear."

Fancy Pants shook his head. "No worries. I'll take him, too."

"You're sure?" Braedon said. "We don't mind—"

"I said I would take him," the man said, not even bothering to look at Braedon. "You have the sword?"

"Yeah, of course," Braedon said. "It's just over here."

"Leave it," the man said. "You've done well."

His eyes never left mine, even while he bossed Braedon around. It was a little disconcerting.

"You and your brothers may leave now," he said. "You've done well, but I no longer require your services for this particular game."

"You don't want some backup?" Braedon asked. "In case they try something?"

"There's nothing here I can't handle on my own," he replied. "And my team will arrive shortly. Go."

"What about... What about our payment?" Braedon asked, crossing his arms over his chest.

For the first time, the smarmy chap turned to look at Braedon. The hardass were-mether might've been a puppy pissing on the floor for the look he received. "Do you think I am not a man of my word, Braedon?"

"Well, it's not that," Braedon said, taking a step back. "It's just, around here, you pay at the time of delivery."

"I'm not from *around* here," the man said, letting a little venom course through his words. "And you will be paid, Braedon. Do not try my patience. Go."

Braedon held his ground a moment longer, then motioned to the others. The brothers slowly shuffled outside, leaving us alone with the man in the business suit.

As soon as they were gone, he moved over to an old stack of pallets and plopped down across from us.

"Uh, hi there," I said, trying to keep my composure.

"So, you're the Blade Mage," he said, clapping his hands together.

"Or is he?" Axel said, shaking his head. "We just debated this with Braedon. Without the blade, is he really the Blade Mage?"

The man chuckled and rose from his seat. He walked over to where Braedon had left my sword, which the brothers had wrapped in an old pearl snap shirt. He removed the shirt like it was covered in filth and carried Dyrnwyn back to his pallet, where he draped the sword over his knees.

"This is it, then?" he asked. "The genuine arcane artifact? White Hilt?"

I didn't reply.

"What do you think would happen if I tried to wield it?"

"You should try and find out," I replied.

He shook his head. "I'm no Blade Mage. Better that I don't get any ideas in my head, right?"

"No, I think you should try," Axel said. "What's the worst that could happen?"

"You must be the infamous Axel Gunner."

"You know my name," Axel said, narrowing his eyes. Then he glanced at me. "Wyatt, he knows my name."

"I heard," I replied.

The man nodded toward August. "And I guess that's the former constable August Bones, yes?"

"But who are you?" I asked.

"And what are your dealings with the Evans brothers?" Axel asked.

"And what are you doing in Lost City?" I asked.

"And what do you intend to do with us?" Axel said.

"All in good time, boys," the man said. "All in good time. But let me just say, you two have been a right pain in my ass these past couple of days. And that, I'm afraid, must come to an end. Now."

Axel and I glanced at each other.

I had a feeling this wasn't going to end well.

# CHAPTER FIFTY-FIVE

Outside, I heard the rumble of an engine, followed by the death of an engine, followed by several car doors.

"It seems my team has arrived," the man said. "I think you're going to like this part."

*"It's him, isn't it?"* Axel asked. *"He's the bad man."*

*"I don't know."*

*"I bet he is. Do you think it's Waya and his Wolf Pack coming in? Or the Ani-kutani? Is this guy the Ani-kutani? He doesn't look like a fire priest. Wait... What does a fire priest look like? Are they, like, covered in flames? Do you think they would look more like the Human Torch or Ghost Rider?"*

*"Axel, I don't know."*

But he was right about the first part. Who else could it be? This man clearly had power and influence. Who else could he be, if not *the* enemy? Why else would he want us captured?

The man made a *tsk tsk* noise at us. "No using mind-speak, boys. That's rude."

*Oh, shit.* Axel *was* right.

*"It's totally him,"* Axel said, ignoring the man's orders about mind-

speak. *"This is the enemy, Wyatt. We've got to kill him. This is our chance. I'll keep him talking. You strike. Go, now!"*

I turned my head and blinked at my friend. What the hell did he expect me to do?

The door opened and the man's team walked in.

It wasn't Waya and his Wolf Pack.

Nor was it any of the other local gangs.

Yet I did recognize them.

It was the Honey Badgers.

The strike team I'd trained with at the Castle.

I blinked at them a few times as well.

Finally, Commander Harris said, "Hey there, Wyatt."

"Uh, hi," I replied, unsure what else to say.

I glanced over her shoulder and saw a bulldog face. "Hey, Garza."

My former training partner didn't even nod in reply.

"Wait, you know these people?" Axel asked, his head whipping between the newcomers and me so rapidly I thought it might pop right off. "How do you know them?"

I turned my attention back to the man in the suit. "Wait, so, you're... Who the hell are you?"

"The Braedons know me as Mr. Jenkins, a wealthy and powerful crime lord." He laughed. "But you, well, you may refer to me as Watcher Rhodes."

"What the hell is going on?" Axel asked. "I'm so lost. Wyatt, explain to me, please."

I turned to Axel. "You were wrong."

"What? No. I'm, like, *never* wrong."

"They aren't the Ani-kutani."

"Well, obviously. They aren't on fire. Duh."

"He's a watcher, Axel. A watcher from the Cabal. And they're the Honey Badgers, a Cabal strike team. I don't know what they're doing here."

"Okay," Axel said, nodding. "That's all well and good, but if they're from the Cabal, then why am I still tied to this bloody chair?"

"Well, that's just it," Watcher Rhodes said. "I'm not sure what to do with you two."

"What does that mean?" Axel asked.

"You bumbling idiots." Rhodes sighed and stood up. "Did you really think the council completely disregarded the tribe's concerns?"

Axel and I shared a look. In sync, we both said, "Well, *yeah.*"

"Of course not," Rhodes said with a sigh. "The Cherokee medicine men and women have long been allies of the Cabal. For them to have a bunch of kids run off and then this talk of dark magic, well, of course the council wanted to lend aid and find out what the hell was going on."

"But what about all the nonsense of wanting the tribe to give up more control?"

Rhodes shrugged. "Politics. That's why they sent me. I've long been undercover in Oklahoma, building up a reputation as some sort of supernatural crime boss. I've been subtlety building a rapport with the gangs around Lost City for years. So, when this came up, Master Watcher Jackson directed me to use my influence to find the truth. And with the help of the Honey Badgers, I'm to snuff out any dark mages, if we are we to find some."

"But they didn't want the tribe to know?" I asked.

"That's the politics part," Rhodes said, shrugging again. "Naturally, the council sees this as an opportunity to gain a more beneficial arrangement with the Cherokee."

"So, when we saw you meeting with each of the gangs?" I asked.

Rhodes smiled. "Mr. Jenkins is a very wealthy man with ties to supernatural crime families. A deal broker, if you will. Like I said, I've been working undercover, building up a bit of a mythos. The Evanses are morons. Small-time drug-dealing morons. I flash a dollar in their face and they'd murder their own grandmothers. The Red Dirt Riders, well, Raymond is clever, but he's always looking for an angle. I just have to provide him one. Fatima and her group? They're tougher nuts to crack. I've had little luck in my dealings with her. Only information trade. So, after I received my orders, I visited each of them, just to see what I could suss out."

"Does that really work?" I asked.

"Oh, yeah," he said, nodding. "People spill their guts when they think you can make them a lot of money. Nothing buys pretend trust like the mighty dollar. If you help someone's business flourish, then they'll tell you things they wouldn't tell their own spouse. At least, that's true for Braedon and Raymond. Like I said, Fatima is a tougher nut to crack. She'll trade information to protect her group, but even that's limited."

"Sounds about right," I said.

"And we're still tied up," Axel said.

"Right," Rhodes said. "Which brings me back to you two. There I was, making lots of progress, when all of a sudden the Blade Mage comes to town and now we've got a supernatural bloodbath. The Red Dirt Riders are on the warpath. Fatima would rather attack than speak to me. This whole thing is spiraling out of control."

"But have you uncovered anything?"

Rhodes glared at me. "No, because two idiots and their drug-addled new friend have gotten in my way."

"Hey, August," Axel said.

I glanced over and saw that August appeared to be asleep.

"August," Axel continued. "He's talking about you."

August raised his head for a moment, then let it lull to the side again. He was in rough shape.

"So, what's your point, Rhodes?" I asked.

"His point," Commander Harris said, "is that you've all but ruined our investigation."

"That's hardly my fault," I said. "If you jerks had let me know, I wouldn't have gotten in your way."

"I find that hard to believe," Rhodes said. "And regardless, Master Jackson ordered me to be discreet and only reveal my identity if it was absolutely necessary."

"And now it is?"

"Yes," he said. "I need to finish my investigation. And I need you out of the way."

That made me laugh. "You haven't even gotten close. In fact, I think you're barking up all the wrong trees."

"Is that right?" he said, folding his arms over his chest.

"I've met the teens three times now. Have you even laid eyes on them?"

"Yeah?" he asked. "And what's your body count? How many Red Dirt Riders are dead?"

"Oh, you've got me there," I said. "But do you know how many Cherokee are dead now?"

Rhodes watched me in silent observation, but Harris's face betrayed her.

"Yeah, amazing what you can learn if you actually talk to the tribe," I said, shaking my head. "There's more going on here than either of you know."

"So, tell us," Rhodes said. "We're allies, are we not?"

"Uh, no," Axel said. "I mean, I like a bit of kink, but this is just getting old. Is there a safe word or something? We're not friends until the binds come off."

Rhodes sighed and motioned toward Harris, who in turn motioned to her team.

Three members walked over to untie us.

Garza came to remove mine.

"Howdy, Blade Mage," he said as he drew a long K-bar from its sheath and stood in front of me. The tone of his voice wasn't as friendly as the words he used. And he stalled for a moment, perhaps considering whether to kill me after all.

I smiled up at him. "Hey there, Garza. If you decide to *accidentally* miss the rope and stab me, aim for my throat. Last night, I had my skull crushed by a tomahawk, and, well, as you can see, that didn't quite do the trick. Severing my jugular might work better."

He grunted and moved behind me, freeing my wrists. Then he cut the ties around my feet.

I rubbed my wrists and slowly stood up, not quite trusting my own feet. My knee still hurt like hell, and there was a dull ache in the back of my skull from the when the Evanses had struck me, but I was getting used to head trauma.

"There," Rhodes said, spreading his hands. "Now we're all friends. Tell me what you know, Blade Mage."

"Why?" I asked. "I'm pretty sure I know where this conversation leads. You want us out of town."

"You don't think that would be for the best?" he asked. "You don't think you've caused enough trouble?"

"We never cause enough trouble," Axel said.

I glared at him. "Let me handle this."

"Right," he said, moving to the other side of the room. "Where are my drumsticks?"

I glanced over and saw August had remained seated.

"He needs medical attention," Rhodes said. "You should take him to the Castle."

I shook my head. "I'll take him to the tribe."

"I don't think you're getting this," Rhodes said. "You *have* to leave."

I shook my head again. "I made a promise, Rhodes. That might not mean shit to you or the Cabal, but it means something to me. I promised the elders I would help save their kids. They're in more danger than you realize, and Elder Morgan has been taken captive, if he's even still alive."

"Elder Morgan has been captured?" Rhodes asked. "Are you sure?"

"Reasonably confident," I said. "So, you see, I can't leave. I made a promise."

We held each other's gaze for a time, and finally Rhodes sighed. "Fine. Tell me what you know, and perhaps we can work together to keep this from spiraling further out of control."

And so I did.

I told them what I'd learned about the gangs. About my meeting with Raymond. I told them a little about the Uktena, though I left out the name or any real details. If the tribe hadn't wanted me to know those details, then they certainly wouldn't want me to share with others. I could respect that. And I told them about my interactions with the teens.

Rhodes called me out on one tiny, minor, itty bitty detail I might've forgotten to mention.

"There's a rumor that Shain Stone is in town."

"Really?" I asked. "Hmm. Wonder what he's doing here?"

"Don't try to bullshit a watcher." Rhodes rolled his eyes. "The council wants me to bring him in, if I can. Where is he?"

"Don't know."

"You're lying."

"Yes, I am." I turned my attention to Commander Harris. "Don't go after Stone. It's not worth it."

"I'll follow my orders," she said.

I shook my head. "This time it'll be a mistake. There are real enemies to worry about. He's not one of them."

She shrugged. "Orders are orders."

"Well, I suppose it's only fair I share something with you," Rhodes said, changing the subject. He pulled a small plastic bag out of his jacket and held it up for me to see. I might've mistaken the contents for pot, if not for the fact the buds were a dark purple instead of green. "Do you know what this is?"

"A good time?" Axel asked.

"Not quite," Rhodes replied. "It's called Zavan. It's from an extremely rare and ancient plant. According to Cabal records, it's extinct. Yet, here it is, in my hand."

"Okay," I said, not sure where this was going. "Is it some kind of drug?"

Rhodes smiled. "You aren't completely inept after all. Yes, it is a very unique drug. Mages think it enhances their magical ability, and to some degree, I suppose they're right. What it actually does is open more of your mind's connection to magical energy. Allows the user to perform more powerful spells than they probably should. Whereas you or I have to spend more time training and practicing our focus to open our minds to greater amounts of power, this... Well, let's say it can give someone the ability to dump their full metaphorical magical load in one go. Like what Ecstasy does with your serotonin. It's pretty dangerous. The consequences can be dire for the user. And often they lack the ability to control their spells, which is dangerous for everyone else."

"Really?" I asked. This was news to me. "I've never heard of such a thing."

"We thought the plants were extinct," Rhodes said. "It hasn't been seen in our lifetime. And there's one real problem: it's extremely addicting."

"Okay, so why are you telling me about this?"

"Because this bag was found at the barn where you met the kids.

One of our dear local constables found it. He didn't mention it to the tribe, and instead sent it back to his superiors at the Castle."

"So, Waya and his little wolf pack are taking this?" I asked.

Rhodes shrugged. "Sure seems like it. The question is, where are they getting it from? My first suspicion was the Evanses, since that's sort of their thing, but it wasn't them."

"So, where?" I asked.

"That's the question, isn't it?" he asked, moving over to August. When the former constable looked up at him, Rhodes held up the bag. "What about you? Have you ever seen this before?"

August shook his head.

"A shame," Rhodes said. "I'd hoped one of you might know something."

"No, but I can make a guess," I said, considering. "And there's something else you should know. Have you ever heard of the Ani-kutani?"

Rhodes shook his head.

"That's who Alyita—or Pathkiller, as she prefers to be called—that's who she said she was serving. They were some ancient religious order. Used to rule the Cherokee. But apparently, they were real assholes and the Cherokee rooted them out. Or so they thought."

"Mages?" Rhodes asked.

"They're called the fire priests, so I'll go with yes."

Rhodes rubbed his chin. "Either way, if there is a dark entity here, someone must know who and where. And that's probably the source."

I shrugged. "Maybe, but we've not had any luck finding them. Although the kids seem hellbent on killing me. Whoever they're working for, they want me dead."

"Hmm," Rhodes said. "Maybe I should have you tied back up and dangled in front of them like a carrot."

I raised an eyebrow.

"That was a joke, of course."

"And while it was an *excellent* joke, I think I'll be taking my staff and sword back now."

"This is a serious matter, Wyatt," Rhodes said. "And I think the best course of action would still be for you to leave the area."

"And you don't think that would be suspicious? For me, Axel, and August to just disappear?"

"We can let them think the Evanses killed you. Or that this Wolf Pack killed you. It doesn't matter. What we need now is subtlety."

"No, what we need is to find the kids. Save them. Save Elder Morgan. And then put a very cruel end to these fire priests or whoever the hell is pulling the strings around here."

"I agree," Rhodes said. "But what are your current leads?"

I sighed. "The only lead we had was the strange man in the black car."

"So, you have nothing, then?"

I glared at him.

"It's true, and you know it. We, on the other hand, have a lead we intend to run up."

"What's the lead?"

He shook his head. "I don't want you involved. I want you to go back to the Castle and let us handle it from here."

"That isn't going to happen."

"I'm not above having you tied up again."

"Yeah, well, you won't find it as easy this time."

Again we held a staring contest.

Commander Harris sighed. "Why don't we agree to a compromise?"

We both turned to look at her.

She motioned to me first. "Give us one day, Blade Mage. Go hang out with the tribe, or go home, or whatever. I don't care. Stay out of our way for one day and let Rhodes see what he can find. Tomorrow, we'll bring you up to speed and agree what's next from there."

Rhodes nodded. "I can live with that. Can you?"

I didn't like it, but I didn't see another way. The fact of the matter was, if they really wanted me out of their way, it wasn't a fight I could win. And it certainly wouldn't help my relationship with the Cabal to have an altercation with the team they'd sent.

I sighed. "Fine. I can agree to a day."

Rhodes smiled. "Well, aren't we all just best friends now? We've done you the favor of bringing your truck here. Feel free to leave."

"How can I contact you?" I asked.

"You can't," he replied. "I'll contact you."

With that, I started toward the door.

It wasn't until we were in the truck that Axel asked, "So, what next?"

I glared at him. "I promised not to do anything for the next twenty-four hours."

Axel nodded. "You're right. *You* promised not to do anything."

As I put the truck in gear, I felt a smile play at my lips.

# CHAPTER FIFTY-SIX

B ack on the road, I glanced over at August, who was riding in the center between Axel and me. "Do you have your phone? Or did they take it from you?"

August fished into his trench coat and produced the old flip phone.

I took it from him and pulled off the side of the road. Flipping through the contacts, I found the number for the tribe's camp and called it. I didn't recognize the voice that answered, but I identified myself and asked to speak to Elder Thomas.

I pulled back on the road while I waited.

"This is Elder Thomas."

"Hey, it's Wyatt. I have a question to ask."

"Go for it."

"I've got August with me. He's in bad shape. Can I bring him to the camp to have your healers have a look at him?"

"He's injured?" Elder Thomas asked.

"No," I said, glancing over at August, who looked completely deflated at the loss of dignity. "Not quite."

"I see," the elder replied. "No, Wyatt. Whatever you do, don't bring him here."

"Okay," I said, not sure what else to say. I wasn't sure what to do about him.

Elder Thomas continued, "Listen, Ahuli is on the warpath. It isn't good. You should get back here as quickly as possible, but don't bring August. You'll understand when you arrive."

"Right," I said. "See you soon."

I ended the call.

There was an awkward silence in the truck for a few moments, and part of that was Axel humming "MMMBop." The other part was the look on August's face.

Finally, he said, "I guess I'm not welcome at the camp. That's for the best. I don't want them to see me like this."

"I don't think it's that. It sounds like something else. We need to get back there."

"But you can't take me," August said. "Pull over. Just leave me on the side of the road."

I didn't reply. Instead, I was thinking. I didn't have time to drive him all the way to the Boston Mountains to drop him off at the Castle. I needed somewhere close so I could get back to the Cherokee's training camp.

And then it hit me. There was one person in Lost City who'd likely be willing to take in an addict struggling through withdrawals.

"I've got a better idea, August. I think it's time you got right with the Lord."

"What?" August said, not following.

Axel clapped and said, "Hallelujah, we're going to church! This motha' fucka' needs Jesus!"

"No," August said. "Don't take me there."

"You've got a better idea?" I asked.

"Dump me off on the side of the road."

"And the Lord saideth unto he," Axel said, using his TV preacher voice, "we shall not leave thee upon the side of the highwayee. Ye shall be taken unto the House of the Lord, amen!"

"Your choice, August. We can take you to Pastor Wright to rest, or you can sit in the truck and listen to Axel's sermon."

August growled. "Fine. Take me to Pastor Wright."

"And all the people rejoiced!" Axel said. "Can I get an amen?"

"Fuck off, Axel," August said, then closed his eyes.

# CHAPTER FIFTY-SEVEN

~

I was glad to see that Pastor Wright was home and not out on one of his walks, or whatever else preachers did when it wasn't preaching time.

The front door of the church was unlocked, and he came out from the back as we half carried August inside. August was really struggling with his withdrawals.

The nervous little holy man rushed forward, either concerned about the state of August or surprised by our unexpected visit.

"Sorry," I said as he approached. "I didn't know where else to go."

Axel slid August into a pew and plopped down beside him. I remained standing.

"What's wrong with him?" Pastor Wright asked. "Is he injured?"

"I'm fine," August said, not looking up at him.

The pastor turned his gaze on me.

I shrugged. "Withdrawals."

Wright's face took on a concerned expression. "Oh, August, I know this must be a terrible experience, but I can assure you, you've made the right decision. Albeit you might be better off at a hospital."

August shook his head. "No hospital. I'll be fine. Just got to get back on my feet is all."

"Can you?" Axel asked. "Can you get back on your feet, August?"

August glared at him but didn't reply.

I turned to Pastor Wright and whispered, "He's not sobering up by choice. His dealer betrayed him."

"I see," Wright said, his eyes still on August. "I have some experience with this sort of thing, though he really looks like he should go to the hospital."

"I don't have time to take him to the hospital," I said, shrugging.

"You're leaving him here, then?" Pastor Wright asked, meeting my gaze.

"That was my hope." Then on second thought added, "but just for a little while."

Pastor Wright sighed. "I'll not turn away one of my flock. Let's get him to the back."

Axel picked August back up again and helped him toward the back. I chipped in a little, but Axel took most of the burden.

We got him back to the spare beds where Axel and I had spent the night and laid him down while Pastor Wright excused himself to go start some tea. I wasn't sure tea would do much to calm the demons in August's soul, but the preacher did make a wicked good tea.

"Wyatt," August said, looking up at me. "I'm sorry."

I wasn't sure how to reply, so I said, "It's okay, August."

"It really isn't though, is it?" August asked. "It's been... Ever since... I haven't had my shit together since Alyita's mom died. I should've told you. I've let you down. I've let the tribe down. I've let everyone down."

I wasn't sure how to reply. Axel was.

"You're right," Axel said, shrugging at August. "We could really use your help right now. And so could the tribe. So could your best friend's child."

"There's a way you can help me get back on my feet," August said, not looking at either of us.

"We aren't going to help you get a fix," I said. "For one, I wouldn't even know where to find anything like that on short notice, and even if I could, I wouldn't. Sorry."

"No, it's me who should be sorry," he said, shaking his head. He let out a miserable little laugh. "To even ask... What kind of person am I?"

"Don't do that," Axel said. "You've made mistakes, but now isn't the time to beat yourself up. You just need to rest and try to get your head clear."

Ignoring Axel, August said, "Well, now you know why I'm not a constable. It started after... Well, you know. And now you know why the tribe doesn't trust me. Why I'm a joke to the Cabal and everyone in this shit hole little town."

"That's not true, August," I said. "You're a good man. You've done what you could to help your friends and they couldn't ask for more. Now it's time to take care of yourself. Leave it with Axel and me. We'll get things sorted."

August turned his head and looked away.

After a moment, I thought he was asleep again.

Axel said, "Leave me with him for a minute."

I nodded and moved out to the kitchen to find Pastor Wright.

"Is he settled?" Wright asked as he continued tinkering with things in the kitchen.

"I suppose," I replied. "I guess this was what you were referring to when you said there were things it wasn't your place to tell me."

"It isn't a secret around Lost City. August has a problem."

"It was a secret to me," I replied. "I wish someone would've told me before now."

"He should've told you," Pastor Wright said. "It certainly wasn't for me or anyone else."

I bit my tongue. Truth be told, I was a little frustrated with the preacher and the tribe as well. We were facing very real danger, and August had been with us for a lot of that danger. While he'd been medicated, he'd seemed in control, but now...

And I was a little disappointed with myself. I supposed I should've seen it. Or Axel should have. Of course, knowing Axel, he might have and decided it wasn't worth mentioning.

I realized I'd gotten lost in my own thoughts and returned to the present. "I'm sorry for bringing this burden to you. I wasn't sure where else I could take him, and Axel and I are in a bit of a hurry."

"Still trying to find the kids?"

I nodded, but I wasn't going to go into any further detail.

"Do you remember when you first arrived?" Pastor Wright asked. "Do you remember what we discussed?"

"Yeah," I said. "You didn't want us in town because you were worried about what would happen."

"And how many are now dead?" he asked, turning to look at me. "I hear things, Wyatt. I might not be the most well informed, but it *is* a small town."

I nodded at him, unsure what I could say.

"Should I expect to hear of more deaths?" Pastor Wright asked. "Should I expect to find out that more of my flock have been culled?"

Again, I didn't have an answer, and I doubted he'd heard about the losses the tribe had suffered yet.

"Death follows you, doesn't it?" he asked.

I nodded again. "Sure seems to."

"Then I ask you again, Blade Mage... No, I beg of you: please leave Lost City. Just go home."

"I'm not sure it'll be better if I do."

"Is that true? Is that what you really believe, or just what you tell yourself?"

I started to reply, but again bit my tongue. It was a fair question, and though it might've annoyed me, I wasn't so sure. And I certainly didn't want to be a jerk when he was helping us.

"Your silence is answer enough," the preacher said, turning from his work in the kitchen to cross his arms over his chest. "Is there anything I could say that would convince you to leave Lost City?"

I met his gaze and slowly shook my head.

"That's what I feared," he said, holding my gaze. "So, all I can do is pray."

"Perhaps," I said. "And we could all probably use a bit of it."

"Will you pray with me then, Blade Mage?"

I shook my head. "No. I've got work to do."

# CHAPTER FIFTY-EIGHT

A s soon as we arrived back at the camp, John came out to greet us. Apparently, he'd been keeping an eye out. He rushed us straight to Elder Thomas, who led us straight to Ahuli. We met him and a few of the other elders in the same conference room we'd first met Elder Morgan in. That felt like a lifetime ago.

The war chief seemed mostly recovered from his injuries, which at one time had seemed life threatening. Of course, I'd been on the edge of death by all accounts, and the Nunnehi had put my head back together. So, it wasn't a stretch to see him looking well.

When we were all seated, I asked, "What's this about?"

Ahuli answered. "War."

"Okay," I said, glancing at Elder Thomas, then back at Ahuli. "Care to explain that further?"

"We have considered what you told us," Ahuli said. "About Alyita and Elder Morgan. All of it. We can no longer stand by and treat our rebellious children as children."

"What are you saying?" I asked.

"Alyita has the Ulun'suti and she has taken Elder Morgan hostage."

"Hold on," I said, putting up a hand. "We don't know that for sure. I mean, it's safe to assume she took the Ulun'suti, sure, but we can't assume she took Elder Morgan prisoner. It's possible he decided to go with her."

"Then we should consider him an enemy as well?" Ahuli asked.

"What?" I asked, stunned by the statement. "No, that's not what I'm saying. Elder Morgan might've chosen to go with Path... Alyita to try to convince her from this path. We don't know."

Ahuli shrugged. "It doesn't matter. A decision had to be made. We can no longer sit idly by."

"What are you suggesting?" I asked.

"He..." Elder Thomas started, then paused. "The tribe has voted, Wyatt. We're going after Waya, Alyita, and their pack...as enemies."

"As enemies?" I asked, hardly believing what I was hearing.

Beside me, Axel laughed. "You intend to fight your own children? To kill them?"

"If we must," Ahuli said. "The Ulun'suti must come back to the tribe. It belongs with the Cherokee. And this mention of the Ani-kutani, it cannot stand. Even if it is but a lie, it is one that must be silenced. Elder Morgan allowed this to go on too long. I have summoned a war council and we have decided."

"You're serious?" I asked. "You intend to attack your own children?"

Ahuli nodded.

"There's more," Elder Thomas said, his gaze on the war chief. "Will you tell them, or should I?"

Ahuli's gaze met mine. "Where is August Bones?"

"Why?" I asked.

Ahuli's glare hardened. "You will not ask questions any longer. You will answer them."

I held his gaze but didn't reply.

He asked again. "Where is he?"

I shrugged. "Haven't seen him. Why are you interested in him all of a sudden?"

"You know Samuel?" Ahuli asked. "He is one of the instructors here."

"I know him, yes."

"He confiscated drugs from one of the kids. Not any drug, but a very special plant which can enhance the effects of our medicine. He thought it was pot at first, the fool."

I nodded, not mentioning I'd only just learned about this very drug.

Ahuli continued, "When Samuel questioned the kid, he said it was August Bones who supplied it to him."

I turned and glanced at Axel, who'd sat forward in his chair, eyes narrowed. "No."

"Yes," Elder Thomas said, nodding at Axel.

"I'm not denying what you were told," Axel replied, smiling pleasantly at the elder. "I'm telling you it's not true, though. August wouldn't have done that."

Elder Thomas gave him a soft smile. "I know you may find it hard to believe, but we all know August has a problem."

"Why would he do that?" I asked. "August was the one who came to the Cabal to get help for you guys. He's been your biggest ally all along."

Ahuli shook his head. "No. We believe that was a ruse."

"Consider it," Elder Thomas said. "I don't want to believe it either, but it makes sense. If August didn't have the money to pay his dealer, maybe his dealer convinced him to bring the plant to our kids in exchange for his junk. How else would they have gotten their drugs into our camp?"

"Can I speak to this kid?" I asked.

Elder Thomas shook his head. "No. Unfortunately he was the last to leave us. It wasn't until he left that Samuel told us what he'd discovered. We believe the youngster was likely hankering for a fix, and that was why he fled to join the others. Perhaps this is how we've been losing them all along."

Elder Thomas seemed genuinely sad, but Ahuli looked... Well, he looked ready for war.

"And what will you do when you find August?" I asked, trying to keep my voice neutral.

"He will die," Ahuli said. "That will be his punishment."

"But you don't have solid evidence," I replied.

"It has been decided," Ahuli said. "We will sit by no longer. Elder Morgan has allowed the lands around our training grounds to become a cesspit. When I came to Lost City and learned of the gangs here, and the drugs, and now our own have abandoned us... No longer."

"What are you saying?" I asked.

"Tonight, the Cherokee go to war," Ahuli said, as though that were answer enough.

"Not just our teens," Elder Thomas said, his gaze pleading with me. "And not just August."

"All the filth will be driven from our lands or destroyed," Ahuli said. "We will have the Ulun'suti and we will have a reckoning, and any of these gangs who get in our way will perish as well. Any who choose not to stand with the Cherokee will be considered an enemy."

"So, you're going after the Red Dirt Riders as well?" I asked. "And the Evanses?"

Ahuli nodded.

"And Fatima's group," Elder Thomas said.

"Fatima's group?" Axel said. "What have they done?"

"All filth must be cleaned from this land," Ahuli repeated. "If this Fatima and her mages agree to stand with the Cherokee, they may stay. Otherwise, they, too, will be seen as enemies."

"So, that's it then?" I asked. "You're just going to take on the whole of Lost City? Haven't you lost enough people?"

"Yes," he said, glaring at me. "We've lost many of our children, and we'll allow it no longer. It has been decided."

We stared at each other for some time and I struggled to keep my patience. There was nothing for me to say. As he'd said, it had been decided.

"Well, this is awkward," Axel said, breaking through the tension. "C'mon, Wyatt. Let's go."

Ahuli shook his head and I felt Dyrnwyn tremble on my back.

I met the war chief's gaze again. "And us?"

"You're either with us or you're against us," the war chief said.

It was a threat.

"You're serious? After everything we've been through trying to help you. You'd name us enemies because we won't take part in your madness?"

"You're with us, or you're against us," Ahuli repeated. "It is your decision."

I rose slowly from my seat. "No, Ahuli. We are neither. In my time here, I've seen that the Cherokee are wise and your medicine is strong. But this... This is madness. And as I told the elders from the start, I'm no child killer. I'll not start now. Not for your threats or anyone else's."

A heavy silence fell over us, and though I couldn't sense their magic the way I could another mage's, the air felt thick, and I had little doubt a working was in play. Ahuli was ready to get his war started.

"In case anyone is interested," Axel said, glancing around the room as he twirled a drumstick between his fingers with casual grace, "I am also not a child killer. I mean... I was accused of kidnapping a child once, but that was all just a misunderstanding. Point is, I second what my dear life-mate said. I will not be partaking in the murder of angsty tweens."

I turned and glared at him. "We are not life-mates."

Axel shrugged. "So you keep telling me."

"This is no joke," Ahuli said, slowly rising to his feet.

"Yeah, I'm afraid it is," I said.

And Ahuli laughed. "Elder Morgan believed in you, Blade Mage, but I can see he was wrong in that as well. You are weak. No better than the other filth who plague our lands."

"Maybe," I said, shrugging. "Maybe I am, at that. In fact, you could ask just about anyone in my Cabal and they'd probably agree with you. But I'll tell you this, Ahuli. Not only will I not help you murder your own kids, but I'm going to do everything in my power to stop you."

"So you are an enemy to the Cherokee, then?" he asked.

"No, I am a friend to the Cherokee. And that is why I won't allow you to murder the tribe's own."

"Wait," Elder Thomas said, forcing himself up on his cane. "Everyone, just wait!"

We all turned our attention to the elder medicine man. His gaze was on Ahuli. "Is this what we're to become? Are we to turn on those who've helped us?"

Ahuli's eyes narrowed. "There is no white chief here, Elder. Only a red chief. And I say it is war, and it is for me to decide who the enemy is."

Elder Thomas shook his head. "Then I'm afraid you'll have to kill this old medicine man as well, War Chief. I will not be a part of this either."

Ahuli seemed about to say something, but John spoke up and cut him off. "That goes for me as well. The Blade Mage fought bravely against the Uktena. We died beside each other, or at least, we would have, but the Nunnehi thought him one of us. I'll not fight him. Nor will I fight our own children."

Ahuli glanced around the table. "Are there any other traitors among us? Any others who will not do what's needed to save our tribe?"

No one answered.

"It is no surprise," Elder Thomas said, motioning around the table. "Most here came with your first war party. Yet I don't think you'll find many among our instructors who will be so willing to kill the youngsters they've trained. But your war party has taken over, hasn't it?"

"It was voted," Ahuli said. "I am War Chief, and we are to make war."

"But not us," Elder Thomas said. "We shall not take part. And there will be others."

"Go, then," Ahuli said. "Leave these training grounds, Elder. Take these cowards with you. Do not return. Watch from afar as the Cherokee reclaim their glory."

Elder Thomas gave the war chief a soft nod. "I fear you will find little glory in this, Ahuli."

"What of Shain Stone?" I asked. "Should we take him as well? I doubt he'll be a willing party to your plans."

Ahuli shrugged. "He is severely injured. He may remain until he heals or dies. This will be over long before he can move on his own feet, that I can assure you."

I refrained from pointing out that Stone might surprise him. I wasn't sure how fast he was planning to start this war of his, but I had the impression it was going to be sooner rather than later.

"Thank you," I said, though it hurt to say it.

Ahuli shook his head. "He was harmed in service to our tribe. These things are not forgotten lightly."

Again I bit my tongue, not bothering to point out that I also had been severely damaged in service to the tribe. It was pretty clear we were getting off lucky by being allowed to leave without violence. And that was all thanks to Elder Thomas stepping in. Perhaps that had been his plan all along, and why he'd told me to hurry back.

Together, our disenchanted group started toward the door.

"Ten minutes," Ahuli said. "I want you gone in ten minutes, or I will change my mind."

"Change your mind about killing the kids?" Axel asked, looking back hopefully.

"No," Ahuli said. "I'll change my mind about killing you."

"Damn," Axel said. "For a moment, I thought that was going to be really easy. Ah, well. Let's blow this popsicle stand. All this talk about killing children is boring."

Axel stomped out the door. The rest of us followed.

# CHAPTER FIFTY-NINE

Elder Thomas was right.

A handful of the camp's teachers joined us in a strategic retreat, including Samuel, who I was glad to see with us. He didn't strike me as the type who'd be too keen on warfare, yet I also wasn't sure he'd have the courage to walk away. It probably helped to have Elder Thomas with us.

They loaded into Elder Thomas's old Bronco while Axel and I jumped in my truck.

As soon as we were on the dirt road, I pulled over in the ditch and got out to wait for them.

Elder Thomas pulled up beside me and rolled down his window.

"What now?" I asked.

Elder Thomas shook his head. "If I knew where to find the kids, that's where I'd go. I'd try to get them out of town."

"But we don't know where they are," I said, biting my lip. "They aren't the only people we can help. I know where August Bones is."

"I figured you might," Elder Thomas said, giving me a forced smile.

"And we should warn Fatima," I said.

"And as much as I hate to say it," Axel said, giving me a knowing look, "we should probably get a message to the Cabal."

"Right," I said, considering our game plan. I turned back to Elder Thomas. "Do you trust John to drive your Bronco?"

"Of course," the elder said, glancing at the younger man.

John shrugged in reply.

Back to Axel, I said, "You go with John and the others to pick up August. If Ahuli marches his war party out of camp, they're more likely to find him before they make it to Fatima, so I want you to have the backup. After you pick up August, head to the constable office to get that message sent. It's right down the road."

Axel bowed. "Thy will be done."

I turned to Elder Thomas. "Why don't you come with me to speak to Fatima? I'm not sure she'll be too pleased to see me roll up on her land again. But she might not attack me outright if you're there."

"That's good thinking," Elder Thomas said, getting out of the Bronco.

I glanced through the window and saw the back seat was already cramped. That would not be ideal for packing in August as well. I glanced at Samuel. "You should come with us."

"Sure," Samuel said.

A minute later, we were back on the road, following behind the Bronco in my truck. Our path would split once we got to town, but for the moment, I was comforted by having Axel and John just in front of us.

The ride was quiet, Elder Thomas and Samuel both lost in their thoughts, same as I was.

When we hit town, I waved at the Bronco. They went left. We went right. I just hoped I remembered how to get to Fatima's camp. If not, hopefully Elder Thomas or Samuel would.

"Do you really think Ahuli will make war with everyone?" I asked.

"Yes," Elder Thomas said. "Of those trained in the ways of Cherokee medicine, there is much division. Some believe we should assert ourselves. Ahuli is loudest among those."

"He's an ass," Samuel said.

"No," Elder Thomas said, shaking his head. "He can be, yes. But don't underestimate Ahuli by thinking he is a fool. He's a good war chief. Not a good peace chief. I believe the decision to engage in war is a bad one. But if it is to be war, then Ahuli is the right one to lead."

"We just have to figure out how to stop the war from occurring," I said, trying to throw in some positive optimism. "You know—"

I never finished my sentence.

Something slammed against the side of my truck and then we were sliding sideways out of control. My reflexes kicked in gear and I steered into the skid, trying to get it back under control. I almost had it when the unseen force struck again.

As we slammed into the ditch, I was reminded of the last time this had happened, and what it had cost to fix my poor beater. And I was reminded of the time in the Cabal's SUV, when the Abasy had knocked us off the road.

Bouncing around in the cab, I was thankful I'd been wearing my seatbelt. And I was just hopeful that whatever was waiting for us outside wasn't a demon or giant emo-boar. Assuming I survived the coming impact, I couldn't wait to find out.

My truck slammed against a tree, then bounced back into the ditch.

It took a moment for my brain to catch up to the chaos.

At least I hadn't blacked out this time. Maybe my luck with wrecks was improving.

I turned my attention to Samuel, who'd been seated in the middle. His eyes were closed, but he didn't seem any worse for wear. Elder Thomas had a small gash over one eye that was bleeding, but there was no noticeable damage beyond that. Of course, with a head injury, there was no telling.

"You guys all right?" I asked.

Samuel's eyes opened and he seemed a little disoriented. "I think I'm okay. Elder Thomas?"

The aging medicine man opened his eyes and glanced between us, seeming a little confused. "I think I hit my head a little."

"We need to get out," I said, trying to peer through my now spider-webbed windshield. "That wasn't an accident. Something hit us. Twice."

Without waiting for a response, I kicked open my door and got out, slowing only long enough to retrieve my sword and staff.

Elder Thomas opened the passenger door and nearly stumbled out. He only kept his feet by clinging to the opened door. Samuel got out behind him and held the older man.

I turned my focus back to looking for threats. They weren't hard to find.

Three robed figures stood before us, their faces hooded. However, there were another five men with them, and they were recognizable. Red Dirt Riders. And one among them was the brute who'd tried to stare me down when I'd met with Raymond.

Seeing he had my attention, he smiled at me. "You don't look so tough now, Blade Mage."

Ignoring him, I eased around my truck and motioned to Samuel to get Elder Thomas behind me. We were surrounded, but my busted-up truck offered some cover.

I forced a smile at the biker brute. "Who are your friends in the robes? I figured you guys had mages in your ranks, but I doubt they dress for Halloween like these over-the-top clowns."

The brute shrugged. "New friends. Raymond has us teamed up with some new allies, and it turns out, we all have something in common."

"And what's that?"

"We all want you dead."

Well, at least I knew they didn't plan to take me alive. That simplified things.

Not knowing the capabilities of the hooded goons complicated them, though.

I also wasn't sure about Elder Thomas's condition, or whether he'd be able to help, but perhaps Samuel could. Either way, I wasn't completely on my own.

I turned my head slightly but kept my eyes on the enemies in front of me. In a low voice, I said, "Samuel, watch out for Elder Thomas. I'll try to keep their attention on me."

Samuel didn't reply.

Instead, I heard Elder Thomas cry out in pain and turned to see the elder fall to the ground. A bone-handled knife protruded from his back.

Samuel backed away slowly. Looking up at me, he said, "The Ani-kutani rise."

"Ah, fuck. Really, Samuel?"

Elder Thomas was on the ground, and judging by the blood loss, he wouldn't live long.

I assumed the three hooded figures knew magic of some kind. With Samuel, that was four. Four enemies who wielded magic I didn't understand. And, of course, the Riders had their guns.

I felt my nerves fire to life and a tremble crept up my spine. I was always nervous before the action started, but fine once it got underway, so I figured we might as well get started.

"You fellas sure you don't want to get some more backup?" Flames raced down Dyrnwyn's blade. "You might need help to make this a fair fight."

It was a bluff, of course, but a bluff was really all I had.

"Wyatt," Elder Thomas said from the ground. "Samuel..."

"I know," I said, keeping my eyes up. "Just relax. I've got things under control."

I sensed him shift and glanced down to see that he'd rolled toward my truck and was in a half-seated position, taking in what was happening. I wasn't sure whether he was still with it or lost in a state of shock.

"What are you waiting for?" the brute asked the hooded figures. "Kill that prick already."

One of the hoods turned toward him and a raspy voice asked, "Would you like to do this?"

The brute shut up.

The hooded figures began chanting.

And a very loud caw sounded.

Followed by another.

Then another.

The sound of cawing drowned out the chanting of my enemies and the sky filled with black fluttering forms.

A swarm of birds swept down around us.

I could only assume I was about to be swarmed again.

Only, this time, it wasn't all different birds. These were ravens.

And it wasn't me they attacked.

They descended on the robed sorcerers first. Then the bikers and Samuel.

A vortex of black feathers appeared, circling around Elder Thomas and me.

Someone screamed and I saw one biker drop to his knees, blood pouring from his face.

Another of them was lifted off the ground and hurled to the other side of the road, where he lay unmoving.

The robed figures were making out better, but only slightly.

I saw flashes of magic as they tried to attack the birds, but the black mass seemed unperturbed and continued its assault.

A darkness began to build around us, and for a moment, I thought it was just the flock blocking our view of the sun. After a moment, I realized it was truly growing darker. As though the shadows were creeping toward us.

*Ah, shit.*

I'd seen this before.

As if I didn't have enough problems to deal with.

One of the robed figures ignored the birds attacking him and stood up straight. He began chanting again. I had to hand it to the guy: there was no way I could've concentrated on magic with that many flapping death birds pecking at my head.

Another of the hooded figures joined the chant.

The Red Dirt Riders attempted to flee, and Samuel raced toward the hooded men while trying to swat birds away from his face.

There was a flash of red and then they were gone.

All of them.

The shadows dissipated and the flock of ravens soared up into the air, rejoining in one black mass before diving toward my feet.

And then my old pal appeared in front of me.

The Valravn.

As always, he appeared as the face-changing man in a pinstriped suit. The creepy fucker always showed up at the oddest times.

Behind me, Elder Thomas gasped.

I looked back at him and saw he was staring at the Valravn, his eyes wide and filled with fear. He looked over at me and said, "Raven Mocker."

The Valravn winked at the injured medicine man, then turned his attention to me. "Hello, Wyatt."

"What are you doing here?"

"Just checking in on one of my investments. You're welcome, by the way."

"I had it under control."

"Did you? My apologies, then, for making your enemies flee."

"What do you want?"

"Straight to the point, as usual," he said, taking out his coin. He flipped it up and caught it in that annoying habit he had. "What do I want? Well, I want you to survive, for one. This little drama you're playing out is interesting, sure, but it's over your head now, isn't it?"

I didn't reply.

"I'd not see you throw your life away in a fight that isn't yours. Certainly not one that isn't mine. I have use for you still, you know?"

I laughed. Right in his stupid, ever-changing face.

"Use for me? What makes you think I'd ever do anything for you?"

"You already have, mate. You've done plenty. And while your intentions aren't the same as mine, the results are mostly to my benefit. I'd like to keep that arrangement in play, at least for a little longer."

"What are you talking about?"

"The enemy, Wyatt. The *real* enemy." He spoke as though I were a child. "I think he fears you lot. All of you Arcane Guardians. And he should. But you, you in particular, you just keep popping along, charging headfirst into these little dramas. Meddling in the lesser affairs of those he's recruited as allies. I daresay, you must be getting on his nerves. You're on my side and I find you annoying. How must he feel?"

"Are you suggesting that what's happening in Lost City is somehow related to your dark conspiracy theories?"

"My *theories*?" the Valravn asked, making a tsk tsk noise. "Have you forgotten all that you've seen? Or are you merely playing dumb with me? I know what you saw, Wyatt. I know what you saw in Memphis when you peeked through the looking glass."

"What did I see?"

"A dark council."

*Well, shit.*

He wasn't wrong, but I wasn't sure I wanted to admit it.

"I don't know what I saw."

"Yes, you do. You saw a dark council, our pal the revenant among them. You know what you saw, Wyatt Draven. You saw a gathering storm."

"And what's that got to do with Lost City?"

"Have you paid attention to anything I've said?" He turned his attention to Elder Thomas, but pointed at me. "This guy, am I right, Elder? Have you ever met someone so thick?"

"I'll not speak to you, Raven Mocker," Elder Thomas said with trembling lips.

His face was paling, and I knew I was running out of time to get him help.

The Valravn scoffed at the medicine man and mumbled to himself. "I really should find some better, morally bankrupt allies."

Turning his attention back to me, he said, "What do any of these incidents have in common? Hmm? Think, Blade Mage. What is happening everywhere? I've already told you... The real enemy is gathering allies. He's opened his doors to every disenfranchised, disenchanted, and disassociated dickhead. Every sorcerer in hiding. Every supernatural being with a score to settle. Every idiot hungry for power. He is offering them their desires, if they only do his bidding, and he has the resources to get them all on his side."

"Like the Ani-kutani," I said.

"Like the Ani-kutani," he repeated. "For hundreds of years, the fire priests have lived, trained, and passed their knowledge through their bloodlines in secret. They've remained hidden, each generation teaching the next, and not just the magic, no, but the ancient hate that goes with it. They are bred to abhor their betrayers, but never before have they had to strength to strike back at the Cherokee. Never before have they been so bold as to try to reclaim their ancient throne. What changed now, I wonder?"

I stared at him, watching his features shift.

"They've made a new friend. Some*thing* crept from the darkness and whispered in their ears. *Someone* promised them the power to reclaim their 'rightful' place as rulers over the Cherokee."

"Why would the 'real' enemy, as you call him, care what happens to the Cherokee?"

I already knew the answer as the words left my mouth. The Valravn patiently waited for me to say it.

I sighed. "Because then he'd have an army of medicine men and women."

"And another potential foe out of his way. He builds his armies even as he tears down any who might oppose him. It isn't so different from what happened in Memphis. Except he knew the Knights would never do his bidding, so he gave aid to their enemies, that they might destroy the Memphis Knights and take them off the table. With the Cherokee, though, well, if the Ani-kutani rule the tribe, then those medicine men who serve them must, in turn, serve him."

"So, we have to stop them."

"No." The Valravn held a hand up to his face in frustration. "How are you so thick? What's happening here is happening everywhere. This one fight is small potatoes, my dimwitted friend. Who cares about the Cherokee?"

"I care."

"They are but one faction." He held up a finger, I guessed because he thought I couldn't count that high. "Good riddance. Let the Ani-kutani have them. You're no match for the fire priests anyway, kiddo."

"Thanks for the vote of confidence."

"I really don't know how else to explain this to you. If you continue this fight, you *will* die. For sure. The fire priests will cook your dimwitted ass, and then who will continue annoying the real enemy, eh?"

I glared at him.

"So, go home! Better yet, go back to your castle and let your Cabal know about the Ani-kutani. Let those stodgy old mages find a solution. This isn't *your* fight. You've more important things to do. Like continuing to be a right pain in my enemy's ass."

I shook my head. "Look, you're right about one thing: I do owe you thanks for saving my life. So, thanks. But I'm not leaving Lost City. And

I'm not abandoning the tribe to be slaves to the fire priests. Now, my friend needs medical attention and I'm going to go get him some help."

The Valravn turned away in frustration and began mumbling to himself again. "Dumb, fucking, stupid, stubborn, ass, dimwitted, good guys. Why, oh, why did I have to align myself on the side of the angels?"

I ignored him and moved over to Elder Thomas. His eyes had closed but he was still breathing. That was something.

To my back, the Valravn said, "Can't you be a little evil, just once? Do you always have to be such a boring, fucking righteous asshat? You don't even have to be evil. Just a little selfish. Just enough to put your own self interests ahead of a bunch of people you only just met. Is that really too much to ask?"

I looked back at my truck and saw the entire bed was twisted awkwardly. Kind of reminded me of my broken leg. Still, I thought I could possibly drive it...until I noticed a wheel was missing.

*Shit.*

I turned back to the Valravn. "I could use some assistance."

"With what?"

I nodded toward Elder Thomas. "I need to get him help."

The Valravn laughed.

"You said you're my ally, right? So, prove it. Don't just sit on the sidelines and root for the angels. Be one."

"I don't care about that man's life."

"No, but you want me to listen to you, don't you? So, prove you're my ally. Besides, Elder Thomas is a wise and powerful medicine man. Won't he be useful to us against the enemy?"

The Valravn scoffed. "The Cherokee are fucked. The Ani-kutani will win. No point wasting time on them."

"You said the enemy has been recruiting. Should we not be doing the same?"

"Sure, but there's no point wasting time on allies who've already lost." The Valravn paused, studying me. "Although... Tell you what, Wyatt. I'll make sure this man survives if you agree to do something for me."

"Name it."

"I'll get him help, but you go home. Deal?"

"I. Am. Not. Leaving." I glared at him as hard as I could. "I am going to stop the Ani-kutani and help the tribe."

"Then fuck off," the Valravn said, pointing toward Lost City. "Town is that way. Enjoy the walk."

"He'll bleed out."

"Then I guess you'd better run."

With that, the Valravn disappeared in a flutter of wings.

*Asshole.*

I turned to Elder Thomas. "I'm going for help. Just hang in there."

I wasn't sure if he heard me or not, but there wasn't time to waste.

I did what the Valravn suggested. Ignoring the shooting pain in my magically-repaired knee, I ran.

I ran like a son of a bitch.

# CHAPTER SIXTY

"A Haven for the Lost."

By the time I could read the Lost City Church's sign, I was out of breath and had a wicked side stitch. Neither of those was as bad as whatever the hell was going on with my knee. I tried not to think about it.

Surely Pastor Wright would help, assuming he was home.

I was happy to see Elder Thomas's Bronco parked out front. That meant Axel and the others were still there. What a relief.

I stopped.

Wait, that didn't make sense.

They would've had plenty of time to pick up August and head for the constable's office.

Why were they still here?

My unease grew as I saw the front door was standing open.

I drew my staff and sword from my back, wiped the sweat from my eyes, and tried to catch my breath.

Something was wrong.

As soon as I stepped into the church, I found the first body.

I recognized her as one of the teachers who'd joined us in exile.

She was sprawled out on the floor, her dead eyes looking up at me.

There was a massive hole in the center of her torso, like an alien had popped out of her chest.

There was only one reasonable conclusion: magic.

I moved slowly down the rows of pews, telling myself I was just being cautious in case I was attacked. The truth, however, was that I was afraid of what I was going to find.

Was Axel's body going to be the next one I discovered?

No.

The next one I didn't recognize.

Which wasn't saying much, considering it looked like he'd been dead for a thousand years. Something had drained him dry. His clothes were familiar, though. It was the same robes I'd seen on my own attackers.

At least one of them had died, then. *Good.*

But how would they have known to attack the church?

Of course...

Samuel was a traitor.

He'd have told his evil buddies that I'd sent the others to the church. They'd moved in and attacked while I was shooting the shit with the Valravn.

*Fuck!*

Ahead, there was another robed mage, lying dead. This one still looked mostly human, though something had burned straight through the front of his robes, leaving his chest blackened and torn asunder.

I knew exactly what kind of magic caused that kind of damage: lighting.

As I passed the last pew, I found three more bodies. One was the other trainer who'd left with us. I'd never caught his name. He, too, had a massive hole in his chest.

The other two were robed.

I heard a floorboard creak from the back of the church, where the living quarters were.

"Shit," I heard a familiar voice say.

"Axel?" I asked.

Axel's head poked around the corner. "Oh, it's just you. Good deal. Hey, man."

He stepped out. John followed. And then, much to my surprise, August stepped out as well. He was back on his feet and appeared his normal self.

"What happened?" I asked.

"Long story. We had some trouble," Axel replied, then glanced past me. "Where're the others?"

"Long story. We had some trouble. And we need to hurry. Elder Thomas is bleeding to death in a ditch down the road."

"Did you wreck your truck again?" Axel asked.

"Yes," I replied. "It wasn't my fault, though."

"That's what you always say."

"Where's Pastor Wright?" I asked.

Axel shrugged. "He wasn't here when we arrived."

I turned to August.

"I...don't know," August said. "I... I slipped off for a bit."

"And you seem to be feeling much better."

"Lecture me later," August said, not making eye contact. "At least I came back. But I'd guess he's probably out looking for me."

I shook my head at him, but said, "Well, if he is, then your poor choices probably saved his life."

August didn't reply.

"Where's Samuel?" John asked. "He's a reasonably good healer. He could help Elder Thomas."

"I don't think he'll be much help, John. He's the one who stabbed Elder Thomas in the back. Literally and metaphorically."

"What?" John asked.

"Samuel betrayed us. He stabbed Elder Thomas in the back with a hunting knife."

"No," John said, staring at me with wide eyes. "I'll kill him."

"We'll get to that. First, we need to get Elder Thomas some help. He doesn't have long, if he's not dead already. Anyone got a phone?"

August pulled his from his trench coat.

"Call the constable office," I said, thinking quickly. "Tell them that Elder Thomas is dying in a ditch down the road and needs immediate first aid."

"Anything else?" August asked.

"What about the message?" Axel asked, winking at me.

"Tell whoever you speak to that this has gotten way out of hand and we'll be there shortly to turn ourselves over to the Cabal."

"We will?" August and Axel both asked at the same time.

"No, but I want to make sure one of them stays at the office. We should see them pass by the church to see which of them goes. If not, we'll call again."

Axel nodded approvingly. "I get it. Clever."

"I don't," August said, giving me a confused look.

Axel explained. "Wyatt wants to get Constable Williams alone."

Well, he'd *sort* of explained.

"I need to get a message to some friends in the Cabal," I said. "Officer Johnson won't help. So, if Williams is the one that goes to help Elder Thomas, that's where we'll go. If Williams is the one who stays, then we're headed for the constable office."

"Coin toss," Axel said.

"All right," August said, nodding. "I'll make the call."

# CHAPTER SIXTY-ONE

Constable Williams didn't seem surprised to see us.

"How did I know that was just a trick to get Johnson away?" she asked, crossing her arms over her chest.

I shrugged. "It wasn't a complete ruse. Elder Thomas really is hurt."

Her expression softened. "Is it as bad as August said?"

"Worse, maybe. I won't lie. There's a good chance he bled out before Johnson could get to him. And if that's the case, then we don't have a lot of time."

"What do you need?" she asked.

"I need to get a message to the Cabal."

She looked from me to August, to Axel, to John, then back to me. "Is this a trick?"

I shook my head. "No, it's very important. All hell is about to break loose."

"And you didn't think Johnson would send a message for you?"

"Not the message I need to send."

"But you think I will?"

"Certainly hoping so. It's very important."

"What's the message?" she asked.

I was about to reply when I heard a boom in the distance. It sounded like thunder, but...

John moved over to the window, looking toward the direction of the school and the few buildings that made up the unincorporated town of Lost City.

"I think it's already begun," John said, turning back toward us. "That wasn't thunder."

As if to confirm, a gunshot sounded in the distance. Followed by another.

I turned back to Williams.

"I'm ready," she said, nodding. "What's the message?"

"Attention Master Jackson," I said, considering my words. For a moment, I couldn't think of what to say. Then it occurred to me. "All hell is breaking loose in Lost City. I can't stick to the arrangement I made with your man. A lot of people are about to die. Help is needed. *Now*. Signed, the Blade Mage."

"That's all?" she asked.

I nodded.

She picked up her phone, dialed a number, and then relayed my message. Well, she didn't say "signed," but she pointed out that the message came from me.

"No, he's not here now," she said into the handset, watching me as she lied about my whereabouts. "Listen, I've got to go. Something is going down here. Get the message escalated, please."

She hung up.

I could only hope whoever she'd spoken to moved quickly and got my message to Master Jackson.

Judging by the growing commotion outside, we were already too late. There was no way the Cabal would get help here in time. But Master Jackson would have a way to reach Watcher Rhodes and the Honey Badgers. I cursed the watcher for refusing to give me a way to contact him directly.

"What now?" August asked.

I moved beside John to look out the window. There was nothing to see, but the sounds of battle were growing.

I answered August's question. "I'm going into town. Not sure what help I'll be, but I'll not stand by while the Ani-kutani destroy the tribe, even if they sort of sent us packing. And the Red Dirt Riders have aligned with them as well. And we need to save the Wolf Pack."

"You realize those two goals may be in conflict?" John asked.

"Wouldn't want it any other way," Axel said as he headed toward the door. "We're used to having the odds against us."

"August, you should get out of here," I said. "Go to the Castle. Tell them what's happened here."

He shook his head. "I'm in until it's over."

I turned to John.

He shook his head. "You don't have to ask me, Blade Mage. These are my people."

"Let's do it," I said. "But when we all end up dead, don't blame me."

"Wait," Constable Williams said, rising from her seat. "I'm coming, too."

"You're sure? We're probably going to end up dead. And if not, you'll definitely get in trouble."

"Aren't you the one who reminded me that I signed up for this job to make a difference?"

"Well, yeah," I replied.

"Then I'm tagging along."

From outside the door, Axel asked, "Are you guys coming, or what? We're going to miss the fireworks."

"All right," I said, nodding at the lot of them. "Save the kids. Save the tribe. Kill the assholes. Easy peasy."

# CHAPTER SIXTY-TWO

The closer we got to the old school, the more people we saw fleeing the area. Most appeared to be human, but there was at least one lizard-looking fellow, as well as a very tall, lanky woman with pale white skin. Behind her was what I thought was a dog until I saw it had a very humanesque face.

As we drew closer, a group of Red Dirt Riders spotted us and moved to engage.

A silly idea on their part.

None of us were in the mood.

I hit the nearest with a force spell that slammed him back against the school wall. He crumpled to the ground. Lights out.

The remaining two went for their guns, but Constable Williams was quicker on the draw. Raising a thin white wand, she summoned a levitation spell that lifted both of them off the ground. This came as a such a shock to the hard-ass criminals that neither thought to shoot their guns.

Williams flicked her wrist downward and both men slammed against the ground.

I gave her an appreciative nod. "If you were trying to show me up, you succeeded."

"Just trying to do my part," Williams said, forcing a smile. "We're going to get in so much trouble, aren't we?"

"Not at all," Axel replied. "We're much more likely to die. Can't get in trouble if you're dead."

"That's the spirit," August said, shaking his head at Axel.

The three Red Dirt fellas were all down and remained motionless. Whether that was because we'd injured them, or they were playing opossum, I couldn't say.

I didn't really care, either.

The kid gloves were off.

Following the sounds of violence, I got the impression most of the chaos was outside the old school rather than within. I didn't relish the idea of fighting our way through the school anyway, so I led us around the corner instead.

Just ahead, I saw Ahuli and a few of the tribe faced off against another gaggle of biker idiots. It was a short-lived battle.

One of the Riders took an arrow in the chest, which ignited and covered his whole body in flames.

Another went down when a Cherokee man appeared behind him and slammed a tomahawk into the back of his skull.

A final man tried to go toe-to-toe with Ahuli, brandishing a long knife. The war chief sidestepped and crushed the man's neck with his war club.

Ahuli turned and saw us.

Our eyes met and I walked calmly forward. "Ahuli, we should talk."

Ahuli pointed his club at us. "We will have a reckoning soon, you can be sure. But now I don't have time for you."

One of the Cherokee women beside him raised her hands and made several quick motions. A black cloud of smoke rose around me, ascending from the earth like I stood in the middle of a brush fire.

My view was cut off and I took a few steps back while struggling to breathe through the black mass. Around me, I could hear the others coughing as well.

Then I heard John's voice chanting in a similar rhythm. Within moments, the cloud dissipated. First the air cleared near John, then pushed away from the rest of us.

"Glad to have you on our side," I said.

He nodded in reply.

"I'm confused," Constable Williams said, glancing between us. "I thought we were helping the tribe."

I glanced at John, who glanced at August, who shrugged back at me. I turned back to Williams. "It's complicated."

"Not really," Axel said. "Ahuli is on the warpath and wants to kill everyone in his way, as well as the missing kids, who've basically fallen to the dark side and are following the orders of some wicked fire priests who want to take control of the Cherokee, and chances are, the fire priests want Ahuli up in arms, so..." He paused for a breath. "We're trying to get to the kids before Ahuli murders them, while also trying to keep Ahuli from walking straight into a trap. All while he wants to kill us for not helping him kill everybody else. Got it?"

"Huh," Williams said, nodding. "Actually, I do think I get it."

"Right, then," Axel said, pointing a drumstick forward. "Onward, buckaroos!"

He started forward, with Williams just behind him.

August turned to me and said, "He's good at that."

"Never let Axel hear you say he's good at something," I replied.

"Too late," Axel called over his shoulder. "You guys coming or what?"

Around the next corner, we spotted Ahuli and his gang again. We also found a pile of Red Dirt Riders, some fire priests, and even a few of the missing kids.

It was a real party.

Aside from all the attendees trying to murder one another.

I recognized Ben, the little boy with the bad habit of losing his action figures.

I thought I recognized another as Jathan, the same teen we'd seen Samuel taking the pot from.

And that made the rest of it click.

Yeah, I know, I should've gotten it sooner, but in fairness, I hadn't had much time to think up to that point.

Samuel hadn't been *taking* pot from the kid. He'd been *giving* him the Zavan drug.

Samuel was the one getting kids hooked and then helping them escape the camp unseen. Had to be. Which was why he'd pinned the whole thing on August. He'd been behind it the whole time. He'd played up being the weakling, and probably had no trouble building a rapport with the loner kids. That was what the elders had said at the beginning. The only common thread between all the missing kids was that they'd been loners. So, Samuel had pretended to take pity on them, had given them the drug to "make their magic stronger," then probably had led them right to the fire priests himself.

Son of a bitch.

Back to our present chaos...

There were no other kids in sight.

How these two had gotten separated from the rest of their pack, I couldn't say, but Ahuli seemed intent on ensuring they never made it back to the group.

There was open warfare all across the playground.

If any Normans happened to pass down the highway, they were going to be very confused and scared. Or they'd think, *Hey, look at all those geeks out there larping. And the special effects! Whoa! These geeks are serious!*

I can't say I was surprised when I saw one of the fire priests hurl a fireball at one of the Cherokee. Kind of went with the whole "fire priest" title.

The tribesman went down screaming, his whole body engulfed, as did the biker who'd been standing beside him.

I wondered what Raymond would think if he knew his new gal pals were treating his people like cannon fodder.

Another of the bikers certainly wasn't happy about it. He lowered his shotgun and turned to the fire priest, giving him a tongue lashing. His tirade was cut short, however, when an arrow struck him in the throat, presumably from one of the Cherokee.

With our enemies focused on the tribe, my little group could join the fray without garnering too much immediate attention.

"Plan?" August asked over the high decibel violence.

"The kids," I replied, motioning toward Ben and Jathan. "Let's try to get them out of here."

Without waiting for a reply, I started forward, racing straight through the chaos.

We didn't go unnoticed.

A fire priest turned his hooded head toward us and raised what appeared to be a short, stubby war club. It wasn't. Or maybe it was. I dunno, but it *was* definitely a wand.

A column of flame shot toward me, tearing right through my magical shield. Fortunately, August Bones was beside me, and his shield held, albeit barely.

Axel hurled a lightning bolt at our attacker, but the fire priest twirled out of the path with surprising grace, his robes swirling around him.

August raised his bone wand and summoned some sort of red spell that shot out toward the priest, but he only laughed in reply. It was kind of embarrassing.

I threw my sword at the prick.

Dyrnwyn changed form to a throwing knife as it left my hand, then took the form of a straight-bladed longsword just as it buried itself in the fire priest's forehead.

He stopped laughing then.

I felt a bit smug, but only for a moment. Killing the fire priest got everyone's attention. The whole battlefield took notice of little ole me.

Oops.

I called my sword back to my hand and kept moving.

A group of riders opened fire on our position, but Constable Williams summoned a shield to stave off their attack.

"I'll take care of the bikers," August said, moving back toward Williams with his wand raised.

The bikers went down a moment later, scratching at their eyeballs.

My focus stayed on the mission at hand.

I had to save those damned pesky kids.

Ahead, a few fire priests were trying to kill us while simultaneously trying to kill Ahuli's group, who was trying to kill the fire priests and the kids.

Jathan and Ben, for their part, were trying to flee.

They might've been the wisest among us.

One fire priest raised two short twigs, which I guessed were his wands. He aimed them toward the heavens and chanted.

Fire began to fall from the sky like droplets of rain.

One of the Cherokee summoned up a green cloud of mist I was pretty sure I didn't want to breathe.

"You know, it's getting really hard," Axel said, pausing for a breath, "to keep track of which of the people trying to kill us I am allowed to kill back. I don't like this game. Can we just kill everyone?"

He fired a lightning bolt at a fire priest while John dodged an arrow from one of his own tribesmen. I hit the archer with a gentle force spell that put them on their ass.

We got separated then as the noxious green cloud spread between us.

I didn't like our group getting split, but it couldn't be helped.

And there was no time to wait.

Ahuli and another warrior were hot on Ben and Jathan's trail.

Ben stumbled, then panicked as he got back to his feet and ran away from Jathan. Ahuli went after Ben and the other warrior went after Jathan.

There was no way I could get to both of them, and I had about half a second to weigh my options.

Fortunately, there weren't a lot of them to consider.

About the only thing I could do was hurl my sword into Ahuli or the other Cherokee's back, then race toward the other.

Problem was, despite everything, I didn't want to hurt anyone from the tribe.

Ahuli was an ass, and I certainly didn't agree with what he was doing, but he hadn't actually killed any kids yet. He was technically on the side of the good guys. Did I know for sure he intended to kill the kids? Could I strike him down without knowing?

In another fortunate twist of fate, I didn't have to make that decision.

Still trying to put distance between himself and the warrior chasing him, Jathan began chanting and raised a short knife into the air. A black liquid crawled out of the ground behind him, spreading across the dirt like black oil.

The Cherokee warrior hit the oil slick, slid, and then busted his ass, like he'd just run over a banana in Mario Kart.

Okay, apparently Jathan was capable of protecting himself.

I shifted my focus to Ahuli and Ben.

The smaller boy had tried to put some ground between himself and the war chief, but when he glanced over his shoulder to check, he tripped over his own feet and went down. Like a rabbit frozen in panic, the kid didn't move. Instead, he stared up wide eyed at the big man racing toward him.

Ahuli raised his massive war club over his head...

I hit him in the back with a force spell.

The war chief stumbled forward, nearly crashing into Ben, and hit the ground.

And what a save that would've been.

I nearly killed the kid by crushing him with the man who was trying to kill him.

What a big damn hero I would've been.

Fortunately, the war chief fell just to the side of the small boy.

He popped back up to his feet with a roar, angry eyes turned my way.

The look he gave me suggested I probably should've just killed him when I had the chance.

I gave him a friendly little wave, then tried to hit him with another force spell.

It amounted to a whole lot of nothing and he charged toward me, closing in way faster than I'd expected.

I only had time to think two thoughts...

First, how the hell was he moving so fast?

Second, defense!

He swung his war club with blinding speed and I swung Dyrnwyn upward to block and hopefully bat the club away. The problem with going sword to club was that the heavier weapon could push the thinner blade aside. However, I'd seen Dyrnwyn cut right through so many weapons I'd began to count on it as a real defensive technique.

Maybe Ahuli's war club had magical protections.

Or maybe my sword thought Ahuli might need his club for good reasons.

Or maybe my sword was just being crotchety.

Either way, Ahuli's weapon was not cut in half, and I nearly ate the business end of his war club.

Normally, when I found myself in a melee against an opponent with a single weapon, they focused on the sword and I could steal the advantage by jabbing at them with my staff.

Ahuli was too fast.

I found myself on the defense with both weapons, trying like hell to keep the club from smashing my skull. One skull crush a week was all my head could handle.

Still, after a few successful parries and seconds of keeping my brain intact, I got smug and tried to strike back. I parried, stepped in, and tried to jab my staff at his ribs.

It didn't work.

Ahuli sidestepped my attack, grabbed the end of my staff with his free hand, and yanked me toward him. As I stumbled forward, I glimpsed his elbow, right before it struck me between the eyes.

I saw the cosmos.

Or dirt.

Probably dirt.

The pain was delayed, but when it arrived, it was furious.

I opened my stinging eyes just in time to see a club descending toward my face and rolled to the side just as the war club buried in the earth where my head had been.

As I dove clear, I swung out blindly with my staff, satisfied with the thud it made as it cracked the war chief in the ribs.

He howled in pain, and I called it a win.

With bleary eyes, I rose back to my feet, trying not to let the sway of the earth throw me off balance.

Ahuli scowled at me. "Enough."

He chanted a few quiet words and raised his arms toward the sky. A strange sheen began to glow around his skin.

I had about a half a second to wonder what that was about, and then he was on me. The attack was so sudden, I could do little but flail wildly with both my staff and sword. One of them managed to stave off the killing blow, but that was about it.

It was as if I was stuck in Jell-O.

No, that wasn't right, I realized.

It wasn't that I'd slowed.

He'd sped up.

Ahuli was moving with inhuman speed.

I was on the ground again.

And I had no idea how I'd ended up there until pain train finally arrived at the station.

And arrive it did.

It felt like there'd been a grenade in my kneecap and someone had pulled the pin.

It wasn't quite as bad as when the Uktena had crushed it, but damn, it was close.

Apparently, that was where I'd been hit, and my body crumpled as a result.

I didn't have time to assess the damage, though, as a blur came into view. I had a split second to recognize Ahuli and realize he had me. There wasn't shit I could do.

Then another blur appeared from stage right and both blurs tumbled offscreen.

I sat up and risked a glance at my knee, expecting to find it twisted and mangled.

It wasn't.

I tried to move it, and though it hurt, it clearly still worked.

That was something.

I turned my attention to the whirling blurs of madness beside me.

As the two separated, I realized my savior was John.

The younger medicine man was going toe-to-toe with his war chief and shared the same magical sheen about his flesh. Suffice it to say that it was some kind of spell that granted superhuman speed.

*Neat.*

I didn't feel so bad about getting my tail kicked.

The two of them separated, circling each other like fighters in a ring.

Ahuli had his giant war club while John carried a tomahawk in one hand and a knife in the other.

Then they launched themselves at one another. Their movements blurred once more and I could scarcely tell the two apart. Sparks flew as their weapons struck.

I turned my attention back to find the kids and caught a brief glimpse of Jathan holding the younger boy's hand as they slipped around the corner of the school.

They were safe for the moment. I decided that was a win.

Testing my busted-up knee, I forced myself back to my feet.

It hurt to move, but it still worked. Once the swelling set in, I doubted it'd be the same story, but I probably wasn't going to live long enough to have to worry about that.

I considered how I might be of use to John, but at the speed they were moving, I couldn't even tell which was which. There was nothing I could do to help. Or so I thought.

John hit the ground much the way I had, and Ahuli lumbered over him, intent on smashing his skull, just the way he'd intended to smash mine. Without a moment's hesitation, I repaid John's favor by firing a force spell directly into his war chief's back.

Once again, Ahuli tumbled forward, landing in a patch of tall grass.

Ahuli was on his feet again in a moment.

He glared at me, then at John, and yet again decided there were higher priority targets worthy of his attention.

Raising his fingers to his lips, he whistled loud enough to be heard over all the chaos. I had to admit I was impressed. I was never much of a whistler.

He made a few hand gestures that didn't mean squat to me, then turned and raced in the direction the boys had fled.

I almost thought that was a good thing until... Well, it's like this... Ninjas get all the credit for being able to slip into the shadows. Now granted, my experience with ninjas was limited, but at that particular moment, I decided that reputation was more deserving of the Cherokee.

One second, Ahuli's entire group was engaged in battle. A second or two later, there wasn't a single Cherokee, save John, left in sight.

There were, however, still several Ani-kutani fire priests and a whole mess of Red Dirt Riders standing around, and all were real interested in seeing us dead.

Not good.

I knew we shouldn't have allowed ourselves to get separated.

Constable Williams was pinned down and trying to maintain a shield against gunfire from three separate groups of bikers. Meanwhile, August Bones was busy trading magic spells with one of the fire priests. I wasn't sure where Axel had gotten off to.

Another fire priest had switched his attention to John. And one more was looking my way—or it at least appeared he was from under his cowl.

I had a bit of a limp already, but I was still mobile.

I wasn't sure that would do me much good against someone with flamethrower magic. More than that, I had zero confidence my shield could protect me, based on how it had disintegrated the last time one of these pricks had slung magic in my direction.

No, I was pretty sure if the fire priest launched a spell my way, I was screwed.

I never had to find out.

A gray, misty smoke cloud appeared just behind the priest, which I assumed had something to do with some spell he was planning to cast. I raised my sword, prepared to throw it at him, hoping I was faster on the draw.

Instead, a familiar figure materialized in the smoke, just behind the hooded fire priest.

Watcher Rhodes.

He was still dressed to kill, but in one hand he held a sleek black wand. In the other he held a black bladed knife.

I didn't think the fire priest ever knew what hit him.

Watcher Rhodes slammed the knife into the side of the priest's neck, then ripped it clear, spraying blood out across the grass. His body began convulsing before it ever hit the ground.

The watcher winked at me, then disappeared into the fog once more.

I turned to check on my companions and saw John first. The medicine man was racing toward a fire priest who was hurling fireballs at him. The priest, however, was unaware that Commander Harris of the Honey Badgers was at his flank.

She raised a staff that looked like gnarled driftwood. Three blueish pink shards shot from the end and slammed into the fire priest like daggers. He screamed and staggered forward, smoke pouring from his wounds.

Couldn't say what the spell was, nor could I say whether it would've killed him, because John closed the distance and tore through the bastard's neck with his tomahawk.

On the other side of the field, Garza barreled through a whole pile of Red Dirt Riders, tossing them this way and that. It looked like his skin was made of stone, like he was The Thing.

Where John and Ahuli's magic increased their speed, Garza's enhanced his strength.

As I watched bikers sail through the air like rag dolls, I again found myself grateful he hadn't decided to kill me when he'd had the chance.

In a few seconds flat, the Honey Badgers had taken over the field. All our remaining enemies were dead, dying, or running like their lives depended on it, because they did.

Watcher Rhodes popped out of a puff of smoke a few feet away, dusted off his suit, and strode casually toward me. "I thought we had an understanding."

"Some things changed," I replied, motioning across the playground. "Guessing you got my message?"

"I did," he replied. "But can you enlighten me on just what the hell is going on?"

As I gave him the short version, Commander Harris moved in, along with Garza. The rest of her team was focused on locking down the perimeter, just to ensure we weren't surprised by any additional magic-wielding psychopaths.

As I finished, Commander Harris said, "Lost City is a goddamned warzone."

"You're telling me," I replied. "This wasn't how I planned my day."

"Nor me," Axel replied.

I turned, not realizing he'd been standing right behind me. "Where the hell did you go?"

"How many times do I have to explain how super sneaky I am?"

I ignored him and turned my focus to Watcher Rhodes, who was giving me a suspicious look.

"What?" I asked. "Something wrong with my explanation?"

"No, that's not it," he said, rubbing his chin. "I'm going to be honest, Wyatt. Upon receiving your messages, my orders were to scoop you up and get you out of Lost City before...and these aren't my words: 'you cause a major disaster.' But it seems we've got a disaster on our hands regardless."

"Right," I said, hopeful but cautious about his orders. No reason not to put it all on the table. "And I'm not leaving. Not by choice."

Rhodes gave me an innocent smile. "I understand. But what's your plan? What do you hope to achieve by throwing yourself into the middle of this drama?"

"Well, I'm glad you asked," I said, which was really just an attempt to stall as I considered his question. Once again, I decided to go for broke. "I'm going to get the kids away from the Ani-kutani while protecting them from Ahuli's wrath. I'm going to rescue Elder Morgan from the fire priests. I'm going to convince Ahuli not to burn the world down while also pointing him at the actual enemy. Then I'm going to help him stop the Ani-kutani and their new friends, the Red Dirt Riders."

"Those are some pretty tall orders," Commander Harris said, crossing her arms across her chest.

"Well, the good news is we don't have to do them in any particular order," I replied.

"Oh, I like that," Axel said. "We could write them all down on little sheets of paper, then pull them out of a hat one at a time. I hope save the kids is first on the list. That seems the most noble. Though killing the fire priest does seem more fun. *But,* I'm kind of burned out on killing bikers. Been there, done that."

It took him a moment to realize everyone was staring at him.

"What?" he asked, glancing between us. "Right. Time to shut up."

"Do you think you can succeed?" Watcher Rhodes asked, his eyes locked on mine.

"Not alone," I replied. "And not if we waste the clock."

The watcher turned his attention to Harris. "What do you think, Commander?"

She glanced once at me, then back at Rhodes. "It's a death sentence if we stay. I think we should stick to our orders, but it's your op. You call the plays, Watcher."

Rhodes nodded and was quiet for a moment.

Constable Williams, John, and August all moved closer as well, each with their own separate concerns about the appearance of the watcher and the Honey Badgers.

"I may regret this," Watcher Rhodes said, "but the Blade Mage is right. It's our job to protect people from things that go bump in the night. It sounds like these fire priests want to do a whole lot of bumping. And the Cherokee are our allies. We need to help them."

"On your command," Harris said, though she didn't look happy.

And if she wasn't happy, the look Garza gave me said he really regretted not murdering me. Ah, well. That was his problem.

Watcher Rhodes, on the other hand, offered me a pleasant smile. "Lead the way, Blade Mage."

# CHAPTER SIXTY-THREE

I did the lead the way.

In fact, I led us all right into a trap.

In fairness, it wasn't a trap for us, and it had already been sprung, but it was a trap just the same.

I basically just ran toward the constant thrum of gunfire and magical explosions, whirling noises, and other oddball sounds we magic types produce.

From afar, magical warfare can best be compared to an out-of-tune orchestra miserably flailing about during a fireworks show. Add gunshots over the top, and that's usually a collection of sounds I would run in the opposite direction of. Any sane person would.

Around the back side of the abandoned school was a rather large and abandoned bus barn. Caddy corner from there was a maintenance building. Together, the three were set in a triangle pattern, with a small yard in the middle. I wondered idly if the architects who'd worked up the spec had planned on creating the perfect killing field for an ambush. If so, they'd nailed it.

Ahuli and the other Cherokee medicine men and women had been lured right into the yard. Atop each roof was an assortment of fire priests and Red Dirt Riders raining magic and bullets on the Cherokee.

They'd also closed off the gaps between each building, trapping Ahuli and the others in the center.

I came up short and assessed the situation.

It wasn't good.

I'd already identified Ani-kutani fire priests and Red Dirt Riders atop each roof. Additionally, I spotted at least a few of the Wolf Pack scattered among them, though I didn't see Waya or Pathkiller.

There were also fire priests standing alongside the Red Dirt Riders at each of the possible exits, but more importantly, directly across from us on the far side of the little yard stood four of the Ani-kutani, and they had prisoners. I recognized Elder Morgan immediately, as well Pastor Wright. I didn't know the others personally, but there were at least two Cherokee I'd seen around the camp, and three others I assumed were just townsfolk. I didn't know why they'd taken them all, but I suspected they hadn't won a raffle for a free duck boat ride.

"Well, this looks fun," Watcher Rhodes said from beside me.

"Right," I replied, unsure what else to say. "Change of plan. We can't complete our objectives in *any* order. We've got to rescue Ahuli and the Cherokee."

"You don't say," the watcher replied, giving me a wry grin. "Any particular plan you have in mind there, Blade Mage?"

"Kill the bad ones," I said.

"Save the good ones," Axel added from just behind me.

"Try not to get killed," August Bones added.

I nodded enthusiastically. "Solid plan all around."

Commander Harris scoffed while Watcher Rhodes rolled his eyes. Then he asked, "Do you have a plan of attack?"

I considered, not wanting to look like more of a fool, but also, and more importantly, I didn't want to get everyone killed.

"Look, I don't know what you or the Honey Badgers are all capable of, so it would be stupid for me to make a game plan for you. So, I leave that up to you. Axel, August, John, Constable Williams, and I will attack this first gap and try to give Ahuli an escape route. Then we'll try to shield them long enough to get out of the shit. You support however you can, and Commander Harris will direct her people. Yeah?"

Watcher Rhodes glanced at Commander Harris, who nodded in reply. Rhodes turned his attention back to me. "Deal. Let's move."

Commander Harris ordered her squad with hand gestures while Watcher Rhodes disappeared into a puff of smoke. The Honey Badgers spread out and dissolved into the scenery. They weren't as sly as Rhodes, but damn near as efficient. In seconds, the entire team was out of sight.

I turned to my small band. "You guys ready?"

August Bones gave me a nod.

Constable Williams supplied a nervous shrug.

John stared straight ahead, his eyes on his tormented people.

Axel yawned.

I started for the gap, which was being guarded by one fire priest and three bikers.

They weren't facing our direction, so I thought we might be able to make quick work of them and break right through to Ahuli.

I thought wrong.

Just as I raised my sword arm to hurl Dyrnwyn at the fire priest's back, I caught a blur of motion from the corner of my eye.

"It's a trap!" I screamed like Admiral Ackbar, then dove clear.

Something whizzed right over the top of my head and thudded into the dirt several feet away. A tomahawk.

I glanced back in the direction it came from in just enough time to see Pathkiller bearing down on me. She had another tomahawk in one hand was drawing a third from her back as she raced toward me. Apparently, tomahawks were sort of her thing.

As soon as I was on my feet, she closed the distance and took a swipe at my head. I ducked, dodged, and took a step back, trying to give myself some space. Also, I wanted to get an idea of just how screwed we were.

I risked a quick glance around the battlefield.

*Yup, pretty screwed.*

There were some rather impressive bushes growing up beside the school, but not impressive enough for the number of ambushers who'd been waiting for us. I suspected they'd laid their trap via magical camouflage.

Pathkiller and five fire priests had been waiting for us. If they'd waited a moment longer and attacked us from behind, they probably would've killed us all. Instead, Pathkiller had jumped the gun and my warning had saved the rest of my team. Now, we had our own magic-slinging Fourth of July fireworks display.

I didn't know where Watcher Rhodes or Commander Harris had gotten off to, or whether they could see the predicament we'd found ourselves in. Nor was I sure they would come to our aid if they did. Neither had been particularly keen on my plan. I wouldn't have put it past them to just sit back and wait to see whether we actually broke the gap for Ahuli before they decided whether to engage.

Pathkiller charged me again, the determined look of an ax murderer in her eyes. I figured she probably had some hard feelings toward me, mostly on account of how she kept failing to kill me. Failure could be hard on a teenager.

I raised my staff and fired a force spell in her direction.

She dodged to the side, avoiding my attack. Apparently she'd learned from our last encounter. Her education nearly cost me my life.

She darted to the side, then back at me like some kind of damned spider monkey, and closed the distance between us. Her tomahawk came down and my sword went up to block, only this time, Dyrnwyn sliced right through the haft and the razor-sharp head flew by my face, grazing my cheek.

*What the hell, sword?*

It had spared Ahuli's war club but chopped right through Pathkiller's weapon. Why?

I dodged another strike and took another step back.

What did that mean?

Had Dyrnwyn decided that Ahuli, though misguided, wasn't evil, and was therefore worthy of keeping his weapon? If that was the case, what was it trying to tell me?

That Pathkiller was beyond redemption?

That there was no way to save her?

Even as the thought occurred to me, the sword vibrated in my hand as if to say, *Yeah, you got it, sport.*

*Stupid sword.*

Why couldn't is just talk to me or something? That would've made things so much easier.

Pathkiller cursed and took a few steps back. This was normally the portion of the fight where I'd crack a joke or taunt whatever evil asshole was trying to kill me. In this particular case, however, I still had hope, even if my sword didn't.

I took a moment to steady my breathing and said, "Pathkiller, listen to me. This has to stop. Don't you care about the tribe?"

"Of course," she replied, not even winded. Damned teenagers. "And that is why we must be strong again."

"Again? Look around you. You *are* strong."

"No," she replied. "We aren't strong enough."

"Where's Waya?" I asked, trying to stall. "I've not seen him."

She didn't reply.

"Look," I said, nearly pleading. "If nothing else, get your pack out of here. Some are too young for this much bloodshed. You'll never forgive yourself if one of the little ones gets hurt."

She was no longer listening.

Her eyes rolled back in her head and she lifted her chin toward the sky as she began to chant.

It didn't take being a wizard to know she was summoning some kind of spell.

On reflex, I nearly hurled Dyrnwyn. If she'd been any of the other evil pricks I'd fought, I certainly would've buried the blade right in her chest.

In truth, by that point, perhaps my sword was right and I should've just done it.

But at that moment, I thought of Katie, Tyler, Aarav, Ashley, and Mallory, the teens who'd visited my camp on the front lawn of the Castle. I remembered how they'd spoken about their dreams and ambitions. Their plans for the future. I couldn't bring myself to take that from Alyita—or Pathkiller.

Instead, I raised my staff and fired a force spell at her.

In front of her, a swirling of colors had formed. My magic collided with hers and a whole lot of nothing happened as mine harmlessly dissolved against her more powerful spell.

So much for being the great and mighty Blade Mage. A fucking tween had just cracked my magical attack without even trying.

The swirling of colors shifted into orange hues of a setting sun, like flames twirling before her. The flames merged, forming a twisting, throbbing orb with floaty shit swirling around it. I had no idea what it was.

She finished her spell and raised a finger to point at me.

"Oh, no, you don't," a voice said from beside me.

And then Axel jumped in front of me just as the swirling mass shot forward at Pathkiller's command.

"Ah, shit!" Axel said, then turned and fled.

For a moment, I thought Axel had heroically flung himself in front of me in a bid to save my life, then had thought better of it and gotten out of the way again. I was very confused by all of this, and it took me a moment to put it all together.

Truth be told, I didn't really understand until I wasn't murdered by the oncoming swirling mass and watched it chase my friend.

Then it clicked.

It wasn't just some overcharged fireball, nor a Ryu Hadouken, nor was it even an attack spell.

It was a summoning.

Like a wisp or some shit.

Pathkiller had intended for it to kill me, but at the last moment, she'd been pointing at Axel, and now the thing only had eyes for him.

"Shit!" Axel repeated, diving to the side as the wisp hurled a little fireball at him. Back on his feet, Axel fled, the summoning in hot pursuit. "Shit. Shit. Shit."

I wasn't sure how to help him, nor did I get a chance. He sprinted away from the battlefield toward the bus barn, the wisp hot on his heels.

I turned my attention back to little miss Always-Trying-To-Kill-Me.

She was pouting with all the enthusiasm of a teen who's been grounded by their *just* awful parents.

Only, she hadn't been grounded and she was upset because I just kept refusing to die. How many times had she tried to kill me now? I'd lost track.

I took another moment to assess the battlefield.

August, Williams, and John were holding their own against the fire priests. Ahuli and the Cherokee were still in a lot of trouble. Rhodes and the Honey Badgers were still nowhere in sight.

I switched my focus back to Pathkiller.

She had a tomahawk at the ready, and I suspected she was planning her next attack.

"Where's Waya?" I asked again.

She didn't respond, but her eyes narrowed, if only a little.

That was interesting.

"Where's your boyfriend? Did something happen?"

She charged and I prepared for her to launch herself at me. Instead, she hurled her ax at my face, then raced to the side.

I dropped to the ground, letting the hatchet sail over my head, then popped back up to my feet, prepared for another attack. Pathkiller was gone.

I turned in a slow circle, still expecting another attack. None came. She'd fled.

*All right, then.*

I turned my attention to my allies and saw that John was just about to get flanked by three Red Dirt Riders. I hadn't even seen them join the party, and frankly, I was a little surprised they were still dedicated to the cause with all this magic flying around. At least they were smart enough to try a sneak attack.

A moment later, I had one of the three pinned to the side of the school with a magical sword through his abdomen.

Yeah, brutal, I know. But play time was over.

The remaining two bikers looked at their friend, then at me, then back at their friend. Then their eyes widened further as I summoned my sword back to my hand and their friend's body slid to the ground.

They ran.

John and the fire priest he was dancing with took notice of the commotion. John offered me a little nod, which I returned, while the fire priest took a few steps back, realizing that the odds were no longer in his favor. He caught an ancient magical sword in the forehead just the same.

As soon as his foe was down, John turned his attention to Williams and charged one of her attackers from behind. The fire priest never had a chance as John swung his tomahawk up between the priest's legs.

Once upon a time, when I was in training, we'd done a course on combat triage. I distinctly remembered the trainer telling us, "You can't triage a taint." Of course, he was referring to knife wounds. Couldn't imagine what he'd say about a tomahawk implanted in the same region.

The final fire priest attacking August tried to flee, but Constable Williams hit him in the back with a force spell that caused him to stumble forward. At the same time, August hit him with that weird spell that made people clutch at their eyes. John and I were both a little more practical. The priest hit the ground with a sword and tomahawk embedded in his back.

I retrieved my sword and started through the gap, not bothering to check whether my companions were behind me.

I knew they were.

The gap was clear and I had a line of sight to Ahuli and the others who were still struggling against an onslaught of magical attacks. A few were already down, and I had little confidence the rest could hold out much longer.

Getting to them wouldn't be hard.

Getting them out was another story.

And for all I knew, Ahuli might just attack us on sight. We needed a plan. Fortunately, Axel provided one.

My friend, still fleeing the wisp on his heels, ran straight through a group of enemies. It turned out the wisp's aim wasn't all that good. I watched with grim satisfaction as a fireball meant for Axel lit up a fire priest instead.

It was such a spectacle that for just a moment, everyone on the battlefield turned their attention to Axel and the wisp.

I took the opportunity to charge in, hurling my sword at a Red Dirt Rider who was taking potshots at the Cherokee from cover.

Then I yelled at Ahuli.

The war chief turned and glared at me, but when I motioned toward the open escape route, he nodded in what I hoped meant understanding.

Unfortunately, that was the exact moment the garage door exploded off the bus barn.

I had just enough time to cover my head before the light metal door slammed into me and knocked me off my feet.

I saw the cosmos again.

Or maybe it was just the bus barn door I was buried under.

Either way, it was nice to have a peaceful moment to myself. A relaxing time to consider all the life choices that had brought me there.

I considered just lying there for a while, but some helpful asshole lifted it off of me, and someone's hands pulled me to my feet.

I looked up and saw that it was August Bones. His eyes were wide with terror, which I mistakenly believed was due to concern over me.

"Hurry!" he said, near panic. "We've got to run!"

I might've been a little disoriented because I couldn't see what the fuss was. I felt the urge to explain that the aluminum door wasn't all that scary, nor had it caused me any actual harm.

It was then it finally occurred to me that I didn't know *what* had blown the giant door right out of its frame.

I turned and saw a brutish figure strolling from the bus barn. Its skin appeared to be made of stone, as if the Gray Hulk had made a love child with The Thing. It had to duck its head to step through the clearing it had made and staggered forward, putting its weight on a stone cane in its hand.

"What do you think the chances are it's on our side?" I asked, finally catching up to August's sense of urgency.

My question was answered when one of the Cherokee charged the creature with a spear. The stone man reached out and grabbed the front of the spear, tugging the warrior toward him. As the Cherokee stumbled forward, the stone man head-butted him, crushing his skull.

He wasn't done, though.

As the dying warrior sagged to the ground, the stone man lifted him back up and bit right into the fractured skull. There were slurping sounds, like he was sucking milk out of a coconut.

The stone man let out a satisfied sigh and glanced around the battlefield.

For a moment, I thought his face was familiar somehow. Obviously I was still disoriented, because my inner Rolodex didn't have an extensive section for stone people.

"Come on, Wyatt!" August said.

"Oh, right," I replied. "Time to run!"

I scooped up my wits and turned to find Ahuli again.

We were past due for a daring escape.

But of course, our enemies had strategically placed the stone man in the bus barn to prevent our retreat if the fire priests and thugs were defeated. Which they were. I just hoped they didn't have any more cards up their sleeves. And frankly, I was okay not leaving by the route we'd arrived by. The opposite gap had more enemies, sure, but that was also where the hostages were. So, not only did it give us more enemies to kill, but it also gave us more hostages to save. What a bargain!

As I closed distance with Ahuli, I realized just how haggard the war chief was. His arrogance was deflated, and what was left, well, it wasn't confidence.

He didn't even try to attack me.

"We've got to get out of here," I said.

He only nodded.

I took a quick assessment of our allies, realizing roughly half the tribe were still on their feet. The other half... Well, they'd not be joining our grand escape attempt.

"There's more help coming," I told the war chief. "We should push toward the hostages and try to escape that way."

"There're more enemies that way," he replied.

I almost repeated the part about the hostages but held my tongue. Ahuli didn't care about the hostages. Of course he didn't. They weren't part of his tribe.

Instead, I said, "Exactly. Which means they won't expect it. It also means there's less likely to be another big surprise, like our stone buddy back there. We just need a clever plan, or a distraction."

Ahuli nodded again, but offered no suggestion.

Realizing the broken war chief would not be any help, I tried to think of a plan on my own. Fortunately, Axel came up with one for me.

Still running to and fro like a wiener dog jacked up on Mountain

Dew—and a fire-chucking wisp on his tail—Axel ran right into the gaggle of fire priests blocking our exit.

Chaos ensued.

Two priests ended up with their robes aflame.

I would've thought "fire" priests would've been a little more welcoming to fire, but these two howled like... Well, like they were on fire.

The remaining priests shifted their focus to killing both Axel and the wisp.

A pink blast of energy knocked one of the priests off their feet. Glancing in the direction it came from, I spotted Commander Harris finally leading the Honey Badgers into the fray. And there I'd thought they'd abandoned us.

Another of the fire priests managed to take out the wisp.

Axel slid to a stop beside the hostages and doubled over, clearly out of breath. It wasn't the best place to stop for a rest, but in fairness, I would've collapsed much earlier.

One of the nearby priests turned toward Axel, but before he could act, Watcher Rhodes appeared behind the priest, his dagger at the ready. The watcher relieved the priest of his throat, then disappeared again.

I moved from the protective circle and started toward Axel, hoping I could avoid damage and get there in time to help him with the hostages.

Axel took a long breath, then glanced at the hostages, perhaps only then realizing they were right beside him.

He moved to Pastor Wright first and freed his hands. Then he motioned for Pastor Wright to help another while he freed Elder Morgan.

The next few moments would haunt my dreams...

As Axel turned to free the next hostage, Pastor Wright rose up behind him, a knife in his hand.

Our dear, friendly preacher buried his blade in my best friend's back.

Axel yelped as his eyes widened in surprise.

Then he crumpled.

His face hit the ground, the knife still stuck in his back.

I screamed.

I only know I screamed for the trembling vibrations in my throat.

All I could hear was a hollow drumming in my skull.

All I could see was red.

It was as if, in that moment, all the threads of reality came undone, and I was standing apart from the rest of the universe.

Axel was down.

My best friend had just been stabbed in the back.

The soft-spoken, awkward little pastor—the one who'd let us sleep in his church and had begged us to leave to protect his flock—looked up at me and smiled.

The final piece clicked.

For the first time, something that should've been obvious finally occurred to me.

The teens had only been disappearing from camp recently. The only new figure to move into the area was the friendly and unassuming Pastor Wright.

He was one of them.

Of course he was one of them.

His charade up, he turned his gaze from me and began barking orders at the fire priests.

*Holy shit.*

He wasn't just one of them.

He was the leader. He *was* the bad man.

And behind him, writhing on the ground and dying, was my dearest friend.

Between us, the pastor's army.

I was going through them.

Every.

Goddamned.

One.

"Wyatt, wait," a voice behind me said.

I turned and realized it was Watcher Rhodes. I'd neither seen nor heard him appear.

Without another word, he disappeared in a puff of smoke.

I whipped back around and saw him reappear beside Axel.

Another puff and Axel was on the ground at my feet, the watcher beside him.

"I dare say I think that man is the ringleader," Rhodes said, nodding toward Pastor Wright.

I heard what he said, but was focused on the knife embedded in Axel's back. He was no longer writhing. He'd gone limp instead. And there was a lot of blood. A *lot*.

"I've got this," August said, kneeling beside me. "I'll take care of Axel. You focus on getting us out of here, Blade Mage."

"I can help," Constable Williams said as she began drawing sigils in the dirt.

I was just about to ask who she meant to help, but before I could, her eyes rolled back into her head and she began to chant. A wave of energy pulsed from her wand, washing over everyone in the immediate vicinity.

For a moment, it felt like plunging through water, then I came out the other side.

I was about to ask how the hell that was supposed to help when I realized I felt different.

I wasn't as tired.

I'd been pushing through on pure adrenaline, sure, but in the back of my mind, I'd known I was wearing down. Now, though, I felt refreshed. Like one of those fools in the old Irish Springs commercials. Even the pain in my knee withdrew a bit.

I glanced around and saw the others seemed to experience the same feeling.

"Do you think he's in charge?" Watcher Rhodes asked again.

"The pastor?" I asked, but then realized of course that was who he meant. "Yes."

"Good enough for me. Time to get to work."

"Wait," I said, but he was already gone.

I swiveled my head in time to see the watcher appear just behind Pastor Wright and...

In a blur, the false preacher spun away and Watcher Rhodes stabbed out at vacant air. Wright grabbed hold of the knife and ripped it from the watcher's hand.

With his other hand, Pastor Wright grabbed Rhodes's throat.

He lifted the watcher from the ground with one arm and casually tossed the stolen knife up in the air, catching it in a reverse grip. Then he stabbed the watcher in the gut with his own knife.

Wrenching the blade clear, he stabbed again. And again. Over and over, Pastor Wright stabbed and ripped the blade clear.

Watcher Rhodes howled, but the false preacher wouldn't let up.

Satisfied at last with his carving, Pastor Wright turned and held up his prize for all to see. Blood pumped from Rhodes's stomach, painting his torturer's arm and the ground beneath them.

Wright's voice, somehow magically enhanced, boomed out across the battlefield for all to hear. "Cherokee and members of the Cabal dying together. It is a beautiful thing, is it not?"

Watcher Rhodes tried to strike Wright in the head, but Wright simply caught his hand and crushed it under his grip.

Rhodes howled again.

"War Chief," Wright said. "Come now. Surrender. I don't seek the decimation of your people. I seek your servitude. We are the Ani-kutani, and we have come to take our rightful place as your leaders. Nothing to have a fuss over."

All around the battlefield, the fighting paused.

Wright continued, "Do you really think you can use your medicine against us? Who do you think taught it to you, War Chief? We were your religious leaders. We were the holders of knowledge. It was the Ani-kutani who taught you. Surrender."

"We will never surrender!" Ahuli yelled back. "The Cherokee will never surrender!"

"A shameful waste." Wright turned his attention to the watcher he still held captive. "And what of you, Cabal dog? Will you tell your hounds to lay down their weapons? Surely you can see the battle is lost."

Watcher Rhodes's voice was little more than rasp, but I'm pretty sure his last words were, "Go to hell."

"A shame," Wright replied as he grasped the knife still embedded in the watcher's abdomen and gutted him from groin to sternum.

The watcher's screams gurgled from his throat as his innards spilled out on the ground.

Pastor Wright tossed the dead man to the ground and shifted his focus to his priests. "Kill them all. Leave none alive."

"How about that?" Axel's voice said from the ground beside me. "And there I thought their plan was to kill us all this whole time. What a *shocking* turn of events."

I stared down at him, noting that his eyes were closed. Yet just the sound of his voice made my heart soar.

He wasn't dead. Not yet, at least. And there was life enough in him to make bad jokes.

That was something.

I glanced back up and saw Pastor Wright turn and leave the battlefield. Pathkiller and a handful of the priests followed, dragging their hostages with them. At least that was a few less to contend with, not that it would help much. Wright had his arm over Pathkiller's shoulder, like she was his daughter. It sent my creep radar to eleven. *Gross.*

"Any clever ideas, Blade Mage?" Ahuli asked, reeling me back to more immediate concerns.

"Yeah," I replied, forcing my best smile. "Let's take as many of them with us as we can."

Despite my attempt at levity, we were clearly screwed. They had the high ground like Obi-wan. The only difference was their high ground advantage actually made sense. The similarity, of course, was that the fire priests wanted to bake us well-done like Anakin.

Commander Harris and the Honey Badgers had made an impact when they'd revealed themselves, but like the rest of us, they were on the defensive now as well.

Behind our little center circle, John and a handful of the Cherokee were playing Keep Away with the stone man. Well, sort of. It was more like a game of tag, really. The Stone man was "it," and if he caught them, he got to suck their brains out of their skulls.

At any rate, they were screwed, we were screwed, and everyone on our team was pretty well screwed.

And then something amazing happened.

A burst of light knocked one of the priests off the roof of the bus barn. He screamed as he fell, but that didn't last long because he hit the ground like a brick and didn't move.

Another, slightly more fortunate priest came under a barrage of multi-colored magics and jumped from the roof on his own.

A moment later, all the priests on the roofs were under attack and seeking cover.

A very cartoon-like car horn sounded over the chaos and an old beat-up Chevy appeared between the bus barn and the maintenance shed. Whoever was driving, they had the pedal to the floor and the fire priests guarding that gap had to dive out of the way.

The truck slid to a stop just in front of us and I realized Fatima sat in the passenger seat.

She met my gaze and pointed her thumb at the truck bed. "Get in."

I was just about to point out there wasn't enough room for everyone when I realized two more trucks were coming through the gap.

"May want to hurry," she said.

While the bed of a pickup offered little in the way of protection, I knew better than to look a gift Chevy in the grill.

I helped August and Williams dump Axel in the bed, along with our other injured.

The truck beds started filling up.

Timing was everything. The trucks were easy targets, but wherever Fatima's other people were attacking from, they were keeping the fire priests busy.

Ahuli and I were the last to load from the center, then it was just down to John and his fellows to join us. The first two trucks were already squealing tires as Ahuli and I tried to get John's and the others' attention.

The stone man had its sights on John, so the other two turned and fled for the truck, leaving the young medicine man on his own with the stone man. I didn't like it, but I wasn't sure what to do to help him.

But John didn't need my help. Or anyone else's.

He stood his ground as the stone man charged him. At the last possible second, he dove out of the way, rolled up to his feet, and raced toward us.

The stone man was quick, but not as quick as John.

He bolted to us and leaped into the back of the truck. The rest of us grabbed for him like a pack of zombies while yelling for the driver to go.

Our driver hit the gas and the truck sped away, kicking up dirt in the stone man's face.

The fire priests, realizing we were about to escape, began throwing fireballs, but it was too little too late. Next thing I knew, we were on the dirt road and headed back toward the camp.

And somehow, we were still alive.

Some of us, anyway.

# CHAPTER SIXTY-FOUR

The chaos at the camp could've rivaled the chaos at the school. For everyone but me. I couldn't remember a time I felt more useless. Healers ran from person to person, trying to help everyone who'd sustained injury. Members from both Fatima's group and the Honey Badgers assisted, as well as August and Constable Williams.

For my part, I stood near Axel, thankful the Cherokee medicine men made time for him, despite him not being one of their own. He was no longer conscious, and his skin was pale from the loss of blood. I desperately wanted an update on his condition, but I also didn't want to interrupt their work. Each time a medicine man or woman moved from him, I'd ask, but they'd only shrug in reply.

It wasn't a good sign.

They'd put him in his bed at the cabin. Shain Stone was still out cold on the other side of the room, so I supposed, in a sense, he wasn't alone.

I sat in a chair in the corner, letting my gaze shift between the two of them.

We'd really outdone ourselves this time, and I didn't see any way out of it.

There was no clever trick that might save either of them. No clever scheme I could pull to stop our enemy. There was little doubt Wright would march his army up to the camp. And when he did, I wouldn't be able to protect my injured friends.

I wouldn't be able to protect anyone.

I could barely walk as it was, and my magic was no match for our foes.

They would be coming.

It was only a matter of time.

If I had thought it was safe to move either of them, I might've high-tailed it for the Castle. In fact, I'd thought to suggest that to Ahuli for the whole group, but when I'd sought him out, I was told he was too busy. Frankly, I was too beat up to argue. So, I just limped back to the cabin and watched over Axel.

That was what I was doing when August came to find me.

He didn't look any better than I felt.

"Any word?" he asked, nodding toward Axel.

I shook my head.

He nodded and changed the subject. "Ahuli wants to see us. I was asked to come get you."

I forced myself back to my feet, trying to ignore the searing pain in my knee. When everyone else was cared for, I'd have to see about getting a healer to look at it for me. For the moment, though, they had much more pressing concerns. Like Axel.

I limped behind August, barely able to walk to the conference room.

There were not as many elders present now, but the vacated seats were filled by Fatima, Commander Harris, and Constable Williams.

I turned my gaze to Ahuli. Gone was the arrogance and pride that had driven him earlier. Now he just looked defeated.

And apparently, August and I were the last two he was waiting on. Before we even had a chance to sit, he began to speak.

"First, I wish to thank you all for supporting our tribe," he said, eyes toward the table. "If not for your intervention, I fear our losses would've been worse."

No one replied.

"Second, we must assume that an attack on the camp is inevitable," he said. "We cannot defend this position against what is coming. It seems the Ani-kutani have truly returned, and they seek to re-take control of our tribe. If we try to face them here..."

His words drowned away.

After a moment, he looked up, but his eyes had a faraway look.

"We must prepare an evacuation."

"We should get everyone to the Castle," I said. "You'll be safe there."

Commander Harris nodded her agreement. "I agree."

Ahuli shook his head. "No. The Cabal cannot save us from this threat. There is but one option to preserving our knowledge and the ways of our tribe."

"You're sure?" one of the other elders asked. I didn't know their name.

Ahuli nodded. "Yes. It is the only way."

"Can someone fill the rest of us in?" August asked.

"We will split up," Ahuli said. "Our students will be divided up among the remaining medicine men and they will flee to every corner of the world, and we will continue training from hiding."

"Okay," I said. "That makes sense, but it will take some time to plan and put in motion. There aren't even enough vehicles here to get everyone out in one go. The fire priests could show up at any time."

"Yes," Ahuli said, lowering his head once more. "Which is why I asked you here. You've all done much to help us, and it shames me to ask, but will you help us just a bit longer?"

When no one else spoke up, I did. "What are you asking?"

Ahuli took a deep breath and said, "I'm asking you to help protect the camp until we can ready everyone for an evacuation."

"How long will it take?" I asked.

"We will need a couple of hours."

"I'd be willing to bet Pastor Wright doesn't intend to give you that long," August said, sharing a look with me. "You can't move any faster?"

"We will try," Ahuli said. "But we will need time."

"What of your injured?" Constable Williams asked. "Many won't be safe to move."

"I fear we will have to leave them," Ahuli said, looking down once more. "The continuation of our medicine is paramount. We cannot risk losing the knowledge. You must understand."

"We do," I said, nodding. "We all get it. But we need a plan."

"What if the Cabal will help with that?" Commander Harris asked. "What if I can get them transported to the Castle?"

"Yes," Ahuli said with a nod. "That would be a great help, though I suspect that will take even more time. Will you help defend us until then?"

His gaze moved around the room, looking at each of us in turn.

"I should report back to the Castle," Commander Harris said. "This was Rhodes's operation. With him gone... I need to report back to my superiors. Constable Williams should join us, and I dare say the Blade Mage should as well."

I met her gaze, but fortunately Fatima spoke up before I could answer.

"This isn't our fight," she said. "Frankly, I shouldn't have gotten my people involved. We need to make our own evacuation. But for what it's worth, you should take the Blade Mage's advice and get everyone to the Castle."

"So, you will not help defend our camp?" Ahuli asked, though instead of his brash anger, it seemed more like an accepted defeat.

"We'll stay long enough to stabilize the wounded, but after that, we're out," Fatima said.

"Same for my team," Commander Harris said. "Besides, if we want the Cabal to help with the injured, the sooner I communicate with my superiors, the better."

"What of Elder Thomas?" I asked, changing the subject. "Has there been any word from Constable Johnson?"

No one answered, which meant no one had heard whether the constable had gotten him to a place safe.

"And what of Elder Morgan?" I asked. "Will you leave him to the Ani-kutani?"

"Elder Morgan would want us to ensure the safety of our knowledge," Ahuli said. "We may not have agreed on much, but in this, I am confident he would want us to leave him behind."

I bit my lip, knowing he was probably right.

"I'll stay," August said. "For as long as you need me."

"Thank you," Ahuli said, not hiding his disappointment.

For my own part, I didn't reply.

# CHAPTER SIXTY-FIVE

I stepped back out into the night air and considered my options.

Abandoning the tribe wasn't one of them, of course. Not to mention that Axel wasn't in any condition to move. In fact, there were a lot of injured that were in no condition to be moved. Even if Commander Harris was right and the Cabal was willing to transport everyone, that, too, would take more time than we had.

So, what did that mean?

It meant that even if Pastor Wright refrained from marching his army to the camp before the tribe could evacuate, when they did show up, they'd probably find me limping around by myself, waiting for a ride to show up to move all the severely injured.

We'd be easy pickings.

The only way this would work was if Pastor Wright procrastinated a bit. From the sounds of it, that asshole had dedicated his life to this cause, so I didn't suspect we could count on that. Instead, my suspicion was that at that very moment, he was preparing to march on the camp.

And frankly, even if Harris and Fatima had agreed to defend the camp, I knew we'd probably get spanked anyway.

We needed time.

Time for Harris to get the Cabal to evacuate the injured.

Time for Ahuli to get all the kids separated and shipped off with their teachers.

It was all about time.

We needed something to stall Pastor Wright.

And I could only think of one thing.

I limped my way back to the cabin and stood over Axel. There wasn't a healer present, which I took to be a good sign. But he was still nearly as pale as his sheets and I could scarcely tell if he was breathing.

I reached out and squeezed his arm. He didn't react.

"I'm sorry, Axel," I said, my eyes locked on his peaceful face. "I'm sorry I got you into this. I'm sorry..."

I paused, considering my words. Despite the fact I knew he couldn't hear me, I wanted to get this right.

"You know, Axel, you're the only one who ever believed the sword chose right. So, I guess... I guess I'm sorry I never became the Blade Mage you believed me to be. I'm sorry I let you down."

I wiped a tear from my cheek and started for the door.

But I paused and glanced over at Shain Stone. "And I'm sorry to you too, Stone. Sorry I couldn't be the Blade Mage my father was. Gods, I wish he were here now. But he's not, and this, I think, is what he would do. I think it's the only option I have left, you know?"

He didn't reply.

I let the door of the cabin swing shut behind me and looked for a vehicle that still had the keys in it.

# CHAPTER SIXTY-SIX

I parked in a vacant lot down the road from my destination.

My knee was cranky, and I hoped if I walked on it a bit, maybe it'd warm up before I really needed it. Spoiler alert: it didn't.

The church was just ahead.

I had no real reason to suspect that was where I'd find them, but that was what my gut told me, so I went with it.

I'd only made it a few steps when a familiar voice asked, "What are you doing?"

Her tone was calm, simply curious, yet I nearly jumped out of my shoes anyway.

I turned and saw the Nunnehi walking beside me. She'd appeared from thin air, as far as I could tell.

"I, uh..." I wasn't sure what to say. "I'm just going for a walk, is all. What are you doing?"

She raised an eyebrow but continued alongside me. "Your enemies are ahead."

"Yes, they are," I agreed.

"I saw the battle."

"Did you?"

"Yes," she said. "And I know you cannot hope to defeat them alone."

"Well, that's where you're wrong," I replied, still limping along. "I *can* hope to defeat them alone."

Her brow furrowed. "You play with words. You know what I mean. You cannot defeat them."

I sighed and finally stopped, turning to face her. "No, I cannot."

"Then what are you doing?"

"I'm going to face them."

"Even though you cannot win?"

"Even though I cannot win."

When she didn't respond, I turned and started forward again.

"Why?" she asked finally.

I stopped once more and turned back to face her, but I didn't know what to say.

"It makes little sense," she continued. "You are mortal. Your time is so limited. Why would you squander it?"

"I'm not squandering it," I replied. "I'm going to try to stall them, if you must know."

"I don't understand."

"The others need time to escape. I'm hoping to give them that time."

"You intend to sacrifice yourself?"

"That's... That's not what I'd call it. I mean... Maybe there's a chance I can take on the Ani-kutani and their allies all on my own. Who knows?"

"You know you cannot," she replied. "You can barely walk."

"Listen," I said, growing more annoyed and uncomfortable with the conversation, "if you just came here to point out my shortcomings, it's going to take a while, and I don't have that much time."

"I am seeking to understand."

"What's to understand?"

"Why you are planning to die?"

I stared her in the eye, noticing how innocent she looked. Perhaps she really didn't get it. Perhaps as an immortal fairy-like being, it didn't make a lot of sense to her. Fact was, it didn't make that much sense to me. It was just the only card I had left to play.

I sighed. "Look, my best friend is back at the Cherokee camp. Do you understand friendship?"

She nodded. "The Cherokee are our friends."

"Right," I said. "And when they needed you, you helped them."

"Yes."

"Well, this is the only way I can help my friend. And the Cherokee. They're my friends, too. And August Bones. Shain Stone. All of them. This is the only way I can help them. Do you understand?"

"By dying."

"No," I said, shaking my head. "That's the cost. What I'm giving them is time. If I can stall our enemies for just a few minutes, that's a few minutes longer they'll have to escape. A better chance that they can survive."

"But what if the Ani-kutani just kill you immediately?"

I waved the notion away. "Bad guys never kill anyone straight away. They always want to talk about how awesome they are . Besides, even with a limp, surely I can hold my own for, like, three or four seconds."

"You *are* going to die," she said, a look of sadness in her eyes. "You cannot survive this."

"Yeah," I replied while refraining from giving her a sarcastic thanks. "I probably am."

"And you won't turn back?"

"Not a chance," I said as I started walking again.

"I could teleport you away."

"Well, don't," I said over my shoulder. "Don't take away the only gift I have left to give."

With that, our conversation was over.

And when I glanced back over my shoulder, she was gone.

The church was just ahead.

I continued limping forward, trying not to dwell on the extremely positive message of the Nunnehi.

*You are going to die.*

*Yeah, thanks, fairy lady. Just wanted I wanted to hear. Super encouraging.*

I forced down these thoughts, took a breath, and limped into the church parking lot.

A handful of Red Dirt Riders stood out front, but they hadn't noticed me yet.

"Hey, assholes!" I said. That got their attention. "Are you supposed to be on guard duty?"

The two nearest shared a look and one of them said, "Yeah."

"Cool," I replied. "Then you should probably alert your new friends that the enemy has arrived. Right?"

They stared at me, dumbfounded.

"Sound the alarm," I offered. "Light the beacons. Make bird noises. Whatever it is you dipshits do. Look, it's going to be really awkward if I limp over there and chop your fucking heads off before you alert anyone I'm here. This isn't exactly a sneak attack."

"Hello, Blade Mage," Pastor Wright's voice said.

# CHAPTER SIXTY-SEVEN

"Hello, you evil, lying, jerk face," I replied. "Good to see you again, ya cheery, miserable fuck. Also, your guards suck."

"Good help is hard to find," Wright agreed, nodding.

He came down the church steps and started toward me. Behind him, several more robed figures stepped out from the church. Behind them were the members of Waya's Wolf Pack, but no sign of Waya or Pathkiller. Lastly, two robed figures dragged Elder Morgan out and dumped him on the ground.

Pastor Wright stood before me, just as cheerily as when we'd first met.

"What can I do for you, Blade Mage?" he asked.

This was the point where I should've had something really cool to say.

I couldn't think of anything, though.

Not a damned thing.

So, I said, "It would be a big help if you and your pals would just go ahead and kill yourselves. It'd save me a lot of work, and if I'm honest, my knee is *just* killing me."

From the shadows around the side of the church, I saw a hulking figure move in the darkness. The stone man, no doubt.

More of the Red Dirt Riders came out of the church as well, including Raymond.

"Hi, Ray," I said, waving at him. "Glad to see everyone is here."

"Yes, we're all here," Wright said. "In fact, we were just about to come visit you at the camp. Question is... Why are *you* here? Couldn't wait that long to see us?"

"Oh, I'm here to kill you," I replied. "Thought I'd save you the trip."

"Is that so?" he asked, raising an eyebrow. "And you plan to do this all alone?"

"Yup, reckon I do."

"And how do you think that's going to work out for you?"

"Reckon we'll find out."

"Well," Pastor Wright said, opening his arms as if in invitation. "At your convenience."

*Well, shit.*

I'd hoped to get him to talk a little longer than that.

Time for some Axel-level stalling.

"Thank you, Pastor. That is most kind."

"Please," he replied. "There's no need to keep up the disguise any longer. You no longer need to refer to me as 'Pastor.' "

"Was 'Wright' a fake name, as well?"

"It was."

"Huh," I replied. "But why?"

"Why what?"

"Why choose 'Wright' as your fake name? It's so boring."

"I chose 'Wright' because I like to be *so* wrong."

"Ewww," I replied, putting up a hand. "Just. No. Gross. Please, never say that again."

"No?" he asked, falling short on his chortle.

"That is the least funny thing I've ever heard another human say. I mean, that would fall short even by dad joke standards. Just... No."

"Fair enough," he replied. "Jokes aren't really my wheelhouse. I'll take it under advisement."

"You do that. I have another question." I let my gaze slide over the kids huddled between the fire priests. They looked scared. "Where's Waya, huh? And Pathkiller?"

"I don't see how that is any of your concern," Wright said.

"That's the whole reason I came to this forgotten little Okie town, remember? The sad part is I think I know the answer. At least for one of them."

Wright just stared at me, waiting for me to continue.

I stalled a few moments longer, then shouted to the darkness, "Hey, stone man, why don't you come out here? Don't be shy now."

The stone man stepped out of the shadow and into the light.

As I got another look at his face, my suspicion proved true. "What did you do to him?"

"I made him better," Wright said. "Our young Waya is so much more now than he ever would've been as a mere medicine man."

"Waya, are you still in there?" I asked. "Are you still you?"

There was no reply.

"Waya is gone, Blade Mage," Wright said. "As I said, he's become something more."

"And Pathkiller?" I asked. "Alyita?"

"It's fortunate you arrived when you did," Wright said. "You might enjoy the show."

"What show?" I asked.

"Bring her out," Wright called over his shoulder. "Let the Blade Mage see."

A few moments later, three fire priests dragged Pathkiller outside. She writhed and jerked against them, but her eyes were rolled back in her head and she was foaming about the mouth.

"What have you done to her?"

"I have given her what she asked for," he said, leaning down to gently pat her head while she continued seizing on the ground. "She's becoming something more, Blade Mage. Something great and lost to our people."

"Really? Because she looks like a teenager having a drug overdose."

"She'll be fine, I assure you. Better than fine, even."

"And the others?" I asked, pointing toward the kids. "What about them? Are you going to turn them into monsters, too?"

"It's unclear at this juncture," he replied, also assessing the group with his stare. "I'm not sure any of them are truly worth keeping. I may just rid myself of the burden, to tell you the truth. Once the Cherokee bow their heads to me, I'll have the pick among their students. Some may join the ranks of my priests. Others, the weak, they'll be cast away or made stronger."

"And what of Elder Morgan?"

"Ah, yes, that reminds me," he said, turning to the priests holding the elder. "I thought I said I wanted him awake. I want him to see his failure. I want him to see his granddaughter change."

The fire priests set to work, trying to wake the older man.

"See, there for a moment I thought you were a reasonable bad guy who was just the 'any means necessary' type. But I can't think of any good reason to wake Elder Morgan up, other than to be an evil dick."

"We all have our weaknesses." He shrugged. "Now, on to other matters. It's clear you came here hoping to stall us, which I will say was quite brave and endearing of you. However, as you can see, we were waiting for Pathkiller to finish her transition before we proceeded to the camp anyway, so your efforts were in vain. So, would you like to die now, or would you care to suffer the ache in your knee and living with your failures just a bit longer?"

"I, uh, suppose I would live a bit longer, if it's all the same to you."

"By all means," he said. "I much prefer your continued suffering. In fact, I'd be glad for you to try to convince Pathkiller to change her mind."

"Change her mind?"

"Oh, yes," he said, nodding way too enthusiastically. "This was her decision. Her choice. Try to talk her out of it. Go on."

"You know, you really are a sick fuck."

"Hurry," he said, motioning toward Pathkiller. "You're running out of time. It won't be long now. Don't you want to try to save her?"

I wasn't a complete moron. I knew he was toying with me, but I also suspected he was telling the truth. He didn't believe there was any turning back for Pathkiller. It seemed Ahuli had come to that same conclusion, as had my sword. I'd certainly wondered over it myself, but in my own stubborn way, I'd refused to give up.

There had to be a chance.

All I had to gamble was a little pride.

What did I care if Wright got to have a laugh at my expense?

Elder Morgan was awake now. His gaze met mine, then turned to his granddaughter. The old medicine man began to cry.

I moved closer to Pathkiller and dropped down to my knee.

"Can you hear me, Pathkiller?" I asked.

She convulsed and twitched, paying no attention to me. I noticed her face had begun to distort a bit and her flesh had paled. What the hell were they doing to her?

I decided on another tactic. "Alyita. Can you hear me, Alyita?"

For a moment, her seizure seemed to increase in intensity, but whether that was because I'd used her former name or not, I couldn't say. It was something, though.

"Your grandfather is here, Alyita. He's watching this happen to you. And when it's over, they're going to kill him. You understand that, don't you?"

Still nothing.

"The others are scared, Alyita. The other kids that followed you. They're frightened. Waya is gone, and you're all they have left, and they are scared. They need you. Your tribe needs you. They say this is your choice. That you want to become something else. But will you still be in there? Will you still be yourself?"

Silence.

"Jesus," I heard Raymond's voice say. "This is cruel, even by my standards."

A few of his men laughed, but they were nervous laughs, pretending at cruelty. At least some of the Red Dirt Riders had finally realized they were in over their heads.

I ignored the interruption and focused on the teenager in front of me.

I called out to her over and over. I reminded her of the tribe, of her friends, of her family, over and over.

At the last, I begged and pleaded. I don't know how long I tried, but it felt like a lifetime.

And still, nothing.

Her skin took on a grayish tone and one of her fingers seemed to elongate and grow. She was changing, and it didn't seem there wasn't a damned thing I could do about it.

"Step away now, Blade Mage," Wright's voice finally said. "You've had your chance. It seems our little Pathkiller has made her decision, no?"

I looked up at him, then back down at her, and I whispered my final plea. "Alyita, you've tried to kill me more times than I can count. By all rights, I should've given up on you. Everyone else has. Maybe I'm just a fool, but I won't. I believe you can still do the right thing. I believe deep down that you want to. And I'm probably going to be dead in a few moments, so don't prove me wrong. You chose the name Pathkiller because you had the choice. You still do."

Her eyes opened and she looked at me.

For a moment, I thought I'd convinced her.

Then I dove to the side as she jabbed at me with her long, spindly finger.

It had grown a few more inches in the few seconds I'd been speaking, and I saw it had sharpened into a point.

Wright laughed at me. "Careful there, Blade Mage. Spearfinger has a taste for human flesh. Specifically the liver, in case you're wondering."

I looked up at him. "So, this is your big plan, huh? Turn the tribe's teens into monsters to use against them?"

"Pretty much," he said. "Listen, I don't want to hurt the tribe. We aren't here to destroy them."

"No, you just want them to serve you."

"That's right. We were once their leaders. We will be so again."

"Why now?" I asked. "It's been, what... Hundreds of years? Thousands? I can only assume your order has been in hiding all this time."

"Yes. At first, we hid among other tribes. Our line continued and each new generation was trained in secret. When the white man came, we felt the tribe had gotten what it deserved for turning on us. But then we saw an opportunity. And so, we continued to pass our heritage down through the years, waiting for our chance."

"But why now?" I asked again. "Why today?"

"Because I always knew I was the one," he said, shrugging. "I knew I'd be the one to lead us to reclaim our rightful place."

"Yeah, yeah. Of course. You're the chosen one and all that. But why did you choose today? What spurred you to come to Lost City when you did?"

He stared at me for a moment before replying. "You're more clever than I gave you credit for."

"You had some help," I said. "You aren't the only player in this game."

"That's true. We have had some help. New allies, if you will. There're other changes coming, Blade Mage. And we want to be on the winning side."

"And what side is that?"

"The side you aren't on." He grinned. "You're moments from your death, and you will go to your grave with your questions unanswered."

It was my turn to shrug. "That's all right. I can piece most of it together, anyway. Your new pals offered you some assistance in pulling off your coup. Though obviously not too much, because they aren't here. However, in return, you're going to help them pull off theirs. Typical evil asshole stuff, really. And frankly, whoever this baddy is, you aren't his or her favorite gal. I've already seen this play out a few times. And you know what else? I don't really care who is pulling your puppet strings. Just another asshole with delusions of grandeur."

"I see," Wright replied, though I suspect I might've irritated him a bit. *Win.* "Then, if you're all done, would you like to get on with killing us all now? Or do you wish to stall a little longer?"

"A fair question. On one hand, I would like to get on with killing the lot of you. On the other hand, I would like to stall a little longer, but I don't really want to talk to you anymore. Would it be rude if I just stalled over here by myself? You guys can totally pretend I'm not here."

Before he could answer, Pathkiller cried out, her screaming echoing through the night. One part teenage girl, one part rock scraping stone.

And then she was still.

"I think we're just about done here," Wright said. "Time to go visit the tribe."

I heard him, but I was focused on Pathkiller, who was in the process of standing up. If I didn't know it was her, I wouldn't have recognized her. Where Waya the stone man had kept a few of his own features, just enough to recognize his face in the granite, Pathkiller hadn't.

It looked as though she'd accomplished what she'd set out to do. She'd killed her path. Gone was Alyita. But gone, too, was Pathkiller. Now she was just Spearfinger.

And her cold eyes were locked on mine.

Well, so maybe she hadn't forgotten everything. She still wanted to kill me.

"Farewell, Blade Mage," Wright said. "I'm glad you could be here for our moment of triumph. And to tell you the truth, I think my new friends will be overjoyed when I bring them your head."

"Always glad to be a help," I replied, readying myself. I had my sword in one hand and my staff in the other.

I considered whether there was something clever I could do to catch them off-guard and came up empty. I considered making a run for the priests to see if I could cut down a few. Or maybe just try to kill Raymond, at least. Instead...

I threw my sword at Wright.

The leader of the Ani-kutani sidestepped and my sword hit the gravel behind him.

*Shit.*

"It's not going to be that easy, Blade Mage."

"Well, I'd certainly hope not," I replied as I summoned my sword back to my hand. "I'd at least want you all to have a fighting chance."

Spearfinger and Stone Man charged me.

Banter time was over.

It was time for me to die.

At least I was going to die knowing I *had* stalled them for a little bit longer. *Win.*

Spearfinger closed the gap first and I dove to the side, right into the path of Stone Man. That was okay, because I immediately dove again as he tried to crush me. That put his hulking frame between me and Spearfinger.

I nearly struck out with my sword, but stopped myself at the last second.

For one, I wasn't really sure Dyrnwyn would cut through stone flesh.

Mostly, though, I was a bit worried it would. Maybe I was just a fool, but I still couldn't bring myself to harm the kids, regardless of what Wright had said about them being gone.

And that's pretty much what caused me to get knocked on my ass.

I deftly dodged a strike from Spearfinger, but when the weight came down on my damaged knee, I staggered. That was just enough time for Stone Man to backhand me to the ground.

It was like getting hit in the chest with a cinder block.

I hit the ground and stared upward as the bulky fella closed in, intent on smashing me to mush.

# CHAPTER SIXTY-EIGHT

S omewhere in the back of my mind, I heard a raven's caw and assumed it was just my adrenaline-addled mind playing a final trick on me before my timely demise. I said "timely" because honestly, it was only fair my luck had finally run out.

Feathers filled my vision.

Hundreds upon hundreds of black feathers.

Instead of a single caw, now I was hearing hundreds of caws, singing out of harmony like... Well, like a bunch of angry birds.

And then I felt a sense of weightlessness, like I was being lifted off the ground.

Was this what dying was?

Not really at all what I'd expected.

And then I was on my feet and a tornado of birds was pulling away from me, separating and taking flight.

The first thing I realized was that I was now a good hundred yards from the church.

The second thing I realized was that the Valravn now stood just beside me.

"Uh, hey there," I said, glancing at him.

He straightened his suit and then shook his head at me. "Why do you insist on throwing your life away on lost causes?"

"Keeps me on my toes."

"I already told you," he said, hooking a thumb back toward the church. "This is not the true enemy."

"Well, yeah," I agreed. "But he is a real asshole, so...meh."

As if on cue, Wright's magical voice boomed across the distance between us. "Raven Mocker. What are you doing here?"

With an equally loud magical voice, the Valravn responded, "Checking up on an investment."

"You know our mutual friend will not be pleased."

The Valravn shrugged. "That's kind of the point, isn't it? We're not really mates anyway, him and I."

"A shame," Wright replied. "It's one thing to refuse his gracious help. It's another entirely to meddle in his affairs. He'll not be pleased to hear of this."

The Valravn waved the notion away, as though Wright were standing just beside him. "Believe me, he doesn't care about anything going on here. He only cares that you serve. At any rate, I'll be on my way now."

He turned back to me. "Come along now, Blade Mage. Let's get you from this certain death."

I stared at his shadowy, twisting face for a moment, then turned and started limping back toward Pastor Wright and his fellow assholes.

Look, I know you aren't supposed to look a gift horse in the mouth.

I also know you aren't supposed to look a supernatural gift raven who just saved your sorry carcass in the mouth, but hey, I've always been stubborn.

And frankly, the Valravn kind of got on my nerves. He'd saved me, sure, but he wasn't my friend. He was an asshole, too. It just so happened he had ulterior motives that clashed with some of the other assholes. Didn't make him stink any less.

And my mission wasn't complete. I was there to stall for my friends. The actual good guys.

"What are you doing?" the Valravn asked.

"Oh, just having a nice little walk," I replied over my shoulder. "The hell does it look like I'm doing? I going to kick names and take ass, or *something* like that."

"You'll just be killed."

I cursed my limp for not letting me move quicker. "Yeah, I know, dingus. But the job ain't done."

"I just gave you a way out, and you're just going back. For nothing?"

"Not for nothing."

"You know I could just whisk you further away."

"Who says 'whisk' like that? Do what you've got to do. I'll just start walking back this way again."

For a moment, I thought he was gone, then I looked up again and realized he was casually walking right beside me.

"You know, I find you incredibly frustrating," he said.

"Good. I wouldn't want you to start thinking we're pals."

"Fine, Blade Mage. Have it your way. I thought, perhaps, you might yet be of use for the greater good. But I see now that perhaps you're just too stubborn and stupid."

"You're just now picking up on that?"

"Fine. Go get yourself killed, then."

"I mean... You could help, if you're that worried about it."

"No. I think I'd rather let you die and hope someone more sensible reclaims your sword."

"Ha! Everyone in the Cabal has been hoping for that. Ask them how it's going."

"You're a fool."

"And you're a creepy bird man. We all have our flaws. Now, if you aren't going to help, then flock off."

He didn't even reply to that.

His body disintegrated into a flock of birds and he did, in fact, flock off.

Pleased by my darling sense of humor, I got back to the mission of limping my way to death.

I would like to say that it was a really impressive walk. You know, the kind in the movies where they're boldly strolling into the last battle, head held high. Thing is... It's hard to look like a badass when you're limping worse than a grandpa who's misplaced his cane.

And my enemies were no help either, really. They just kind of watched me approach, as if they couldn't believe I was stupid enough to walk right back toward them. It took me a *good* few minutes. Guess I was just lucky that these particular assholes were patient.

When I felt I was close enough, I said, "So, where were we?"

"You really don't know when to quit, do you?" Wright asked, shaking his head. "It might be impressive if it weren't so sad."

He motioned toward Stone Man, who started toward me again. Spearfinger had disappeared from sight, and while I was curious where she'd slunk off to, I had a much bigger problem to deal with.

I raised my staff and considered whether any spell in my retinue would be of any help against the hulking brute. I decided probably not. I again considered my sword, but knew that if it did work, it would be lethal. Somewhere inside Stone Man was Waya the wolf, and somewhere inside Waya the wolf was Salal the squirrel. I couldn't kill the kid.

When Stone Man was within ten paces, I tried a simple force spell, just to see if I could stagger him a bit. If nothing else, I thought perhaps I could slow him down.

I summoned the energy through my staff, manipulated it the way I wanted it, and fired.

*Boom.*

The night lit up as the space in front of Stone Man erupted in flame.

# CHAPTER SIXTY-NINE

Even from where I stood, I felt the concussion and was knocked off my feet.

Looking up, I saw that Stone Man had fared little better. He landed on his back, smoke billowing off his chest.

My ears rang and my head swam. My senses were so disoriented that for a moment, it felt as though I were dreaming.

I looked down at my staff, then back up at Stone Man, then back down at my staff.

I heard Steve Urkel's voice in my head ask, *Did I do that?*

Ahead, I saw Wright and all his pals were also staring at the scene with confusion and dismay. So at least I wasn't the only one flabbergasted by whatever the hell had just happened.

Then I saw one of Raymond's goons drop to the ground, followed immediately by another. The rest of the a-hole pack started moving like scurrying ants.

I finally got the bright idea to look behind me.

And there was Shain Stone, moving forward with his eye tucked behind the optic of an M4 with a grenade launcher attachment, firing round after round as he sped-walked closer to the church.

*No, Urkel, you don't have to take the blame for this one,* I thought as I watched the scene unfold with a sense of wonder. Hey, at least I wasn't going to die alone.

Turning back toward our enemies, I saw movement from the darkness to the left and a series of what I could only describe as energy daggers take down a fire priest. Oh, who was I kidding? They looked like lasers. Behind the lasers, I saw Commander Harris with Garza and the rest of the Honey Badgers.

Glancing to the right side of the battlefield, I saw one of Raymond's goons go flying through the air and Fatima appeared from the darkness, her gang behind her.

The area in front of the church descended into chaos as Wright and his goons were attacked from all sides. I watched in amazement as Shain Stone and the wizards pressed the attack, forcing my foes on the defensive.

A hand grab me from behind and I turned to find August Bones standing over me. Constable Williams was just beside him. Together, pulled me to my feet. Both were speaking, but I was still deaf from the explosion.

The whole ringing ears thing was really inconvenient because I had a lot of questions I would've liked answered. Well, no, actually, just one question—what the hell were they all doing here?

Instead, they started half-carrying and half-dragging me away from the recovering Stone Man. It seemed their plan was to get me away from the fighting, which I was torn on. On one hand, I was a wee bit injured, but on the other hand, I was inspired by their arrival and ready to wipe the smug smirk from Wright's face. He might've had his way up to this point, but this was something he hadn't expected.

At least, that's what I was thought right up until to the moment everything froze.

I'd just glanced back over my shoulder when the chaos froze in place.

It literally just stopped.

Like someone had pressed the pause button.

No one was moving, good guy or bad.

Confused by this unexpected change, I tried to turn my head back to the others to see if they'd noticed, but I realized I couldn't turn my head. I couldn't move.

Was *this* what dying was?

All the world just frozen in my final moment?

And then I saw movement.

One single figure casually strolled about the battlefield without a care in the world.

Wright.

He'd done this. Somehow, he'd frozen everyone in place. What manner of power was this? I'd never seen anything like it. If he was capable of such magic... We were screwed.

I was surprised when I heard his voice over the ringing in my ears. I had to admit that his magical volume enhancer was even more effective than I'd realized.

"A valiant effort," he said. "Really. I am impressed that you all gathered here, just for me."

"Not for you," a familiar voice said.

A fog appeared, sweeping across the ground. As fast as it had appeared, it was gone and the Nunnehi stood in its wake. With her were Ahuli, John, and the rest of the Cherokee.

Even at a distance, I saw Wright was taken aback by her appearance.

*There, ya prick. Finally, something you weren't expecting.*

"For him," the Nunnehi said, glancing over her shoulder at me. "He is their friend. He was about to sacrifice himself for them. And so, he is our friend, too. And together, we have decided that we could not leave him to face the darkness alone."

Ahuli took a step forward. "We are Cherokee. And we will never bow to you, Fire Priest. Nor will we abandon our allies. Today, we fight as one."

"And so you will die together," Wright said, but for the first time, he was off his game.

"We shall see," the Nunnehi said, raising her hand.

And like that, the freeze ended.

Chaos reclaimed the field.

Stone Man rose to his feet, eyes set on Ahuli.

The war chief dropped to one knee, as though he were praying. The Nunnehi reached out a hand and touched the back of his head.

Ahuli rose to his full height, but now he was slightly bulkier than before, and his skin no longer looked like flesh, but instead looked hardened, like he, too, was made of stone. He still was only a third the size of Stone Man, but he charged right toward the brute and slammed into him.

It sounded like two mountains crashing together.

"Hey!" I heard myself say. "I can hear again!"

"You couldn't before?" Williams asked.

"Not a bit," I replied. "My ears were ringing."

"No wonder you were ignoring us," Bones replied. "How injured are you?"

"I'm all right," I said, showing them I could stand on my own. I'm sure my wince didn't fill them with much confidence, but I followed it by saying, "I can fight."

The look on their faces told me they weren't convinced, so I said, "We need to go after Wright. He's the ringleader."

"And clearly the most powerful," Williams said.

"You have a plan for that?" August asked.

"I thought I'd throw my sword at him, for starters," I replied.

"Is that effective?" Williams asked.

"Nope."

"You're in no shape to fight him," Bones said.

"You're probably right," I agreed, biting my lip. "While everyone else is waging war, though, we should try to free Elder Morgan."

"That's a plan I can get behind," August said.

Williams nodded and slid her arm through mine and up over my shoulder. "Come on."

"I can walk, you know," I replied.

"Not very well," she replied. "I'm certainly not slowing you down, anyway."

"A fair point," I replied.

And then I looked up and right into the eyes of Spearfinger. If looks could kill, I would've been rotting already. I wasn't sure how much of Alyita, or Pathkiller, was left in there, but there was at least some memory of me, and the great frustration I'd caused her by refusing to die. One look told me she was confident she could get the job done now.

"Who's that?" August asked.

"That delicate little flower is our old friend Alyita."

"What?" he asked, glancing between me and Spearfinger. "It can't be..."

"It is," I replied. "I watched her change."

"How?"

"Now is not the time for lengthy explanations about things I don't understand myself."

"Can she be changed back?"

"I don't know."

"Wyatt..."

"I don't know, Bones," I said, meeting his gaze. "One problem at a time. If anyone can help her, it's her grandfather. Get him freed. I'll hold her off."

"Bullshit," Williams said, letting go of me and holding her wand up. "You can barely walk. I'll try to hold her. You two go."

"Williams," I pleaded, but before I could argue further, Spearfinger charged.

Constable Williams closed her eyes, chanted a few quick words of power, and a bright blast shot from the end of her wand. It hit Spearfinger in the chest, and though it didn't seem to do any damage, she froze in place, similar to how we'd all been trapped a few moments earlier.

Over her shoulder, Williams said, "I'm not sure how long I can hold her. Go."

"Thank you," I replied, letting August help me move.

"And Wyatt," she called. "Forget what anyone else says. You're everything a Blade Mage should be."

"Thank you, Constable Williams."

With that, Bones and I limp-sprinted across the church lawn. All around us was chaos. Wizards, medicine men, fire priests, Raymond's thugs, the Nunnehi, and bloody-as-you-like, one-of-a-kind Mr. Shain Stone were tearing the hallowed grounds apart like this was World War Three. Losses were heavy on both sides, but this was it.

There was no backing down now. Both sides were in it until it was over.

Ahead of us, a fire priest turned his attention our way. I was just about to warn August when a long, thorny whip came out of nowhere and wrapped around the priest's throat. He yelped as the thorns pricked his neck, then screamed as he was ripped off the ground and flung off into the darkness.

My gazed followed the length of the whip back to its owner, the Nunnehi. Noticing she had my attention, she offered me a friendly wave and a pleasant little smile. I returned the favor, thankful she was on our side.

Ahead was Shain Stone. Beyond him, our route to Elder Morgan was clear. I didn't see Pastor Wright anywhere, which I didn't take to be a good thing.

As we closed in on Stone, he nodded my way as he threw a fresh mag in his rifle. "What's the play, kid?"

"We need to get to the elder," I said, pointing.

"I'm with you," he replied, following in step with us.

Unfortunately, we only made it about three steps when John smashed into the three of us and we all went down in a pile. Naturally, I ended up on the bottom.

"What the hell, man?" I asked as the pile separated.

"Sorry," John replied. "Stone Man. Way stronger than I expected."

"No, kidding," I replied.

"Uh, fellas," August said.

I glanced up and saw that Stone Man was racing toward us. Apparently, he still wanted to finish the job he'd started on John. Ahuli was behind him, but he wasn't going to catch the brute in time.

"Clever ideas?" I asked.

No one replied, and there was no time to think of anything. I went for my sword.

But just before I threw it, Garza sprinted past us with his staff pointed at the ground behind him. The end glowed and took on the ethereal shape of a war hammer. Just as Stone Man closed in, the wizard swung his staff upward, smashing the magical battle hammer into the brute's head.

Stone man's jaw snapped back and he staggered a few steps, then fell to the ground. Before he could get back up, Ahuli jumped on him again.

Garza glanced back at me. "I'll hold off the big guy."

"Thanks, Garza," I replied.

"Yeah," he replied. "Glad I didn't kill you, Blade Mage."

"Me, too, buddy. Me, too!"

With Garza helping Ahuli, John decided to stick with us. That was fine by me, because ahead of us on the left, one of the fire priests had taken notice of us. To the right, Raymond, surrounded by what remained of his gang, had also switched his focus to us. We probably seemed the easier targets, compared to some of the others.

The fire priest took a few steps forward and flung back his hood, revealing Samuel's face.

"This one is mine," John said, stepping away from the group. He held his tomahawk in one hand and a long knife in the other.

Samuel tossed aside his robe and withdrew a knife and hawk as well. He smiled at the friend he'd betrayed. "I've been waiting for this for a long time."

"You were like a brother to me," John said.

"No," Samuel said, shaking his head. "You were the favorite. I was the disappointment. But I always knew I was better than you. Today, everyone else will know it, too."

John didn't reply. Instead, he charged.

"I'll keep Raymond and his pals busy," August said, letting go of me. "He's had it out for me for a while, anyway."

"I can help," Stone said. "Wyatt, can you get to the elder on your own?"

"So long as there're no extra surprises between here and there."

With that, they split off.

I kept my gaze on Elder Morgan, but kept my magical shield up just in case of a random attack. Didn't want to get caught with my pants down, so to speak.

Elder Morgan was just ahead. He was sitting on the ground with his hands tied behind his back. It didn't appear that they'd roughed him up and his eyes were alert as he watched me approach.

I was nearly to him when he yelled, "Watch out!"

I dove forward and hit the ground in a roll, coming up just in time to see Spearfinger stabbing at where my head had just been. My first thought was of Williams and what this meant for her. Where was she?

There wasn't time to focus on that, though, as Spearfinger came at me again.

I jabbed my staff upward, intent on hitting her with a simple force spell. She slammed into the front of my staff even as I fired. The impact knocked her back and put her on the ground, but only for a moment. She bounced right back up and dove at me.

Another figure slammed into the side of her as she came down on top of me, moving her just enough that the razor-sharp finger missed my head and stabbed into the ground instead.

Williams.

The two fell off the top of me, still locked in a tussle.

When they separated, Spearfinger came up first.

Williams didn't come up at all.

Glancing down, I saw the front of her shirt was coated in blood. Even through the mess, I could see she'd been stabbed twice. Once just then, and I suspected once before. Yet, somehow, she'd fought her way over to save me, refusing to give up.

Now, though, her eyes were glazed over and blood was trickling from the side of her mouth.

Spearfinger raised her hand, intent on finishing the job.

# CHAPTER SEVENTY

~

A cold fury swept over me and I summoned every bit of effort I had left to hit her with the hardest force spell I could.

Spearfinger was knocked off her feet again.

"No, no," Elder Morgan said, scooching closer to Williams. Tears poured from his eyes as he turned to look at the thing his granddaughter had become.

Spearfinger rolled back to a crouch but didn't pounce. Her eyes studied me, Williams, and her grandfather.

"What have you done?" Elder Morgan asked, staring at her. "What have you done?"

He repeated the question over and over, chanting it as his gaze moved from Constable Williams to his granddaughter.

For my part, I dropped to the ground beside Williams and pressed my hands over the wounds, trying to stem the bleeding.

It was no use.

The constable's eyes met mine, and she looked as though she were trying to say something, but her body went slack and her head rested on the ground.

I felt for a pulse, but couldn't find one.

She was gone.

Constable Williams was dead.

She'd died to save me.

The sounds of battle melted away into nothing but screams and I looked up, realizing the sky had opened and it was raining fire. Droplets of flame were falling among enemies and allies alike. Everyone was either seeking cover or attempting to protect themselves with magical shields.

Only the area directly in front of the church was not impacted. We were safe.

August Bones, Stone, and Raymond's group were mostly safe, though at least half of Raymond's crew were dead. A few others didn't survive the fiery rain.

And a few feet away, John and Samuel were still hacking at each other. Neither of them was hurt, either.

"It's beautiful, is it not?" Pastor Wright asked.

He now stood just a few feet away, his gaze up at the sky.

I threw my sword at him.

He sidestepped and Dyrnwyn missed.

Pretending that hadn't just happened, I tried to keep my cool and asked, "Proud of your work?"

"Shouldn't I be?" he asked. "Look at how much I've accomplished."

"You haven't won yet," I said, then turned my gaze toward August and Stone.

It was perfect timing, too, because just then, Stone laid down some cover fire while Bones charged straight into Raymond's thugs. His strange, long, bone-carved wand took on a red glow and a scythe appeared from the end of it.

Raymond's eyes went wide in the moment before Bones swung it through his neck, decapitating him.

His remaining bodyguards were so surprised by this turn of events that they didn't see Stone step around the other side.

I turned back to Wright. "There's one ally down."

He shrugged. "Raymond had already outlived his use. He served little purpose beyond distraction."

"And what of Samuel?" I asked, my gaze already switched.

John stood over the man he'd once considered a brother. His knife was embedded in Samuel's chest.

"Same, really," Wright said. "Samuel had some potential, but truth be told, he was weak. His only real use was being my eyes in the camp, getting the children hooked on Zavan, and sending them to me."

"And all of your fire priests who have died?"

Again, he shrugged. "Once the Cherokee bow to me, I'll have an endless supply of students to train. I may even seek recruits from other tribes. Might even steal a few of your Cabal's wizards, though the magic is different, as you've seen. Besides, look at the battlefield. My students are still many. Your numbers are dwindling."

It was my turn to follow his gaze.

Out across the flaming rain, I saw what he'd said was true. There were far too many medicine men and wizards on the ground. We were losing.

But I also caught sight of something else.

Where the Nunnehi stood, the flaming rain didn't touch her. In fact, the entire area around her was clear of flame. She walked calmly toward where Ahuli, Garza, and the Stone Man still fought.

It was clear neither Ahuli nor Garza had the strength of Stone Man, but they were the more experienced fighters, and had managed to get Stone Man on the ground. Now the two of them were struggling to keep Stone Man down. It served little purpose but to keep the monster out of the fight. Yet that was something, though it could only last for so long.

When the Nunnehi closed in on them, she reached a hand down to touch Stone Man on the back of the head. From this distance, I couldn't hear what she said, but saw that she spoke a few words.

The brute froze in place for a moment, and then went slack, falling to the ground.

Ahuli and Garza rose to their feet beside her. Stone Man didn't move.

I turned back to Pastor Wright. "And what of Stone Man?"

"Ah, now that would be a loss," he said, shaking his head. His gaze returned to mine. "Still, though. Compared to Spearfinger, he, too, is weak. She holds the Ulun'suti. She is powerful. And I am her master. Watch."

He turned his attention to Spearfinger. "Finish them, dear. Start with the Blade Mage."

Spearfinger began to rise.

"No, Alyita," her grandfather said. "No more. Do you not see what you've done?"

She looked at him, confusion on her face.

"Look," Elder Morgan said, using his head to point at Williams's still form. "Look what you've done. Is this what you wanted? Is this the power you sought? Is this truly your path?"

"Give it up, old man," Wright said. "Your granddaughter is gone."

"No," Elder Morgan said. "No. She is in there. Alyita, please, listen to me. I love you, granddaughter. I love you and I forgive you. No matter what, I will always love you."

Spearfinger stared at her grandfather, then back at Wright.

"Go on," Wright said. "This is the path to true power."

Her gaze shifted to me.

"No, it isn't," I said, locking eyes with her. "This isn't power. You are not stronger now than you were before. You are weaker. This man isn't going to help you find true power. It's a lie. Somewhere in there, you know this. Look what he made you become. Look what happened to Waya. Is he stronger? Are you truly stronger?"

"What would your mother think?" Elder Morgan said. "She paid the ultimate price for her mistakes. Would she want the same for you? I don't."

"Enough of this," Wright said, clearly annoyed. "Kill them!"

Spearfinger started forward.

"I love you, Alyita," Elder Morgan said. "And I'm sorry. I should've done better by you. By your mother. This is my fault. And I am sorry. I love you."

Spearfinger moved at blinding speed. Little more than a blur, I had half a second to realize I was about to die.

But she went past me and leaped at Pastor Wright instead.

The head priest of the Ani-kutani raised a hand and Spearfinger flew back the way she'd come, end over end, bouncing across the ground until she finally came to a stop.

Wright didn't look happy.

So, I smiled at him. "Huh, well, I guess that's another one down."

"Do you think it matters?" he asked, his voice a hiss.

I looked at Elder Morgan and met the older medicine man's eyes. "Yeah, I think it matters."

"You two will still die, along with all your allies. I can kill you all myself, if need be." He turned his attention to Elder Morgan. "And as for your granddaughter, don't celebrate just yet. When this is over, she will still bend her knee to me or she will die, too."

"Do your worst, fire priest," Elder Morgan said, glaring up at him. "The Cherokee defeated you once. We will do so again."

Wright sneered. "We shall see."

"No, we won't," a new voice said.

It came from just behind the fire priest, but there didn't appear to be anyone there.

Wright attempted to turn around but came up short. His eyes widened and he reached for his throat, as though something had a hold of him. He struggled, panic running across his features.

His eyes met mine, but I could only shrug.

I didn't know what the hell was going on, and I certainly wasn't prepared to gloat until I did.

One thing I did notice was that his fire rain had ceased, which meant that his priests could get back to trying to kill my allies. And they did.

Only... There seemed to be more figures on the battlefield now.

People I didn't recognize.

Wizards, to be exact.

Lots of them.

And they were all... Fighting the fire priests.

*What the hell?*

Wright struggled against the unseen force choking him. He tried to raise a hand, which I could only assume was an attempt to cast some form of magic at his unseen foe. Instead, his hand twisted in a strange way, followed immediately by the sound of snapping bone.

The big boss fire priest might've screamed if there were any air in his lungs, but instead his eyes just widened further.

"Now, now, none of that," said the voice, which I was sure I knew. "You know, I really don't like it when someone murders one of my people. Doesn't sit well. I'm sure you understand."

A figure materialized just in front of me, one hand wrapped around the throat of Pastor Wright. He was dressed in a two-piece suit. A *very* expensive two-piece suit.

Master Watcher Giovanni Jackson.

It was the Cabal.

They were here.

The master watcher's voice remained pleasant and calm. "Furthermore, the Cherokee are our allies. And you've hurt them, as well as some of the Cabal's people. Under normal circumstances, I would arrest you. However, you might be a bit too dangerous for that."

He turned to me.

"Would you agree, Blade Mage?"

I nodded.

"Good," he said, offering me a friendly smile.

Then he crushed Pastor Wright's neck with his bare hand.

The dead fire priest crumpled to the ground.

I blinked a few times.

Pastor Wright, or whatever his name actually was, had been capable of turning Waya into the hulking Stone Man. He'd transformed Pathkiller into Spearfinger. He'd frozen a whole battlefield full of people. He'd made it rain fire. He'd caught Watcher Rhodes and had killed him effortlessly.

He was one of the most powerful assholes I'd ever faced.

And Master Watcher Giovanni Jackson had just killed him like he was a tick.

I glanced back at the battlefield. With the Cabal's numbers, the fire priests were going down fast. I even recognized Parker Grimm in the mix.

Turning my attention back to Elder Morgan, I began inching my way toward him so I could finally get him untied.

"Ah, please, allow me," the Master Watcher said.

He stepped over behind Elder Morgan, untied his hands, and helped the aging medicine man to his feet.

Elder Morgan set off immediately to his granddaughter. He wrapped his arms around her and squeezed, the tears streaming down his cheeks. Already, her features were returning to normal.

I stared at the two of them for a moment until I finally felt like I was invading their privacy.

Fortunately, Master Jackson snapped me back to reality.

"Well, this is a bit of a mess," he said, eyes moving around the battlefield.

"Right," I said. "I hope you won't think it's rude of me if I just go ahead and pass out right here."

"Not at all," he replied. "I think we've got the situation in hand."

My head was already on the ground, but I raised an arm to give him a thumbs up.

# CHAPTER SEVENTY-ONE

B etween the Cherokee, Fatima's group, the Honey Badgers, and the overwhelming number of reinforcements from the Cabal, the rest of the fight was short-lived.

The Ani-kutani fought to the last, though. I had to give them that.

They wouldn't be taken alive.

I raised my head from the ground just long enough to see Ahuli kill the last of them, calling an end to the fight.

There was no celebration, however.

I could see from the faces of my allies that none felt particularly victorious.

The losses had been too great.

Many medicine men and women were dead, their losses tremendous. Fatima's group and Commander Harris's Honey Badgers were no exceptions.

Worst of all, perhaps, was Waya.

Salal, the Squirrel, as he'd once been called, had been Stone Man too long. In that, at least, Pastor Wright had told the truth. When the Nunnehi had changed him back, there was nothing left of the young man. He was gone.

Alyita hadn't awoken from her transformation, but she was still breathing. No one knew whether she'd wake up, and if she did, how much of herself she might've lost. It was a waiting game.

The rest of the kids had made it, and that was no small thing to be thankful for.

One figure had disappeared from the battleground entirely.

Shain Stone was nowhere in sight. I noticed that none among our allies mentioned or asked about him, which meant he must've have slipped away before the Cabal realized he was there.

I wasn't going to be the one who sold him out.

Most of us loaded up and headed back for the camp. We brought our injured and deceased with us and left a number of the Cabal reinforcements and a few of the Cherokee to secure and sort the rest of the mess.

I dozed in the back of the truck during the bumpy ride. When we arrived, John helped me down onto my angry knee.

Once standing, I realized I was dizzy and nearly fainted. After I got over that, I ignored the exhaustion and pain and hobbled to the bunkhouse.

I needed to check on Axel.

I found him fast asleep, snoring peacefully.

That was a positive change from earlier. I took it to be a good sign.

I considered collapsing in the other bed, but decided it would be wise to make sure Axel hadn't been forgotten among all the fresh injuries. The Cherokee had enough of their own problems to worry about, but now that the Cabal was here, surely I could convince them to help him.

On the other hand, I didn't really want to move, either. That shit hurt.

August Bones found me there once again.

"He looks better," August said as he moved to stand alongside me.

I nodded. "Have you heard anything about his injuries?"

"Oh, right, I meant to tell you, but then things were a little crazy."

"What?"

"Before we left, the Nunnehi assured Ahuli that she would see to all our injured. They're all like this, Wyatt. Sleeping peacefully. Even the ones in the worst conditions."

I nodded. Considering what the Nunnehi had done for my knee, that was the best news of the night.

"So, Axel may be all right."

"It's probably early to get our hopes, but yeah, he just might be."

"Is she still here?" I asked. "I would like to thank her for... Well, for everything."

He shook his head. "She disappeared right after the fight."

We stood in silence for a moment, both staring at Axel. Finally, I said, "I've got a question for you, Bones."

"What's that?"

I turned to face him. "When we first met on the Castle lawn, did you have any idea you were dragging me along for such a messed-up time?"

"I'm afraid I didn't," he said. "But I'm glad as hell I did. You're all right, Blade Mage. I don't want to think of how much worse this might've played out if you hadn't been here."

"Same for you," I replied. "I mean... Sure, there's a part of me that's like, why couldn't August have just stuck with his first impression and found me unworthy? Then I wouldn't be here. But on the other hand, if you hadn't taken the actions you did, things would be a lot worse."

"I feel like I caused a lot of deaths," he said, looking away.

"No, you didn't," I said, shaking my head. "None of this is on you. Well, except the part where we got caught by your dealers. That part *is* your fault. The rest of it, though, no, you don't get to take any blame. Your actions saved more lives."

"Still a lot of dead, though."

"But we got the kids back safely."

"Not all of them."

I sighed, considering my next words carefully. "You know what? You're right. We didn't save all of them. And yeah, a lot of good people got hurt, and some have been lost. There's nothing I can say that's going to unburden your guilt. Fact of the matter is, I feel it, too. Logically, I know I did the best I could. I know *we* did the best we could. But I will carry this with me always, and I will always wonder what I could've done better. And that's just part of it. I like to think that's part of what makes us the good guys."

"You think that's true?" he asked. "That we're the good guys?"

This time, I bit my lip. "I don't know, August. I used to think so. You know, my dad seemed to handle this role like a champ, and I've spent a lot of time thinking how he would've done things differently. I've even questioned what kind of monster I'm becoming. But now I wonder... Did he feel this immense guilt? Did he always feel like a failure?"

August nodded and we stood together in silence for a few moments longer.

Finally, he coughed and said, "I was, uh, asked to come fetch you."

"I was thinking to collapse on that bed."

"Elder Morgan and the Master Watcher want to see you. Told them I knew where you'd be."

"All right, then I guess I better go see what they want," I said, hobbling toward the door. I took one look over my shoulder at the empty bed calling my name.

# CHAPTER SEVENTY-TWO

A haggard and weary-looking war chief stood alone outside the main building.

I paused in front of him and forced a smile. "You look like crap, War Chief."

He nodded. "Then I must look considerably better than I feel."

"Was that a joke?" I asked, raising an eyebrow. "The wonders just won't stop tonight."

He snorted. "You can barely walk. Has a healer seen to you?"

"Not yet," I said, shaking my head. "There're graver injuries than mine. Figured I'd give them time to get the others sorted, then just when they think their long night is over, I'll surprise them with a bummed knee."

Again he nodded, but then went quiet, staring off into the dark forest.

"What are you doing out here by yourself, anyway?" I asked.

"Just getting some fresh air."

"Is it helping?"

"No," he said with a heavy sigh. "Go on, Blade Mage. The others are waiting for you inside."

I started forward, then paused, thinking of a question. "Has there been any word on Elder Thomas?"

"Yes," Ahuli said. "Constable Johnson was able to stabilize him and stop the bleeding. He then took him all the way to the Castle on his own."

"Ah," I said, nodding. "And that's probably why the Cabal knew to come precisely when they did. Or Commander Harris reported back. Either way, guess it was good they showed up when they did."

"Yes."

I stared at his face, noting that his eyes hadn't met mine yet.

"You know, Ahuli, if there was a market for guilt, we'd all be rich after tonight."

He glanced my way for just a moment, then looked away again.

"You can't take all the blame, War Chief. Leave some for the rest of us."

"I failed as Red Chief," he replied. "I made many mistakes."

"Yeah, you did. Made mistakes, I mean. So did I."

"My mistakes cost lives," he said, finally meeting my gaze. "I was supposed to lead the Cherokee into battle. Instead, I led my people straight into an ambush. I thought I was wise, but in the end, I was just arrogant and foolish."

Just like with August, I considered my words carefully, but in the end, decided on a more brash approach. "You're right. You were an arrogant ass. And yes, your mistakes had a heavy cost. But do you really think any of the others would've done better?"

He didn't reply.

"Look, at the end of the day, you did what you thought was right. You risked your own life for that of your tribe. You did what—I can only assume—a War Chief was supposed to do. And sure, you can wallow in the guilt of your mistakes, but also wonder, then, if you hadn't been there to lead, how much worse would it have been? You may not, but I know the answer to that. You saved your tribe tonight, Ahuli. Take some solace in that, at least."

He was silent for a moment, then said, "Perhaps your council is wise, Blade Mage."

"That is...not something I hear every day."

"You are not of my tribe, and I have seen that I can trust your discretion. Can I ask you a question?"

"Sure."

"I am thankful for Elder Morgan's return. Not just because he is my friend and important to my tribe, but also because I am grateful to relinquish the burden of command. The war is over, and so the Red Chief can step aside and let the White Chief lead once more. Do such thoughts mean I am unfit to be War Chief? Does that make me weak?"

"No, it makes you human," I replied. "You know, I've always believed that deep down, one of the things that makes a great leader great is that they understand the burden of leadership, and they don't want it. They don't seek it. But understanding that burden is what makes them best suited to lead. The best leaders aren't seeking glory and power for themselves. They're seeking success for those they're responsible for. And I think yesterday, you were in the previous category. You wanted to be War Chief for the sake of pride. Today, though, you understand what it really means, and I suspect it will serve you well going forward."

Again he was silent for a time. Finally, he said, "I'm glad I didn't kill you, Blade Mage."

"Yeah, me, too," I replied. "And for what it's worth, I think you should stay as war chief. Call it gut instinct, but I think there may be more trouble coming for all of us. And when it rears its head, I, for one, will be glad to know the Cherokee have Ahuli as their war chief."

"Thank you," he replied. "That...actually means a lot coming from you, considering how poorly I treated you."

"Well, hopefully, if we work together in the future, it will be under better terms."

"You can count on it," he said with a smile. "Now get in there, Blade Mage. I believe your Master Watcher was looking for you."

I limped my way inside and saw John straight away.

Noticing my limp, he frowned at me, then came over and helped me walk the rest of the way to the conference room. Once I was seated within, he told me he'd let the others know I'd arrived. Then, much to my surprise, he returned a minute later with a glass of water and a couple of Advil. He was quickly becoming my new favorite person.

A few minutes later, a pile of people began streaming into the conference room.

None of them looked any better than I felt.

First were two elders whose names I couldn't remember.

Next was Ahuli, still brooding.

Then Fatima, who looked uncomfortable and annoyed. If I had to guess, she probably wanted to go home, but had been asked to hang out a few minutes longer than she desired.

Master Watcher Giovanni Jackson and Commander Harris entered the room next and took seats. Of all the participants, the Master Watcher was the only one who didn't look like he'd been in a battle. His pressed suit was as clean as the day he'd bought it.

Parker Grimm strolled in next, his eyes meeting mine.

"Wyatt."

"Parker."

"Shamus Grimm," Master Giovanni said, not even bothering to look up. "My apologies. I hadn't intended for you to participate in this meeting. If you would wait outside, please?"

The shamus, who reported directly to the Archmage, looked up at the master watcher with something like shock and awe. Apparently, he had just assumed his spot in... Well, whatever this post-fight recap meeting was all about. But the master watcher had just thrown his weight at the shamus.

It was hard to hide my smile.

I mean... *So* hard.

So, I didn't.

Parker Grimm glared at me for half a second, then switched to an appropriate professional face for the Master Watcher. "My apologies... I will, uh, just be outside if you need me."

"Thank you, Shamus Grimm," the Master Watcher said with a pleasant smile. "Your services will not be needed for this, however."

Parker Grimm replied with an awkward nod, glared at me again, then stepped out of the room.

I refrained from thanking the Master Watcher.

Elder Morgan was the last to join us. Despite not fighting in the battle, he had been a prisoner and looked even more exhausted than the rest of us.

"Apologies," he said, as he slowly sat down. "I was seeing to my granddaughter."

"Of course," Master Jackson said. "And I apologize for requesting this quick gathering. After the day's events, I know all of you must be exhausted and still have much to do. So, I appreciate you taking a few minutes to meet with me."

That raised my eyebrow. I hadn't realized the master watcher had called this meeting.

"What did you wish to discuss?" Elder Morgan asked.

"The terms of our relationship. That of the Cabal and the Cherokee, to be very specific."

"Right now?" I heard myself ask. I glanced around the table for support. "This can't wait until, like, you know, until everyone has slept for a week or two?"

"And why am I here at all?" Fatima asked, crossing her arms.

Ignoring her, Master Jackson offered me an easy smile. "It certainly can, Wyatt. No question. And if you think that's best for all parties, we can certainly delay this conversation. However, it will then go before the council and get dragged out through negotiations."

"And something different will happen if we do it now?" Elder Morgan asked.

Still grinning at me, the master watcher said, "Well, you see, among the Cabal, our dear Blade Mage has a reputation for being brash and independent. Therefore, the council would not be surprised to learn that the Blade Mage had agreed to new terms with the Cherokee on their behalf."

His gazed shifted to Fatima. "Or even a group of local mages in the Lost City area."

"But..." I said, raising an eyebrow at him. "The council would just apologize and say I didn't have any authority to negotiate on their behalf."

"That is a possibility," he agreed. "However, if a senior member of the Cabal—let's say a master, in this case—happened to be around, and the Cherokee wanted assurance the Blade Mage's new terms were valid, he might have little choice but to reluctantly agree to uphold the terms the rogue Blade Mage offered. At which point, the council would have little choice but to begrudgingly accept those terms."

It got really quiet as all the eyes in the room turned toward me.

"Holy shit," I said, staring at him in disbelief. "You're going to get me in *so* much trouble. I mean... You're going to get me in more trouble than I could possibly have managed on my own."

He spread his hands. "Your choice, Wyatt."

"It would be better, I think," Elder Morgan said, meeting my gaze, "if you were the one to negotiate the terms of our relationship. Even prior to my capture, I had thought to broach the concept with the other elders, to see if we might demand you be involved. If what the master watcher says is true...this may be our best opportunity."

"So, you see why it is I've rushed pulling us all together, despite the circumstances," the master watcher said.

"And why you kicked Parker out of the room," I said, biting my lip. "Otherwise, he'd just go tell the Archmage this was all your idea. As it is, I'm the only one who incurs the wrath of the council. Thanks for that."

"You do it so well," Master Jackson replied. "Old hat for you, really."

I scowled at him. "Aren't you worried Harris might sell you out?"

Commander Harris shook her head. "I'm just a strike team leader. I wasn't around when Wyatt negotiated terms with the tribe. He sure as hell didn't ask my opinion. I didn't know what he agreed to, either."

"Wow," I said, nodding. "You guys suck."

"So," Master Jackson said. "Since you are the one who will incur the council's wrath, I think it's only fair that you are the first to share your views on what the terms should be."

Again, all eyes in the room turned to me.

This was a pivotal decision for me. Any thoughts I had about building a better relationship with the council would be shot to hell if I did this. I wouldn't be back at square one. It was one thing to cause a ruckus, but it was another entirely to negotiate on their behalf without their blessing. Especially on something that should be decided by the council itself. This was a dangerous decision.

"Okay," I said, gathering my thoughts. "First, I think the Cabal should offer to lend additional manpower until the tribe is back on its feet. That means having a greater constable presence to keep the supernatural element around Lost City in check. I don't know how many of Raymond's Red Dirt Riders survived, if any, but I don't want them to just start rebuilding and run rampant. The Cherokee aren't prepared to police the area yet themselves."

"A fair point," Master Jackson said. "Completely reasonable. Elder?"

Elder Morgan glanced at his fellow elders and Ahuli, then nodded. "Yes, that would be a great benefit."

"Wonderful," the master watcher said. Then back to me, "What else?"

"It is my opinion that we should maintain a greater constable presence in Lost City, and they should be more involved with working with the Cherokee. Having them just sit in a shack all day is a waste of resources. Constable Williams wanted to help the people she was meant to protect. In the end, she gave her life to do just that, knowing full well she would've gotten in trouble...had she lived. The constables should be more involved. And the Cherokee can specify the number of constables in Lost City, within reason."

"Within reason," Master Jackson repeated. "I like that. What very professional language, Wyatt."

"I also think this should extend to Fatima and her group," I said. "They aren't just a band of nomads. They are their own coven and should be treated with the respect of a mutual ally. They, too, should be considered protectors of Lost City. Fatima?"

"I can agree with that," she said. "We don't mind doing our part. If nothing else, this ordeal has shown me that we should be more friendly with the tribe, at the very least."

"Which brings me to my next thought," I said. "There should be at least a weekly meeting between the Cherokee, the local constables, and Fatima's group. Even if just to say hi and talk about what's going on in the community. There should be an open discussion about any potential threats."

"Agreed," Elder Morgan said.

Everyone turned to Fatima. She sighed. "Well, shit. Fine. Turn me into a damned social butterfly, why don't you?"

"Additionally," I said, figuring the other shoe might drop on this one, "The Cabal will not seek more control over Cherokee territory when the Cherokee request aid. That stops. Today."

"Agreed," Master Jackson said. "What else?"

I blinked a few times, thinking that was going to be the one he pushed back on. Since he didn't, I turned my attention to Elder Morgan. "Your medicine must remain a secret to your tribe. However, ours is not sacred knowledge for us alone. So, going forward, I would offer that if there are kids who would rebel, give them the option to come train among the kids of the Cabal for a time. Learn our way of magic. Like a foreign exchange student."

Elder Morgan considered for a moment. "Our numbers have dwindled, and while I'd hate for any Cherokee kid with the gift to abandon us, I see wisdom in this offer. For myself, I would've much preferred my granddaughter went to the Cabal to learn wizardry before turning to the Ani-kutani."

"I don't think it's necessarily about abandoning it," I said. "In my mind, I was thinking that any kid who wanted could come for a year or something. Learn a bit about how we apply our craft. Then come back and continue their education in medicine. I suppose if they truly wanted to switch to become a mage, we should allow that, but it's not my intent to steal your children away from you."

"You're right, Blade Mage," Ahuli said, speaking up for the first time. "I think it is a good offer."

"And a better opportunity for future generations to build a good working relationship with the Cabal at a younger age," Elder Morgan said, nodding. "The more I think about it, the more I like this idea. If it takes a student an extra year to finish their education in medicine, so be it. It would be a great opportunity for them."

"I agree," Master Jackson said. "It will be good for the Cabal as well. I think those are good terms, Wyatt."

"I have one more."

"Okay," the Master Watcher said. "Which is?"

"The Cabal will commit to helping protect the secrecy of Cherokee medicine. We will do our part to ensure our ally's sacred practices can continue into the future, and we will do so without ever trying to take the knowledge ourselves."

The master watcher was silent for a moment. "That is an honorable request. Though there may be some nuance to work out. You've seen the great library and understand how much knowledge is contained there. It is of little doubt our own historians have uncovered some about their craft. And our own efforts in research are to understand all kinds of magic."

"Sure," I said, considering. "And I'm not suggesting we burn our books or throw away any historical findings. What I am suggesting is that we never taken any unethical action which seeks to uncover the knowledge of their sacred art. If we can't agree to that, then the Cherokee shouldn't be our friends anyway."

"Ah, I see," the master watcher said. "Then fear not, Blade Mage. Those terms were already agreed with our friends in the Cherokee many years ago."

"And have we made good on it?"

"Are you asking me as master or watcher?"

"I'm asking you as the spymaster."

"So far as I know, we've upheld our end. Any who would try would be punished severely."

"Good enough for me, then," I said, shrugging.

"So, are we all happy with these terms?" Master Jackson asked.

Again Elder Morgan looked at his peers. They each nodded in turn.

"Yes," Elder Morgan said. "Yes, we are. Thank you, Wyatt, and Master Jackson. Commander Harris. Fatima. All of you. If not for your efforts, we might not be here to discuss new terms. I can only hope this is the beginning of a better working relationship for all of us."

"As do I," Master Jackson said. "And you know, I don't think the council will be that displeased with the terms."

"Really?" I asked.

"Oh, don't look so relieved, Wyatt. They'll certainly want your head."

With that, the meeting was adjourned.

As I started out the door, Fatima moved alongside me. In a quiet voice, she said, "You know, Wyatt, if there were more people like you in the Cabal, I might've never left."

Before I could respond, she shoved past me and headed for the exit.

From behind me, Elder Morgan said, "Wyatt, a moment, please."

I stepped to the side and waited for the others to clear out, then moved over alongside Elder Morgan.

"You should get some rest," I said. "You look like someone who got captured by an evil asshole."

He forced a smile. "I will rest soon. There's much to be done yet."

"How's your granddaughter?" I asked.

He shook his head. "She is still asleep. It remains to be seen what happens when she awakes."

"I see," I said, unsure what else to say.

"I wanted to thank you," he said. "For... Well, for everything."

"Not sure you should be thanking me. This could've gone a lot better."

He nodded. "It could have, sure, but if not for your actions, I fear it might've gone much worse. We might not be here to discuss it."

"Some aren't."

"That is true," he replied. "But there's enough guilt for us all to share on that front."

"Funny. I just had a similar discussion with some of the others."

"And I'm guessing you aren't taking your own advice," he said, and this time, his smile was genuine. "You did a good thing here. Take it from an old medicine man: don't put too much blame on your own shoulders."

I nodded. "I'll do my best."

"That's all you can do. It's all any of us can do."

"Thank you, Elder Morgan."

"No, Blade Mage, it is you who is owed thanks," he said, putting out his hand. "Your father would be proud."

As I took his grip, he nodded toward where Master Jackson seemed to be waiting for me near the front door. "When everything settles down, I would like to speak with you more. There is... I would like to speak to you about what you did that night with the Uktena."

"Right," I said, nodding at his knowing look. "I would very much like your wisdom around that."

"For now, though, I'm sure you need to get back to the Cabal."

"Do I have to?" I asked.

He smiled once more, then began moving away. "I need to get back to Alyita."

"Of course," I said.

I started toward the master watcher, who looked up at me and said, "We should get back to the Castle. The council will want a debriefing."

"What of the mess here?" I asked.

"You aren't a medic, and we have plenty of people to stand guard over the camp, though I believe this threat has been neutralized."

I nodded. "With Wright dead, you're probably right. Hopefully this is the end of the Ani-kutani and they can disappear back into the pages of history."

"One can hope. You've done all you can for the tribe today, Wyatt. We should get back."

"What about Axel?"

"From what I've been told, the Nunnehi saw to his wounds."

"That's what I've been told as well, but I don't know what that means as far as the severity of his injuries."

"He's stable. And if he's well enough in the morning, we'll have him moved to the Castle. There is little else to be done here."

"Actually," I said, a thought occurring to me. "There is one more thing we could do to help the tribe before we go back. One more threat we could help them neutralize."

"I'm listening," the master watcher replied.

# CHAPTER SEVENTY-THREE

I banged my fist against the front door.

From within, I heard a commotion followed by a stream of curses.

A few moments later, the door opened and Braedon Evans appeared with his shotgun at the ready.

"You," he said, somewhat surprised.

"Yeah, me," I replied. "And I know, I know. I'm supposed to be dead and all that. Listen, I'm too tired for witty banter, so I'll make this quick. Your friend in the suit was actually a member of the Cabal. And you've broken a lot of rules, so I'm here to arrest you."

His eyes narrowed.

"Or you can resist and I get to kill you. Either way works for me."

Braedon Evans opened his mouth to speak, but before he could, the voice of Master Watcher Jackson spoke within the trailer behind him. "Now, Wyatt, that certainly wasn't very professional."

"It's a little late for niceties," I replied, speaking past Braedon. "Honestly, I kind of hope this moron and his brothers try to fight us."

Braedon swung around and saw the watcher standing in the middle of his living room.

"How can anyone live like this?" Master Jackson asked, shaking his head.

"Who the hell are you?" Braedon asked.

"Oh, right. Introductions," I said. "My bad."

Braedon whirled on me. "You have two seconds to—"

"Save it," I said. "You might like your odds against me, but the man standing in your living room is one of the Cabal's own masters."

Braedon's eyes widened and he turned once more to the threat behind him.

"Hello, there," Master Jackson said, offering him a little wave.

An uproar of noise tore through the Evans's personal little trailer park.

"Ah," I said. "Looks like your brothers have all been invited to the party as well. So, what's it going to be?"

Braedon cursed and dropped his shotgun to the ground.

# CHAPTER SEVENTY-FOUR

I slept in the car on the way back to the Castle. Master Jackson assured me someone would bring my truck back to me.

It was closer to morning than it was night when we rolled through the front gates.

This time I was allowed directly into the Castle proper. It helped that I had an armed escort led by the master watcher himself. I was also given a room, too. I was starting to think that was a sure sign I was in some sort of trouble.

Either way, I was getting used to how all this worked. I caught a quick shower, ate something, and passed out while I waited for my summons. I didn't know how long I slept—or what time it was when they came for me, because my small accommodations didn't have windows—but I felt I'd only slept for a few minutes.

At last, I found myself seated before the Archcouncil once again.

The Archmage was seated directly across from me. His eyes were studying me with the sort of amusement one might have when staring at a puppy who'd just dug through the trash. The rest of the faces were a mix.

Grand Enchanter Gunner looked as grumpy, as normal.

Grand Shaman Naomi Nguyen maintained her typical pleasant

smile.

And Grand Curator Noah Begay's features held no emotion.

So, pretty typical for the four guardians.

The masters were a mixed bag. Some glared at me with open hostility, like Master Diviner Agatha Brown. She bore the same unamused expression she'd worn when she'd berated me at the library.

Master Battlemage Zephyrine Castillo looked as though she were annoyed she couldn't just kill me already. I supposed that went with the role, though, and I didn't take it personally.

On the other side of the spectrum, a handful of them looked rather amused. Master Librarian Santiago Serrano looked as happy as a clam, as usual. And Master Spiritualist Matteo Gray at least smiled at me.

When all were seated and there had been just enough awkward silence, the Archmage asked me to explain what had occurred from my side of the story.

And as I had done on the previous occasions, I was mostly honest with them. I left out certain details that I thought the Cherokee might prefer kept secret. I didn't bother hiding the fact that Shain Stone had been present. Surely they'd have figured that out, but I didn't mention his role in the last battle, or the fact the Cherokee had nursed him. I also didn't point out Master Watcher Giovanni Jackson's part in suggesting I work through the deal with the Cherokee. I considered it, though.

When I was done spinning my yarn, I yawned and said, "So, I don't suppose you guys need a few hours to deliberate all my sins, do you? I could really use some more sleep."

"To deliberate your sins, no," Master Agatha Brown said, still scowling at me. "Though it might take us the better part of a day just to unpack your many mistakes."

Master Serrano snorted. "Didn't you beat up on him enough at the library?"

I nodded my agreement.

"I fear we don't have the time for a recess," the Archmage said. "We all have much work to do, and I would see this matter concluded sooner rather than later."

"Great," I said, forcing a smile. "Who wants to go first?"

"How about you, Wyatt?" the Archmage said.

"Uh, what?" I asked.

"If you believe there are members among this council who will disagree with certain actions you took, why don't you tell us what you think they are? And perhaps what you think you might've done differently?"

I glared at him. It was too early for this.

But then I remembered the whole reason I'd come to the Castle in the first place. Not this time, but before, when I'd camped on the front lawn. My goal had been to get them to see another side of me, and I'd almost blown it right out the gate in this meeting. Perhaps the Archmage was giving me an opportunity to correct course.

I took a deep breath and swallowed my pride. "Hmm, where to start?"

"You could start with that whole charade you pulled by camping on the front lawn," Master Shamus Abigail Yazzie said.

Before I could reply, the Archmage held up his hand. "Let's save that discussion for another time. I want to focus on his time in Lost City."

"I suppose a few of you might not be too happy that I bargained new terms with the tribe without any authorization." I felt my gaze move toward Master Jackson, who had just the poker face one might expect of the king of spy wizards. "I could see where some of you might not agree with that decision."

"You think?" Grand Enchanter Gunner asked. "You think the leadership of the Cabal might've wanted to be included in negotiations with one of our allies?"

I gritted my teeth. "I think that my perception was that the Cabal didn't intend to help the Cherokee. My impression, when someone sent August Bones to speak to me, was that it was meant to get him gone. So, I went and tried to help."

The Grand Enchanter narrowed his eyes at me. "And while negotiating with the Cherokee, did you allow them an over-exaggerated perception of your authority within this organization?"

"Not at all," I said, shaking my head. "In fact, I strongly suggested that I did not, in fact, have any authority to negotiate on behalf of the Cabal."

"And yet you did," Grand Curator Noah Begay said, his tone emotionless. "Please explain."

"Did they bully you into these terms?" Master Elementalist Thibault Washington asked. "Or threaten you?"

"No," I said, shaking my head. "Look, it was like this: I made my position clear up front. But by last night, I knew the Cherokee would need our help. And Elder Morgan made it clear that when it came time to negotiate terms, he was only going to speak to me anyway. So, I considered the options. Frankly, I don't feel I'm any more a part of this Cabal as I am a member of the tribe. But, by the sword choosing me, I'm stuck with you and you're stuck with me. And I knew the tribe needed help we could provide. So, I did what I felt was right and agreed to terms that would be beneficial to both parties, albeit less beneficial to the Cabal."

"Yet those were terms you had no right to offer," Master Artificer Martin Fuentes said. "Did you not think we might call the deal null and void?"

"No, I knew you'd uphold them," I said. "It would permanently damage the relationship if you didn't. So, yeah, I made a rogue move, knowing you guys might not like it, but it was an opportunity to do the right thing for one of our allies."

"Your brashness is almost unforgivable," Master Brown said.

"Yet the terms were fair," Master Jackson said, finally chiming in. "I can hardly find fault in his decision to move without us. Many of us once showed the same brashness, as you put it. Otherwise we wouldn't have ascended to the roles we hold today. Am I wrong?"

The Archmage gave the master watcher a very long look, as though he were seeing right through him. Something told me that Archmage Magnus Holmes might've suspected Giovanni Jackson's part in this particular scheme. But if he did, he didn't mention it. Instead, he said, "I agree the terms are fair. It might not have been precisely what some of you might've sought, but at the time, you also didn't know an ancient enemy of the Cherokee was to return to plague them. Given the circumstances, I would've offered much the same. Let us not forget why this organization exists and what we're meant to uphold."

Inside, I sighed with relief. Then the other shoe dropped.

"On the other hand, Wyatt, I do not approve of..." He paused for a moment, his eyes scanning the room, pausing a moment longer on the master watcher than anyone else. "I do not approve of the type of game you chose to play here."

I was about to reply, but he held up his hand.

"I am also equally displeased with any among our leadership who sought to use this opportunity to take advantage of an ally's weakness to garner for ourselves more power and control. That is *not* who we are."

If only I'd had a camera, because the amount of butt-puckering in that room was serious. For once, all the ire wasn't pointed at just me, and I loved every second of it.

"We will uphold the agreement our Blade Mage made," the Arch-mage said. "But in the future, Wyatt, I ask that you approach the Arch-council directly before bargaining on our behalf."

I nodded.

"What else?" he asked.

"Well, I suppose you guys might've liked earlier notice that every-thing was going to hell, but I assumed Watcher Rhodes was all over that. I also reckon most of you probably don't approve of me ignoring Constable Johnson's warnings that I was supposed to return to the Castle." I paused and bit my lip. "I can't say I would do anything differ-ently, though. I think the onus is on you guys for this one."

Grand Enchanter Gunner leaned forward in his seat, his eyes meeting mine. "Is that so?"

"Yes," I replied. "My assumption was still that you just weren't going to help and wanted me to stop interfering. Had I known there was a watcher involved, I could've worked with him. As it was, I had committed to helping the tribe, regardless of your wrath."

"I agree with him on this one," Master Serrano said, giving me an approving nod. "Prior to this incident, Wyatt came to Castle in good faith to try to work with us. Most among us couldn't spare him a few minutes. So, what else was he supposed to believe?"

There were some grumbles at this, but Grand Shaman Naomi Nguyen put up her hand and everyone shut up. "Master Serrano makes a valid point."

"With all due respect, Grand Shaman," Master Battlemage Castillo said, "it may be a fair point, but it doesn't change the fact that Wyatt's actions inevitably led to the deaths of several of our own, including Watcher Rhodes."

"That will be the end of that," Master Jackson said, his icy gaze meeting hers. "Watcher Rhodes lost his life in a fight against a terrible foe who would've hurt many more people. I will not hear his sacrifice sullied, nor lain upon the shoulders of the Blade Mage."

"I meant no disrespect toward Watcher Rhodes," said the Master Battlemage. "Only that Wyatt's actions led to unfortunate circumstances, including loss of life."

"I disagree," the master watcher said. "By all accounts, Watcher Rhodes, Constable Williams, and the members of the Honey Badgers volunteered to aid the Cherokee when they realized how serious the threat was. They faced a more powerful foe with little hope of victory because they believed in the principles we stand for. Wyatt did as well."

"Axel, too," I said, turning to look at Grand Enchanter Gunner. "You know your son was injured, right? It was pretty bad."

"I've been told he's recovering well," Gunner replied without emotion. "His condition is not the topic at hand."

"Fine," I said. "I'm sure there may be other things you all would like to berate me for, but there's another matter I wish to discuss. August Bones should be made a Cabal constable again, and he should be put over the office in Lost City."

This request was met with considerable silence.

"You believe he's fit for the role?" the Archmage asked. "Even knowing his troubles with addiction?"

"Yeah," I said. "We're wizards. Surely there's something one of the healers can do to help him."

"There are some magics that can help, yes," Master Healer Cassandra Carter said. "Though we've seen time and time again that it helps only if the person is truly willing to recover."

"Fair enough," I said. "Then August Bones should be reinstated with the understanding that he'll get help."

The Archmage smiled at me, perhaps suspecting I'd planned to get the response I'd gotten. What can I say? I was learning.

"He may be reinstated under those terms," the Archmage said. "However, for the time being, he will not be placed in Lost City. I would have him here until he has confidently recovered from his affliction. Then we'll see where he might best fit. He has too much emotional attachment to the tribe to be assigned to their area while working through his recovery. Besides, there may be another issue he's better suited to help us with."

"Which is?"

The Archmage nodded toward Abigail Yazzi, Master Shamus.

She turned to me. "This isn't the first time we've seen this drug. It has popped up in a few different places recently."

"In Cabal territory?" I asked. This was news indeed.

Master Watcher Jackson nodded. "Yes, and we've yet to identify the source."

"That means..." The reality of it hit me like a bomb.

Master Jackson finished my thought. "It means that whoever the Ani-kutani was supposedly working with is possibly the source of this drug."

"Which means we might actually have a lead," I said. "For the first time, we might actually have a lead on whoever this is stirring up all the supernatural thugs."

"Perhaps," the Archmage said. "Although it's just as likely the source of the Zavan is just another pawn. Still, though. It's a lead. And it's something we want out of our territories."

"And you think August might be able to help?" I asked.

"Maybe," he replied. "First, we'll have to see if he agrees with our terms."

"Fair enough," I replied. "So, where do we start with this investigation?"

The room got really quiet.

"What can I do to help?" I added.

"Stay out of the way," Master Agatha Brown said.

"Come now, Agatha," Master Spiritualist Matteo Gray said, shaking his head. "There's no call to be rude."

"Oh, sod off," she said, snapping her head at him. "I didn't intend to be rude, but there's also no reason to sugarcoat it. This type of work requires subtlety. We don't need our errant Blade Mage setting fire to half the Ozarks looking for drugs."

"What are you saying?" I asked. "You guys don't want my help with this?"

All eyes turned to the Archmage.

"We have a number of people already engaged," he said. "A number of task forces have already been assigned. In fact, we have a number of narcotics investigators on staff for just this sort of thing. Several ranking constables have been put on the task. Additionally, Master Jackson has provided a few of his watchers and Master Yazzie has supplied a few shamuses. I'm confident we have the right people on the case."

"But not the Blade Mage?" I asked.

"Not the Blade Mage," he said with a smile. "There is...perhaps another bit of work I may seek to have you undertake."

"You can't seriously still be considering that?" Master Abjurer Darshan Williams said.

The Archmage turned to stare at him and the Master Abjurer melted in his seat.

"What's the job?" I asked.

"It is still undecided," the Archmage said. "There is some delibera-tion yet to be had. Others among the council aren't convinced you're right for this particular piece of work, either."

"So?"

"So, I will hear out their concerns as any proper leader would. And then I'll make a decision, whether they like it or not."

"And I can't know what it is?" I asked.

"You're catching up," he replied. "When my decision is made, I'll reach out to you. Until then, the best thing would be for you to return home. And Wyatt, I'm directing you to stay away from the Zavan inves-tigation. Axel, too. Understood?"

I opened my mouth to protest, but the Archmage held up his hand.

"If you wish to earn the respect of this council, and others among the Cabal, then you'll have to play by our rules at least some of the time. Fair?"

I nodded.

"Good," he said. "Meeting adjourned."

# CHAPTER SEVENTY-FIVE

It was the first in what would be a long afternoon of funerals.

Axel stood beside me, having mostly recovered from his injuries. As promised, he'd been moved from the Cherokee camp to the Castle, and I'd stayed there to see that he recovered. I didn't have to move back out to the front lawn, either. They let me keep my room.

It had been an uneventful couple of days, and I hadn't seen any of the council members since. Nor anyone else I knew, save Parker Grimm. Lucky me.

At least he'd let me know about the funerals, and had even helped me secure a suit for myself and Axel both.

So, there we were, awkwardly standing off to one side.

Constable Williams's service was the first in order for the day, which was good, I supposed, since I knew it would be the hardest for me.

I hadn't known her all that well, but when we'd needed her, she'd been there. And in the end, she'd died trying to save me.

I couldn't help but think the world might've been better off if we could've swapped places. I kept thinking about her last words to me as she'd stood against Spearfinger. She'd said I was worthy to be Blade Mage, regardless of what anyone else said. She'd died for that belief. Died to save me.

All I could do was try to live up to that. I just didn't know how.

I tried to force down my brooding thoughts and studied the faces of the other attendees.

There was a better turnout than there had been at Malik's funeral. Probably because Constable Williams had been a better person. And also because several probably intended to attend all the services. But overall, I got the sense that Constable Williams had had more friends. Perhaps people she'd trained alongside or had gone to school with. And there were a lot of crying faces. It made sense.

Constable Johnson was there. Occasionally I noticed his glare pointed in my direction.

Most of the masters were in attendance as well. And the four Arcane Guardians, including the Archmage himself. Likely, his presence was only revealed since there were going to be several back-to-back.

Grand Enchanter Marius Gunner never once looked at his son. That was no big surprise, considering he hadn't come to check on him in the hospital, either. I would never understand how he and my dad had been so close.

Parker Grimm was there as well, though he didn't go out of his way to be seen talking to Axel or me.

In fact, Axel and I held a nice big patch of grass to ourselves.

It seemed no one in the Cabal wanted to be seen standing too close to us.

The remaining members of the Honey Badgers were there as well. I gave Commander Harris the benefit of the doubt and assumed she was there because Constable Williams had fought alongside her crew, and not just because her fallen were next in line for service.

Just as the service was about to begin, a whole horde of vehicles pulled up and parked. I wondered idly how so many wizards had managed to run late in sync, but then I realized they weren't from the Cabal.

It was the Cherokee.

Elder Morgan walked at the front of the tribe with Ahuli beside him. Around them were the other elders, save Elder Thomas, who was likely still recovering. There were many other faces I recognized, including John. And even more to my surprise, I saw Alyita, or Pathkiller, whichever name she'd kept.

August Bones walked behind the Cherokee, with them, but not at the same time. He was cleaned up in much the same way he'd been the first time we'd met, but still wearing his trench coat.

And at the very back was Fatima and her gang of wizards. They, too, had come to pay their respects to fallen wizards of the Cabal.

All eyes turned to the newcomers, who nearly doubled the total attendees by their arrival.

Elder Morgan silently led the parade toward an empty spot near the back of the crowd. Then his gaze met mine and he altered their course. The Cherokee, August Bones, and Fatima's group all shuffled in and filled the space around Axel and me.

Moments earlier, we'd stood alone. Pariahs among our own Cabal. We'd been the outsiders. And then the other outsiders had shown up, and they'd stood by us.

Elder Morgan stood just beside me. August Bones stood beside Axel. Ahuli, John, and even Alyita piled in around us.

The rest of the attendees, all members of the Cabal, watched with silent fascination. Even a few among the masters seemed surprised by this.

My gaze met the Archmage's and I realized he was watching me. When he saw my eyes meet his, he gave me the slightest hint of a nod.

And then the ceremony began.

Malik's funeral had seemed more a formality. Despite the kind words they'd said about him, there had been little emotion. The same could not be said for the funeral of Constable Williams. As Master Battlemage Zephyrine Castillo spoke of her sacrifice, many tears fell, both among the Cabal and the Cherokee.

And when the Master Battlemage finished, a man took the podium to speak about his time training with Williams, followed by an elderly woman who'd been her teacher once. Person after person took the podium, telling story upon story about her life.

A life she'd given up saving me.

As stories continued, I noticed Alyita had moved closer and squeezed in between Elder Morgan and me, perhaps so she could better see the speaker. Tears sped down either of her cheeks and she was trembling, yet she held her head up high, refusing to look away.

Whatever I guilt I felt, this young woman's had to be worse still.

Yet she stood and listened, embracing her mistake, and what her anger and desire for power had led to. It didn't matter that she'd lost control of her own mind. She'd made the foolish decisions that had led her to that point, and now a good person was gone, dead by her hand. There was little doubt the weight of her actions were taking their toll.

And despite everything, some part of me felt bad for her.

Yeah, even before she became Spearfinger, she'd tried to kill me, sure. But she was just a kid.

And who didn't make dumbass mistakes when they were a teenager?

I mean, sure, most people didn't end up killing someone for the sake of power, but the point remained.

She'd been influenced, no, manipulated into believing she was doing the right thing. And the cost was that she'd had to grow up real fast.

Reluctantly, I raised my hand and set it on her shoulder.

She turned and her red-rimmed eyes met mine.

Then she hugged me, burying her face in my chest and squeezing the air out of my lungs. Through her sobs, I heard her say over and over, "I'm sorry. I'm sorry. I'm sorry."

I returned her embrace and in a quiet voice only she could hear, I said, "I forgive you, Alyita. And Constable Williams has too, I'm sure of it."

A few moments later, the service ended and Alyita finally pulled away from me. She moved to her grandfather, whom she also hugged.

I felt a strong hand slap me on the back. When I turned, Ahuli gave me a nod. "We have taken a vote. All agreed. You are forever named a friend to our tribe. Your enemies are our enemies. If ever you need aid, you have but to ask and the Cherokee will be there, Blade Mage."

With that, he turned and stepped away.

I moved over to August and Axel, both of whom were smiling suspiciously.

"Wyatt, did you hear?" Axel asked. "August has been asked to come back to the Cabal. They're giving him his job back!"

"Really?" I said. "That's great news, August."

He rolled his eyes. "They told me it was you, Wyatt. They said the Blade Mage recommended it to the council and somehow convinced them."

Axel's jaw hit the floor. "Whoa, way to abuse your position, Wyatt! I always knew you could do it!"

I shrugged, ignoring Axel. "You *should* be reinstated."

"There are certain requirements," he said, looking away.

"Yes," I said. "It's your choice, August. No pressure."

"Bullshit," Axel said, shaking his head. "It's loads of pressure. But it's also a second chance. And that's just what August needs, am I right?"

"Uh, yeah," he said. "I suppose you are."

"Of course I am. I spoke, didn't I?" Axel said. "Besides, you can beat your addiction. If anyone can, I'd bet my money on you."

"Thank you, Axel," he said, then turned back to me. "And thank you, Wyatt. Both of you. When I first met you two, I didn't know what to think. Certainly didn't expect to get my job back and a second chance at life. I'll be forever in your debt."

"No," I said, shaking my head. "You don't owe us anything. No debts between friends."

"Blade Mage," another voice said.

I turned and found Constable Johnson standing a short distance away. When he saw he had my attention, he said, "May I have a word?"

I moved over to where he stood, a short distance from everyone else, which meant I could only assume he wanted to speak with me privately.

As I approached, he said, "It was a nice service, wasn't it?"

I nodded my agreement.

"Williams was one hell of a constable," he said.

"Yes," I said, nodding again.

He leaned in closer and whispered, "And she's dead because of you. I want you to remember that, you piece of shit. She's dead because she thought you were some kind of fucking hero. She followed you and now she'd dead. And that's on you."

He was trembling with rage, his face beat red.

"I'm sorry," I said. There was nothing else to say.

"I don't want your fucking apology. I want you to go away and die.

But until you do, I want you to remember it's your fault she's dead. You don't deserve that sword. You don't even deserve to be alive. A curse on you, Blade Mage."

With that, he turned and walked away.

I stood alone for a few moments and finally sighed.

# CHAPTER SEVENTY-SIX

Axel and I finally made it home.

And after everything, I wanted nothing more than to crawl into my bed and not wake up for at least a year. I was ready to put it all behind me.

But when I stepped onto my porch, I saw there was a manila envelope taped to my front door.

I turned to Axel, who shrugged in reply.

I tore open the envelope and reached inside. The contents were a cheap cellphone and a note.

The note read, *We should talk. Keep this phone handy. – Stone.*

The End

# DEDICATION

*Rebel Medicine is dedicated to you, dear reader. Especially those of you who waited for its release. Don't worry. The next one is done and being edited already. Spoiler alert: I think it's pretty awesome.*

# ACKNOWLEDGMENTS

As always, I have to give credit to J.H. Fleming for not only editing my work, but for putting up with me. I am a handful. But I'm also super awesome, so she's pretty lucky, if you think about it...

∾

Shout out to the Best Smelling Author crew! J.H., Julie, J.C., Becca, Tracy, Billiam, and even, pfft...Shayne, I guess. You guys rock!

∾

Shout out to real-life Axel for being our go-to person for enthusiasm about our work. Sometimes you finish a book, or an album, or a piece of art, and it's like... Hmm, cool, no one cares. But as J.H. would say, real-life Axel always has the right amount of excitement about our creative endeavors. To my fellow creatives, if you're ever feeling down about your work, get a real-life Axel.

∾

And shout-out to my dear friend Chrisafer the Magnificent, who has been a stalwart Blade Mage supporter since day one. He's been waiting for this one longer than anyone. When I completed the final draft, I sneakily uploaded it to our private chat in Discord. Much to my dismay, he missed it. Finally, when I gave him a prod, I got back a response that went, "Oh, sheeeeeeet!" This is why Chrisafer is the best. #ChrisSoundsHot

# AUGUST BONES'S BUTTER BEER

## A FALL FAVORITE

No alcohol involved. Not for Bones. You could add some, if you like. Maybe some Baileys, fresh out of a shoe.

This isn't the most complicated recipe. Nor does it require actual measurements. You should be safe to wing it.

Ingredients:

- Milk
- Butter
- Butterscotch syrup (the kind you put on ice cream)
- Brown sugar
- Cream soda
- Whipped cream

Pour a cup—or two, or however much you want—into a pot. Set it to medium heat. When it starts to warm up, throw in a fat glob of butter. Then dump in some amount of brown sugar. It doesn't really matter how much.

Stir like your life depends on it. Or whisk. Or whatever the right term is.

When all of that goodness has melted and mixed in with the warm milk, start squeezing in some butterscotch. Again, dealer's choice for how much. If I'm making a pot to serve multiple people, I'm probably dumping in half the bottle. If I'm making a single cup for myself, well, I'm still squeezing in half the bottle. You might prefer a little less.

When you've got all of this goodness near a boil, it's time to start pouring cream soda into the mix. Now, this is going to cool your concoction, so you might want to continue stirring it until it's nice and hot again.

Now it's time for the tricky part: figure out how to get it into a cup without burning the shit out of yourself. Honestly, if you master this step, you're a better kitchen sorcerer than I'll ever be. I either burn the crap out of my hand or lose a bunch in the sink. Every. Freaking. Time. Last time, I managed to do both.

And finally...the whipped cream. If it doesn't look like a snowy mountain in the middle of a landslide, are you even trying?

Drink it up, Buttercup!

*(In no particular order - Phill, Real-life Axel, and a Predator. You guess which is which.)*

## About the Author

Phillip Drayer Duncan has written over ten novels and is the only author who has ever sponsored a racecar...probably. He is a co-host of the Future Best Seller Podcast. His work has been published by Yard Dog Press, Pro Se Productions, Seventh Star Press, and Happy Omega Publishing.

Along with reading and writing, he enjoys kayaking, fishing, video games, and telling bad jokes. Phillip's natural habitats include the rivers and lakes of the Ozarks, but he may also be spotted at a con or concert. During the cold season, he hibernates beneath a pile of books and video games. He is generally an approachable creature; however, it's best to give him snacks to ensure he won't bite. Cookies are best.

His earliest books were acted out with action figures and scribbled into notebooks. Today, he uses a computer like a real grownup, though he refuses to act his age the rest of the time. If it would pay his bills, he'd be playing with G.I. Joes right now.

His greatest dream in life is to become a Jedi, but since that hasn't happened yet, he focuses on writing and eagerly awaits the next season of *Firefly*. He demanded we mention that he is a best smelling author.

PhillipDrayerDuncan.com
FutureBestSellerPodcast.com

# CATALYSTS

A BLADE MAGE & MOONSHINE WIZARD COLLECTION

# PHILLIP DRAYER DUNCAN

Don't forget to pick up your **FREE** digital copy of

## *Catalysts*

featuring the Blade Mage prequel shorts...

*The Generic Mage*
&
*The Last Great Blade Mage*

Join Wyatt and Axel as they hunt down a wicked clown goblin and live the experience of Wyatt being chosen as Blade Mage.

Get Catalysts **FREE** by signing up for the Phillip Drayer Duncan Newsletter at...

**PhillipDrayerDuncan.com**

Happy Reading!

# ALSO BY PHILLIP DRAYER DUNCAN

**Catalysts** – Featuring 2 Blade Mage & 1 Moonshine Wizard Story. FREE & only available by signing up for the Phillip Drayer Duncan Newsletter.

∼

**The Blade Mage:**

**The Blade Mage**

**Of Song and Shadow**

**The Memphis Knights**

∼

**The Moonshine Wizard:**

**Moonshine Wizard**

The Distilled Shorts Collection:

*First Job*

*The Ogre & The Primates*

*A Sword Named Sharp*

*Hunting one Like Us*

*The Monster Beneath the Bed*

*The Hunt for the Dark Wizard*

∼

Assassins Incorporated:

Assassins Incorporated

Assassins Incorporated: Rehired

www.ingramcontent.com/pod-product-compliance
Lightning Source LLC
Chambersburg PA
CBHW020919020726
47495CB00002B/257